SPECIAL AGENT'S PERFECT COVER

BY
MARIE FERRARELLA

MILLS
BOON

First published in Great Britain 2012
by Mills & Boon, an imprint of Harlequin (UK) Limited,
Eton House, 18-24 Paradise Road, Richmond, Surrey TW9 1SR

Special thanks and acknowledgement to Marie Ferrarella for her contribution to the PERFECT, WYOMING miniseries.

© Harlequin Books S.A. 2012

2in1 ISBN: 978 0 263 89517 9

46-0412

Harlequin (UK) policy is to use papers that are natural, renewable and recyclable products and made from wood grown in sustainable forests. The logging and manufacturing processes conform to the legal environmental regulations of the country of origin.

Printed and bound in Spain
by Blackprint CPI, Barcelona

USA TODAY bestselling and RITA® Award-winning author **Marie Ferrarella** has written more than two hundred books, some under the name Marie Nicole. Her romances are beloved by fans worldwide. Visit her website at www.marieferrarella.com.

To
all the wonderful readers,
who give me
such a great audience
to write for.
You make it fun.

Prologue

Micah Grayson wasn't sure what had possessed him to turn on the TV in the pristine, upscale hotel room that he was occupying for the day. He wasn't exactly the kind of man who craved company or needed to fill the silence.

Hell, in his particular chosen "line of work," silence and stealth were two of his best tools. He had no desire to listen to music or watch anything that might be on the big screen TV that came with the price of the first-class room. For that matter, he only kept up on world affairs insofar as to learn about what region of the world he'd most likely be going to next.

But after methodically going through his own mental checklist and making sure that the room was clear of bugs—not the kind with legs but the kind that could get a man killed—he'd absently switched on the set and sank down on the bed, thinking about his next move.

The grim voice of the newscaster didn't even penetrate his consciousness.

Not until her picture was flashed on the screen.

Very little caught Micah off guard these days. His life was literally riding on this fact, that he was always prepared for any and all contingencies and could act accordingly.

But seeing her face knocked the wind out of him. More than that, it was as if he'd just been on the receiving end of an iron fist aimed straight for his gut.

Because according to the newscaster, the woman in the photograph was dead. And when he had last seen her, a million years ago, before life had gotten so immensely complicated and they had gone their separate ways, Johanna had been very much alive.

Alive, but no longer his.

"In keeping with what seems to have become a bizarre ritual, the body of Johanna Tate was found yesterday outside of Eden, Wyoming. The victim suffered a single gunshot wound. The coroner has concluded that that was the cause of death. This is the fifth such female body found in as many years. Police are asking anyone with any information about this latest murder victim to please step forward. Any informant's identity will be kept strictly confidential. Rumor has it that this young woman was a resident of Cold Plains, a town located some eighty miles away, but this has not been confirmed yet."

A resident of Cold Plains.

Yes, she was from there, Micah thought, bitterness filling his mouth like bile.

As had he once been.

Johanna had been the reason he'd remained in that godforsaken blot on the map for as long as he had. And ultimately, she'd been the reason why he had abruptly left without so much as a backward glance. Because after being his, after planning to share all her tomorrows with him, she'd allowed herself to be charmed away from his side by the very devil himself.

Charmed away by Samuel Grayson.

Never mind that Samuel was his twin brother. He and that underhanded, despicable excuse for a human being were as different as night and day. *He* had never pretended to be anything but what he was, never made any excuses for himself. While Samuel wove elaborate tapestries made of intricate lies to ensnare those he wanted to own, to control for his own unstated purposes.

Crossing to the TV monitor, Micah Grayson turned up the volume.

But the story was over. The dark-haired newscaster had gone on to talk about the unseasonably warm April weather, exchanging inane banter with an overly ripe, barely legal-looking weather girl sporting a torrent of blond hair that appeared to be almost longer than her dress.

Johanna had been allocated less than a sound bite.

Micah hit the off button. The screen on the wall went instantly dark as it fell into silence.

"Damn it, Johanna, I told you he was trouble. I *told*

you you'd regret picking him over me," Micah said in frustrated anger.

That had been the extent of his fight to keep her. Telling her that she'd regret her choice. He'd felt that if he had to convince Johanna to stay with him, then he'd already lost her, and it hadn't been worth his breath to argue with her.

Taking out his worn, creased wallet, the one that carried his current ID stamped with his current name—one of many he'd assumed since he'd left Johanna and Cold Plains behind—he opened it. Beneath the handful of bills he always kept in it and the false ID was a tiny close-up of a sweet-faced girl with pale brown eyes and long, straight black hair.

Johanna's high school picture.

The same picture that was embossed in his brain. He couldn't say that it was embossed on his heart because he no longer had one. One of the hazards of his job. A heart only got in the way, slowed a man down, kept him from a laser-like focus on his assignment.

A wave of fury flared through his veins, and Micah crumpled the faded photo in his hand. He drew back his arm, about to pitch the tiny paper ball across the room, then changed his mind.

Exhaling a long, slow breath, he opened his hand, letting the small wad fall onto the bed. He carefully flattened it out again, then slipped the now-creased photograph back into his wallet.

Samuel couldn't be allowed to get away with this, Micah swore vehemently. He didn't know any of the particulars, but Samuel had to be behind Johanna's death. His twin brother's prints were all over this. He'd bet his soul on it.

The corners of Micah's mouth curved in a humorless smile.

If he had a soul, he corrected silently.

Micah knew someone who could look into things. Someone who could take Samuel's so-called paradise, strip it of all its gingerbread facade and expose it for what it was: hell on earth. Someone who he'd known all those years ago and had himself left for greener pastures, so to speak.

Someone, Micah thought as he tapped the numbers lodged in his memory out onto the cell phone's key pad, who still had a soul. And who knew, maybe even a heart, too.

The cell phone on the other end rang a total of six times. Micah decided to give it to the count of ten and then try again later.

A man in his profession didn't leave messages.

But then he heard someone picking up on the other end and a deep voice say, "Special Agent Bledsoe."

A glimmer of a smile passed over Micah's lips.

His brother was going down. It might take a while, but he was going down. And he would pay for what had happened to Johanna.

"Hawk, this is Micah. Grayson," he added in case the agent was having trouble remembering him. It had been a while. "I need to see you." He paused and then said cryptically, "I've got a not-so-anonymous tip for you about those murdered women on the news."

Chapter 1

Okay, so where is he?

Special Agent Hawk Bledsoe paced about the hotel room, which grew progressively smaller by the moment. His frown deepened significantly as impatience drummed through him.

He had a really bad feeling about this.

About *all* of this.

To say that he had been surprised to hear from Micah Grayson out of the blue yesterday after so many years gave new meaning to the term "understatement." Micah and he both had the very same connection between them that had just recently come to light about the five murder victims: they came from the same region in Wyoming. Micah was born in Horn's Gulf, while he had the misfortune of actually growing up in Cold Plains.

A great place to be from, Hawk thought cynically,

the heels of his boots sinking into the light gray carpet. He made yet another complete trip around the room. *Nothing good had ever come from that town. Except for—*

No! He wasn't going to let himself go there. Those thoughts belonged in his past, buried deeper than the unearthed five victims apparently had been.

The victims, he'd already decided after reviewing the notes made by past agents, had all been buried as if the killer had expected them to be discovered. Eventually, if not immediately.

Why? What was the sense in that? What did these women have in common other than having the bad luck of being from Cold Plains? And of course, other than the fact that they had all been murdered, execution style, with a single bullet to the back of the head. Their sins—whatever they were—had obviously been unpardonable to someone.

But who?

And why?

And where the hell was Micah, anyway? He was supposed to be here. The urgency in Micah's voice was the reason why he'd driven straight through the night to get here.

It wasn't as if he'd called the man—a man who he knew through various sources made his living by hiring out to do things that others either could not or would not do—or were just unable to do. Be that as it may, it was Micah who had called *him,* not the other way around.

Called him and had said just enough to get him hooked. That he needed to talk to him about the five murdered women who had been found scattered through isolated areas in Wyoming.

Did that mean Micah knew who was responsible? Or that he at least had a viable theory? He wished he could have gotten Micah to say more, but the man had been deliberately closemouthed, saying he'd tell him "everything" when he got here.

So where was he?

Hawk knew that Micah Grayson had once dated Johanna Tate. Was *that* why the man had gone out of his way to call him? Had he called in reinforcements? As far as he knew, that wasn't Micah's style.

Either way, it looked as if he wasn't about to find out now. He'd gotten no more out of his one-time friend than that: to come meet him in this off-the-beaten-path hotel. Room 705. Micah didn't believe in saying much over the phone, even one that most likely was one of those disposable models, which could be discarded—and rendered untraceable—at a moment's notice.

So rather than clear anything up, Micah's call had merely added to the mystery that was already so tightly wound around the dead women it reminded Hawk of a skein of yarn whose beginning was so well hidden, it defied discovery—or unraveling.

Yarn.

Where the *hell* had that come from?

And then he remembered.

She had liked to knit. He'd teased her about it, saying things like it was an old-lady hobby. Carly, in turn, had sniffed dismissively and informed him that it suited her just fine, thank you very much. He recalled being fascinated, watching her fingers manage the needles like a master, creating articles of clothing out of straight lines of color.

As he recalled, she had professed to absolutely *love* creating things.

Again, he banished the thoughts—the all-too-vivid memories—out of his head. But not quite as force-fully this time as he had initially. Hawk supposed that it was inevitable. After all this time, he was about to be dragged back to the little pimple of a town he'd once left behind in his rearview mirror.

He recalled driving away as fast as he could all those years ago. At the time, he'd thought he was leaving per-manently. Obviously not.

He was making too much out of this. The thoughts he was having about Carly just went to prove that he was human, just like everyone else. Nothing more.

The problem was, he didn't want to be human. Es-pecially not now of all times. If nothing else, being human, reacting emotionally, got in the way of effi-ciency. Being human was a distraction, and he had a case to unravel and a murderer—or murderers—to track down. That had to come first. He couldn't afford to be distracted, not even a little.

Memories and thoughts of what could have been—and *hadn't* been—had no place here. Or anywhere in his life.

Though his expression gave no evidence of his emo-tional turmoil, Hawk was too tense to sit down. So he went on pacing about the small hotel room where Micah had said he would meet him.

He'd been waiting for over an hour.

To the best of his recollection, Micah was *never* late. It was one of the things they'd had in common. Because of the directions that life had taken them, they both believed that time was a tool to be used, not frivolously ignored or disregarded.

Micah *wouldn't* be late. If the mercenary wasn't here it was because he *couldn't* be here.

Which meant that something was wrong.

Which in turn meant that he, as the special agent who had recently been put in charge of this case, couldn't put off the inevitable for very much longer.

The only thing that Micah had confirmed over the phone was what he'd already just learned: that all the victims were women from Cold Plains. In order to conduct the investigation properly, he would have to go up to Cold Plains, Wyoming, himself.

Looks like the prodigal son is coming home, he thought wryly.

Except that, in this case, he hadn't been prodigal so much as smart. Leaving Cold Plains had been the smartest thing he'd ever done. By the same token, returning might turn out to be the stupidest.

Hawk looked at his watch again. When he'd gotten here—and found the room empty—he'd mentally promised himself to give Micah approximately ninety minutes to show up. But right now, he was feeling way too antsy to wait for sixty more minutes to slip beyond his reach.

With a sigh, he crossed back to the hotel room door that had been deliberately left unlocked for him.

Damn it, Micah, I hope you haven't gotten yourself killed, he thought irritably. Because he was fairly certain that nothing short of death would have kept Micah Grayson from keeping an appointment that he himself had set up.

He needed to see the county coroner before he made his way to Cold Plains, but a visit to Cold Plains was definitely in his immediate future.

Biting off a curse, Hawk let himself out of the room and closed the door behind him.

It seemed rather incredible to Carly Finn that the two times she made up her mind to finally, *finally* leave Cold Plains, something came up to stop her.

And not some mild, inconsequential "something" but a major, pull-out-all-the-stops "something."

The first time she'd been ready to test her wings and fly, leaving this soul-draining speck of a town behind her and eagerly begin a fresh, new chapter of her life with the man she knew deep down in her soul she was meant to be with, her infinite sense of obligation as well as her never-ending sense of responsibility to her family had added lead to her wings and grounded her with a bone-jarring thud.

The problem then was that her father had been a drunk, a dyed-in-the-wool, leave-no-drink-untouched, hopeless alcoholic, and while there were many men—and women—with that shortcoming who could be considered by the rest of the world to be functioning alcoholics, her father hadn't fallen into that category. He hadn't been even close to a functioning alcoholic, and she knew that if she left with Hawk, if she accompanied the man she loved so much that it hurt so he could follow his dreams, she would be abandoning not just her father but her baby sister to a very cruel, inevitable life of poverty and, eventually, to homelessness. The baby sister she had promised her dying mother to look after all those years ago.

So she knew that in all good conscience, she had to remain. And remain she did. She remained in order to run the family farm and somehow juggle a job as a waitress, as well, the latter she undertook in order to bring in some extra, much-needed money into the household.

She remained while sending Hawk Bledsoe on his way with a lie ringing in his ears.

There was no other choice. She knew that the only way she could get Hawk to leave Cold Plains—and her—so that he could follow his dreams was to tell him that she didn't love him anymore. That she had actually *never* loved him and had decided that she just couldn't go on pretending anymore.

Because she knew that if she didn't, if she let him know how much she really loved him, Hawk would stay in Cold Plains with her. He would marry her, and eventually, he would become very bitter as he entertained thoughts of what "could have been but wasn't."

She couldn't do that to him. Couldn't allow him to do that to himself.

Loving someone meant making sacrifices. So she'd made the ultimate sacrifice: she'd lied to him and sent him on his way, while she had stayed behind to do what she had to do. And struggled not to die by inches with each passing day.

But the day finally came when she had had enough. When she had silently declared her independence, not just from the farm but from the town, which had become downright frightening in a short period. Cold Plains had gone from a dead-end town to a sleek, picture-perfect one that had sold its soul to the devil.

She'd reached the conclusion that she had a right to live her own life. That went for Mia, the baby sister she had always doted on, as well.

She didn't even want to pack, content to leave everything behind just so that she and Mia could get a brand-new start. But she was in for a startling surprise. Somehow, while she was doing all that juggling to keep the farm—and them—afloat, Mia had grown up and formed opinions of her own—or rather, as it turned out, had them formed for her.

When she had told Mia that the day had finally come, that she'd had enough and that they were leaving Cold Plains for good, her beautiful, talented baby sister had knocked her for a loop by telling her flatly that she was staying.

It got worse.

Mia was not just staying, but she was "planning" on marrying Brice Carrington, a wealthy widower more than twice her age.

"But you don't love him," Carly had protested when she had finally recovered from the shock.

The expression on Mia's face had turned nasty. "Yes, I do," her sister had insisted. "Besides, how would you know if I did or didn't? You're always so busy working, you don't have time to notice anything. You certainly don't have any time for me. Not like Samuel does," she'd added proudly, with the air of one who had been singled out and smiled down upon by some higher power.

The accusation had stung, especially since the only reason she had been working so hard was to provide for Mia in the first place. But the sudden realization that while she'd been busy trying to make a life for them, trying to save money so that they could finally get away from here, her sister had been brainwashed.

There was no other term for it. What Samuel Grayson did, with his silver tongue, his charm and his exceedingly handsome face was pull people into his growing circle of followers. Pull them in and mesmerize them with rhetoric. Make them believe that whatever he suggested they do was really their idea in the first place.

Why else would Mia believe that she was actually in love with a man who was old enough to be her father. Older. Brice Carrington was as bland as a bowl of unsalted, white rice. He was also, in the hierarchy of things, currently very high up in Samuel Grayson's social structure.

Maybe Brice represented the father they'd never really had, Carly guessed. Or maybe, since their dad was dead, Mia was looking for someone to serve as a substitute?

In any case, if Mia was supposed to marry Brice Carrington, it was because the match suited Grayson's grand plan.

The very thought of Grayson made her angry. But at the moment, it was an anger that had no suitable outlet. She couldn't just go railing against the man as if she was some kind of a lunatic. For one thing, most of the people who still lived in town thought Samuel Grayson was nothing short of the Second Coming.

Somehow, in the past five years, while no one was paying attention, Samuel Grayson and a few of his handpicked associates had managed to buy up all the property in Cold Plains. At first, moving stealthily but always steadily, he'd wound up arranging everything up to and possibly including the rising and setting of the sun to suit his own specifications and purposes.

These days, it seemed as if nothing took place in Cold Plains without his say-so or close scrutiny. He had eyes and ears everywhere. Anyone who opposed him was either asked to leave or, and this seemed to be more and more the case, they just disappeared.

At first glance, it appeared as if the man had done a great deal for the town. Old buildings had been renovated, and new buildings had gone up, as well. There was now a new town hall, a brand-new school, which he oversaw and for which he only hired teachers who were devoted to his ideology. And most important of all, he'd built a bright, spanking, brand-new church, one he professed was concerned strictly with the well-being of its parishioners' souls—and that, he had not been shy about saying, was the purview of the leader of the flock: Grayson himself.

To a stranger from the outside, it looked like a pretty little, idyllic town.

To her, Cold Plains had become a town filled with puppets—and Samuel Grayson was the smiling, grand puppeteer. A puppeteer whose every dictate was slavishly followed. His call for modesty had all the women who belonged to his sect wearing dresses that would have been more at home on the bodies of performers reenacting the late 1950s.

Maybe her skepticism was because she'd grown up listening to her late father's promises, none of which he'd ever kept. Promises that, for the most part, he didn't even recall making once a little time had gone by.

Whatever the reason, she didn't trust Samuel Grayson any further than she could throw him. And he was a large, powerful-looking man.

Her sense of survival was urgently prompting her to leave before something went wrong—before she *couldn't* leave.

But no matter what she felt about Cold Plains's transformation and no matter what her sense of survival dictated, she was not about to leave town without her sister. And Mia had flatly refused to budge, declaring instead her intentions of staying.

She was, Carly caught herself thinking again, between the proverbial rock and hard place.

Common sense might prod her to make a run for it, but she had never put her own well-being above someone else's, especially that of a loved one.

That was why she'd lied to Hawk to make him leave Cold Plains and why she was still here now, doing her best to pretend to be one of Samuel's most recent converts even though the very thought made her sick to her stomach.

In her opinion, Samuel Grayson, once merely a very slick motivational speaker, was now orchestrating a utopian-like environment where allegiance to him was the prime directive and where, by instituting a society of blindly obedient, non-thinking robots, he was setting the cause of civilization back over fifty years.

Women in Samuel's society were nothing more than subservient, second-class citizens whose main function, Carly strongly suspected, was to bear children and populate Grayson's new world.

She'd heard, although hadn't quite managed to confirm, that Samuel was even having these devoted women "branded." Horrified, she'd looked into it and discovered that they were being tattooed with the small letter *D,* for devotee, on their right hips. That alone made the man a crazed megalomaniac.

Although it sickened her, Carly knew she had to play up to Samuel in order to get her sister to trust her enough so that she could eventually abduct her and get her away from this awful place. Nothing short of that was going to work—and even that might not—but she had no other options open to her.

Hoping that Samuel would eventually grow tired of his little game—or that someone would get sick of his playing the not-so-benevolent dictator—and send him on his way was akin to waiting for Godot. It just wasn't going to happen.

So she'd gone to Samuel and insisted that she was qualified to fill the teaching position that had suddenly opened up at the Cold Plains Day Care Center. A smile that she could only describe as reptilian had spread over Samuel's handsome, tanned face. Steepling his long, aristocratic fingers together, he fixed his gaze intently on her face.

He paused dramatically for effect as the moment sank in, then said, "Yes, my dear, I am sure that you are more than qualified to fill that position, and may I say how very happy I am that you have come around and decided to come join us." He'd taken her hand between his and though his smile had never wavered, it had sent chills through her. Chills she wasn't quite sure how to dodge. She'd never felt more of a sense of imprisonment than she had at that moment.

"You will be a most welcomed addition," he had assured her.

She remembered thinking, *Over my dead body*, and she had meant it.

The problem was she was fairly certain that the coda, although silently said, would not be a deterrent to Grayson. He was a man who allowed nothing to stand in the way of his plans. To that end, he was perfectly capable of cutting out a person's heart without missing a beat.

She *had* to get Mia away from here. And she would, even if it wound up being the last thing she ever did.

Chapter 2

"Hi, Doc. This is going to have to be quick. I've only got a few minutes to spare," Hawk said by way of a greeting as he walked into the county coroner's office.

In reality, since Micah hadn't shown up for their appointed meeting, he should have skipped coming here altogether and gone on straight to Cold Plains. But the coroner had called, saying there was something that he needed to tell him. And if he was being honest and had his choice in the matter, he would have gladly stalled and remained here indefinitely, at this temporary FBI outpost. But he didn't have a choice, and he could only spare a few minutes.

At this point, he would have welcomed being sidetracked by anything, and this included an earthquake, a tornado or a tsunami, none of which ever occurred in this rough-and-tumble region of Wyoming. But although he would rather do *anything* than go on to Cold Plains to investigate exactly how these five murdered women were connected, Hawk was first and foremost a dedicated FBI agent, and he wasn't about to let any of his past personal feelings get in the way of his trying to solve this case.

Not bothering to shrug out of his jacket, Hawk crossed over to the coroner. He'd only met the man a few days before but the coroner took his job very seriously.

"Why did you call me?" Hawk asked. "Did you find out anything new?"

"Not exactly," Dr. Hermann Keegan replied, measuring his words out slowly, as if he wanted to be sure they were absolutely right before he uttered them. He looked at Hawk over the tops of his rimless reading glasses. "Actually, what I found was something old."

His mind on the ordeal that lay ahead of him, Hawk had very little patience with what sounded like a riddle. "Come again?"

"Once the fact that they were all connected came to light, I pulled the autopsy records of the other four victims," he explained. "Were you aware of the fact that the 'tattoo' the deputy coroner found on victim number two's right hip washed off when he was cleaning the body?"

Victim number two was the only female they hadn't been able to identify yet. All the others had names, but this one was still referred to as Jane Doe four years after she'd been discovered. The woman's DNA and fingerprints turned out not to be a match for anyone currently in any of the FBI databases.

"Tattoos don't wash off," Hawk pointed out.

Doc Keegan smiled, making his spherical, moonlike face appear even rounder. "Exactly. According to the notes, the letter, a *d,* appeared to have been drawn in with some kind of permanent, black laundry marker or maybe a Sharpie." He raised his eyes to Hawk's. "You know what that means, don't you?"

"Yeah," Hawk answered crisply. "Either this woman had a penchant for marking up her body—or she wasn't really one of the cult's followers but was pretending to be for some reason." Being a law enforcement agent, the first thing that struck him was that Jane Doe might have been one, as well. "She might have been undercover," he concluded.

Keegan's head bobbed up and down. "My money's on that."

Hawk looked at the five manila folders that were fanned out on top of the coroner's extremely cluttered desk. Each was labeled with the name of a different victim. Besides Jane Doe, there was Shelby Jackson who had been found first in Gulley, Wyoming, five years ago, Laurel Pierce, found in Cheyenne three years ago, Abby Michaels, discovered in the woods outside of Laramie last year and Johanna Tate, found in Eden last week.

Johanna Tate.

Micah's former girlfriend, Hawk suddenly remembered. The name had been nagging at him ever since he'd heard the news. Was that why Micah had called him? Because of Johanna?

Did Micah know more than he'd alluded to? Had he decided to take matters into his own hands? Going outside the law had become a way of life for him, and he would have thought nothing of avenging Johanna's murder. Had it backfired on him because he'd let his emotions get in the way?

Damn it, he needed answers, Hawk thought, frustrated. Nodding toward the folders, he asked, "Mind if I take those with me?"

Stepping away from Joanna Tate's lifeless body he'd finished sewing together, Keegan scrubbed and then pushed the files together into one pile. "Be my guest," he told Hawk. "I've already made copies of them for you."

Hawk scooped up the files. Already familiar with all the victims, he wanted to review the files in depth and was grateful to the coroner for making copies for him. Still stumped, he needed all the input he could get his hands on.

"You're pretty thorough," Hawk commented.

Keegan raised his slopping shoulders and let them fall again. "I've got the time to be. This is the most amount of action this office has seen in a very long while."

"What do you do the rest of the time?" Hawk asked, curious what occupied the man's time when he wasn't conducting an autopsy. He sincerely doubted that Wyoming was a hotbed of homicides.

Keegan's answer surprised him.

"I'm a vet," the older man replied. "Technically," he explained as a look of disbelief came over the special agent's face, "I don't even have to be a doctor of any kind in order to become a coroner. I just have to be unusually observant and display a high tolerance when it comes to the dissection of dead bodies. Like this one." He nodded at the draped body on his steel table.

"Good to know," Hawk quipped. Holding the files to his chest, he crossed to the door. "Thanks again for these."

"My pleasure," Keegan answered, adding, "so to speak."

Closing the door behind him, Hawk blew out a breath. "Yeah," he muttered to himself in a low voice. "So to speak," he echoed.

He squared his shoulders and made his way out of the building and back to his car. He was all out of excuses and reasons to delay his departure. He'd already gotten in contact with his team and told them to temporarily set up a "satellite FBI office" in a cabin several miles out of town.

They were probably already there, he thought. Now it was his turn. Hawk turned his key in the ignition and listened to his car come to life.

Next up: Cold Plains.

Ready or not, here I come.

Carly was standing outside the school where she had so recently taken a position, supervising the children as they made the most of their afternoon recess.

That was where she was when she first saw him. First saw the ghost from her past.

That was what she initially thought she was seeing, a ghost, a figment of her wandering imagination. A momentary hallucination on her part, brought on by a combination of stress and anger and the overwhelming need to have someone to lean on—just for a little while.

For her, the only one she had ever had to lean on had been Hawk, but that had been a very long time ago. At least ten years in her past, she judged.

Maybe even more.

The bottom line was that there was absolutely no reason for her to see Hawk Bledsoe getting out of a relatively new, black sedan. The vehicle had just pulled up before the pristine edifice which housed The Grayson Community Center as well as the living quarters of several of Samuel Grayson's top people.

Or, as she was wont to think of them in the privacy of her own mind, Grayson's henchmen.

Her mind was playing tricks on her, Carly silently insisted. Any second now, this person she had conjured up would fade away or take on the features of someone else, someone who she knew from town. Someone she was accustomed to seeing day in, day out.

She waited, not daring to breathe.

He wasn't fading. Wasn't changing.

Suddenly feeling very light-headed, Carly sucked a huge breath into her lungs.

Ordinarily, fresh air helped clear her head. But it wasn't her head that needed clearing, it was her eyes, because she was still seeing him.

Or at least a version of him.

The boyish look she'd known—and loved—was gone, replaced by a face that, aside from being incredibly handsome, was thinner and far more somber looking. Otherwise, it was still him, still Hawk. He was still tall, still muscular—the navy windbreaker he wore did nothing to hide that fact. And he still had sandy-blond hair, even though it was cut shorter now than it had been the last time she had laid eyes on him.

And when he made eye contact with her from across the street, she saw that the apparition with Hawk's face had the same deep, warm, brown eyes that Hawk had had.

Eyes that could melt her soul.

She felt her pulse accelerating, her heart hammering as if it was recreating a refrain from The Anvil Chorus in double time.

Why wasn't this image, this apparition, this ghost from the depths of her mind fading? Why was it coming toward her?

Carly's breath caught in her throat, all but solidifying and threatening to choke her. Even so, for the life of her, Carly just couldn't make herself look away.

She was still waiting for the image to break up—or for the world to end, whichever was more doable—as the distance between them continued to lessen.

When Hawk had first driven slowly through the town, heading for its center, its "heart," Hawk had to admit that he was rather stunned. The town appeared to have gone through an incredible amount of changes.

When he had left, Cold Plains looked to be on the verge of simply drying up and blowing away, a dying town abandoned by all but the very hopeless. Those who were devoid of ambition and who couldn't make a go of it anywhere else had chosen to remain here and die along with the town.

There was no sign of that town here.

This was more of a town that could take center stage in a children's storybook. All around him, there were new buildings. The ones that looked remotely familiar had all been restored, revitalized, given not just a new coat of paint but a new purpose.

The streets were repaired and clean. Actually clean, he marveled, remembering how filthy everything had appeared to be when he was growing up here.

The smell of fertilizer was missing, he suddenly realized. Cold Plains now seemed like a town on its way to becoming a city rather than a hovel disintegrating into a ghost town.

For a moment he thought that he was in the wrong place, that he had somehow gotten turned around while coming here and had managed to drive to another town. A brighter, newer town.

But then he saw a few faces he recognized, people he'd known growing up. That told him that this *was* Cold Plains. At the same time, he began to take note of not just the newly constructed buildings but the people, as well. Briskly moving people. People who seemed to have a purpose.

He saw several parents holding on to their children's hands, heading for what appeared to be a playground.

He did a mental double take. A playground? Since when was that part of the landscape? Or an ice cream parlor, for that matter?

"Excuse me, young man, didn't mean to almost walk into you." An older man laughed, sidestepping around him at the last moment. Hawk couldn't help staring at the white-haired man. He wore color-coordinated sweats, fancy, high-end sneakers—running shoes?— and he was holding navy-blue-colored weights in his hand that looked to be about a pound each.

He was power walking, Hawk realized.

Had everyone lost their minds?

He looked around again. All the people who were out and about appeared to be smiling. *Every last one of them.* It was almost eerie. And then he looked closer at the women who were passing him. Smiling, as well, they were all modestly dressed. No jeans, no scruffy cutoffs or overalls. Each and every one of them, young or old, children or adults, they were all wearing dresses.

Dresses that came down past the middle of their calves.

Hell, they all looked like extras from a movie about Amish life, Hawk thought. All that was missing were those hats or bonnets or whatever those things that all but hid their hair were called—

Hawk froze.

A second ago, he'd been busy scanning the immediate area, trying to reconcile what he was seeing with the Cold Plains citizens he remembered from his past. Lost in thought, he'd forgotten to get himself prepared, and so he wasn't.

Wasn't prepared to have the sight of her, wearing one of those ridiculous, sexless dresses, slam into him like a runaway freight train sliding down a steep embankment. Plowing straight into his gut.

He had to concentrate in order to draw in half a breath.

Carly.

Carly Finn.

The woman who had led him on, then skewered his insides and left him without so much as a backward glance. Left him to live or die, no matter to her.

Why the hell hadn't he realized that she would probably still be here? Still be living on the outskirts of Cold Plains?

This was where that stupid farm was, the one that meant so much more to her than he did, of course she was still going to be here.

Still here and, despite the unbecoming, shapeless brown sack she wore, still as beautiful as she'd ever been.

More, he amended.

Even at this distance, he could see that Carly, with her long, blond hair pulled back into a ponytail, was even more beautiful than he remembered. Maybe that was because he'd been trying so hard to bury her image, to scrape it from his mind.

His hands were clenched at his sides. Fury raged through him, but there was no outlet. He couldn't afford to allow himself one.

Damn it, he wished he could just walk away. This minute. Wished he could get into his car and just drive until he ran out of gas or purged her image from his mind, whichever happened first.

But he couldn't, and he knew it, so there was no sense in wishing. He owed it to the Bureau to see this through, and he owed it to those five dead women to find their killer or killers. He wasn't a kid anymore who could just think of himself. He had responsibilities, even if he no longer possessed a viable heart.

Incensed, stunned, angry and a whole vanguard of other emotions he couldn't even begin to catalog yet, Hawk found himself striding straight for the woman clad in the unflattering brown dress.

When she saw him heading for her, Carly's very first reaction was to want to bolt and run.

But she didn't.

She had never run away from anything in her life and she was not about to start now—no matter how much she wanted to and how much easier it would have been than to wait for him to reach her.

Leaning for support against the white picket fence, which ran along the length of the school yard, Carly raised her chin, said a silent prayer that she *wasn't* losing her mind and waited for the approaching man to turn into someone else.

He didn't.

So much for the power of positive thinking.

Her thoughts did a complete one-eighty. Okay, so it *was* Hawk. What was he doing here? Of all the times she'd yearned for him to return, this was the worst possible one.

She couldn't allow herself to forget what she was still

doing here. She had to remember why she'd taken this job at the day care center and why she forced herself to smile at Samuel Grayson when she would rather just drive a stake through his heart, grab her sister's hand and run.

"Carly?"

The second she heard his voice, a wave of heat, then cold, then heat again washed over her. For the tiniest split second, the world shrank down to a pinprick. Only sheer willpower on her part caused it to widen again, chasing away the blackness that threatened to swallow her up whole.

Taking another deep, calming breath, she responded, "Yes?"

"Carly," Hawk repeated, his voice more somber this time, more forceful. His dark brown eyes all but bore into her. "It's Hawk."

She hadn't wanted to run her tongue along her lips in order to moisten them, but if she didn't, she wouldn't have been able to utter another sound.

"Yes," she answered quietly, praying he wouldn't hear her heart pounding. "I know."

A sixth sense she'd developed these past five years warned her that she was being observed. Observed by someone whose loyalty was strictly to Samuel and who in all likelihood reported everything he saw directly to the man. She had to be careful. Everything was riding on making Samuel believe that she, like all the other women in the sect, was under his spell as well as firmly under his thumb. It went against everything she was, everything she had ever stood for, but to save Mia, she was willing to play this part.

That meant that she had to seem almost indifferent to the man she'd once loved above all else.

A man she still loved.

Carly swallowed as unobtrusively as she could and then forced a bright, mindless smile to her lips as she asked cheerfully, "So what brings you back to Cold Plains after all this time?"

Chapter 3

It *looked* like Carly. Even in that ridiculous, shapeless sack of a dress, it still looked like a slightly older, but definitely a heart-stoppingly beautiful version of Carly.

But it didn't *sound* like Carly.

Oh, it was her voice all right. He would have recognized her voice anywhere, under any circumstances. There were times he still heard her voice in his dreams, dreams that had their roots in a different, far less complicated time. And then, when he'd wake up in the dark and alone, he would upbraid himself for being so weak as to yearn for her. An emptiness would come over him, hollowing out what had once been his heart.

Yes, it was her voice all right. But there was a decided lack of *spirit* evident in it, a lack of the feisty, independent essence that made Carly who she was. That made her Carly.

The bright, chipper, vapid question she'd just asked sounded as if it had come from a Carly who had been lobotomized.

Which was, he now realized, exactly the way he could have described the expressions on the faces of several of the men and women he'd just watched walk by. It really looked to him as if nothing was behind the smiles on their faces. Granted they were moving about with what appeared to be a sense of purpose, but they all came across as being only two-dimensional—as if they had been cut out of cardboard and mounted on sticks.

Damn it, talk, *Hawk,* Carly thought. *Say something so I can go on with this charade. You will never,* never *know how much I've missed you, how many times I'd lie awake, wondering where you were and what you were doing. Wondering if you missed me even just a little.*

Carly had never allowed herself to regret sending him away. It had been the right thing to do. The right thing for *him.* But oh, how she regretted not being with Hawk when he had left town.

And now he was here, standing before her, larger than life—and she couldn't tell him anything. Not how she felt, not why she was going through the motions of being one of Samuel Grayson's devoted followers.

"So?" Carly prodded, still keeping the same wide, vacant smile on her lips. Her facial muscles began to cramp up. Playing mindless was a lot harder than it looked. "What brings you back?" she asked him again.

Carly knew it couldn't be a family matter that had caused him to return. His mother was dead—she had been the only thing keeping him here in the first place—and he never got along with his father who, although kinder in spirit than hers, had the very same romance going with any bottle of liquor he could find, just as her late father had had.

"You're about the very last person I would have ever expected to see coming back to Cold Plains." That much, at least, was truthful.

He laughed shortly as he shook his head. The sound had no humor in it. "Funny, and I figured you had enough sense to leave here," he replied, his tone sounding edgier than he'd meant it to.

Carly shrugged, momentarily looking away. But the children were all playing nicely. No squabbles that needed refereeing on her part. She had no excuse to leave.

She tried to tell herself that Hawk's words didn't sting, but it was a lie. Even after all this time, his opinion still meant a great deal to her. It probably always would.

"Something came up," she said by way of an excuse—and, again, she was being truthful. Something *had* come up to keep her here. Her sister's marriage bombshell.

Hawk's eyes skimmed over the dress she wore. He tried to do his best not to imagine the slender, firm body beneath the fabric or to remember that one night that she had been his. He hadn't realized then that he was merely on borrowed time.

"Yeah," he said curtly. "I can see that."

She sincerely doubted that he hated the dress she had on as much as she did, but wearing it was necessary. It was all part of convincing that hideous megalomaniac that she was as brainwashed as everyone else who had joined his so-called "flock."

"You still haven't answered my question," Carly prodded gently, her curiosity mounting. "Why are you back in Cold Plains?"

He minced no words. The days when he had wanted to shield her were gone. "I'm trying to find out who killed five young women and left their bodies to rot in five different, remote locations in Wyoming."

She looked at him sharply. Had he struck a chord? Did she actually know something about these women who had been cut down so ruthlessly? But then the look vanished, and her expression became completely unreadable. He swore inwardly.

The next moment, a strange smile curved her lips. "So you did it," she concluded, nodding her head with approval.

Hawk narrowed his eyes in annoyed confusion. "Did what?"

He'd told her that he wanted to do something adventurous, something that mattered. He wanted to leave the world a better place than when he found it. It was why she'd made him leave. Someone like that couldn't be happy in a town the size of a shoe box.

"You became a law enforcement agent. A U.S. Marshal?" she asked, guessing which branch he had ultimately joined. It had to be something along those lines in order to give him the authority and jurisdiction to investigate a crime like the one he had just mentioned.

Hawk shook his head. Then because she was obviously waiting for a clarification, he said, "I'm with the FBI."

"Even more impressive."

Working for the FBI wasn't impressive as far as he was concerned. It was a job, something that allowed him to move about, to keep from being tempted to put down roots in any one place for long. And it allowed him to keep the rest of the world at bay. For that, he had her to thank. After she had broken his heart, telling him that she had never loved him, he'd decided that he would never subject himself to that kind of pain again. The only way to do that was not to allow anyone in. Not to form any attachments.

Ever.

So what was he doing, standing here, feeling as if he'd just walked through a portal and gone back in time again? What the hell was he doing *feeling* again? It seemed that no matter what his resolve, all it took to undo everything he'd built up in the last decade or so was to be in Carly's presence again for a few minutes.

It just didn't seem right, but there it was, anyway.

"It's a job," he told her, shrugging off her compliment.

She heard the indifference, the callousness, even if he wasn't aware of expressing them. A wave of concern came over her. Maybe she shouldn't have turned him away. Not if it had turned out all wrong.

"Then you're disappointed?" she asked.

The thought that he was disillusioned sliced away at her heart. She had made what to her was the ultimate sacrifice, sending Hawk away so that he could follow his dream. If his dream had turned out not to be what he really wanted, then all these lost years had been for nothing.

"Yes," he answered coldly as his eyes skimmed over her again.

He wasn't talking about his job, she realized. Hawk was talking about how he felt about her. More than anything in the world, she would have loved to have set him straight, to tell him what she was really still doing here, but if she did that, she would wind up instantly throwing away everything she'd done up until now. It would mean sacrificing all the work she'd put into making Samuel believe that she was one of the faithful. One of the "devotees" he took such relish in collecting and adding to his number.

"Why are you dressed like that?" Hawk demanded, frowning. He looked around as he asked the question, adding, "Why are all the women out here dressed like that?"

"Not all," Carly pointed out, doing her best not to let her relief over that little fact show through. "There are still holdouts."

Thank God, she added silently.

"'Holdouts,'" he echoed her words. "As in, not having found the 'right path'?"

She widened the forced smile on her lips, hating this charade that circumstances had forced her to play. "I see you do understand."

He felt contempt. Had she always been this weak and he hadn't noticed, blinded by the so-called sacrifices she'd made to keep her father's farm running?

"Not by a long shot," he answered, disgusted. Again, he looked around. From all indications, they were standing in the center of town. And yet, it was all wrong, conflicting with his memories. The town he had left behind had been a rough-and-tumble place, a place where people existed without the promise of a future. A place where grizzled, weathered men came in to wash the taste of stagnation and failure from their parched throats at the local bar.

The bar was conspicuously missing as were other establishments that he remembered having once occupied the streets of Cold Plains.

"Where's the hardware store?" he asked. There was a health club—a damn health club of all things!—standing where he could have *sworn* the hardware store had once been.

Since when did the people who lived here have time to idle away, lifting weights and sitting in saunas? Health clubs were for the pampered with time on their hands. Nobody he knew in Cold Plains was like that. They had livings to scratch out from an unforgiving earth.

Or, at least, nobody had *been* like that when he'd left all those years ago.

Obviously things had changed.

"The owner had to relocate to Bryson," she told him, mentioning the name of a neighboring town. "He couldn't afford the rent here anymore." She saw confusion in Hawk's sharp eyes as he cocked his head. It took everything she had not to raise her hand and run her fingers along his cheek, the way she used to when he would look at her like that.

With effort, she blocked the memory. "New people came in and started buying up the land—investing in Cold Plains," she explained, quoting the official story that had been given out about the changes. Changes, everyone had been told over and over, that were all "for the better."

"And the diner?" Hawk asked, nodding toward a place down the block. The diner was clearly gone, replaced by another, far more modern-looking restaurant with a pretentious name. "Exactly what the hell is a 'Vegetarian Café'?"

"Just what the name suggests it is," she replied, then added, "They serve much healthier food than the diner ever did."

The name indicated that no meat was served on the premises. From where he stood, that just didn't compute. "This is cattle country," Hawk protested. "Men like their steaks, their meat, not some funny-looking, wilted green things." As he spoke, it struck him that the people who continued to walk by him all seemed to have the same eerie, neat and tidy and completely-devoid-of-any-character appearance as the new buildings did. "Speaking of which, where the hell *are* all the men?" he asked.

She knew what he meant, but of necessity, she pretended to be confused by his question. "They're all around you," she answered, indicating the ones who were out with their families or just briskly walking from one destination to another.

"No, they're not," he bit off. He'd grown up here, had lived among them. The men who had lived in Cold Plains when he was a teenager spent their days wrestling with the elements, fighting the land as they struggled to make a living, to provide for their families and themselves. The men he saw now looked too soft for that. Too fake. "These guys look like they're all about to audition for a remake of *The Stepford Wives*."

"Lower your voice," Carly said, using a more forceful tone than he'd heard coming from her up until now. *That* was the Carly he remembered, he thought.

But it bothered him that she was looking around, appearing concerned. As if she was afraid that someone would overhear them.

What the hell had happened to Cold Plains?

To her?

"Or what?" he challenged. "Whatever great power turned all these guys into drones will strike me dead for blaspheming?" he demanded angrily. "Who *did* all this?" he asked. "Who made everyone so damn fake?" But before Carly had a chance to answer him, Hawk shot another question at her. "You can't tell me that you actually *like* living this way, like some mindless pre-programmed robot."

Though his tone was angry, he was all but pleading with her to contradict his initial impression, to let him know somehow that she was here looking like some 1950s housewife against her will. That she didn't *want* to be like this.

Carly forced herself to spout the party line. "Samuel Grayson has generously done a great deal for this town," she began, the words all but burning a hole through her tongue.

"Grayson?" Hawk repeated. She was talking about Micah's twin brother. The smooth talker of the pair. He remembered thinking that the man could have easily been a snake oil salesman in the Old West. Last he'd heard, Grayson had hit the trail, spouting nonsense. They called that being a "motivational speaker" these days. Still a snake oil salesman in his book. "Samuel Grayson did all this?"

She nodded, forcing herself to look both enthusiastic and respectful at the mere mention of the man's name. "He and the investors he brought with him," she told him.

She hated the look of disbelief and disappointment she saw in Hawk's eyes, but she knew she couldn't risk telling him the way she actually felt. Couldn't tell him that she knew Grayson, charming though he might seem at first, was guilty of brainwashing the more gullible, the more desperate of the town's citizens. These were people who had tried to eke out a living for so long that when they had been given comforts for the very first time in their lives, they'd willingly fallen under the man's spell. They had given their allegiance to Grayson gladly, never realizing that they were also trading in their souls. Samuel Grayson accepted nothing less than complete submission. He fed on the power he had over the growing population of the so-called, little utopian world he had created.

So the rumors and his first impression were right, Hawk thought grimly. This was what Micah had vaguely alluded to when he'd asked to meet with him. Samuel Grayson had established a cult out here, preying on the vulnerable, the desperate, the easily swayed. He'd used all that against them to establish a beachhead for his particular brand of lunatic fringe.

"And where is Samuel Grayson right now?" he asked.

Again, the words all but scalded Carly's tongue, but she had no choice. She'd seen one of Samuel's henchmen come around the back of the school yard. The man didn't even bother pretending that he wasn't watching her. It was enough to make a person deeply paranoid.

"Samuel is wherever he is needed the most," she replied.

Without fully realizing what he was doing, Hawk took hold of her shoulders, fighting the very strong urge to shake her, return her to the clearheaded, intelligent woman he'd once known—or at least believed he'd once known.

Exasperation filled his veins as he cried, "Oh God, Carly, you can't possibly really believe what you just spouted."

Carly forced herself to raise her chin the way she always used to when she was bracing for a fight. "Of course I believe what I just said. And I'm not 'spouting,' I'm repeating the truth."

Hawk rolled his eyes, battling disgust.

"There a problem here?" someone asked directly behind him.

The low, gravelly voice belonged to the town's chief of police, one Bo Fargo. It was a job title that Fargo had apparently bestowed upon himself. The title elevated him from the lowly position of sheriff, a job he had just narrowly been elected to in the first place. But he did Grayson's bidding and, as such, was assured of a job for life, no matter what.

Carly's eyes widened.

"No, no problem," she declared quickly, hoping to avert this from turning into something ugly, given half a chance. She knew how Fargo operated. The stocky man didn't believe in just throwing his weight around but in using his fists and the butt of his gun to do his "convincing," as well. She didn't want to see Hawk hurt. "I'm just telling Hawk here about all the changes that have been introduced to Cold Plains—thanks to Samuel—since he left here."

The name obviously struck a chord. Fargo squinted as he peered up into Hawk's face.

In his fifties, the tall, husky man was accustomed to having both men and women alike cowering before him whenever he scowled. He enjoyed watching the spineless citizens being intimidated by him. He went so far as to relish it.

"Hawk?" Fargo echoed as he stared at the outsider through watery blue eyes.

"Hawk Bledsoe," Carly prompted by way of a reminder. "You remember Hawk, don't you, Chief?" she prodded, watching the man's round face for some sign of recognition.

"Tall, skinny kid," Fargo said, deliberately taking a derogatory tone.

Hawk gave no indication that he was about to back away. "I filled out some."

There was another moment of silence, as if Fargo was debating which way to play this. Hawk was not easily intimidated, and Fargo clearly didn't want to get into a contest where he might wind up being the loser. So for now, he laughed and patted his own gut.

"Haven't we all?" he asked rhetorically. "So what brings you back, Bledsoe? You thinking of resettling here in Cold Plains now that it's finally got something to offer?" he asked.

Hawk's eyes never left Fargo's. "No, I'm here to investigate the murders of five of your town's female citizens."

To back up his statement, Hawk took out his wallet and held up his ID for the chief to see.

If he didn't know better, Hawk thought, he would have sworn that Fargo turned pale beneath his deeply tanned face.

Chapter 4

The next minute, Hawk saw the chief of police pull himself together. What appeared to have been a momentary lapse, a chink in his armor, disappeared without a trace. Instead, a steely confidence descended over the older man's features again, eliminating any hint that he had been unnerved by talk of an investigation.

"I'm afraid that someone's been pulling your leg, Bledsoe," Fargo told him in a measured, firm voice. "We don't allow any crime here in Cold Plains."

Talk about being pompous, Hawk thought. The man set the bar at a new height. "Well, whether you allow it or not, Sheriff—"

"Chief," Fargo corrected tersely. "I'm the *chief* of police here."

Hawk inclined his head. If the man wanted to play games, so be it. He could play along for now, as long as it bought him some time and he could continue with his investigation. Not that he thought Fargo would be of any help to him. He just didn't want the man to be a hindrance.

"Chief," Hawk echoed, then continued, "but those five women are still dead nonetheless."

Minute traces of a scowl took over Fargo's average features. "I run a very tight ship here, Bledsoe. Everyone's happy, everyone gets along. Look around you," he instructed gruffly as he gestured about to encompass the entire town. "In case you haven't noticed, this isn't the town you left behind when you tore out of here after graduation." His eyes narrowed with the intention of pinning his opponent down. "I've been the chief of police these last five years and I don't recall anyone finding any bodies of dead women in Cold Plains," he concluded, closing the subject as far as he was concerned.

"That's because they weren't found here," Hawk explained evenly. "The bodies were discovered in five different locations throughout Wyoming over the last five years."

The expression on Fargo's face said that the matter was settled by the FBI agent's own admission. "Well, if you know that, then I don't understand what you're doing here, trying to stir things up. We're a peaceful little town, and we don't need your kind of trouble here."

A "peaceful little town" with a whole lot of secrets in its closet, Hawk was willing to bet. Out loud he said,

"All the women are believed to have been from here at one time or another."

"Hell, what someone does once they leave Cold Plains isn't any concern of mine." Though he continued to maintain the mirthless smile on his lips, Fargo's eyes seemed to bore into the man he considered an interloper—and possibly a problem. "If they found you dead, say in Cheyenne, that wouldn't be a reflection on the place where you were born, now, would it, Bledsoe?"

Hawk knew when he was being threatened and none-too-subtly at that. He had a feeling that Carly knew, too, because he saw her grow rigid, and just for a moment, that empty smile on her face had faded. She almost looked like the Carly he remembered, the Carly he still carried around in his head, despite all his efforts not to.

"It would be if I was killed here and then *moved* to Cheyenne," Hawk countered calmly.

He saw a flash of anger in the watery eyes before the chief got himself under control. "Is that what you're saying, Bledsoe? That these women were killed here and then somehow magically *lifted* and deposited in different places, all without my knowing a thing about it?" He drew closer, more menacing. "You think I'm that blind?"

"No, I don't," Hawk answered evenly. "And what I'm saying is that I need to investigate their deaths further, and that since they did come from Cold Plains, I wanted to ask a few questions starting here."

Fargo crossed his arms before him, an immovable

brick wall. *Daring* the other man to say the wrong thing. "Go ahead."

Their battlefield would be of his choosing, not Fargo's. "When I have the right questions," he told the chief mildly, "I'll be sure to come look you up."

Fargo's eyes narrowed into pale blue slits. "You do that." He shifted his gaze to Carly, who had been, for the most part, silently witnessing this exchange. Though there was a smile on the older man's lips, he looked far from happy. "Looks like recess time is over, Ms. Finn." He waved at the children behind her. "You'd best get those little ones back to their classrooms."

It was a veiled order, and Carly knew it. Nodding, she let the chief think that she appreciated his prompting. There was no point in digging in now. She needed Fargo to believe she was as mindless as all the other women who had chosen to cleave to Grayson's remodeled version of paradise on earth.

"Right you are, Chief."

Turning, she deliberately avoided making eye contact with Hawk, afraid he would see too much there, things that would give him pause. Because if he thought that what she was doing might all be an act, she was certain that Fargo, who was smarter than he actually looked, would pick up on it.

Worse, the chief might act on it. She didn't want any harm coming to Hawk. Though it might sound callous to someone else, she didn't care about the women whose murders were being investigated. They were dead, and nothing would change that. But Hawk wasn't. She didn't want Hawk getting hurt, and if he stayed here any length of time, he just might become a target.

It wasn't safe here anymore.

Hawk had always shot straight from the hip, and around here, that was dangerous. Fargo wasn't a man to cross and neither was Grayson or any of his cold-blooded henchmen. The only way to deal with any of them was to pretend to play the game.

As Carly withdrew, Fargo remained standing where he was, his right hand resting on the hilt of his holstered weapon as he regarded Hawk.

"Anything else I can do for you?" Fargo asked.

Hawk knew the value of retreat in order to regroup for another time, another battle. "I'll let you know, Chief," he promised noncommittally, just before he turned and walked away.

"You won't have any trouble finding me," Fargo called after him. "I patrol these streets pretty regularly. Seeing me among 'em is what keeps folks on the straight and narrow."

"Got it," Hawk replied without bothering to turn around. He did his best not to sound dismissive.

When he had initially left town, he remembered that Fargo had been a deputy, not the sheriff and certainly nothing as pretentious sounding as "chief of police." In addition, the man had also been the town bully, more given to causing trouble than to quelling it. Fargo took over, according to the information that he'd collected, when the old sheriff died in a freak accident.

He wondered just how much of it had been an accident and how much had involved a freak. Might just be something else to investigate, Hawk thought, after he cleared up this matter of the five women's murders.

Crossing to his car, Hawk blew out a breath. Just what the hell had happened here in the past five years or so? Five years was also about the time that the first body had turned up. And *that* coincided with another piece of information that the Bureau had discovered about Grayson and his band of not-so-merry-men. They had descended on the town, under the guise of being business "investors," and started buying up property with the intention of making renovations five years ago.

He'd read the reports that had been compiled, but he'd never dreamed the extent to which all this actually went. Grayson had transformed everything, as well as everyone he encouraged to remain in the town, creating what he freely touted as being "paradise on earth."

There was no such thing and they all knew it, Hawk thought, getting into his car. Or were supposed to know it.

After closing the door, he fastened his seat belt. What Grayson had really created was a town of zombies. Key in hand, Hawk remained sitting in his car, observing the people on Main Street for a few more minutes. He was acutely aware that Fargo was watching him watch the good citizens of Cold Plains.

It struck him in less than another minute that there was something *really* wrong with this scenario, something that went beyond the inane smiles and the overly neat clothing. Didn't anyone get dirty anymore? Not even the kids? What he noticed was that there wasn't a single neutral expression in the whole lot.

It wasn't possible for *everyone* to actually be happy at the same time, just as it wasn't possible that they all looked so perfect. No one was limping or stumbling, no one was coughing or sneezing. What the hell had the great God Grayson done, outlawed allergies, colds and imperfections? Had the man also managed to outlaw plain people? Because there were no plain people on these streets, certainly not ugly people, at least as far as his eye could see.

Something was very, very wrong here.

Fargo, apparently, had decided to surrender his passive role as observer, because the man was now on the move, heading straight for him, Hawk realized. In response, Hawk switched on his ignition and started his car.

For now, he wanted to get back to the cabin outside of town to make sure that the task force he'd put together was settled in. He'd picked good people, but he had an uneasy feeling that before this was over, they would need reinforcements.

Lots of them.

Carly could feel her insides shaking.

From the first floor window of her classroom, she'd covertly watched Fargo and Hawk regarding one another, two stags about to lock horns. She'd prayed that Hawk would have the good sense to leave before something bad happened.

When Fargo started walking toward Hawk, she thought her pounding heart would break one of her ribs. Fargo was like a bull moose and Hawk—Hawk was too damn stubborn for his own good. He might be the younger of the two, but the Hawk she remembered didn't fight dirty. He was nothing if not honorable. Fargo wasn't shackled by any such noble conventions. To Fargo, the prime directive was to get rid of any obstacles that might get in his way and those who might ultimately impede Samuel's control over Cold Plains.

Oh God, the sooner she could get Mia out of here, the better, she thought, still watching the two men. Desperation stole over her when she thought of Mia. Her sister wouldn't listen to reason. That left having to find a way to kidnap her, to drag Mia kicking and screaming out of Cold Plains before she was forced to marry that man.

Brice Carrington had been married once before, and no one knew exactly what had happened to the first Mrs. Carrington, other than the fact that one day, Carrington had haltingly announced that she was "gone from this earth."

Just like that, the woman was no longer among the living. Not unlike, Carly recalled, what had happened to the chief of police's wife. She had disappeared, as well, making Bo Fargo a widower—or so the man had claimed. No one really questioned him about it. One day the man was married, then the next day, he wasn't.

It occurred to Carly that the men in Cold Plains did not get divorced. If they found themselves suddenly alone and widowers, it was because they had conveniently "lost" their wives.

What if these women were not "lost" but rather eliminated? What if Carrington's wife and the chief's wife had been killed, just like those five women whose deaths Hawk was investigating?

And what if there were a lot more dead women buried throughout the state, women who had come from Cold Plains and who, for one reason or another, had fallen out of favor with Samuel?

Now that she thought of it, Carly vaguely remembered hearing someone say that Brice Carrington had wanted children to carry on his legacy and the first Mrs. Carrington hadn't been able to have any children. Was that her sin? The inability to conceive and produce little disciples for Grayson? Was *that* why Carrington was marrying Mia, so she could become the baby machine he both wanted and expected?

Oh, Mia, Mia, how can you be so blind? They just want to use you. And you're letting them.

"Is something wrong, Carly?"

The question, coming from behind her and quietly worded, nearly caused Carly to jump out of her skin. Even at its lowest point, it struck her as a very creepy-sounding voice.

Samuel.

Looking out the window, she hadn't heard him come into her classroom. The man moved like smoke—or like the devil, except that his cloven hooves were muted, hidden inside of hand-stitched shoes, which cost more than a lot of the farmers and the ranchers in the area managed to earn in any given year.

Samuel Grayson, movie-star handsome, with a tongue that was smoother than sweetened whipped cream, and blessed with hypnotic eyes that could easily hold a soul in place, had left the tiny town of Horn's Gulf years ago to make his mark—and his money—as a motivational speaker.

Increasingly more and more successful, he toured the Southwest and gave seminars to hapless people who wanted nothing more than to be half as dynamic as the man who had captured their attention and fired up their souls.

So they plunked their money down and listened in rapt attention, hoping for miracles to strike, miracles that would transform them into veritable clones of the stirring speaker. And as they prayed, Grayson went about the business of separating these desperate would-be disciples of his from their "contributions."

Contributions, Carly knew, a good many of them could ill afford to give. But that didn't bother—or stop—Grayson from collecting what he obviously felt was his due.

Eventually he grew bored and sought new challenges. Not content with moving from city to city, reaping money and unconditional adulation, Grayson had apparently decided to return to his roots and seek out a place to transform and make his own. A place that appeared to be dying. Cold Plains fit the bill.

Whether his own motivation came out of a desire to revenge himself on someone or from a need to come full circle and take over a town that reminded him of the place where he'd once been regarded as a ne'er do well, she didn't know and, frankly, she didn't care. What mattered was that he hadn't sucked her into his vortex no matter how hard he had tried.

The meaningless, empty smile she'd displayed for Hawk earlier curved her lips now as she looked up at the man who professed to being the town's "gentle, guiding conscience."

"No, Mr. Grayson," she replied politely, "nothing's wrong."

Grayson surprised her by slipping his arm around her shoulders in a familiar manner she instantly resented. Carly could feel herself screaming on the inside. But she didn't have that luxury right now, nor could she shrug him off—or push him away—the way she would have so much preferred.

"Now Carly," Grayson chided, "what was it I told you?" He looked at her pointedly.

For a second, because she was still recovering from the absolute shock of seeing Hawk back in Cold Plains, Carly's mind went blank.

And then she realized what Grayson was so coyly referring to.

"You said to call you Samuel."

"Yes, I did. There is no hierarchy here," he assured her, an insincere smile vouching for the veracity of his statement.

The hell there isn't, and you know it, Carly thought as she deliberately mirrored the smile on Grayson's thin, pursed lips.

"Now come on," he coaxed, "let me hear you say it."

"There's nothing wrong, *Samuel,*" Carly repeated sweetly.

Samuel made a show of peering into her eyes, as if

he was looking into her soul, as well. It was all part of the act, and they both knew it, Carly thought.

"Are you sure now, Carly?" Grayson asked solicitously. Then before she could reply again, he continued, "I thought what with Hawk's unexpected return here to Cold Plains, you might find yourself having to deal with some 'issues' the two of you might have had." He singled out the word, emphasizing it like a television pop psychologist.

That blindsided her.

There were times when the man really did seem to know everything, Carly thought uneasily. At those times she could almost believe Grayson *was* omnipotent, the way some of his followers claimed.

But no man was, and Grayson was definitely *not* the exception but the rule.

"No, I'm fine. Really. Hawk and I were over a long time ago," she told him staunchly.

Grayson nodded, his expression unreadable and all the more unnerving because of that. She didn't know if he believed her or was just playing her.

"That's good," he replied in a tone that equally revealed nothing. "But if you ever find yourself wanting to talk or just in need of a friendly, nonjudgmental ear, my door is always open," he told her, punctuating his words with a warm squeeze of her shoulders, which was hardly quick in nature.

It took everything she had not to allow her revulsion to show through.

Instead, Carly forced herself to assume a beaming,

grateful expression. "Thank you, Samuel. You're very kind."

"I can be kinder," he assured her, his voice pulsing with promise as their eyes met.

Not even if hell freezes over and the fate of the world depended on it, she thought.

Any second now, she was positive she would throw up. Time to retreat.

"I'd better be getting back to the children," she told Grayson. She gestured toward the rows of eerily quiet seven-year-olds who were sitting at their desks, their hands folded. "I can only count on their behaving themselves for just so long."

Grayson's magnetic green eyes met hers. "I was just thinking the same thing."

Carly knew that she had just been put on notice. If she was going to get Mia out of here, it would have to be soon.

Very soon.

Chapter 5

Thinking that their conversation was over, Carly hoped that Grayson would finally leave the classroom. But the self-appointed leader of the renovated Cold Plains community made no move to walk out. Instead, the man remained where he was, uncomfortably close to her.

Carly instinctively braced herself for round two.

"You know, your sister is coming along very well," Grayson said. "She is going to be a fine addition to our peaceful, little community once she and Brice are finally married."

Every word out of Grayson's mouth sounded so terribly wrong to her, especially this. After going through the motions of this charade she was forced to play for the past couple of months, if the man had said that the grass was green, she would have expected to look down and see that, instead of green, it was actually a shade of blue.

Wanting desperately to point out how horribly patronizing and chauvinistic he sounded, Carly bit her tongue, swallowing the hot words that instantly rose to her lips. Instead, she forced herself to say what she knew Grayson was waiting to hear.

"I haven't had much time to talk with Mia," she told him, "but I know that she's very excited about the wedding."

"The ceremony's only three weeks away," Grayson needlessly reminded her.

Or was he actually just goading her? With him it was difficult to tell. The only thing she would have sworn to was that there wasn't a drop of human kindness in the man's entire body. Not only that, but he was lecherous, as well. She'd seen the way Grayson looked at some of the women in the community, married and unmarried alike. The look in his eyes definitely did *not* belong to a man who was "pure of heart," the way he claimed.

Somehow, she managed to keep her vacant smile in place. "Yes, I know."

Just how much longer was she going to have to pretend that Grayson wasn't looking at her right now as if she were a piece of barbecued meat and he hadn't eaten in a month?

Mia, think of Mia. You tell this charlatan what you think of him, and Mia's lost.

Carly curled her fingers into her palms, digging her nails in to keep from saying something that would make her feel better but would ultimately ruin everything.

"You know, you might think about finding some-one and getting married yourself, Carly," Grayson suggested. She could almost *feel* his eyes touching her. "After all, at thirty-one you must be hearing your prime reproductive minutes ticking loudly away."

If she were having a normal conversation with a normal, albeit opinionated and annoying, man, she would have been tempted to haul off and hit him for the demeaning way he was talking to her. But giving in to her more primitive instincts wasn't going to help rescue Mia. So again, Carly forced herself to pretend to agree with him.

"Actually, I do, but so far, there hasn't been anyone I would want to spend the rest of my life with."

Grayson waved away the excuse. "Nonsense, I know plenty of eligible men I can introduce you to. You're just being too picky, Carly," he chided, although he continued to smile at her. "But I do sense a certain wavering within you," he confessed. "It's only natural," he assured her. "Some people come to the right path after taking all the wrong ones, and they can't bring themselves to believe they've finally found the right road. I could give you some private lessons if you like," he offered. "Share with you the benefits of all I've seen and learned about this way of life."

Though she gave no outward indication, Carly was instantly on her guard. They were shadow boxing. She could sense it. Grayson was trying to make her slip up, to let her true intentions show through.

Don't hold your breath, Grayson. I've fooled a better man than you, she thought, remembering the look on Hawk's face when she told him she really didn't love him.

"I couldn't impose on you that way." Carly paused a moment, then added his name to her declaration, enunciating it slowly, melodically, "Samuel. You're much too busy a man. I'd feel guilty taking up your time like that."

He laughed off her protest. "I'm never too busy to spend some quality time with one of the community's good citizens, Carly." His peppermint-laced breath seemed to form a cloud all around her, making it difficult to breathe. "You'll find, my dear, that I can be *very* approachable."

Yes, she just bet he could be. She'd heard that he had "approached" at least half a dozen women within the transformed sectors of Cold Plains since she began paying attention to what was happening here, to the place she called home.

"I shall keep that in mind," she promised. "But now I really do need to get back to my lesson plan." She smiled up sweetly at him, entertaining herself with the thought that some day that man would get what was coming to him. And maybe having Hawk here signaled the beginning of the end of King Samuel's would-be reign. She relished the thought. "Otherwise," she continued, "the children won't be able to do their homework assignments tonight."

"Careful, Carly," he warned with a warm smile. "You don't want the little ones thinking that you're a slave driver."

Instead of just being enslaved by a man with a golden

tongue, she countered silently. Because that was what Grayson did, enslave an entire community of people who now moved about like automatons, with compliant, moronic smiles on their faces.

Were all the people here so easily brainwashed? Were they all so desperate for something new, something different, something supposedly "better" that they would blindly obey a man whose real agenda was still hidden?

The thought made her very uneasy—as did the realization that she wasn't really safe. Grayson had all but put her on notice. She would have to be on her guard against him. No doubt, he had plans for her, plans that very well just might make her wind up the same way that those five women whose bodies were scattered throughout the state had ultimately wound up.

She had no proof, but in her heart, Carly just *knew* those dead women were somehow tied to Grayson.

She also knew she should be afraid, really afraid, but somehow, just knowing that Hawk was in the area quelled her uneasiness. He'd always had the ability to make her feel safe. Maybe it was unrealistic to think that he still gave a damn what happened to her, but somehow, she sensed that he did.

The children, thirty seven- and eight-year-olds in total, finally began to grow restless. Had they been a normal bunch they would have gotten that way much sooner.

For now, she turned her attention to them, putting any and all thoughts of Grayson, Mia and Hawk on the back burner. Or at least trying to.

She was successful on two counts, but Hawk's image refused to take a backseat to *anything*.

Two out of three wasn't bad, Carly consoled herself.

The minute he'd driven away from the center of town—and away from Fargo's steely gaze—Hawk pulled over to the side of the road and took out his cell phone. By now he knew the number by heart.

Punching the numbers in, he tried to reach Micah Grayson again. He'd been trying the number periodically ever since the man hadn't shown up for their appointment or called to explain why.

And as with all the other times when he actually *could* get through—and reception out here left a great deal to be desired—Hawk heard the phone on the other end ring once, then immediately after that heard his call go to voice mail.

There was no need to leave yet another message. He'd already left three. Still, Hawk bit off, "Where the hell are you, Grayson? I swear, if you're not dead, you will be."

With that, he jabbed at the word *End* on his phone and terminated his unsuccessful call before jamming the cell phone back into his pocket.

Sitting there, he impatiently drummed his fingers on the dashboard. Ordinarily, he wasn't a man who worried. He just calculated worst-case scenario and the probability percentages that such a scenario would actually occur. But the problem was that this time he *was* worried. Really worried. Micah Grayson was nothing if not a consummate professional and completely business oriented, even though the business he was in was utterly unorthodox.

In the old tradition, Micah was as good as his word, which was his bond. If he had said he'd show up somewhere, then he'd show up. Unless something really dire had happened to him, preventing him from keeping the appointment.

And if that was the case, had this "dire something" happened because of his chosen occupation, or was it somehow tied to what Micah wanted to tell him about the murdered women?

Since there were no answers right now, why should he make himself crazy? Hawk thought. There was already enough of that going on. His mind reverted back to his last exchange with Carly in the school yard.

Damn but this land, which was cruel and hard on everyone, had somehow been good to her. She'd lost weight, he'd observed. Just enough weight to make her hauntingly beautiful, not enough to make her appear weathered and worn.

There was no justice in the world, he thought. If there was, he would have found her off-putting and frazzled, with a pack of little kids squabbling at her feet.

But that, he reminded himself, would have meant that someone had to have been with her. Touching her. Making love to her. And that would have clearly torn him apart.

Was this any better? he silently demanded. Seeing her and finding out that he still wanted her? Maybe more than ever?

His cell phone began ringing. It took him a couple

of rings to extract it from his pocket again. Glancing at the number, he realized that he was still nursing the hope that Micah would turn up as mysteriously as he'd vanished and call back.

But the caller wasn't Micah, it was Boyd Patterson, one of the three special agents he'd recruited for this mission.

"Bledsoe," Hawk snapped as he answered his phone. In return, he heard a high-pitched noise on the other end, followed by static and then a voice that sounded as if it actually belonged to an extraterrestrial attempting to make first contact. "Patterson?" Hawk asked dubiously. Other than the caller ID on his screen, he hadn't heard anything to correctly identify the person on the other end of his squawking phone.

In response to his single word question, Hawk heard more static, now joined by an ear-shattering crackling noise.

Civilization, he thought in frustration, was still only moderately flirting with places like Cold Plains. Full contact with the inventions of the past ten years was still a patience-trying league away.

"Listen, I can't hear you," Hawk finally said into the phone, raising his voice in case the reception on Patterson's end was better than what he was hearing on his. There was no point in continuing to try to make out what, if anything, was being said on the other end of this call. "If this *is* Patterson, I'm about fifteen minutes out and heading back to the cabin. Stop draining the damn battery and turn your cell off for now. Maybe you'll have better luck using it later."

With that, Hawk ended his call and instead of putting the cell phone back into his jacket pocket, he tossed the small smartphone onto the passenger seat, leaving it within easy reach in case a miracle happened and decent reception actually put in a public appearance for more than a ten-second spate.

The phone remained silent for the duration of his trip.

It wound up taking him less than the promised fifteen minutes to reach the secluded cabin. He'd already been here a number of times to check out its accessibility as well as to ascertain just how much visibility was available from within the cabin. He wanted no surprises—just in case he and his team needed to make a stand here.

To the untrained eye, the modest little cabin looked like the perfect getaway home, a place where a busy executive might take off for a few days to unwind and become one with nature.

What it *didn't* look like was a place where four FBI special agents were conducting an investigation into Samuel Grayson's comings and goings, his land holdings as well as the "investors" he had brought along with him. All this while actively maintaining surveillance on the man and his main residence.

The cabin's rustic appearance suited Hawk's purposes just fine.

Though there was no one in the area, Hawk left nothing to chance and was not about to drop his guard or grow lax. He parked his vehicle behind the cabin, out of sight. The other three agents, he noted with approval, had already done the same. If someone did happen to drive by in the coming days, nothing out front would arouse curiosity or create the need for speculation.

Walking into the three-room cabin through the rear door he'd had put in, Hawk was instantly enveloped in a warm, welcoming scent. One of the agents was cooking. Unless he missed his guess, the agent was making stew. The tempting aroma reminded him that he hadn't really eaten today. Seeing Carly again had thrown him off and killed his appetite. Things like food and eating had temporarily been banished to a nether region.

But now hunger returned, barreling through him with a vengeance. He could hear his stomach growling, making demands.

He passed the agent who had been on the other end of the unsuccessful call. Special agent Boyd Patterson looked as if he was currently at his wit's end, trying to coax a little cooperation from his Bureau-issued laptop.

"Smells good," Hawk commented, nodding toward the tiny kitchen in the rear.

The other agent barely glanced up. "Rosenbloom bought supplies," he explained, preoccupied. "He figured since we're going to be stuck here, he might as well make us all something decent to eat."

Hawk smiled, nodding his approval. "Knew I brought him along for a reason." Then he raised his voice and called out to the rear of the cabin, "Someday you're going to make some woman a wonderful wife, Rosy."

Lawrence Rosenbloom paused momentarily to stick his head out of the alcove. The tall, thin special agent had initially trained to become a world-class top chef before he'd succumbed to the enticing, so-called promise of adventure and excitement while in the service of his country.

He took his superior's comment in stride, firing back, "I'd be careful what I said, Bledsoe. When I worked at a famous five-star restaurant in New York, I saw servers spit into the food they were bringing out to customers who irritated them."

Hawk nodded, as if this revelation was news to him. "Any of these customers have a gun?" he asked the other agent mildly.

Rosenbloom went back to slowly stirring his creation. "Can't say that I ever saw any."

"Therein lies the difference," Hawk told him, his voice still incredibly friendly. "*I* have a gun. I ever catch you even thinking about doing what you just said, I'll use it."

"Point taken." Rosenbloom grinned. "Guess that makes this a standoff."

"Guess so," Hawk agreed.

"So?" Patterson interrupted impatiently. He wasn't one of those types who regarded camping as something even remotely recreational. He preferred skyscrapers to grass every time. "Did you find out anything?" he asked with interest.

Yeah, I found out I'm still in love with Carly Finn even after all these years. I found out I'm not the robot I thought I was. And it sucks!

Out loud, Hawk replied, "Yeah, I found out something. I don't know *why* Samuel Grayson came in with his men and bought up huge chunks of property, but he's managed to turn the whole damn town into the movie set straight out of *The Stepford Wives*."

Patterson blinked, trying to follow what he was being told. But Hawk had lost him with the reference. "The what?"

"It's a cult classic," Rosenbloom's disembodied voice came floating out of the kitchen alcove. "All the wives in Stepford were brainwashed into being obedient and subservient to their husbands. They moved around the town like a bunch of smiling, mindless robots."

Temporarily pushing back from the table and his computer, Patterson grinned. "Sounds great. Where do I sign up?"

"Spoken like a man who hasn't been married," the third agent, Stephen Jeffers, a twenty-year veteran both of the Bureau and marriage, remarked. There was a note of pity in his voice.

Taking a momentary break, Rosenbloom left the stove and walked out into the main room. "If that's all you want out of a relationship, Patterson, get yourself a dog from an animal shelter. Me, I like intelligent conversation and a woman with some proven fighting spirit."

The grin on Patterson's face turned wistful as he allowed his mind to drift for a second. It was a general known fact that Rosenbloom's wife was not just intelligent and feisty, she was exceedingly sexy, as well.

"Spirit sounds good," Patterson agreed.

"Right about now, *anything* sounds good to him, Bledsoe," Rosenbloom explained as he turned back to the meal that was almost ready. "I think he's getting cabin fever."

Patterson had been the last of the four of them to arrive here.

"After only twelve hours?" Hawk asked incredulously. They hadn't even gotten their feet wet yet. And while he was hoping that he could find enough evidence to quickly wrap up the case, he was too realistic to pin his hopes on that.

"Doesn't take long," Patterson volunteered. "You forget, I'm a city boy. What the hell do people do around here for entertainment—besides watching paint dry and grass grow, I mean."

"I don't know about 'other people,'" Hawk told him, "but you're going over anything we can find on Samuel Grayson. That includes his background from the minute he was born as well as the people he's associated with since then."

Patterson glanced toward the front window, and Hawk could almost read the other man's mind.

"And under no circumstances," he went on to warn, "are you or Rosy or Jeffers to go into Cold Plains. Strangers stand out like sore thumbs there. I don't want Grayson getting it into his head that I didn't come alone." They didn't have much going for them, so this at least gave them the element of surprise if they needed it. Every little bit helped.

"What about supplies?" Rosenbloom wanted to know. "I can't make this stew last for more than a couple of days, Hawk."

"No one's asking for the miracle of the fishes and

the loaves," Hawk replied, walking into the alcove for a moment. He nodded at the stove. "Where'd you get those?"

"Little town thirty miles south of here," Rosenbloom answered. "Hadleyville, I think it was called."

The name sounded vaguely familiar to him. "Then that's where you'll go to get anything else. Cold Plains is full of grinning zombies. I could use a little leverage on my side, and it looks like you three are going to be it."

"Zombies?" Patterson questioned with a touch of confusion.

Hawk snorted. "They might as well be. From what I saw, they look like the only thoughts they had in their heads were the ones put there by Grayson."

"Is everyone on board with this guy?" Patterson wanted to know.

"That's what I intend to find out," Hawk answered, then added with a grin, "After I have some of Rosy's stew, of course."

"Coming right up, Fearless Leader," Rosenbloom sang out. The next minute, he walked into the living room, using a makeshift tray he'd created out of a board of wood to carry four bowls of hot stew.

The warm meal didn't quite wipe away the cold, tight knot that had formed in Hawk's stomach the moment he had seen Carly, but he had to admit that it did help. Some. At least he now felt ready to face the very definite possibility of seeing her again.

Chapter 6

A week went by.

A week involving what turned out to be mostly painstakingly fruitless observations and smoldering, growing frustration. Though he would have been the first to say he'd severed all ties to Cold Plains, the truth was that Hawk did *not* like what he saw happening within the town he'd once called home. The more he watched, the more annoyed he became.

He grew more convinced that, at the very least, Samuel Grayson was out to line his own pockets at the expense of the weak-minded sheep who had so easily fallen under his spell. It was as if they had no backbone, no will of their own.

He continued to try Micah's number at least once a day, with the same frustrating results. Micah wasn't picking up and he was nowhere to be found.

Hawk's bad feeling continued to escalate.

He and the three special agents who comprised his team went on gathering information both on Grayson and on anyone in the man's employ. They relied on both covert, firsthand observations as well as doing intense research as they went over old records and current databases.

Every night, before he finally returned to his hotel room in town, a hotel room he was certain Grayson had bugged, Hawk would find himself driving over to the farm where Carly still lived.

The farm that had come between them because she had remained to operate it for her father and sister, and he had left to find his true destiny.

All the other nights, he had just driven past it, glancing to see if the lights were on.

They always were.

But tonight, tonight was different. Instead of continuing on his way, he'd stopped. Not slowed down as he'd initially intended, but stopped dead. He turned off his engine.

Hawk leaned back in the driver's seat, willing the knots out of his shoulders. He told himself that he was here because he had questions for her. Questions about what was going on in town. Questions that pertained to the five murdered women.

After all, if she hadn't left town, hadn't moved on in all this time, who better to talk to about Cold Plains and the changes that had taken place than Carly? She was an observant woman, she should have insight into these things. The fact that he'd had feelings for her shouldn't matter.

Shouldn't.

But it did.

Because he still had feelings for her. He hadn't realized just how much or how strong until the second he'd seen her a week ago.

Hell, the whole damn world had just stopped dead on its axis, freezing in place. The only sound he'd heard for a split second was the sound of his own heart banging against his rib cage, fit to kill.

So much for telling himself that he was over her. That he would *ever* be over her, for that matter.

Hawk squared his shoulders. Well, he wouldn't get any questions answered like this, sitting inside his car, watching darkness creep in and surround her house.

He allowed anger to get the better of him. It got his blood pumping, and that, in turn, forced him to get out of the car.

She'd been home for over half an hour now. That was how long he'd sat out there, watching the house. Debating his next move.

He'd followed her from the school, where she'd remained far longer than her students had. Though he told himself not to be, he had been consumed with curiosity about what she was doing and what had kept her there until almost seven, practically four hours after parents and school buses had shown up to transport students back to their homes. Was she grading papers? Talking to other teachers?

Spending time with Grayson?

A flash of something hot, unwieldy and unreasonable shot through him. Hawk refused to identify or put a label on it. Jealousy was for other people, not him. Certainly not now.

For a second, he focused on Grayson. He knew that Samuel Grayson and Micah, his missing informant, were twins, and at first glance, the two men did look alike. But while Micah was a natural for his chosen line of work, a methodical, keenly observant man of few words who could terminate a man's existence with a minimum of moves, Samuel was outgoing, gregarious and not only played up but relied on his looks.

No matter how you dressed him up, Samuel Grayson still reminded him of a snake oil salesman. And from what he'd heard, Grayson actually *was* selling something. Grayson had his people collecting, bottling and preparing half liter bottles of "healing" tonic water.

The water in question came from the creek behind the community center. Legend had it that the water had immense healing powers and that, some said, it actually had some of the elements of a fountain of youth in it, as well.

Bottles of this "healing water" were placed on sale—"offered" at twenty-five dollars a pop—in the community center. The water that flowed in the creek was no longer available to the citizens of Cold Plains except through Grayson. He had seen to that, buying the land on both sides of the creek and turning it into private property.

Not only were bottles placed on sale independently, but they were also on sale at the weekly seminars that he gave. Regular attendance was mandatory if those in his flock wanted to remain in good standing with both Grayson and the rest of the "community." Purchase of the bottled water was mandatory, as well. And with each purchase, Grayson's coffers became a little fuller.

The man had a hell of a racket going for him, Hawk couldn't help thinking. He could understand how a lot of the people who lived here had gotten ensnared. They'd been trapped by dreams of well-being and contentment that Grayson seemed to be able to market so effortlessly. The people of Cold Plains had had so very little to cling to, and Grayson dealt in hope. Albeit unrealistic hope, but when a person was truly desperate, any hope was better than none at all.

That was their excuse, he thought, dismissing the other citizens he'd seen herded into Grayson's "meeting center." But what was hers?

Carly had never been a woman to wallow in self-pity or one who allowed herself to be sidelined or defeated by dwelling on worst-case scenarios. When they were growing up, she had always been the one to buoy him up, to make him feel as if he could put up with it all, because there was a better life waiting for him—for them—on the horizon.

Granted she'd dashed it all by telling him that the one thing he had clung to—that she loved him—was a lie. But even that wouldn't explain why she had been transformed from an independent, intelligent young woman to an obedient, mindless robot.

He couldn't have been *that* wrong about her, Hawk told himself.

Finally climbing out of the car, Hawk resisted the temptation to slam the door in his wake. Instead, he merely closed it, then strode over to her front door—just the way he had done so very many times in the past.

He ached for things that lay buried deep in years gone by.

Hawk rang the bell—and heard nothing. No one had ever gotten around to fixing the doorbell, he realized. It had been broken when he used to call on her.

Some things never changed.

Too bad that other things did.

Raising his hand, he knocked on the door. Then goaded by impatience, he knocked again. He'd just raised his hand to knock for a third time when the door finally opened.

Carly, with her hair pinned back from her face, stood in the doorway. She wore frayed jeans and a T-shirt that had seen one too many washings.

She'd never looked more beautiful to him.

He saw surprise, instantly followed by uneasiness, pass over her face. Her eyes darted from one side to the other, as if checking the area. Then rather than asking him what he was doing here or what he wanted, she ordered sharply, "Get inside," and stepped to one side to give him access.

All but yanking him in, she scanned the darkening, flat terrain one last time, then quickly closed the door behind him.

Whirling around to face Hawk, she finally spoke. "What are you doing here?"

The question was tersely asked and no empty, mindless smile accompanied her words. She wasn't smiling at all. Instead, she appeared agitated.

That was more like it, he thought. But was she agitated? Did it have to do with finding him here—or was Grayson behind her display of uneasiness?

"What the hell is going on here?" he demanded. "And what the hell happened to you?"

"You don't answer a question with more questions," she informed him, snapping out her words. It was a defense mechanism. Because she was afraid where this would wind up taking her.

Taking them.

"I don't want an English lesson or a grammar lesson, Carly," he retorted in the same exasperated tone she had just used. "I want an answer."

All promises to hold on to his temper had flown out the proverbial window. He cut the distance between them from several feet down to less than a few inches.

He was in her space and she in his, and the air turned hot and sultry between them, despite the fact that outside, the April night was crisp and clean. And more than a little cold.

"Damn it, Carly," he shouted at her, "this isn't you."

"This is me," she countered stubbornly.

Hawk's brown eyes darkened as they narrowed. "I refuse to believe that."

"Well, unfortunately for you, you don't have a say in it. It is what it is, no matter what you say to the contrary," she maintained stubbornly. "Besides, you've been gone for ten years, you have no idea what kind of transformations have been going on and taking place here," she pointed out.

"Maybe not." He agreed to the general principle she'd raised. "The town looks like it's gone to hell in that handbasket our grandmothers were always talking about."

She would have smiled if this wasn't so serious. "The town has prospered," she contradicted, dutifully spouting the party line. For all she knew, he was now in Grayson's employ, too. He was out here to trip her up for some reason she hadn't figured out yet. "Just look around the next time you're on Main Street."

"I have." His expression told her that he was far from impressed with the changes. She would have been—had they not come at such a high price. "It's like they all made a deal with the devil." He paused, his eyes pinning her. "Did you do that, too, Carly? Did you make a deal with the devil?"

She should have taken it as a compliment, because it meant that she was playing her role well and was convincing. But instead, she felt insulted that he thought so little of her.

Isn't that what you wanted? To come across as one of Grayson's mindless minions?

The answer was that she both wanted it, and she didn't. A part of her felt he should have known better than to think this of her.

Her feelings were getting in the way of her common sense and her plan.

She tossed her head, her eyes blazing. "I don't know what you're talking about."

Carly began to turn her back on him, but he caught her by the wrist, holding her in place. "I think you do," he told her.

"What you think really doesn't matter to me," she lied, doing her best to ignore the wild turmoil going on in the pit of her stomach. She attempted to pull free but only succeeded in having him tighten his hold on her. "You're hurting me," she accused.

"Am I?" he retorted angrily. "Am I hurting you?" Struggling with himself, he opened his hand and released her. Anger continued to flash in his eyes. "Well, it's nothing compared to what you did to me."

Carly raised her chin contentiously. "I didn't hurt you, Hawk," she informed him. "What I did was set you free."

Had she lost her mind? Did living under Grayson's thumb completely destroy her ability to think? "What are you talking about?"

After all this time, she would have thought it might have dawned on him. Apparently not. She spelled it out as much as she could.

"You left here to become something. To make something of yourself. To follow your dream. And from what I can see, you succeeded. So in the long run, you should actually be grateful to me. Because of me," she concluded, "you got to be happy."

How the hell had she come to that conclusion? "Wrong on both counts," he told her, cynicism clinging to every syllable.

He was just saying that to get back at her for hurting his male pride by rejecting him all those years ago.

Couldn't see the forest for the trees, could he? Neither could he see what her sacrifice had ultimately cost her. Maybe he wasn't as smart as she'd initially thought.

"But this is what you wanted, isn't it?" she pressed, trying to get him to admit it. "Authority, adventure, moving from place to place, making a difference. Helping people." She repeated to him everything he had once told her.

At the top of his list had been leaving Cold Plains. Well, she'd gotten him to do that. The rest, she'd assumed at the time, had followed and fallen into place. Finding out he was an FBI special agent just reinforced that for her.

"What I wanted," he shouted hoarsely into Carly's face, unable to hold himself in check any longer, "was you!"

She didn't believe him. Because if that were true, she would have never been able to get him to leave, no matter what lie she told him. Or, if he'd left, he would have come back in a short time, saying something about being determined to get her to change her mind—or words to that effect.

But he *had* left and he *hadn't* returned, not for ten years, and now it was a case that brought Hawk back, not her.

"Let's see." She raised her right hand as if she was cupping some invisible object, weighing it. "Me," she announced, nodding at her hand. Then Carly raised her other hand for a moment. "Versus a lifetime of adventure and achievement." She indicated that what her left hand was holding was heavier by letting it sink a lot lower than her right hand. "Doesn't seem like much of a contest to me."

Hawk took hold of her hand in his, pulling her in and eliminating the last tiny bit of space that was still left between them. His eyes, blazing fiercely now, were on hers.

"No," he all but growled as he struggled to contain his temper and keep it from exploding. "It's not."

This time, she had a feeling that he wouldn't release her.

"Let go of me, Hawk," she ordered in a steely voice that gave no indication she was quaking on the inside. Her ability to hold him at bay, to resist her own mounting desires, quickly diminished. Any second now, it would all plummet to her feet.

Frustrated, worried, Carly made one last attempt to yank her wrist away from his grasp. She got nowhere. She might as well have been trying to pull it out of a bear trap. He had what amounted to a permanent hold on her.

"I said, let go!" she ground out between clenched teeth.

"Or what?" Hawk challenged. "You'll call Grayson and have him and his henchmen stick me into one of those unmarked graves he seems to favor so much?"

How can you even think that, you idiot? And then she thought of Mia and the very real danger her sister was in if this actually turned out to be true. Up until now, she'd thought of Grayson as a cold-blooded manipulator out for his own selfish interests. She hadn't thought of him as a killer.

This put a whole different, chilling spin on things.

"How do you know that Samuel's the one who is doing this?" she asked, wanting to hear his reasoning. She refrained from telling him her suspicions.

But Hawk noticed something else; something had caught his interest. She hadn't protested, hadn't cried out indignantly that Grayson would never be capable of such heinous actions.

Why?

Did she suspect that the former motivational speaker *was* behind it—or did she have information she wasn't telling him?

Open up to me, Carly. Trust me. You used to, remember?

Out loud he told her, "Grayson's the one who is obviously running the show here." He continued to hold her hand, afraid if he released it, she'd run off. And he wanted to hear the truth about this two-bit creep who'd hypnotized her into being one of the faithful—if not more. "He's a megalomaniac who's not about to allow anyone else to have any authority or share the spotlight with him. It's all about him, it always has been, always will be. And even though we haven't found the direct connection yet, every one of those five dead women— including the one without a name—lived in Cold Plains at one time or another."

With every passing second, her concern for Mia's safety grew. "How do you know that the woman without a name lived here?" she asked.

"That's on a need-to-know basis," Hawk retorted tersely. He grew acutely aware that he was still holding her wrist, acutely aware of how close they were. Just standing here like this was filling his senses with her very essence. "And you don't have a need to know," he informed her.

Her eyes met his. Though she didn't say a word, she pleaded with him silently, praying with all her heart that there was still a tiny trace of the connection that had once been so strong between them. The connection that allowed them to finish each other's sentences, to finish each other's thoughts.

Oh, but I do, Carly thought frantically. *I really do. I have a need to know* everything *that's involved in this case. Because Mia's life might just depend on it.*

Chapter 7

Hawk's deeply hypnotic eyes continued to hold her prisoner. Her nerves rose close to the surface and the very ground beneath her feet seemed to sink.

"I just can't figure out what you're still doing here," Hawk finally said. "Why you didn't leave when Grayson started buying up everything, changing everything? Turning people into grinning puppets?"

"Where would I go?" she asked. "This is *home*."

"Where would you go?" Hawk echoed incredulously. "Anywhere is better than this." She had to see that. The Carly he knew was too smart to be taken in by the gingerbread, by the pretense. The Carly he remembered would be able to see that Grayson was not out for the greater good, but the greater haul—*for him*.

"First of all, I would *never* leave without Mia." He had to know that. "And she wants to stay here, and second, I can't just abandon Cold Plains because some silver-tongued Pied Piper decided to lay claim to it and would be changing things around."

Her description of Grayson was far from flattering, which immediately told him that unlike so many of the other town residents, she hadn't elevated the man to the level of a god. And the fiercely protective tone in her voice when she'd mentioned her sister gave him the hope that Mia was the real reason Carly was still here.

Which in turn meant that she hadn't fallen under the charlatan's spell, unlike Mia. This version of Carly at least bore some resemblance to the bright-eyed girl who had taken up so much space in his young life.

Hawk suppressed a sigh. He'd really thought that they were going to spend the rest of their lives together, grow old together. Funny how things turned out.

"So what's your plan?" he finally asked her. "Are you going to somehow covertly confront and then fight Grayson? Winner gets to keep Cold Plains, loser has to leave town, that kind of thing?"

Carly took offense at both the question and his tone. "You're making fun of me," she accused.

He thought of the way she'd been in the school yard that first day he returned to Cold Plains.

"No, I'm trying to understand why the spirited, feisty woman I once knew would allow herself to be ordered around like some mindless lackey. You can't possibly be taken in by Grayson's act. You're way too smart for that," Hawk insisted.

Despite the fact that she felt a very real desire to tell him what she was doing, maybe to ask for his help, she couldn't risk it. If this came to light, her chance of rescuing Mia would go down the drain.

So instead, she challenged, "Did you ever think that maybe you're being too cynical? That just maybe Samuel's on the level?"

A look of contempt came over his features. Whether it was directed at Grayson—or her—was difficult to tell from where she was standing.

"Yeah, and maybe the moon's made out of green cheese." His eyes narrowed to sharp green slits. "Look, I don't know what your so-called plan is, but I want you to stay away from Grayson, understand?" It wasn't a request, it was an order. "The man's dangerous."

She had *never* liked being ordered around, and now was no exception. "You have no right to waltz into town ten years after you left and think you can start telling me what to do."

The sharpness of her own reaction surprised her. Why was there this wealth of anger, of hurt, bubbling up within her? She had no right to resent him. After all, she had been the one to send him away. She'd been completely aware of what she was sacrificing, and she'd done it, anyway. Done it because she loved him. She couldn't resent him for doing exactly what she'd orchestrated for him to do—

And yet—

And yet, there was a part of her, a small, selfish, lost part of her, that had wanted him not to leave back then, no matter what she'd done to get him to go. Or, if he did go, she'd wanted him to dramatically return and announce that he wasn't going anywhere, not unless she came with him.

You can't fault him, she told herself sternly. *He'd tried. God knows, he'd tried. He even told you that he was willing to take Mia along when the two of you left town. It was your choice to stay, your choice because you thought that you and Mia were going to be like an anchor for him and his dreams, dragging him down.*

Besides, hadn't Hawk just admitted that what he'd wanted most in the world was her? What more did she want from the man? She was being irrational. But then, she'd heard that love did that to a person, made them entirely crazy and irrational. Made them want things that weren't possible.

Like living happily ever after.

"I'm a special agent with the FBI. I have every right to tell you what to do," he corrected, all but shouting into her face.

She felt no such need for restraint. "Go to hell," Carly shouted defiantly.

That tore it for him. The last fragile hold on his temper snapped like a dried twig underfoot after a long draught. "Not without you!"

The few seconds that followed were all a blur. What happened next was certainly not something he'd foreseen himself doing, even though, if he was being honest, it had taken place a thousand times in the half dreams that littered his mind, occurring just before dawn each morning.

One moment they were shouting at one another, their emotions completely exposed, raw and bleeding. The next, instead of shouting, he was kissing Carly with all the passion, the feelings that had just been uncovered and had spilled out.

And she was kissing him back with the same amount of verve.

The eruption was inevitable.

The magnitude of their emotions could only be contained for so long. The moment his lips touched hers, the second they came together, they both knew that there was no turning back. That whatever stories they had told themselves, saying their relationship had long been over, were all lies, pretenses to get them through the day, the week, the month. They'd all been very useful at the time, but still lies.

The moment they kissed, it was like two halves of a whole finally coming together. Like rain falling on a parched terrain to make it finally flourish again.

They *needed* one another to be complete.

God help her, she *needed* him.

Even though she knew she was going to regret this, knew that she should have remained strong and vigilant, she also knew that this was what she had been craving ever since she'd stood on the hill, keeping well out of sight, watching Hawk's car on the road that led away from town—away from *her*—grow smaller and smaller on the horizon.

She'd missed him since that moment, and if that was weak, well, so be it. She'd never claimed to be an invincible warrior.

Even though the tiny shred of common sense she still possessed told her to end this, to pull away, Carly couldn't help praying that this kiss would go on forever. Praying that he wouldn't abruptly pull back, look at her with perhaps a small trace of smugness and say something to the effect that he'd known all along that she still wanted him.

Because she did.

And this proved it beyond a shadow of a doubt. When it came to Hawk, she had no defenses, no resolve. No shame.

It was a terrible thing for Hawk to realize that after ten years of strict self-discipline that he couldn't even think straight.

Hell, he couldn't think at all.

Not a single thought that rose in his mind lived to see completion. Only broken fragments seemed to exist in his brain, and he swept those away, because they got in his way, got in the way of his being able to just savor this moment.

And if for some reason she was playing him for a fool, well then, he'd deal with that later. Right now, all he wanted to do was to fill his hands, his senses, his very *soul* with her. With the taste and feel of her.

With the very sound of her breathing, excitement radiating within each breath.

He was vaguely aware that they'd started out fully dressed, and then somewhere along the line, they weren't anymore. Whether she'd undressed him or he her—or they'd undressed one another or just themselves—none of that left an impression or even fleetingly registered in his memory bank.

None of that mattered.

What mattered, what left its indelible mark, was making love with her. What mattered was giving himself up to the heat, the passion, the demands that all but raged within him.

He couldn't get enough of her, but he kept trying.

He'd missed her, he admitted to himself, missed her the way he would have missed the very air had it been taken away from him.

Because in a way, it had.

Until this very moment.

Each soft curve that he touched, every pliant inch of skin he kissed brought back memories. Memories that had gone a long way in sustaining him.

And yet, somehow it almost felt as if this was the very first time he'd had her. He couldn't make sense of it, and he stopped trying. Stopped doing everything except enjoy her the way he'd yearned to for so long.

The very first time they had ever made love, they'd been in her father's barn, up in the hayloft. It was close to midnight, and moonlight had streamed in through the cracks in the uneven shutters, highlighting her face, adding to the glow that radiated from her.

Though each time they made love together had been special, he never forgot that first time. Never forgot the sense of awe that had pulsed through him. Making love with Carly, he'd felt as if he'd captured a sunbeam in his hands.

That wondrous sense of "something special" hadn't faded. If anything, it felt as if it had been utterly underscored.

His heart racing in his chest, he kissed Carly over

and over again, fanning flames that were, even now, already over the top. Flames that threatened to incinerate them both and reduce them to a single fused, burnt, shriveled crisp.

Ten minutes, Carly realized somewhere at the height of her surrender, ten minutes was all it had taken. Ten minutes from the time Hawk had knocked on her door until she was here like this with him, her body nude and wanting.

Aching.

All it had taken was ten minutes to make her abandon her charade and silently own up to how much she still wanted him.

How much she still yearned for him.

On the floor, with nothing between them but red-hot desire, Carly immersed herself in the sensuality of the world that had temporarily opened up for her. There was almost a frantic sense of urgency to avail herself of all this.

Instinctively she knew that soon, very soon, everything would recede, and she would go back to doing what she had to. Back to being the responsible one. The only one who could rescue her sister from a life of servitude and hell—if not worse.

But for now, for this moment frozen in time, she was just Carly Finn, madly, hopelessly and eternally in love with Hawk Bledsoe, and nothing and no one else mattered outside of this.

Outside of the two of them.

Her body primed, her pulses visibly throbbing, Carly

arched beneath him, silently making him aware that she was ready.

More than ready.

Ready for their union. A union of the body and the soul.

She wondered if he knew that she was his for all eternity. That she was wedded to him until all time ceased, even though words to that effect had never been said over them.

No priest, no minister or justice of the peace could have cemented their union more indelibly.

She was married to him and always would be, no matter what separate directions their two paths in life would ultimately take them. She knew that now.

Once more sealing his mouth to hers, he wove his fingers through hers, and then Hawk thrust himself into her. He was home. It was completed. Their union was reinforced.

And then, after a heartbeat had passed, they began to move in unison, melting into the same dance that they had discovered up in that hayloft so long ago.

The languid tempo stepped up, growing more demanding and urgent with each passing second until the final crescendo found them, sending them crashing over the edge still clinging on to one another, holding on for support, for love.

Slowly, his heartbeat began to slow down until it finally reached a rate that didn't threaten to match the speed of light. And as it slowed, his breathing returned to normal.

Hawk became aware that he held her to him with one

arm wrapped around her, while with his other hand, he gently, slowly, stroked her hair. The ends of it were splayed out along his chest, her head cradled against his rigid pectorals. He could feel her heartbeat mingling with his. Or maybe the two had merged into one.

He found the latter thought comforting.

It was as if the past ten years had never happened. As if his heart hadn't been ripped apart by the callous words she'd uttered.

Words he no longer believed to have been true.

For some reason, she'd lied to him to make him leave town. Why didn't seem important, at least not right now.

It took Hawk more than a couple of minutes to find enough breath to enable him to speak.

The words left his lips slowly, as if languidly coasting on a spring breeze that had yet to come. "Nice to know some things haven't changed."

"What do you mean?"

Too tired to lift her head, Carly asked the question with her cheek still pressed against his chest, unaware that her warm breath was tantalizing his skin with each word she uttered.

"I think that's rather obvious," Hawk answered with a soft laugh. Then because her silence made him think that perhaps it wasn't so obvious to her after all, he said, "You can still reduce me to a palpitating mass of desires, needs and emotions faster than a speeding bullet. I find that pretty impressive."

This time Carly raised her head to look at him. The admission he'd just made left him momentarily vulnerable, exposed, and she knew he was aware of that. If she said something flippant, she'd be protecting herself, but it was a safe bet that it would also succeed in making him pull back, away from her.

Because he was vulnerable, she didn't want to hurt him, didn't want to make him feel that he was the only one in this relationship who felt that way. The only one who was exposed.

So she smiled at him, allowing the sentiment she felt to reach her eyes as she said, "Right back at you, Hawk." And then she took a breath before adding, "But this really doesn't change anything."

He wasn't so sure about that, but he knew better than to say so at a time like this. "We'll talk." The word "later" was an unspoken given.

Before she could even think to challenge his assumption, Hawk surprised her by shifting. With his hands on her waist, he deftly moved her so that she was now over him.

It was hard to carry on any sort of a serious argument with their more than warm bodies pressed against one another like this.

She let him win the round.

For now.

Because in doing so, she won, as well.

And winning, as they said, was everything. As long as it was with Hawk.

Chapter 8

So much for staying strong, Carly upbraided herself as she slowly descended back to reality and the demands of the world around her.

Now what?

Although she was incredibly aware of the man lying beside her, that didn't change the situation. They couldn't actually progress anywhere from here. The earth might have stood still and caught on fire when they made love just now, but that didn't block out the years gone by or even start a new chapter in their lives.

What had just transpired between them, she supposed, could be thought of as an aberration at best. A single aberration.

"So," she finally said, unable to take the silence anymore, "same time, same place ten years from now?" She was doing her damndest to sound chipper and not like a woman who expected promises.

Hawk turned to look at her. "Don't," he chided. His face appeared as if it was carved out of stone.

"Don't what?"

"Don't do that."

Same old Hawk, she thought. No one could ever accuse this man of running off at the mouth. There were times when he doled out words as if each one came from a rare collection.

"Don't do what?" Carly pressed a little more sharply.

"Don't be flippant."

Well, she couldn't deny she was guilty of that, but it wasn't because she was being cynical. She was just behaving the way she thought he'd want her to. Like the women he was probably accustomed to encountering— both in and out of bed.

"Okay," she said gamely, "what would you like me to be?"

His eyes held hers for a moment before he said, "Honest."

Was he accusing her of lying? About what? He couldn't possibly be referring to their last conversation ten years ago, so what was he talking about?

"I'm always honest," she fired back defensively, then prayed he wouldn't delve too deeply in order to point out the contradiction.

The expression on his face when she said that told her that he knew better—or that he thought he did.

But he didn't take her to task for the lie she'd just uttered or challenge the words she'd told him ten years ago that had sent him packing and on his way—the words she'd used to tell him that she didn't love him. He knew Carly well enough to know that she could have never made love with him, especially like that, if love wasn't at least a factor.

"Carly, I want you to tell me the truth," he began.

Carly headed him off, teasingly saying the words that she'd heard many a man wanted to have the woman he'd just bedded say. "Yes, the earth moved."

Hawk didn't laugh the way she'd hoped he would. His subject was too serious for him to laugh.

"That's not what I'm asking you," he replied evenly.

Nerves began to dance throughout her body again. Hawk had always seen right through her, except for that one time. Her words had hurt him too much for him to see beyond the pain, to guess why she was saying what she had.

But now he seemed deadly serious, and his eyes felt as if they were boring into her very soul, lifting words, reading thoughts.

Wanting to momentarily escape, she started to rise. Before she could stand up, his fingers tightened around her wrist.

She wasn't going anywhere.

"I thought you had murders to investigate," Carly reminded him.

That was the whole point, didn't she see that? "I do, and I don't want you to wind up joining that unholy number."

Was it that he actually cared about her, or that she

represented extra paperwork? *Don't get carried away, remember? No future, you know that.*

She waved away his voiced concern. "I'm fine. In case you weren't paying attention, I'm alive and well."

"I was paying very close attention," he assured her. "And for the record, I want to keep you that way—'alive and well.'"

Hawk really did need to lighten up. She relaxed a little as she asked, "What makes you think anything is going to change?"

That was a safe bet. Her remaining safe was not. He had a feeling that Grayson might already see through her act—because what else could it really be? Carly was way too intelligent, too savvy to be taken in by a second-rate motivational speaker no matter how slick he tried to be.

She'd had him going at first, Hawk thought, but he saw through it now. Because she really *was* still Carly, for all her protests to the contrary.

"That's simple enough," he told her, then warned, "Grayson doesn't like being played."

"Who's playing Grayson?" she asked innocently.

Hawk didn't buy the act for a second and rather resented that she was continuing with this charade after they'd made love. She was definitely not being honest with him.

"You are," he bit off. When she opened her mouth to protest, he ordered curtly, "Save it. You're still the same woman you were ten years ago. *That* woman wasn't a fool."

"I don't know about that," she murmured under her

breath, remembering the way she'd ached, sending him away. Maybe she shouldn't have.

Granted he was more successful now, but he didn't look any happier than he had back then. As a matter of fact, he looked less so, and she certainly wasn't ready to do cartwheels over the course her life had taken. She was still struggling to make a go of the farm, or had been before she'd decided to walk away from it and Cold Plains. That plan had involved being determined to start over somewhere else.

But she wanted to start over not just for herself but her sister, as well, something that was proving impossible to do since Mia wanted to remain here to become the Bride of Dracula—or at least his first lieutenant.

"She wasn't a fool," he repeated. "She was noble, loyal and giving. And she was the type to make sacrifices."

He knew, she thought as she looked into his eyes. Hawk knew. Knew what she'd done all those years ago, knew what it had cost her. But until she confirmed it, he had only his speculation to go on. "You're giving me too much credit," she said dismissively.

Lying there, he began to stroke her thigh as he spoke. "And you're not giving me enough. I want you out of here, Carly. Grayson is trouble. He has blood on his hands, and despite the wide, artificial grin on his face, he wouldn't hesitate to eliminate whoever gets in his way—male or female." Hawk's meaning was very clear.

For a moment, she thought about continuing her act. But then she decided not to keep up the pretense, which meant trying to defend Grayson's character and actions.

She wasn't *that* good an actress. She loathed the man and what Hawk was saying really scared her. Not that she was afraid for herself—she could take care of herself—but she was exceedingly worried about her sister. Mia was apparently an integral part of Grayson's plans for the future.

"I can't leave Mia," she told him flatly, thinking that was the end of the discussion.

Hawk surprised her by saying, "I know how you feel, but Mia's a big girl, she can look out for herself."

She'd forgotten that in his case, his sense of family left something to be desired.

"No, she can't," Carly insisted. "If I don't do something, Mia's going to get married in two weeks to a man she doesn't love. A man who's too old for her. A man whose first wife went mysteriously missing. I don't want the same thing happening to Mia, not when I can stop it."

She was *finally* being honest, he thought. Took her long enough. "So I was right."

That caught her up short. "Most likely," she allowed, "but about what?"

"That you're still in Cold Plains for a reason. That you're not hanging around because Grayson charmed you into remaining." His mouth curved for the first time, his smile stirring her the way it always did. "I knew you weren't that empty-headed."

Carly laughed shortly. "Still have that silver tongue, I see."

He knew she was taking exception to the word *empty-headed,* but he made no attempt to apologize because that had been his concern, that she'd somehow lost all her common sense and that almost seemed inconceivable.

"You could always think for yourself," he continued, "not follow the crowd like some lemming, programmed to drop off the edge of a cliff straight into the ocean."

In all honesty, she hadn't wanted him to think that she was captivated by Grayson. That was just too demeaning. "So you understand that I have to stay until I can get her to see reason—or until I can find a way to kidnap the bride before the wedding? At this point," she confessed, "I don't care which way I do it as long as I can keep Mia from marrying that man."

He wondered if she'd thought through the consequences or, if she had, if she was turning a blind eye toward them. "If you wind up having to kidnap her, she's going to hate you."

Carly shrugged. Mia already blamed her for what she considered her unhappy, deprived life. "Won't be the first time."

Hawk sighed. He might have known trying to talk her out of it was useless. "So you're not going to listen to me and get out of Cold Plains?"

"I'll get out of Cold Plains—after I have Mia," she assured him. "Not before."

They were lying here, carrying on a conversation, dressed in nothing but the warmth of their own body heat. Body heat that reached out to the other.

Hawk slipped his arm around her and drew closer to her. He propped himself up on his elbow and looked down into her face. "Were you always this stubborn?" he asked her.

"Always," she whispered.

Hawk shook his head. "Funny, I don't seem to remember that."

"What do you remember?" she asked.

The smile that came over Hawk's features told her exactly what he remembered. The same thing she did. The lovemaking that nurtured their souls and kept them both sane, making their stark world bearable.

Rather than say anything, Hawk showed her.

He stayed the night, even though when he'd first stopped on her doorstep, he'd had every intention of returning to his hotel room at the end of the evening. Somehow, he just never made it out of the room.

When Hawk finally woke up the next morning, he reached for her.

And found only emptiness beside him.

Carly was gone.

He was programmed to think the worst in any given situation, and all traces of sleep and contentment instantly fled. He was alert and ready to go searching for Carly.

But the next moment, the scent of freshly brewed coffee mingling with the tempting smell of bacon and eggs frying registered. He sincerely doubted Grayson or any of the man's robotlike minions were here, making him breakfast.

Pausing only to pull on his jeans, Hawk padded down to the kitchen in his bare feet.

He was relieved to find Carly there, standing over the stove, making breakfast. Instead of wearing her own clothes, she had on the light blue shirt he'd worn last night. It hung down to her knees, and he had the feeling that she was completely naked underneath.

He had difficulty reining in his imagination. The sight of Carly like that made him ache for her all over again.

Moving quietly as he'd been trained to do, Hawk came up behind the woman who had rocked his world last night, rocked it the way it hadn't been, even remotely, these past ten years.

He stood behind her and slipped his arms around her waist. He felt her stiffen as she grabbed for another skillet, her hand wrapping around the handle as if she intended to use it as a weapon.

"Down, tiger, it's only me," he whispered against her ear, managing to all but singe her very skin with his warm breath.

Carly breathed a sigh of relief. She released her grip on the skillet, leaving it on the back, dormant burner.

"There is no 'only' when it comes to you," she informed him. Then before he could explore her comment, she told him to "Sit down, breakfast is almost ready."

Pulling over the two plates she'd set out on the counter, Carly began to divide up the eggs and bacon. She topped it off with the toast that she'd just finished buttering.

She then set the pan down and gave Hawk the larger portion. As she remembered, he always had an appetite first thing in the morning. Conversely, hers always took a couple of hours to kick in.

"By the way," she said as she set his plate before him, "some FBI agent you are. You didn't even stir when I slipped out of bed this morning. I thought you guys are supposed to sleep with one eye open."

He took the fresh coffee she'd just poured for him. It was as black as he imagined Grayson's heart was. For a second, he savored the heat that rose up from the cup before taking a deep, life-affirming sip.

"You completely wore me out," he said matter-of-factly, then added, "I'll have to work on that."

Was that last part just an off-the-cuff remark, or did he mean something by it, she wondered. "Working on it" made it sound as if she would be there to see if he succeeded.

Don't read anything into it, she warned herself. This was nice, being here like this with him, but it too was an aberration. The man was here for a reason, and she wasn't it. He had a job to do, and then he would be on his way.

She had to remember that, Carly silently insisted. Otherwise, she left herself open to devastation. She couldn't go through that twice, loving him and watching him walking away from her. She wouldn't survive a second time—if she allowed herself to love him again.

So this time, it's going to be just fun, no strings.

"You haven't lost your touch," Hawk said after taking a hearty bite of his breakfast. He looked at her for a long moment, then added, "Not with anything."

She could feel warmth creeping up the sides of her

neck, reaching her face. Any second now, she would turn a really embarrassing shade of pink, she thought, upset with her inability to bank down feelings.

"So what's the plan?" she asked abruptly, trying to change the subject. Hawk was exceedingly focused, so if she could just get him to think about his reasons for being here, she thought it was a safe bet that she could turn lime-green and he wouldn't notice. At least not immediately.

"With Grayson," she added, in case he thought she was asking about their future together.

She already knew the answer to that one. They had no future together. She'd taken care of that when she'd initially sent him on his way. This was just a lovely, quick trip down memory lane, but she wasn't going to make herself crazy by thinking that maybe they were getting a second chance to do it right this time.

They were both too far along on their separate paths for her to think that life offered any kind of "do-overs." It didn't. One had to live with the consequences of one's actions, and she was prepared to do just that, even if it felt as if she were swallowing razor blades.

"The plan is that I continue rattling cages, asking questions, trying to get someone to testify against Grayson and to hopefully give us the missing evidence that ties that bastard to the five murders. I know in my gut he did it—or ordered it done—but I can't prove it.

"So far, the guy's been a slick devil. We've connected the women to Cold Plains, but we haven't been able to connect them to Grayson—yet." He thought of Micah and wondered again where the man was. Grayson's twin still wasn't answering his phone, but he refused to think that Micah was dead. Men like him brought death to people; they weren't mowed down by it.

If he could just get a hold of Micah and ask him some key questions, maybe things would clear up a little.

At any rate, it was something he was going to look into—as soon as he finished breakfast. Granted he was indulging himself, but he rarely did that, and who knew when he could get a home-cooked meal again?

"Everything okay?" Carly asked as she sat down on the stool next to his at the counter.

"The meal's fantastic," he said in a tone that told her he was leaving out more than he was saying.

Fork raised, she forgot about eating for a moment. Leaning her head against her hand, she looked at him.

"So what isn't okay?" she asked.

What wasn't okay was that he suddenly had her to worry about. She wasn't one of those women who stood off to the side, observing or waiting to be rescued. She was the kind of woman who charged out and took matters into her own hands. She was the kind of woman who made him worry and kept him up at night. Knowing the answer he was going to get, he gave it a shot, anyway. "Any way I can convince you to leave dealing with Grayson up to me?"

She smiled and shook her head. "Not even a repeat performance of last night," she answered. There might have been a smile on her lips, but her eyes, he noted, were very serious as she added, "I take care of my own, Hawk, you know that. And Mia's my sister, that makes her my problem."

"She's old enough to make her own decisions," he pointed out again.

"Only if she makes the right ones," was Carly's good-humored albeit stubborn response.

It was futile to argue with her. She would only succeed in getting him to lose his temper.

Same old Carly, he couldn't help thinking.

Despite his concern, Hawk caught himself grinning for the remainder of their time together. It was way too late for them after all these years had gone by—but that didn't mean that he couldn't savor the small moment that had unexpectedly been carved out for them at this junction.

He could.

And he would.

Chapter 9

After breakfast, just before he and Carly went their separate ways that morning, Hawk decided to try one last time to talk a little sense into Carly, to no avail.

She listened quietly as Hawk continued to enumerate all the reasons—again—why what she was doing was tantamount to juggling with loaded pistols. When he was finished, he could tell by the expression on her face that he had made no headway whatsoever in making her come around to his way of thinking.

Instead, rather than arguing with him, she pointed out the upside of having her continue to pose as one of the faithful in Grayson's circle.

"Think of it this way, Hawk. You need to have a person on the inside to be your eyes and ears. I'll be that person."

That was all well and good, if she were a trained special agent—and someone else. But she wasn't trained in undercover work, and she was Carly, someone he didn't want taking any risks.

So he shook his head and got ready to leave. He looked down into her eyes one last time. "I don't want to see anything happening to you."

Carly smiled at his concern. She wouldn't have been able to explain why, but the very fact that he was worried made her feel safe.

"That makes two of us," she assured Hawk. "Don't worry, I'll be careful."

He really wished he could believe her, Hawk thought, walking over to where he had left his car last night. But where her sister was involved, Carly would take whatever risks she felt were necessary in order to save Mia.

Getting into his vehicle, Hawk blew out a long breath. The best way to protect Carly at this point was to nail Grayson as quickly as possible for at least one of the murders. Once he had that, once he could point to Grayson's connection to one murder, he had a feeling the rest would fall into place.

Preoccupied, he inserted his key into the ignition. Just as he was about to start the car, he saw that there was a folded piece of paper on his dashboard.

Staring at it, Hawk frowned.

He was positive that hadn't been there last night when he drove up to Carly's house. His hand automatically covered the hilt of his service revolver as he looked around slowly, deliberately. But other than Carly's house, the barn and the corral, nothing was visible for miles. Whoever had broken into his vehicle and left the paper on his dashboard was long gone.

Not knowing what to expect, he took out his handkerchief, and holding it by the edge, he opened the folded paper and read:

"Please meet me at the Hanging Tree at 10 this morning. I urgently need to speak with you. Come alone."

That was it. Three terse sentences. No signature, no indication what this was about. For all he knew, he was being set up.

But this could also be on the level. It might be one of Grayson's people who'd had enough, was unable to break away and was willing to trade information for help in getting out of the cult—because at this point, that was what it was. A cult.

Hawk glanced at his watch. The note said to be there by ten. Because he'd lingered over breakfast—and over Carly—he didn't have all that much time to spare. The reference to the meeting place made him think that perhaps he was dealing with someone who was a native of the area. Outsiders didn't know about the oak tree's nickname.

The Hanging Tree had gotten its name because of a story that had made the rounds over a hundred years ago. The biggest branch on it was uniquely bent and actually pointed down. The story had it that an outlaw gang caught the sheriff who had been pursuing them, and that they hung him from the biggest, strongest branch of this massive tree and then just rode away, leaving the sheriff to die. The branch miraculous bent down far enough for him to reach the ground with his feet. Freeing himself, he went on to track down and avenge himself of each of the outlaws who had left him to die.

When he was a kid, Hawk liked to pretend he was that sheriff, hunting down outlaws and dispensing his own brand of justice. After a while, the lines between reality and make-believe blurred a little. He supposed that story had gotten him thinking about becoming a law-enforcement agent.

Before he took off for the appointed meeting place, Hawk called Rosenbloom at the cabin. "I just wanted you to know where I'm going in case I don't get back."

"You want backup?" Rosenbloom asked.

The agent sounded eager to get out of the cabin. Hawk couldn't blame him. But he also couldn't use him right now. "The note said to come alone."

He could almost *hear* Rosenbloom's frown over the phone. "Since when do you listen to notes?"

Since I don't want to jeopardize this case, I'm in a hurry to wrap it up and keep Carly safe, because the woman doesn't have enough sense to stay the hell out of this.

"I didn't call you to argue," he told the other man. "I just want you to know where I'm going."

"Got it."

Hawk hung up and drove straight to the appointed place. Taking precautions, he got out of the vehicle and slowly circled around. The man he saw standing by the tree and impatiently shifting from one foot to the other was a stranger to him.

But as he drew closer, Hawk realized that this was someone he'd seen recently. But where? And with whom?

Was it a setup? Hawk wondered again. Whoever this guy was, he definitely appeared uneasy. Why? Because he was afraid of being watched? Or because he was afraid he might get cut down in the cross fire?

Dr. Rafe Black looked at his watch. It was three minutes past ten.

Where the hell was Bledsoe, anyway?

He dragged a hand through his black hair. Three months ago, he had been blissfully unaware that Cold Plains, Wyoming, even existed. And then he'd received a phone call from a woman he'd been involved with a little more than nine months ago for exactly one night. At first, when she told him her name, he couldn't even place her.

And then he remembered. She was a sweet-faced, almost timid young woman.

Abby Michaels had tracked him down and was calling because she thought he should know that he was now the father of a newborn, healthy baby boy named Devin.

Stunned by the news, he took a moment to recover. When he began firing questions at Abby, the line went dead. He tried to shrug it off as a practical joke that one of his colleagues was playing on him, but he had the uneasy feeling that it wasn't.

And he was right.

A week later, he received a brown envelope with a photograph of a male infant. It could have been his own photograph taken at that age. The child had the same dark eyes, the same dark hair that he'd had. In addition, the baby had his mother's nose and small, rosebud mouth. One look, and he *knew* this was his child—and Abby's.

A letter was included with the photograph. In it, Abby asked him for ten thousand dollars to help care for the baby, instructing that it be wired to a bank in Laramie.

He did as she asked, going down to Laramie with the hopes of finding Abby, his son and some answers. However, none of it materialized. Abby and the baby were nowhere to be found. Wondering if he'd been duped, Rafe nonetheless seriously considered hiring a private investigator to track down Abby and his son.

He was still debating that course of action when he saw the news story about the five murdered women being found in different locations. In all honesty, after a long day at the hospital, he was only half paying attention when he saw Abby's photo being flashed on the screen. That got his attention immediately. She was one of the dead women.

Rafe had tuned in just in time to hear that all five women, including a Jane Doe, had Cold Plains, Wyoming, in common. He started packing immediately.

Cold Plains was where the answers were. Once he arrived, he went about the business of opening up a practice, thinking it would help him blend in. He was hoping to pick up enough information to enable him to locate his son. After all, people told their doctor things they didn't share with their friends or families. Maybe he would hear something useful that would help.

He'd hardly been in Cold Plains more than two weeks when he heard that there was an FBI special agent in town looking into the deaths of these women. Into Abby's death.

Confident that this was the break he'd been looking for, Rafe had decided to contact Special Agent Bledsoe and share what he knew about Abby. However, Rafe instinctively understood the need for caution and secrecy. Apparently, there was a killer loose, and he didn't want to attract undue attention, which might result in his son being harmed—if the boy was actually here, something he hadn't established yet.

"Who are you?" A deep, low voice behind him growled out the question.

Caught completely by surprise, Rafe spun around, not knowing what to expect and wishing he'd brought some kind of weapon with him. Half braced to be staring into the face of a killer, Rafe exhaled a loud sigh of relief when he saw that the man facing him was the FBI special agent he was waiting for.

"Damn, but you scared me," Rafe told him, his hand splayed across his chest.

Hawk made no apologies. "Didn't know if I was walking into a trap."

Seeing the ironic humor in the situation, Rafe laughed shortly. "That makes two of us." He put out his hand to the special agent. "I'm Dr. Black. Rafe Black," he added.

After a beat, Hawk took the offered hand and returned the handshake.

He glanced over his shoulder at the Hanging Tree. "Well, Dr. Black, I can't say that this is exactly a typical meeting place. Why did you want to meet me out here and not in your office?" Hawk asked.

That, at least, was a simple question to answer. "Because I didn't want anyone overhearing what I had to tell you."

Hawk was still waiting to find out what this was all about and if it in any way helped to shed some light on the murders he was investigating. "Which is?"

Rafe took a deep breath and then plunged into his story. "I had a relationship with one of the murdered women, Abby Michaels."

His interest piqued, Hawk continued to scan the area, making sure that they weren't caught by surprise. So far, they appeared to be alone out here.

"Go on."

Rafe backtracked a little. "Well, not so much a relationship as a one-night stand."

Hawk did his best not to sound impatient, but it wasn't easy. The level of his adrenaline was rising. "Which is it?"

"A one-night stand," Rafe said definitively. "At least I thought that was all it was. But three months ago, I got a phone call from Abby saying that she'd just given birth to a baby boy and I was the baby's father."

Hawk looked at him sharply. This was the first he'd heard about a baby. Would they find yet another, much smaller body somewhere out there? "Did the numbers work out?"

"Yeah, that's about the time we hooked up. Abby sent me a photograph of my son." He took it out of the pocket of his jacket and glanced at it before holding it up for the special agent. "This could have been a picture of me as a newborn."

Hawk took the photograph and studied it for a moment before handing it back to the doctor. "You are aware that most babies look alike."

Rafe knew what the agent was implying, but he was convinced that this was his son. And just as convinced that he had to find him somehow.

"No, this one's mine," he said with conviction. Then because the agent was looking at him a bit skeptically, he added, "It's a gut feeling. I *know* he's mine, Bledsoe," he told Hawk.

"I'm the last one to dismiss a gut feeling," Hawk assured him. A gut feeling was what had gotten him this far. Granted it was by no means an exact science, but he'd found that his instincts were right over seventy percent of the time. "Why are you telling me this?" he asked.

"Because I need your help," Rafe said without any fanfare. "I can't find him. I came as soon as I saw the story on TV about the murdered women all being from Cold Plains. I thought maybe she'd left my son with her relatives, but I'm beginning to think that maybe she didn't even come back here between the time she called me and the time she was killed. I've been asking around if anyone's heard anything about a motherless baby somewhere in the area, but so far, nobody seems to know anything. Or," he amended, "if they know, they're not saying."

"Yeah, I get that a lot," Hawk told him with a dismissive laugh that had no humor to it. "Did you go to the police chief with your story?" he asked out of curiosity. Fargo definitely wouldn't have been his first choice, but then maybe the man was different with the people of his town.

"Yes, I did." Rafe's frown told him just how far that had gotten him. His next words confirmed it. "Man's not very friendly," Rafe testified. "Said he hadn't heard anything about any of the women in his 'community' having any unwanted children, but I get the feeling that he's not telling me the truth."

Welcome to the club, Hawk thought. "I'll keep my eyes open and let you know if I find out anything," he promised the doctor. In exchange he was hoping the doctor would do the same. "Listen, since you got me out here, maybe you can answer a question for me."

Was it his imagination, or did the doctor look a little apprehensive before finally saying, "Sure, if I can."

Hawk's question concerned the newly constructed clinic that Grayson had had built according to his specifications. For a medical clinic, it was exceedingly cold, sterile and unwelcoming.

"I noticed that the town now has this Urgent Care Center that Grayson was responsible for building." When he'd left town initially, any medical care had to be sought outside the town, over in a neighboring county. "I'm picking up things that don't seem right to me."

Rafe knew exactly what the special agent was referring to. He'd become aware of strange practices himself, practices that went against the norm. He'd also noticed that he hadn't been asked to join the care center. Was that because he was new to the town, or was it because of some other reason? Such as, if he knew exactly what was going on behind closed doors, he would request an investigation?

"By that, you mean like the fact that people aren't allowed to leave the facility until they get a complete, clean bill of health from the attending physician— even if they have ongoing conditions such as diabetes or heart trouble?" Rafe asked.

Hawk nodded his head. "That's what I mean." What had gotten his attention in the first place was finding out about the unorthodox case he was now recounting. "I talked to someone the other day who said that her cousin accidentally hit his head on the pavement, so he went to the Center to get some stitches—and he hasn't been heard from since. This cousin also has a heart murmur, according to the woman I talked with."

Rafe nodded. That didn't surprise him. "Sounds about right. People who have started coming to me looking for treatment are people who don't want to have anything to do with the care center. Margaret Chase—" he brought up the name of one of the town's oldest residents "—told me that some of her friends have gone missing, and the last time she'd heard from one of the women, she was going in to the clinic to get treatment for a persistent cough that just wouldn't go away."

He'd already noted that the people he'd seen around town who belonged to Grayson's dedicated followers all seemed to be robust, healthy-looking specimens of humanity. Now that he thought more about it, he couldn't remember hearing anyone even coughing or sneezing. No one seemed to have so much as a hangnail. Everyone seemed to be the flourishing picture of health.

Was that by design?

Where were all the sick people, the ones with disabilities? For that matter, where were the homely ones? The ones who were not perfect?

This was beginning to sound eerily gruesome, Hawk thought.

For all he knew, Grayson might actually be trying to fashion some perfect society filled with movie-star-handsome men, women and children.

And Carly was right in the thick of it, he thought suddenly.

Damn but he needed to get her to back away from all this for her own good. Maybe if he swore to her that he would rescue Mia the first chance he got, he could get her to listen to him and leave Cold Plains before Grayson found out what Carly was up to and things became really ugly.

But even as he thought it, Hawk knew that there was no reasoning with Carly, not once she made up her mind. There'd been a time when he'd admired her strong will and strength of character, but right now, it could be the very quality that could get her killed. He had no illusions about Grayson, not after he'd reread the report on the man's background.

"Look, Doc," he proposed out of the blue, "if I promise to keep my ears and eyes open for any information about an orphaned newborn, will you see what you can find out about what's happening to those people in the Urgent Care Center? I mean, it's not like a circus clown car when dozens of people go in and then don't come back out again." Rosenbloom had compiled a list of people who had gone into the care center in the past six months but hadn't been seen or heard from afterward.

So where were they? Had they been asked to leave town or, he thought darkly, were they merely eliminated if they didn't cooperate? It sounded almost absurd. He could easily see Grayson justifying this action because he wanted to purify the strain, form a society of healthy, pretty people.

The man wasn't a charming hypnotist, he was a crass, manipulative bastard, and the sooner he could take Grayson down, the better.

It was a thought he hung on to as he drove back to the cabin. He needed to fill his team in on this newest twist, and it was done better in person.

Chapter 10

Depositing the three, extra-large containers of dark roast coffee on the table, Hawk looked at the three men who gave every indication of having severe cases of cabin fever. "How are we doing with our Jane Doe? Any progress finding out who she really was?"

Rosenbloom pried the lid off his giant container and took a long swig of the still-hot coffee before giving him an answer. Only after the black liquid had wound its way through his system did he frown critically at his container.

"What did they use to make this, trail mix?" he asked.

"I guess gourmet coffee hasn't made an appearance in Cold Plains yet," Jeffers quipped, seemingly grateful to have something black and hot to sustain him.

"Hey, it's better than nothing," Patterson commented, downing all but the last third of his container.

"Jane Doe?" Hawk prodded, looking from one man to the next. All three shook their heads.

And then Jeffers put it into words. "We haven't found any missing persons report matching her description so far. At least not in Wyoming in the last four years. I'm going to check the out-of-state reports next." His expression said he didn't hold out too much hope. "But after four years, this seems like a pretty cold case."

That wasn't what he wanted to hear. "Well, then, warm it up," Hawk instructed.

Rosenbloom turned his chair back to face the laptop on his side of the table. "By the way, how's life in the outside world?" he asked. "The sky still blue?"

"Do people still get to listen to the news?" Patterson put in.

Hawk ignored the flippant remarks and filled the men in on his meeting with the new doctor and the latter's hunt for his missing son. He went on to tell them about the physician's theory about what he believed was going on in the Urgent Care Clinic.

Jeffers ate up every word. "You know, once we wind this up, we've got the makings of one hell of a movie script here," he commented.

Hawk laughed shortly and shook his head. "Yeah, if we ever *do* wrap this up." Right now, he had his doubts about that happening. There was no denying that Grayson was slick. Nothing seemed to stick to the man. And without the information that Micah was supposed to provide, who knew if they would ever be able to pin anything on the so-called community leader.

"Do I detect a lack of faith?" Jeffers asked with a touch of surprise.

It wasn't so much a lack of faith at play here as a healthy respect for the reality of the situation. On the average, more cases remained open than were closed. "It's just that everywhere we turn for answers, all we find are more questions."

"Well, my money's on us," Jeffers said cheerfully. "Don't forget, we're the good guys," he reminded his superior.

"Yeah, well, if we don't get out of this cabin soon, we'll be too stiff and out of shape to do anybody any good," Rosenbloom complained. He was far from happy about being confined this way.

Patterson's nerves were getting frayed. "Maybe if you started cooking something that wasn't exclusively made up of fat, salt and sugar, we wouldn't be *getting* out of shape."

He had to nip this before it got out of hand. Ordinarily, the three men worked well together, but that was when they weren't living in one another's pockets 24/7. "You three keep this up, and I'm going to have to send you to your rooms without your supper," Hawk warned, looking from one to the other.

He got his point across. They were bickering like children. Not that he didn't secretly sympathize with them. Staying in the cabin for an indefinite amount of time, waiting to finally be able to spring into action, could drive anyone crazy. But playing the waiting game was all part of the job. Not a pleasant part, but a part nonetheless.

The moment Hawk started toward the door, Rosenbloom was instantly alert. "Where are you going?" he asked.

"It's time to see if I can rattle the head honcho's cage and hopefully get him to make a mistake." Hawk paused by the door just before leaving. "If I'm not back by tomorrow, pick him up for questioning," he told Rosenbloom.

"You think he'd actually try something?" Jeffers asked.

"He does know you're an FBI agent, right?" Patterson asked.

"He does, but desperate men resort to desperate measures. Especially if they think they can get away with it."

He had no illusions about Grayson. If he had had those women murdered, then what was another body more or less? At this stage, having gotten away with so much, Grayson had probably developed a god complex, he reasoned. Or at the very least, thought he was invulnerable.

So far, he was right.

"Remember, one day," Hawk reminded his men as he went out. The way he saw it, it was always better to be safe than sorry.

Rather than corner Grayson alone in his office and ask him questions that the man was probably going to respond to with lies, Hawk decided to observe the man in his full glory first. He wanted to see for himself exactly what all the excitement was about.

Hawk was aware of several motivational speakers who had managed to do very well for themselves, building up an empire based on books, audio tapes and speaking engagement fees. He'd heard that Grayson had had a modest amount of success following that route, but obviously the man wasn't strictly interested in making a living or even in the "calling" of helping people fulfill their true potential, something that was the supposed cornerstone of every motivational speaker's philosophy.

The only one Samuel Grayson wanted to help was Samuel Grayson, and apparently the way he did it, at least in part, was to boost his ego by seeing just how many people he could get to pledge their undying loyalty to him.

As he stood in the back of the room, near the door he'd used to slip into the auditorium, Hawk watched Grayson become a dynamo of barely harnessed energy. Moving about the entire stage and remaining in perpetual motion, Grayson created the illusion of addressing each person in the room individually. He singled them out, as if that particular person was the only one who mattered at that particular time.

It was a pretty neat parlor trick, Hawk couldn't help thinking. Admittedly, it was a skill that not that many people had.

What was the man's end game? he wondered. Was Grayson just doing this to see how many people he could get under his thumb, vowing to follow him to the ends of the earth—and beyond? Or did he have almost a *physical* need for all this adulation? Was he stirring everyone up for a reason, for some personal gain at the end of the line, or was it all just a power trip?

Most of all, how had he benefited—if he actually had—from the deaths of those five women? Why *those* particular women? And were they the only dead bodies to be found, or were there more that they just hadn't come across yet?

Hawk had an uneasy feeling it was the latter, but for now, he shut the thought away and observed Grayson in his element.

"You can't let life drag you down," Grayson said, his words and gaze taking in each and every person seated at the seminar. His voice swelled as he asked, "What do we do with negative thoughts?"

"We flush them away," the audience chanted in response.

Grayson cupped his ear as if trying to make out a faint sound. "I can't hear you," he announced in a singsong voice.

The audience responded with enthusiasm, repeating what they'd said, only louder this time. However, it still wasn't loud enough to suit Grayson. He kept egging them on to say the phrase louder and louder until they were all shouting the words.

Only then did he smile with approval, an approval his audience ate up and reveled in, like children allowed to temporarily sit at the adult table.

The guy's a real puppet master, Hawk thought, his eyes sweeping over the faces of the audience that he was able to see from where he stood. They looked as if they were in the throes of rapture. It reminded him of a black-and-white film clip he'd seen on one of the history channels, chronicling a dictator's rise to power just before the fateful second world war.

A chill went down his spine.

Hawk saw no difference between the dictator and Grayson. Both appeared enamored with the sound of their own voices. And with the desire to seize power through the people they so obviously commanded.

It was enough to make a man sick.

As Grayson moved about the raised platform he'd had specially built according to his exact specifications, focused on working up his audience the way he did every day as he brought each of his seminars to a close, his eyes met Hawk's.

Hawk was immediately alert. There was no quizzical pause, no indication that Grayson didn't know who he was looking at. Instead, there was an evident smugness, as if he was well pleased with his performance and satisfied that he had created the impression Grayson wanted him to witness.

"That's all for tonight," Grayson finally announced. Taking a hand towel from the podium, he wiped the perspiration from his brow. "I want you all to go to your homes and think about how you can improve upon what you're doing and how you can enrich your neighbors' lives through your own evolvement."

Yeah, and how to put more money into your fearless leader's pockets, I'll bet, Hawk thought cynically. Grayson was as phony as a three-dollar bill. If he hadn't believed it before, he did now. What completely mystified him was how nobody seemed to be able to see through the other man's facade. It was all sparkling glitter and hyped-up rhetoric.

As the meeting broke up, Hawk watched the people in Grayson's audience rise to their feet, applauding wildly. Those who *didn't* swarm around the speaker began to file out of the auditorium.

A few hung back, neither trying to gain Grayson's attention nor leaving just yet.

He realized that Carly was in that third group. Why was she lingering?

And then he had his explanation. A girl who looked vaguely familiar—was that really Mia, all grown up now?—was part of the circle clustering around Grayson. They all appeared to be eagerly vying for the favor of the speaker's momentary attention.

Carly's sister smiled broadly as he heard Grayson say, "Mia, I need a word with you, please."

"Of course, Samuel," the young woman replied.

She sounded just like a robot, Hawk couldn't help thinking.

Despite the fact that there was half a room between them, his eyes met Carly's and he could see she was thinking the same thing. And that it really upset her. Small wonder.

Grayson, with his lofty seminars and flattering words, with his attention, which made the members of his circle feel as if they were being singled out by God, had managed to brainwash a room full of easily manipulated people, young and old.

To what end? Hawk wondered again.

Was it just to feed his ego, or was there some darker purpose in all this? A dark purpose he wasn't seeing just yet.

He could see why Carly was worried. Hell, he'd been worried himself before he realized that Carly was only putting on a show for Grayson's benefit.

And it was a pretty damn convincing show at that, he thought now, watching her. Though it took some restraint, Hawk made no effort to approach her. As far as he knew, Grayson wasn't aware that he and Carly had a history, and he wanted to keep it that way. Not knowing that little fact would keep Carly a lot safer at the moment. He didn't want to think what might happen if Grayson suspected she had a connection to an FBI special agent—no matter how innocent that connection might actually be.

He watched as Grayson took both of Mia's hands in his. "The ladies have selected a wedding dress for you," he informed her. "You need to make yourself available for a fitting." He bestowed a benevolent smile on the young woman whose hands he still held. "You wouldn't want to offend your husband by not appearing perfect at the ceremony."

"Oh no, Samuel, I would never do that," Mia assured him with immense feeling in her voice.

His voice was patronizing as he said, "That's my girl."

Hawk stole a covert glance at Carly. That was the kind of remark that would have had her seeing red in the old days. Seeing red and putting someone like Grayson in his place.

But she looked perfectly serene now, as if the man's smarmy remark made absolutely no impression whatsoever.

She really was one hell of an actress, Hawk thought again, silently tipping his hat to her. This was a side of Carly that he'd never seen before, hadn't even suspected existed. All he knew was that there was a time when she would have instantly made her feelings about Grayson's crass assumption known.

Hell, she might have even contemplated gutting the man—or making him think that she would.

Hawk suppressed an amused smile. The next moment, he saw that Grayson's eyes had shifted in his direction. Hawk was instantly on his guard.

Walking over to him, hands outstretched as if he were greeting a long-lost brother, Grayson asked in a booming voice, "Am I in the presence of a new convert?" he asked.

Rather than tender a negative answer to the question, Hawk identified himself instead. Taking out his wallet, he opened it to display his ID and held it up for Grayson's perusal.

"I'm special agent Hawk Bledsoe with—"

"The FBI," Grayson concluded with a nod of his head, which seemed more of a dismissal. "Yes, I am well aware what makes you so special, Agent Bledsoe," Grayson replied in a humoring tone that Hawk found exceedingly grating. "To what do I owe this pleasure?" he asked, his tone neutral, giving nothing away.

How much did the man actually know, and how much was he bluffing? Hawk caught himself wondering.

Out loud, he announced, "I have a few questions for you, Mr. Grayson."

Though Grayson continued to maintain his welcoming smile, there was a complacency to it that existed just along the perimeter. He thought himself superior, Hawk realized. That was fine with him. As long as the man thought he had the upper hand, he wouldn't be that aware that he was being taken down.

"Everyone does," he told Hawk easily. "I'll do my best to answer them for you. In just one moment," he said, holding up his finger to indicated that he wanted his "guest" to pause his thoughts. "Carly, I'm going to need to see your lesson plan for tomorrow's children seminar," he told her. "If you don't mind, I'd like you to drop it off in my office later this evening. Say around nine?" he suggested, eyeing her. Waiting for her compliance.

"Of course, Samuel. Nine will be fine," she replied in the same obedient, subservient tone that her sister had.

Turning back to Hawk, Grayson clasped his hands together before him and said, "Now then, you said you have some questions for me?"

He had questions all right. Foremost was why did Grayson want to see Carly in his office later this evening? Was he just asking her to drop off the papers, or did he have something else in mind for her?

Though he gave no outward indication, Hawk could

feel anger flare within him. It took a great deal to keep it under control.

Forcing himself to focus on the present, Hawk opened up the manila envelope he had brought with him. As Grayson watched with what he took to be feigned interest, he removed five eight-by-ten photographs, one for each of the women who had been found.

"We're investigating the deaths of these five women," he told Grayson, deliberately substituting the word *deaths* for *murders*. One by one, he shuffled through them, displaying each for Grayson's benefit. He watched the man's face intently. "Do you recognize any of them?" he asked.

Grayson dutifully viewed one photograph after another. His expression never changed, and he gave no indication that he recognized any of the women.

Even so, Hawk could have sworn that the small, blue vein at the man's right temple pulsed as he looked down at the photographs. There was genuine surprise registered there, he thought. Apparently Grayson hadn't thought that these bodies would ever surface.

But he knew them. Hawk would bet his soul on that. Grayson knew each of these women, including their mysterious Jane Doe. Getting him to admit it, though, would be difficult if not impossible.

He needed someone on the inside to bear witness against the man.

Shaking his head, Grayson returned the photographs. "I'm afraid I really can't be of any help to you. I don't recall meeting any of these unfortunate ladies. The faces from my past tend to run together."

I just bet they do, Hawk thought, taking the photographs back and slipping them into the envelope again.

"I have seen so many people—I started out as a motivational speaker, you know," Grayson explained in an aside. "That was before I found my true calling." His hands swept about, indicating the now-empty auditorium.

Hawk continued to watch the man's face, looking for a breech, some telltale sign, however small, to give him a clue to his real intent in taking over Cold Plains. "And that would be?"

"Why, leaving my mark on this wonderful town, of course. Making sure that it is developed to meet its full potential, so that everyone here might benefit. You're free to move about, you know, Special Agent, so you can see for yourself how business is thriving and how well and happy everyone who lives here is. I'd like to think I had some small part in that," he added with studied modesty.

Had the so-called spiritual leader just inadvertently admitted to eliminating the people who weren't "well and happy?" Hawk wondered, because they clearly weren't out and about. Everyone he'd seen so far had the same frozen, unnerving smile plastered on their faces as if anything else was strictly forbidden.

Hawk took the opening to ask, "I've noticed that nobody here seems to be sick. No colds, no allergies…" He allowed his voice to trail off, curious as to what the other man would say.

Grayson laughed. "Well, we've decided to outlaw all that."

He made it sound like a joke, but Hawk had an uneasy feeling that the man wasn't really kidding. It was all about *his* choices, *his* preferences, *his* master plan. Whether he made light of it or not, Grayson was convinced that the world revolved around him—as it should.

Hell, it was clear that Grayson really did think he was God.

Chapter 11

She wasn't home.

There were no lights on in the eighty-year-old farmhouse, and her car was nowhere to be seen. He'd knocked three times, anyway, each time a little louder than the last. Each time with the same results.

There was no answer.

Hawk remained at her front door another minute or so. Then frustrated, he turned on his heel and walked away.

But rather than just shrug it off and proceed on to his hotel room for the night, Hawk got into his car and sat there in the dark, waiting. As he waited, he grew progressively restless and apprehensive with each minute that ticked by.

Where the hell was she?

Carly had told him that she didn't stay in town, that

she liked sleeping here, in her own bed, where she felt she had some sort of control over her immediate surroundings. In Cold Plains, the ever-increasing number of Devotees of Samuel, as the "faithful" sometimes referred to themselves, made her feel uncomfortable, so she preferred to do her sleeping here. He could well understand that.

Hawk tried to distract himself by reviewing the information he had on hand, but his mind kept going back to the fact that he'd heard Samuel asking Carly to come by his office once he finished in the auditorium.

Again, Hawk uneasily wondered why. A series of scenarios kept suggesting themselves in his head, but he blocked them before any of them could completely materialize.

Maybe he should have hung around himself, Hawk thought. His presence, he was certain, would have been taken as a silent warning to Grayson that he wasn't to harm anyone or have any of his henchmen harm anyone. Because if he did, everything the self-enamored egotist had built up would come crashing down around his ears faster than a child's plastic building blocks.

With a frustrated sigh, Hawk debated starting his car and going back to town.

But if he left now, he might wind up missing Carly if she came to the farmhouse via another route. And if he burst in on Grayson in his office or where he lived, that would completely blow the mission. He didn't want Grayson alerted to the fact that he and his people were under FBI surveillance. So far, all the so-called charismatic leader thought was that he was some independent FBI agent asking questions about a bunch of dead women and not getting any useful answers in reply.

The longer he sat in the dark with his imagination attempting to run amuck, the less reasonable and patient Hawk became. He thought about calling Jeffers or Patterson and sending the agent into town to look around, but that, too, would arouse suspicions. Cold Plains wasn't exactly the kind of town that received a steady flow of outside traffic. It was neither a tourist draw— although from what he'd picked up that was apparently part of Grayson's plan—nor on the road to somewhere else. There would be no reason for a stranger to pass through without a specific reason.

Hell, he didn't care if it made sense or not. She could be in some kind of real danger while he sat here, as inert as Hamlet mumbling his "to be or not to be" soliloquy to himself.

Fed up with waiting, Hawk was just about to start his vehicle when he saw headlights slicing through the darkened terrain. Removing his key from the ignition, he watched as they drew closer and the car became larger.

It was Carly's car. He recognized her headlights. The right one was slightly dimmer than the left. While he wanted to leap out of his own vehicle to ask her why she was so late, he forced himself to remain where he was and calm down.

Number one, he had no right to make noises like some overwrought, jealous boyfriend, and number two, the fact that she might not be alone—something that truly bothered him—would make his sudden appearance difficult to explain to whomever was with her—especially if it turned out to be either Grayson or one of his many minions.

So Hawk stayed where he was and impatiently waited. And watched.

When Carly pulled her car up in front of the farmhouse and got out, she was alone.

The second he was sure of that, Hawk shot out of his own vehicle like a hastily fired bullet and cut across the front yard. Taking the porch steps two at a time, he caught up to Carly just as she reached the front door.

Startled, she swung around, her fist drawn back like a prize-fighter in training. She stopped two inches short of making contact and dropped her hand when she saw who it was.

"What are you doing here?" she asked. Damn but this man was going to wind up giving her a heart attack yet.

"Checking on you," Hawk replied, his tone deceptively simple.

She'd been too preoccupied as she approached the house and hadn't noticed his car parked outside. Carly drew in a deep breath, then let it go, doing her best to calm her rather shaky nerves. It didn't really work. She tried again.

Unlocking the door, she let Hawk inside. "Why?" she asked wearily. "Are you afraid that I'll suddenly turn into a Samuel groupie?"

Alerted by her tone that something was off, Hawk moved around to get in front of her. He wanted a better look at her face as she turned on the light. Taking her chin in his hand, he examined her even more closely.

Carly tried to turn her head away, but he held her captive.

"You know better than that," he told her. His eyes slid over her face. Something was wrong. "What happened tonight?"

Carly let out a huge, soul-twisting sigh before answering.

"Nothing." Then raising her eyes to his, she added, "At least not the way you mean, anyway."

Hawk couldn't decide if she was telling him the truth, or merely trying to spare him because that was the kind of person she was, ready to shoulder rather than share the burden. Even when its weight could very possibly break her.

"Grayson didn't touch you?" Hawk demanded.

The small, disparaging laugh had no humor to it. "Oh, he touched me, all right." The next moment, Hawk looked as if he would go charging out the door. She grabbed his arm to stop him from letting his emotions get the better of his common sense. "But again, not the way you mean."

His temper frayed into combustible strips, Hawk shouted, "Then for heaven's sakes, tell me what *you* mean." The next moment, his better judgment resurfaced and he realized that he owed her an apology for acting like a Neanderthal. "Sorry. I didn't mean to start shouting at you."

She knew he wasn't shouting at her, but shouting at Grayson by proxy. The frustration that his hands were temporarily tied had gotten the better of him.

"Apology accepted," she said, leading the way to

the kitchen. "Why don't you sit down?" she suggested, nodding at the table. "I'll make us some tea and tell you what happened."

She was the one who looked as if she needed to be waited on, he judged. "No, you sit down, and I'll make the tea," Hawk offered, reversing the order. "But you *can* tell me what happened."

"Done," she answered with a faint smile. She all but bonelessly slid onto the kitchen chair. For one second, Carly fought the urge to put her head down on the table and just make this evening, as well as the world in general, go away for a little while. She'd been caught unaware, but she'd gotten through it, and that was all that mattered.

Hawk was waiting for her. Taking another breath, she began her narrative of the evening's events, trying to be as succinct as possible. "Grayson decided to welcome me into the fold."

Hawk took the battered, red tea kettle from the back of the stove and brought it over to the sink. Turning on the faucet, he started to fill the kettle with water.

"What does that mean?" he asked guardedly, doing his best to sound calm. The trouble was, where Carly was involved, he had a tendency to remain anything *but* calm.

"He made a devotee out of me," Carly replied quietly, turning her face away from him. She stared out the kitchen window, into the darkness just beyond.

"He indoctrinated you?" Hawk asked uneasily as he put the kettle on the front burner and switched on the gas jet beneath it. Small, blue flames popped up and danced feverishly beneath the round metal surface.

"He tattooed me," she replied through teeth that were slightly shy of being clenched.

The kettle and its contents were forgotten. Hawk came around to where she was sitting and dropped to his knees before her. He knew what she was saying, but he was hoping that, by some fluke, he was wrong.

"You mean...?"

Carly silently nodded. It was stupid to cry, and she didn't want to. She wanted to yell, to be angry—and she was—but tears came to her eyes, anyway. Upbraiding herself for this weak display didn't stem their flow.

She pressed her lips together, drew back the wide, billowing beige skirt from her leg and pulled the material up high so that her right thigh was completely exposed for Hawk to see.

On it was a small, fresh, black letter *D*. The skin just beneath it was an angry red. Hawk cringed when he saw it. He swore he could feel the same needle inking his flesh.

As if his brain was on a five-second delay, he suddenly heard what she'd said. "He does the tattoo himself?" Hawk asked, surprised.

Carly nodded, telling herself that once this was over and behind her, she would have the tattoo removed, no matter what it took or how painful that process turned out to be.

"Seems to really enjoy doing it, too," she told him grimly. "Enjoys the fact that he was inflicting pain 'artistically.'"

Hawk rocked back on his heels, suddenly struck by a thought. What she'd just told him was a brand-new piece of information they hadn't had before. A few tiny pieces of the puzzle came together.

"That's probably why," he said.

Carly looked at him, confused. Was he talking to himself or to her? "What's probably why?"

He glanced up. It made sense now. "I think I know why our Jane Doe was killed. She had a black *D* on her hip, except that hers was done with a black marker. She undoubtedly did it in order to blend in. But she didn't know that the only one who 'awarded' those tattoos was Grayson himself."

As the light dawned, Carly finished his statement for him. "So when he saw it, Grayson knew she had to be an imposter."

"Right, which naturally made him suspicious. Because of what he felt was at stake, he didn't stop to ask her any questions, he just had her executed." That still didn't tell him what the woman was doing there in the first place, but at least they had one of the answers.

"Executed?" Carly echoed uncertainly, clearly confused.

Hawk nodded. "That was a detail we kept back from the media." That way, if a copycat killer suddenly emerged, they would be aware of it. He had no doubts a great many sick people existed who would do anything for their fifteen minutes of fame—or infamy in this case. "Each of the women was shot in the back of the head. A single bullet, execution style."

It didn't necessarily have to be an execution, she

thought. "Or shot when they weren't looking, so they didn't know what was coming—or get the chance to plead for their lives," she suggested.

He hadn't thought of that. Hawk looked at Carly with a flicker of admiration. "That's a possibility, too," he agreed, then grinned. "Not bad."

"Thank you." He saw a small smile struggling to emerge.

The tea kettle began to whistle, calling attention to itself and the water that was now boiling madly. Hawk rose to his feet again and crossed back to the stove. He opened a couple of cupboards before he finally located two large mugs.

"He asked me, you know," she told him, watching Hawk as he poured steaming hot water into the mugs. "Grayson asked if I was serious about becoming one of his 'chosen followers.' If I'd said no or that I had to think about it, he would have slammed the proverbial door in my face, just like that—" she snapped her fingers "—and then I probably wouldn't even be able to get in contact with Mia or talk to her."

Carly sounded almost a little defensive. After what she'd just been through, did she think he was going to give her a hard time? He wasn't completely heartless.

"You don't have to explain anything to me, Carly," he told her.

She would beg to differ, Carly thought. "The expression on your face when you came up behind me just now said that I do. You looked damn angry that I was late getting home."

He shrugged, his shoulder vaguely moving up and down. "I was worried about you."

Carly relaxed a little. *I was worried about you.* That had a nice ring to it.

Carly knew that it didn't really mean anything in the grand scheme of things, because life had taken them in different directions—*since you sent him away,* her mind taunted—and even though their paths had crossed one another temporarily, life would soon be back on its rightful track, and he would have his life and she hers.

But his voiced concern still sounded nice, and just for the slightest moment, Carly indulged herself by letting her mind go to the land of what-if?

What if she hadn't sent him away? What if he'd stayed by choice? Or she had been able to leave without her conscience bleeding, anchoring her here?

What if…?

Snapping out of it, Carly said, "It's been a long while since anyone was worried about me."

He knew how independent she'd always been and, thank God, apparently still was, despite her pretense to the contrary for Grayson's benefit. Truth of it was, he wasn't all that certain what he would have ultimately done if she really had turned out to be one of Grayson's followers.

Probably tried to kidnap her the way she was trying to find a way of kidnapping Mia as a last resort, he thought.

Out loud he said, "Sorry, didn't mean to crowd you or infer that you weren't perfectly capable of taking care of yourself." The words were automatic rather than straight from the heart—the way his flash of anger had been. "No offense intended."

He was backing away. Why? Did he think she wanted him to? Or was it that he didn't want her thinking that there was something still between them when there clearly wasn't?

"None taken," she murmured.

Coming to, he picked up both steaming mugs and crossed back to the table. He placed one in front of her, then placed the second one on the table where he was sitting. He slipped back onto his chair.

Carly looked down at Hawk's masterpiece and then grinned. The man had forgotten one key ingredient.

"You know," she began gently, "it might help to put the tea bags in."

His attention had been completely focused on her, and he'd been grappling with surges of anger and the very strong desire to strangle the man he had under surveillance. Case or no case, when he thought of the man possibly forcing himself on Carly, all bets were off. In that tiny space of time, he was a man first and an FBI special agent second.

Not something his superiors would be thrilled about hearing.

He glanced down at the two mugs. Each was filled to the brim with water. Tea bags, however, were nowhere in sight. He'd forgotten to put them in. He would obviously never make it as a waiter, he thought ruefully.

"Sorry," Hawk muttered under his breath as he started to get up again.

Carly stopped him by putting her hand on top of his.

When he eyed her quizzically, she nodded at his chair and indicated that he should sit down again.

"You sit, I'll get the tea bags," she told him. "I know where they are," she added. "You'll only wind up having to go searching through the pantry," she told him with a soft laugh.

They were right where she'd left them. But when Carly turned away from the pantry, the tin with tea bags in her hand, she found that Hawk wasn't where she had left *him*.

He was right behind her, so close that when she'd turned around, her body had brushed against his. She felt the electric tingle immediately. It blotted out the revulsion she'd been battling with.

"Are you that impatient for tea?" she asked, trying to suppress a grin.

Her eyes were dancing, he noted. And all he wanted to do right at this moment was make her his again.

"The hell with the tea," he answered. His emotions were still all in a jumble, and he was at a loss how to sort everything all out. "I thought that Grayson—I was afraid that you—"

None of this was coming out right. He wasn't accustomed to feeling this confused, as if he was being pulled in two directions at the same time, one labeled duty, the other labeled conscience. And him stuck in the middle.

"Damn it, Carly," he all but exploded, thinking of what *might* have happened to her had Grayson an inkling that she was playing him, "I don't like you taking these kinds of chances."

She knew that, but she still found it oddly comforting to hear him admit it.

"You don't have the right to tell me not to do this, you know," she reminded him, even though she couldn't suppress the hint of a smile curving her lips.

"I know," he answered, "but just thinking that something could have happened to you—"

Hawk couldn't bring himself to finish his sentence. Instead, he abruptly pulled her into his arms and kissed her. Kissed her hard, with all the feeling pulsing through his body.

It took Carly a full thirty seconds to find her breath. "The water's going to get cold," she whispered, not trusting her voice to keep from cracking if she spoke any louder.

He didn't care about the damn tea. "It can be reheated."

His words brought a wide smile to her lips. "Apparently," Carly said with a soft laugh as she pressed her body against his, "so can you."

He brought his mouth down on hers again, this time with even more force than before. Kissing her as if there was no tomorrow because, for all he knew, there wasn't one.

Not for him, not for her and especially not for them.

Chapter 12

Hawk had long ago decided that law enforcement work was a combination of danger and boredom with very little in between. On rare occasions, there was also a glimmer of the satisfaction associated with closing a case. But for the most part, it was the former set of circumstances that prevailed.

The boredom also included more than a little frustration. There was no doubt in Hawk's mind that this particular case, involving dead women and a rampant display of mind control, was the classic example of both of those elements.

It was clearly dangerous because if Samuel Grayson decided that he had become a threat to his utopia, Grayson would have him eliminated without a thought. The frustration in this case was multifaceted, like a Hydra monster straight out of Greek mythology. Hawk found himself frustrated at almost every turn he took. There was the matter of the second victim's, currently Jane Doe's, true identity. She matched no missing persons report or any of the fingerprints that were on file in the various databases.

And as of this moment, the facial recognition program, which Jeffers had been running non-stop for the past day and a half, hadn't found a match, either.

If this woman *was* an undercover operative, it had to be deep cover because, to date, no agency had attempted to claim her.

Maybe the woman had been a private detective, hired to track down and bring back someone Grayson had attracted to his community and subsequently brainwashed. It was a possibility. Hawk had suggested it to Jeffers the instant he thought of it.

"If she was a private investigator," Jeffers had pointed out, "then she'd have to have a license and her prints would be on file somewhere—which they're not," he concluded with a deep sigh.

The only other possibility, Hawk had gone on to speculate, was that the woman *hadn't* been a professional investigator and had undertaken this "going undercover" mission on her own because someone she cared about had been absorbed into Grayson's society.

Their Jane Doe could have very well acted on the same instincts that Carly had, Hawk realized the next moment. The thought was far from comforting.

Damn but he wished he could get Carly to listen to him and give up this charade. He didn't want her turning up in some shallow grave just because her sister was one of the mindless and addle brained who was so hopelessly devoted to Grayson.

Driving through the town like a man strictly out to enjoy the afternoon, Hawk observed the town's citizens, looking for evidence he could work with.

He wasn't sure just how much longer he could keep his mouth shut around Carly about the role she was playing. He made a right at the next corner with the intentions of doing one last round. He'd made his initial protest to her, then had intended to let the matter go because Carly wouldn't be browbeaten or bullied into backing away. When pushed, she had a tendency to dig in, not flee or relent. He'd learned that a long time ago when her father had taunted her that she would never amount to anything. She became the only reason they didn't lose the farm years ago.

But knowing the way she reacted didn't keep him from voicing his opinion rather loudly the other night when he'd thought something had happened to her.

In a way, it had, he reminded himself. She'd been tattooed—branded—by that sick S.O.B. Hawk was now more worried than ever about her safety. Grayson was paying too much attention to her. Whether it was because he was suspicious that she wasn't on the level or because he had singled her out as one of his particular "favorites," Hawk didn't know, and it really made no difference to him. The end result was the same. It placed Carly in danger.

And he didn't like it.

One way or the other, he *had* to get her to leave town for her own good. Even if, by getting her to leave, he would be getting rid of the one bright spot in his life—not just here but in general.

For the past ten years, Hawk had been all about the job, all about his duty and whatever case he was working on. Nothing distracted him, nothing divided his focus. He'd had no real personal life, moreover, no desire to open up that part of himself where his feelings had once resided.

But being with Carly this short space of time, whether he liked it or not, had abruptly changed all that. It made him remember that there was another side to life, a side that didn't involve guns, dead bodies and covert operations.

A side that involved a reason to smile.

Don't get used to this, Hawk silently ordered himself. All of this—the good part—would be in his past in what amounted to less than the blink of an eye. And the less he invested himself in it now, the easier it would be for him to regroup and move on later. He needed to remember that.

"Words to live by," he said sarcastically, under his breath.

The other source of his frustration, currently at the top of his list, was trying to reach Micah. For three weeks now he'd had the same kind of luck: none.

It was as if the man had just disappeared off the face of the earth after that initial communication.

Or, Hawk thought grimly, Micah's brother had had him killed, just like, he was certain, Grayson'd had everyone else who had incurred his displeasure killed.

If that did turn out to be the case, he had no idea

where to begin looking for Micah Grayson's body—other than perhaps in or around the town where Micah had arranged to meet him, he supposed. Still, that was a large area to cover.

Could Grayson have learned about the proposed meeting, seen it as a threat to what he was doing and sent one of his henchmen to eliminate his twin brother? He might have even done it himself, Hawk speculated. Grayson might have taken a certain pleasure in ridding the world of his double, so that there was and would continue to be only *one* person with his face.

Who knew what went through that psychopath's mind, Hawk thought, his frustration mounting as he felt that he was facing yet another brick wall.

There just had to be some faster way to get answers, but for the life of him, Hawk didn't know how.

Carly struggled to keep her smile pasted to her lips. It was far from easy. Not when she was standing in the doorway of the community center's all-purpose room, looking at the ongoing preparations for Mia's upcoming wedding.

Samuel had put several of his more dedicated female followers to work, festively decorating the area. They went about their appointed tasks, fashioning roses out of construction paper and adding gaily-colored streamers to every square inch of the community room.

To Carly, it looked as if a colored paper mill had exploded. In addition to streamers, balloons would soon flood the room. Because of helium's somewhat limited life span, the balloons would be brought in during the last leg of the preparations so that they would appear robust and full of promise on the big day.

Unlike the actual situation.

When one of the women looked up and saw her, Carly suddenly found herself being pressed into service, despite her protests. After all, she was the sister of the bride. Her sense of pride and loyalty should have had her insisting on helping right from the beginning, one of the volunteers, a woman named Janice told her in no uncertain terms.

Carly would have liked nothing more than to leave— for a number of reasons, most prominently her incredibly strong disapproval of this match. But she knew it would look suspicious if she flatly declined Bubblehead Lady's tersely worded suggestion. And that in turn would only wind up calling for a closer scrutiny of her behavior.

So she forced herself to cheerfully say, "Of course," in response to Janice's urgings to "Come help us get ready for Mia's wedding."

She'd give them an hour, Carly decided, then beg off to run some imaginary errand. They couldn't find fault with that, right?

Mentally she began the countdown.

And in the meantime, she worked to create paper wild roses—pink ones—and she listened. She didn't have to listen for very long to hear something distasteful.

"Mia is so lucky that Brice Carrington chose her— and that Samuel approved," one of the other women declared.

And still another agreed, saying, "Brice is quite a catch, you know." She turned her brown eyes to look at Carly. "Any one of the unattached ladies would have been more than thrilled if they had caught his eye. But Samuel thinks that your sister is best suited for him. Samuel says that she is at a perfect age as well as being physically perfect," the woman confided, leaning in toward Carly to "share" her information.

A third woman chimed in, "Samuel believes your sister will make beautiful, healthy devotees."

"Perhaps six, if not more," Janice spouted as if she was repeating the gospel of her lord. Her eyes swept over the others and, for a moment, lingered on Carly as if she was waiting to be contradicted or challenged.

A baby machine, Carly thought with contempt. *Grayson doesn't see Mia as a person, he sees her as some kind of a soulless baby machine for him to operate. I was right all along,* she thought angrily, finding no solace in having guessed correctly.

With all her heart, she wished that Mia could hear this. Maybe *then* she would finally snap out of her trance, see things for what they really were. But this seemed a hopeless venture. Her sister clearly bought into Grayson's vision of the world and was perfectly comfortable with the man's plans for her future.

That only left kidnapping her sister as an option.

Since Mia remained in town each night, she would have to keep her eyes open for an available opportunity to abduct Mia without being noticed or arousing suspicion.

She hated thinking about it, but there was obviously no other way.

In addition to finding the right opportunity to get this all to snap into gear, Carly would probably have to bound and gag Mia in order to get her out of here. Otherwise, her sister was liable to scream her head off and get them both killed.

Or at least her, Carly thought cynically.

Sometime during working on this forced "labor of love," it occurred to Carly that one of the faces she'd become accustomed to seeing around town, and especially around the community center, was missing today.

Now that she thought about it, she hadn't seen the young woman in at least a couple of days. Maybe even longer. With her relationship with Hawk heating up so unexpectedly and so quickly, she'd wound up overlooking everything that wasn't directly connected to Mia.

"Where's Susannah?" she asked the women now, hoping one of them could fill her in. What she hadn't expected was sarcasm.

"Ah, she speaks. I thought maybe you'd gone mute," Janice told her coolly as she worked.

Carly deliberately kept her tone amiable. "I didn't want to interrupt any of you ladies while you were talking," Carly replied, hiding her resentment at the comment.

Besides, she'd found that listening to the people around her talk—if they were Grayson's followers—was far more informative than talking herself.

The woman she was asking about wasn't like any of these women she was working with. Or for that matter, she wasn't like most of the women in town. Susannah Paul was a sweet, young woman with a rather lost, haunted look in her eyes. It was that look that had first drawn her to Susannah. Once they spoke, there was almost an instant bond. Carly had found herself befriending the brand-new mother who had confided to her just the other day that she was having second thoughts about living here under what felt like "Samuel's watchful eye." She'd whispered that it made her feel uneasy.

Carly had tried to be sympathetic without tipping her own hand. She remembered urging Susannah not to do anything hasty without letting her know first.

"I don't want you feeling alone," she had explained. "Or going off by yourself with your baby." Squeezing the young woman's hand, she'd said with all sincerity, "I want to help you if I can. I know it can't be easy, being a single mother with a brand-new baby."

She'd seen a little of herself in that scenario, because after their mother had died, she had all but raised Mia on her own, too. Certainly her drunken father hadn't been of any actual help when it came to that. The only thing the man knew how to do was how to drink, not how to raise a very young girl.

In response to her words, Susannah had given her a quick, grateful smile and had promised to keep her apprised of any decisions she would make.

"You'll be the first one I'll tell," she'd said. "And probably the only one, too."

So where was she?

Carly looked at Janice, waiting for the woman's

answer since she seemed to be into everyone's business. But instead of responding, the woman looked up uneasily, making eye contact with someone behind her.

The next moment, Carly heard Samuel's deep voice saying, "Please don't trouble yourself about Susannah." She turned around to face the man just as he said, "She is where she is supposed to be."

That didn't sound good, Carly couldn't help thinking. "And that is—?" she pressed.

Grayson gave her a beatific smile. "—none of your concern," the man concluded serenely.

Suppressing a sense of horror, Carly still couldn't make herself let it go. "And the baby?" she whispered, almost afraid of the answer.

"Why, with her, of course," Samuel replied. "Where else would a young child be, but with the woman who had given her life?"

Carly's blood ran cold, all but draining from her face. Could Grayson possibly be saying that Susannah and her precious baby were dead? That maybe he had learned that she was vacillating about continuing under his so-called guidance.

Considering his low opinion of people, Susannah's doubts about remaining in Cold Plains and involved in the center made her imperfect in Grayson's eyes, and Carly was beginning to see what the man did with anyone who he deemed imperfect.

Samuel's eyes narrowed, and he made no attempt to hide the fact that he was scrutinizing her as if trying to delve into her thoughts. "Why are you so interested in where Susannah is, Carly?"

"I just thought I could help her take care of the baby," Carly explained innocently. "She seemed a little over-whelmed."

"My perception of her exactly," Samuel agreed with a vigorous nod of his head. The smile he gave her made Carly feel *really* uneasy. "We seem to think alike, Carly, you and I." His eyes were all but holding her prisoner. "I find that very gratifying."

Carly knew enough to pretend to look down de-murely. It was either that or have him see how much she truly hated him for having brought so much evil to her home.

He looked as if he was about to suggest that they continue their "talk" and comparison of thoughts in his office.

She was saved at the last minute. Because just then, someone called to Grayson about needing his final input on several pressing matters involving the construction of yet another new building along Cold Plains's Main street.

"Duty calls," Grayson told her with a heavy, dra-matic sigh as he excused himself from her company. Then just before he left, he leaned over and whispered in her ear. "This conversation is far from over, Carly," he promised.

As he left the room, the women all looked at her with unabashed envy.

Feeling as if she had just dodged a bullet, Carly made herself scarce as quickly as possible. She needed to get away from town, away from Grayson, at least until she figured out how to handle all this unwanted attention.

The man clearly wanted to brand her with more than just the letter *D* that he had tattooed onto her thigh.

"She's missing," Carly announced to Hawk when she let him into her house later that evening.

She had given him a spare key, but Hawk thought it more prudent if he knocked and waited for her to open the door. That way, she would see that it was him, and she couldn't be caught by surprise by anyone else if they attempted to break in on her.

"Mia?" he guessed, since she hadn't mentioned the missing woman's name.

"No, Susannah Paul." Carly could see that the name meant nothing to him. Why should it? As far as she knew, Susannah hadn't spoke to him. Susannah knew nothing about nothing, so there would have been no reason for her to speak with the FBI special agent. "She told me she was thinking about leaving the community."

Well, maybe that was her answer, Hawk thought, following her to the kitchen. Every night since he'd made that first stop to "check" on her, he'd stop to have a little dinner with her and then stay to talk. Except that they hardly ever did. They let their passion do the talking for them.

"Maybe she did," he speculated, but he could see why she was concerned. People didn't just up and leave Cold Plains, not unless Grayson wanted them to. And then it was as if the atmosphere had just swallowed them up.

Carly shook her head. "Susannah wouldn't go without telling me. I made her promise she'd let me know first. And there's something else."

Hawk looked at her, waiting.

"She's just had a baby recently. She wouldn't really be up for a lot of traveling." She glanced at Hawk, but long enough so that he could see the distress in her eyes. God knew, it wasn't without merit.

Carly hesitated for a moment, then asked, "Do you think that Grayson could have—"

"He very well could have, yes, but don't let your imagination go there yet. There could still be a lot of other plausible explanations," he told her soothingly.

But even as he said it, he wasn't nearly as convinced as he sounded for Carly's benefit.

And he suspected that Carly knew it, too.

Chapter 13

Carly was running out of time and she knew it.

Mia's wedding ceremony was less than three days away. For the past two days, she hadn't even been able to get *near* her sister.

Each time she tried, Mia was either already busy working under Grayson's watchful guidance, or if her sister appeared to be momentarily alone and she started to approach her, Grayson would somehow suddenly come swooping down out of nowhere, requesting that Mia join him or come see something, or he'd use a dozen and one other diversion tactics to separate Mia from everyone else.

Mainly her.

Not that she had much hope of miraculously persuading her sister to give up this absurd idea of marrying a man who was more than twice her age. The last time she had gotten to talk to her alone, she had used every argument she could think of to persuade Mia not to make what she considered in her heart to be a "terrible mistake."

Mia hadn't even let her finish. Her sister had looked at her with open hostility and said, "I don't care if you like what Cold Plains has become or not, but I do. I *like* it here, do you understand? For the first time in my life, I have order, I have peace—and I have a place that makes me feel as if I'm important." She'd raised her chin pugnaciously and declared, "For the first time in my life, I feel happy."

For the first time in my life.

That had stung. Badly.

Carly tried hard not to make it about hurt feelings, but it was difficult not to. She had sacrificed everything for her sister, especially her own happiness. She had stayed on here in Cold Plains when she would have much rather just taken off and started a brand-new life with Hawk.

"And you didn't before?" she had challenged Mia with suppressed anger.

Mia had tossed her head, her eyes narrowing as she had looked at her defiantly. "No."

"And life with me was so terrible?" Carly asked.

"What 'with' you?" Mia demanded, throwing up her hands. She upset one of the decorations that had just been hung up that morning. Angry, she picked it up and lovingly dusted it off before carefully reattaching it. "I never saw you," she pointed out accusingly.

How could Mia stand there, throwing that into her

face? There was a reason she hadn't been around and it wasn't because she was out having a good time, enjoying herself. She had run herself ragged, trying to make ends meet.

Didn't her sister understand that?

Apparently not, she concluded. Sighing, Carly gave it her all, trying one more time to reason with Mia.

"That's because I was trying to run the farm and earn some money on the side as a waitress so you could have the little luxuries, you know, like food." She realized that came out sounding rather sarcastic. She hadn't meant for it to, but she was still stunned that, given all those years she'd worked so hard so that her sister could have at least a few things that she hadn't had, Mia wasn't grateful for any of it.

"I would have rather had you," Mia spat out. "I never got to talk to anyone. You were *never* there for me." Her eyes became angry blue flames. "All I ever did was clean up after Dad. And I mean that literally."

"So did I," Carly informed her. They stood facing one another, officially at a standoff. "I worked so that you could have regular meals, clothes on your back, a roof over your head. If I hadn't done what I did, we would have lost the family farm."

Mia drew herself up and went back to working on the decorations for her wedding. "So now I hope you and the farm will be very happy together. And if you can't be happy for me at my wedding," she added curtly, "then don't bother coming. The choice is yours."

Carly stared at the back of her sister's head. How could Mia talk to her this way? How could she be so insensitive as not to see everything she'd given up for her?

"Mia, I—"

"There you are!" a cheerful voice addressing Mia declared.

Charlie Rhodes, one of Grayson's inner circle of handpicked men, who was also going to be best man at the wedding, came up behind them and then took Mia gently by the arm.

At first glance, Charlie had the features of a sweet-faced angel.

He probably would have been one of the fallen ones, Carly couldn't help thinking. In the few, brief exchanges they'd had, Charlie had been nothing but polite to her, but she still couldn't get over the uneasy feeling she would always get in the pit of her stomach whenever she was around the young man. For one thing, his eyes were flat, as if there was no soul, no conscience, behind them.

"Samuel's been looking for you," Charlie told Mia. "He has something to ask you about those children's seminars you've been giving for him. He seemed pretty busy, so I offered to fetch you for him."

Fetch. Just like she was some inanimate object, Carly thought. *Mia, wise up! Please!*

"Well, you found me," Mia declared cheerfully. "Now take me to him."

Said the lamb to the wolf as she was led off to the slaughter. Damn it, Mia, don't you hear *yourself?* Carly wondered angrily.

For a moment, she thought about just grabbing Mia's

hand and running, but she knew how irrational that would seem. For one thing, Mia wouldn't run with her, certainly not willingly. She'd probably just dig in her heels and refuse to go.

That had been her last one-on-one contact with her sister, almost five days ago. Since then, every attempt she'd made had been thwarted one way or another. She may actually have to kidnap Mia and get her out of the community. There appeared to be no other way to save her.

That evening when she came home, she was still contemplating the exact logistics of pulling off her sister's kidnapping. Everything she came up with depended heavily on luck. The only easy part was getting into the compound, and that was because Samuel believed her to be just as brainwashed as the others.

When she'd resisted moving into town, he'd been a little suspicious at first, his hypnotic eyes all but burrowing into her. But she had pointed out that she needed to keep the farm in business. After all, her chickens did provide breakfast for the masses and her dairy cows kept the children in milk.

Using that as her foundation, Carly managed to convince Samuel that she could better serve the community by returning to the farm each evening and working it the hours she was not teaching the children.

So with Grayson thinking she was one of the true believers, she had the element of surprise on her side. That would win her about sixty seconds. After that, she would have to run like crazy, dragging her sister behind her. Either that or get to her just before the ceremony. Ultimately, the plans were the same. One way or another, she intended to abduct Mia before her little sister had a chance to say those fatal words that would seal her doom.

Carly pulled her car up near the house and looked around. Disappointment nudged its way to the surface and hung there. She worked her lower lip uneasily. There was no trace of Hawk.

Funny how quickly that man got to be a habit with her. All it took was looking at him, and she was a goner. He'd been her first love and, as it had turned out, her only love. She had never felt anything for any other man. Not that she had actively tried to find someone, but once or twice, she'd gone out with one of the other men in town. Her ultimate goal had been to find some sort of companionship. Maybe even settle down.

But for her, there was no repeat performance of a magic moment, no chemistry suddenly pulsating through her. Not even the desire to be held and kissed by whoever was taking her out that night.

And so she eventually came to the inevitable conclusion that Hawk would forever be the one and only man she would ever care about, ever love.

And he was out of her life by her own doing.

She had to resign herself to that. So she did.

Until he'd shown up, Carly thought now, letting herself into the darkened house. He had instantly turned her whole world upside down by coming back into town, looking better than any man had a right to after ten years had gone by.

This time, she didn't know how she would survive having him walk away. Because he would. He'd carved out that life for himself that she'd pushed him toward.

A life that didn't include her.

"Don't think that far ahead," she chided herself. "He's still here for now, and all any of us have is now. Make the most of it," she ordered herself as she went around the house, turning on lights and chasing away the gloom.

With the house now well lit, Carly made her way into the kitchen to prepare dinner. It seemed rather ironic because she hardly bothered with dinner when she was alone. Usually it meant just grabbing something out of the refrigerator and eating it over the sink while doing three other things at the same time.

But for Hawk, she prepared dinner. Looked forward to dinner. Even if they didn't speak, she still loved to sit there beside him at the table, watching him eat what she'd made for him. Doing so gave her a warm feeling of normalcy she'd been lacking for longer than she could actually remember.

Maybe that was why Mia wanted to get married, Carly thought abruptly. Why her sister seemed to cleave to this sham of a life she saw being offered to her. Because she wanted what everyone wanted. A little piece of the normal life.

Except that marriage to Brice Carrington wouldn't be normal. Not in the way Mia wanted in her heart. Mia would be nothing more than a baby machine.

After taking the roast she'd made yesterday out of the refrigerator, Carly glanced at her watch. What was keeping Hawk? Not that there was a specific time that had been agreed upon. It was just that Hawk was usually here by now.

Leaving the roast on the counter, Carly suddenly felt an uneasy need to watch for him through the large bay window that faced her private road. The road that led away from the heart of Cold Plains.

Carly picked up her pace and made her way to the living room.

She passed by the gun rack where she still kept her late father's weapons primed and cleaned. They represented the only really good memory she had of the man. On the occasions that he'd been sober when she was a child, her father had tried to take her hunting. When she'd burst into tears the first time because he'd told her they were going to hunt for deer, he'd relented and taught her how to shoot at targets instead. She wound up shooting at pictures of snarling, vicious wolves.

She knew that her father had hoped to get her acclimated to shooting animals, wanting to make sure she would always be safe because animals could turn on her in a heartbeat, he'd explained, but she never did.

Eventually, her father began to drink more and more, and those Sunday afternoons in the woods, shooting at the pictures he'd posted for her, became a thing of the past. But she never forgot how to shoot and, on occasion, still went out to practice on her own. With Grayson and his cronies spreading their scourge here, who knew when that ability—to hit whatever she aimed for—might just come in handy?

Reaching the front window, she got there just in time to see Hawk pulling up.

The smile on her lips spread all through her. He was here!

She was about to hurry to the door to open it when a light in the distance caught her eye. It took her less than half a second to realize that it was actually two lights, not one. Two, like the headlights of an approaching vehicle.

Had Hawk brought someone with him?

But if he had, why weren't they both traveling in his car? And why was he now getting out of his vehicle without so much as a backward glance at the other car? It was as if he had no idea that there *was* another car approaching in the distance.

Nerves stretched taut began to dance through her. She had come to realize that she had grown to be a great deal less trusting than she had once been.

Backing away from the front window, Carly hurried over to the gun rack, the phrase *better safe than sorry* drumming through her head.

The last thing she wanted was to be sorry.

She had just unlocked the chain that she kept threaded through the weapons when she heard it.

A sound pealing like the crack of thunder.

Except that it wasn't thunder. She'd heard it often enough to know the difference between distant thunder and a gunshot.

There was no hesitation.

Grabbing the rifle closest to her, Carly hurried back to the front door. With no children in the house to worry about, she knew the weapon in her hand was fully loaded and ready to be discharged.

Carly threw open the door, then got her weapon ready, just in time to fire at whoever was firing a second shot at Hawk. Carly returned fire even before she realized that Hawk was down, obviously hit by that first shot she'd heard.

Rushing out to him, her heart pounding madly, Carly kept firing in the general direction of her quarry. She was intent on providing cover for herself and, more importantly, for Hawk, who she now realized was bleeding profusely from his left arm.

"Can you walk?" she cried, her eyes trained on the now-retreating back of the man who had followed Hawk here and tried to kill him. "Hawk, can you hear me?" she all but shouted when he didn't answer her. She didn't allow herself even to contemplate the reason why he wouldn't answer her.

"Yeah," Hawk managed to bite off, swallowing most of a string of curses. His arm felt as if it was on fire.

He should have seen that coming, Hawk angrily upbraided himself. But he'd been so preoccupied with the thought of seeing Carly, the thought of *being* with Carly, that he had let his guard slip. He hadn't been as careful as he should have been. And worst of all, he hadn't realized that he had a tail following him.

What a damn stupid rookie mistake, he thought angrily. He should have never allowed this to happen.

Carly was suddenly beside him, down on one knee as she kept shooting, providing their cover fire.

"Here!" she ordered, presenting her shoulder to him. "Lean on me."

Before he realized what she was doing, Carly had her shoulder wedged under his. With one massive effort, she struggled to bring him up to his feet. He did what he could to make it easier, willing himself to be stronger.

Their shadows fused together to appear as one wide, awkward creature, Hawk and Carly made their way quickly into the house, never turning their back on the shooter, even though it looked as though he'd given up and was fleeing.

The moment she had Hawk inside the house, Carly quickly slammed the front door and bolted it. Only then, with her arm wrapped around his middle now, did she half walk, half drag Hawk over to the sofa.

"Here, lie down on the couch," she ordered, all but dropping him there as she released the heavy weight of his frame from her aching shoulders. There was blood all over one side of her. "I'm checking the other windows and doors to make sure we don't get any uninvited pests slithering in."

As good as her word, Carly quickly and methodically checked each and every window, testing its integrity just to make sure it held. She also made sure that the back door was still secure.

"What was that all about?" she asked, raising her voice so that Hawk could hear her.

"Had to be one of Grayson's men," Hawk guessed. He closed his eyes for a moment, gathering his strength to him. The bullet was still lodged in his shoulder, and it had to come out. If they went to the nearest hospital in the next town, he might bleed out before they got there. And there was no way he could go to the Urgent Care Center in Cold Plains. He'd be dead before morning.

No, this was something that Carly was going to have to do. He wondered if she was up to it, or if, ultimately, she'd be too squeamish.

The woman who had come running to his rescue without a thought for her own safety had been magnificent—and not even remotely acquainted with the term *squeamish*.

"I think he feels that I'm getting close to something, although damned if I know what," he speculated. There was no other reason for the man to want to kill him, he thought. And he was sure that Grayson was behind this attack. As sure as he was that the sun was coming up tomorrow.

"He just doesn't want you nosing around, asking questions. It undermines his authority and his hold on 'his' people," Carly called back.

Satisfied that the windows were as secure as she could get them, Carly hurried back to the living room. It suddenly occurred to her, a second before she reached the living room, that by rushing to Hawk's aid, she had blown her cover.

She couldn't go back to the community center to try to see Mia. After she had just fired on one of his men, there was no doubt in her mind that Grayson would kill her if he saw her.

She didn't regret it. In her heart, she knew that if she hadn't been there, or if she'd hesitated and played it safe,

Hawk would be lying dead in her front yard—instead of bleeding on her sofa.

Getting him patched up was all that mattered, she told herself as she hurried over to him.

"Did the bullet go through?" she asked even as she gently began to examine the wound herself. There was no through and through, which could only mean one thing, she thought, her stomach sinking as she heard Hawk answer her question.

"No," he told her, "I think it's still in there." Looking up at her, he said, "You know what you have to do."

Throw up comes to mind, Carly thought, doing her best not to turn a very sickly shade of green.

Chapter 14

This was no time to think about herself, Carly silently chided. There were a number of different possibilities if the bullet was left where it was, none of them good. Besides, it wasn't as if she'd never seen a wound up close before, or cleaned one for that matter. It had just never involved someone she loved the way she loved Hawk.

"You're going to need some alcohol, bandages, a needle and thread—and your sharpest knife," Hawk said from the kitchen chair she'd helped move him to, trying his best to focus on details and not the sharp pain. The amount of blood he'd lost was making him feel light-headed, and he needed to remain conscious so that he could help Carly. He really should go to a hospital but he didn't trust anyone, and for this case, he had to fly under the radar.

She had already returned to the kitchen from the

bathroom, her arms filled with the items he had just rattled off.

"I know," she said, depositing them one by one on the kitchen table, lining them up in front of him. "I've done this before."

He looked at her in surprise. "When?" he asked.

It wasn't one of her fonder memories and up until now, she'd kept it to herself. "Dad and his friend used to go out hunting with enough alcohol in them to stock a small liquor store."

That was after her father had decided that drinking and hunting with his buddies was a lot more fun than going out for target practice with a little girl, she remembered. There was a time when that realization had pinched her stomach and made a sadness descend over her. But that time had long since passed. Now whenever she thought of her late father or anything associated with him, she felt nothing. She was completely removed from that period of her life. It no longer mattered.

"One time his friends came back carrying Dad between them—not exactly an easy feat since they were all falling-down drunk. Seems that one of the guys had accidentally mistaken him for a deer when he was in the bushes, relieving himself, and shot Dad. There was no time to take him to the next town to see a doctor, so I was drafted."

Hawk frowned. She couldn't have been that old. "Why not one of the other men?" he asked.

That would have probably hastened her father's demise. "Would you want someone trying to remove a bullet out of you when their hand was as steady as an earthquake?" To emphasize her point, she held out her hand and showed him how badly the men's hands had shaken.

He saw the point. "Guess not."

She went over to the sink and poured the rubbing alcohol liberally over the knife, disinfecting it. "Well, neither did my dad. He wasn't *that* drunk. So I was elected."

He wondered why she'd never told him about this before. What else hadn't she told him about? At one point he would have sworn that they had told each other everything. Everything because they had so much in common and had come together, seeking solace and comfort in the fact that the other *knew* exactly what they were going through, having an irrational drunk as a father. Now he was no longer so sure.

"Just how old were you?" he asked.

She didn't even have to think about it. "Almost eleven. It was the year after my mother died," she added in a quieter voice. There were times when she caught herself still missing her mother. That was never the case with her father. He had died *years* after he'd been lost to her.

Checking everything she'd laid out on the table, she said, "I need one more thing before I get started." With that, Carly hurried out of the room.

He looked at the items on the table. "What else do you need?" he called out, curious.

"Technically, I don't need it. But you do," she told him as she walked back into the room.

She placed an old bottle of whiskey on the table right

in front of him. The bottle was dusty. It was also un-opened. He glanced at her sharply. If asked, he would have easily bet that there was no liquor in the house. Obviously he would have lost that bet.

"What are you doing with that?" he asked.

Grabbing a kitchen towel, she quickly cleaned the dust on the bottle. She tossed the towel onto the back of a chair, removed the bottle's cap and set it to the side.

"This is the last bottle my father bought. He dropped dead of a heart attack just as he started to open it. I'm not exactly sure why I've kept it all these years, but now I'm glad I did. It's not going to knock you out," she told him, getting a glass from the cupboard, "but at least it might help you put up with the pain a little." Saying that, she poured a liberal amount of the amber liquid into a glass, then held it out to him. "Here."

Maybe it might help, he thought as he accepted the offered glass. Rather than just sip the drink slowly, as was his habit if he drank at all, Hawk tilted the glass back and drank down the contents quickly, draining it. He put it back down on the table with a "thwack" that resounded through the room.

The whiskey dulled his senses, dragging a fire through his belly and his limbs. He was still having trouble focusing, but now he didn't mind as much.

"Have at it," he told her, shifting in his chair so that his injured shoulder now faced her. "I'm ready, Dr. Finn," he declared, deliberately emphasizing the title she had no claim to.

Well, he might be ready, she thought, but she really wasn't. Still, this needed to be done, and the longer she delayed, the worse the consequences might be for Hawk. She brought the knife over to the sink and repeated the ritual of liberally pouring the last of the rubbing alcohol over both sides of it. And while she was doing that, she also did one more thing.

"Your lips are moving," Hawk noticed. "But I don't hear anything."

"You're not supposed to." That was her answer, but he was obviously waiting for more, so she explained very quietly, "I'm praying."

The admission surprised him. He thought for a moment, then found that between the triple shot of whiskey he'd just consumed and the blood he'd lost, he really couldn't do that well.

"Didn't know you did that," he told her.

Carly took a deep breath. The rubbing alcohol was all gone and, with it, her excuse for stalling. She was ready, whether or not God was.

"On occasion," she answered, then nodded at the bottle on the table. "Want another drink before we get started?"

"I'm good," Hawk told her, bracing himself. He had no intention of passing out like his old man had habitually done. Drinking himself into a stupor was his father's usual way of operating. "Go ahead."

Oh God, was all Carly could think, over and over again, as she applied the point of her knife to Hawk's flesh and began to go in. Although she knew that this wasn't his fault, she found that digging for the bullet was exceedingly difficult. For one thing, the muscles in Hawk's arm were as hard as rocks. Pushing the knife into his flesh was far easier in theory than in actual practice.

Amazingly, Hawk wasn't making any noise. Muscles or not, this *had* to hurt. "You all right?" she asked, slanting an uneasy glance at him.

"I've been better," he answered through solidly clenched teeth.

She didn't want to hurt him like this, but she had no other choice. "I'm sorry—"

"Just find it," he ordered, doing his best not to snap at her.

"I can't," she cried, growing more frustrated the deeper she probed for the bullet.

And then, finally, she felt it, felt a definite resistance of another kind. The point of her knife had touched metal.

"I think I found it."

Thank God, he silently cried. Out loud he merely muttered, "Good for you."

"Just a little longer," she promised, hoping she wasn't lying as she angled the knife in her hand, trying to get under the bullet to move it along.

And then, in what felt like a million light-years later, she finally managed to get it out. Such a little thing, causing so much damage, she couldn't help thinking as she put it on the table.

But there was no time to take a breath or admire her handiwork. Without anything to hold it back, Hawk's blood began to flow freely from the hole in his arm. Acting fast, Carly jammed a large wad of cotton against the wound, temporarily stemming the flow until she could reach for her needle. Her stomach, in turmoil, all but rose up into her mouth.

She felt sick. Whether with relief or the thought of what *could* have happened, she wasn't sure. But the one thing she knew was that she wanted desperately just to throw up.

As if sensing what she was going through, Hawk said in a very soothing voice, "You're doing just fine, Carly. Better than I could have hoped."

"I bet you say that to all the women who stitch you up," she quipped, releasing a huge sigh. There were at least half a dozen sighs just like that inside of her, waiting for release.

"Believe it or not, this is the first time I've ever been shot." He'd gone nine years with the Bureau without incident. He couldn't say that about himself anymore.

Something didn't make sense to her. "Then how did you know what I'd need to use?"

He supposed that was a valid question. "It's not the first time I've been around a bullet wound, just the first time I was the one on the receiving end," he clarified.

"Oh."

A sense of triumph suddenly hit her. She'd done it. She'd gotten the bullet out, cleaned the wound and sewn it up to prevent it from bleeding. He was going to make it. The relief continued to flower within her.

She took a large gauze pad, opened it and placed the white square on the wound she'd just closed. She then secured it in place with strips of tape around the perimeter of the gauze. That done, she sat back to look at her handiwork.

"I'm done," she announced with no small pleasure in her voice.

"Nice work," he commended. After making a quick call to his crew to make sure everything was okay there, he leaned heavily on his good arm and pushed himself up on his feet.

She was instantly alert and on hers. "Where are you going?" she asked.

This wasn't the time to sit back and take it easy. Good men lost their lives that way, he recalled. "To look around outside and make sure that the guy who shot me isn't coming back to finish the job."

"Only place you're going is to bed, mister," she informed him, sounding more stern than he could ever recall hearing her. "I can check to make sure that coward hasn't come back."

"I'm not going to bed," he told her firmly.

She knew that tone, knew there was no arguing with it. She compromised. "Okay, then sack out on the sofa if that suits you better. You've got a clear view of the front door as well as the window that way," she pointed out. "But you are not going outside, understood?" she said in a firm, take-no-prisoners voice.

If he'd had more strength, he would have argued with her. But as it was, he really didn't have the wherewithal to conduct an argument. He just was not in control the way he normally was. Between the blood loss and the quickly consumed alcohol, which had gone straight to his head, he felt as if the room insisted on making a circular journey, and it seemed to be spinning more and more quickly.

"Understood," he murmured, surrendering. "Did you get a look at him?" he asked her as, with her help, he made his way unsteadily to the couch. Somehow, the distance had become farther than he remembered.

"Yes, at the very last minute," she told him. And when she recognized the sniper, it was both a shock— and quite honestly—something she'd half expected. "The guy who shot you was Grayson's pretty boy, Charlie Rhodes." She set her mouth grimly as she told Hawk, "He's going to be best man at Mia's wedding." It was the startling contrast of blond hair against the dark night that had triggered recognition for her.

All but collapsing onto the sofa, Hawk looked up at her. His brain was foggy, but he struggled to make sense of what he was being told. Rhodes had clearly seen her coming to help him. It was because of her that he was still alive. That meant that, in Rhodes's eyes, she was a traitor.

Rhodes would go straight to Grayson with that. There was no reason not to. And he knew the consequences.

"The wedding," Hawk echoed. "How are you going to stop it?"

"Now that they know I'm not one of them?" Was this what he was asking her? The answer was heartbreakingly simple. "I'm not. Grayson is never going to allow me to get anywhere near my sister after what happened here tonight." Had she been as brainwashed as Grayson had believed her to be, she would have never even been seeing Hawk, much less coming to his rescue by firing at a member of his handpicked circle of associates.

Even exhausted and weak, Hawk knew how huge a sacrifice Carly had just made to save him. "I'm sorry, Carly."

She forced a smile to her lips, trying to appear as if she'd made her peace. "Not your fault."

But it was, and he knew it. If he hadn't turned up, she wouldn't have had to choose between coming to his rescue or saving her sister. He had to make it up to her. He began to say as much, but discovered to his confusion, that the words just weren't coming out. Not only that, but his thoughts now moved aimlessly about in his head in slow motion, like disoriented puffs of cotton at the mercy of the hot summer breeze.

Hawk couldn't think clearly.

He would have to wait to tell her.

Later, he'd tell her later.

It was the last thought that drifted through his head before his eyes slid closed.

With a sudden, jolting start that played along the length of his entire body, Hawk woke up. Initial disorientation dissolved in increments. There was a blanket partially covering him, the bottom half pooling onto the floor. Daylight forcefully pushed its way into the farmhouse through the bay window. Hawk drew in a deep breath, trying to clear his head.

How long had he been asleep?

Sitting up, he saw that he wasn't alone in the room, the way he'd first thought. Carly was propped up in the dilapidated armchair, her rifle laying across her thighs, giving every appearance of being ready to be pressed into service at a moment's notice.

She was awake and, unlike him, gave no sign that this was a recent event. When he blinked and looked closer, he realized that she looked tired. Like someone who had been up all night.

Again, that was his fault.

"How long have you been sitting there?" he asked.

The tension that had built up in her neck was practically killing her. She tried to rotate her shoulders to alleviate it a little. It didn't help. "All night," she told him.

Guilt burrowed through him and grew. He was the professional here. He was the one who was supposed to be protecting her, not the other way around. "Did you get any sleep?"

"Sleep's highly overrated," she answered flippantly, then added more honestly, "I thought it would be safer if one of us stayed awake, just in case." She saw the concern that passed over his chiseled features, and it touched her that he cared. "I can catch up on my sleep some other time," she assured him. "Right now, I wanted to be sure Charlie didn't decide to pay us another little visit, maybe this time bringing along some of his little friends to finish what he started."

Thinking about it—since she'd had nothing to do all night but watch Hawk sleep, listen for strange sounds and think—it had occurred to her that Grayson's baby-faced disciple surrounded himself with men who seemed downright dangerous.

She put nothing past that crew, including torture,

rape and murder. "The last thing I wanted was for us to be caught by surprise by those happy henchmen."

Carly got up from the armchair, leaning her rifle against it. She watched Hawk with concern. He'd moaned several times during the night, no doubt due to pain, but mercifully, he'd gone on sleeping.

"How's the arm?" she asked.

Right now, it felt pretty stiff and ached like hell. "This wouldn't be the time to take up juggling," he cracked. "But all things considered, it's pretty good," he pronounced, looking at it as if it had just caught his attention. And then he glanced back at her, a grin slowly curving his lips. "You're welcome to stitch me up anytime."

That was one task she didn't ever want to repeat. She'd prefer her stitching to be relegated to mending clothes.

"Don't take this the wrong way, but I'll pass," she told him. "I'm going to make some coffee. You interested?"

"Always," he said, his voice low. And then he added, "And I'd like some coffee, too."

That stopped her cold in her tracks for a good minute. Turning slowly, she looked at Hawk. Their eyes met and held for what seemed like forever. Hawk smiled at her as he began to get up again.

Snapping out of her momentary mental revelry, a revelry that took her to places she told herself he *couldn't* have meant for her to go—there had to be some other kind of meaning behind his words than the one that had instantly popped up in her mind—she said in a loud, authoritative voice, "Sit."

Hawk remained standing, though for the moment, he leaned his hand on the back of the sofa for subtle support. "That might work on your dog, Carly," he began on a warning note. He had always *hated* being ordered around, and she knew it.

"Don't have a dog," she pointed out glibly.

"I don't wonder," he said, taking small steps, each one a little more steady than the last. He was getting his sea legs back, he thought sarcastically. "Any dog of yours would have to run away from home to regain his self-respect." Switching gears, he told her, "I'll 'sit' in the kitchen. Will that make you happy?"

What would have made her happy was if she could have gone back and relived her life, this time making sure not to make the same mistakes that would have brought her to this point.

But there was no point in wishing for what hadn't a chance in hell of coming true. She had to deal with what was in front of her. She always had, and she didn't intend to change now.

So she pretended not to care one way or another and shrugged at what he'd just said. "What you do is entirely up to you."

"Good to know we're on the same page," he replied, a trace of humor in his voice as well as his eyes.

What he needed to do right now was to build up his strength and endurance. He approached the kitchen table, reminding himself of all he had to do. He had another twenty-four hours to get ready—and that included getting his body back to working at, if not maximum efficiency, then at least, an acceptable level.

Carly had risked everything she held dear to save him. He intended to pay her back for that. It was the least he could do.

Chapter 15

They were cutting it so close to the actual time of the ceremony, Carly felt she could barely breathe.

But they had to cut it this close, Hawk had explained to her, and she both understood and fully agreed. Understood that their biggest asset here was the element of surprise, and the timetable for that had to be precise. Since the front door was no longer a viable option, she and Hawk would be gaining access to the community center from within, via an old, long-unused underground route.

She'd all but forgotten that it even existed.

There was an old network of underground passages threading their way beneath the various buildings erected in Cold Plains. Since none of the passages were remotely straightforward and had been dug almost two hundred years ago, not many were aware of their existence, and the few who were had no occasion to mention them.

But Carly did.

She suddenly remembered the stories her mother had told her years ago, passed on from her grandfather, about how the tunnels were initially dug to protect the early Wyoming settlers from the wrath of outraged Native Americans looking to rid their land of the scourge that had oppressed them: the pioneers who were settling all over their precious land.

"And I know that there's one right under the community center," Carly had told Hawk yesterday as they were trying to come up with a way to rescue Mia from what Carly considered a fate worse than death. "It comes up right into the old storage room at the back of the building."

"Great." That gave them a way into the community center, but that still left the little matter of getting into the tunnel to begin with. "Do you know where that particular tunnel starts?"

Carly did her best to remember. Vague fragments, mosaic pieces from her childhood, tumbled about in her mind, like a kaleidoscope, at first refusing to come together to form any whole.

She concentrated harder, refusing to give up and eventually, it came to her. "One of the ways into the tunnels was this old, abandoned mine shaft right outside of town."

That sounded vaguely familiar to him, like something he'd seen when he was a kid here. "They struck a vein of silver back at the turn of the last century," he recalled abruptly. It surprised him how easily memories from his childhood came back to him, despite all his efforts to block that part of his life—both man and boy here in Cold Plains—from his mind.

But then, he reminded himself, he'd never forgotten a single thing about Carly, and she was a huge part of that time.

She nodded. Tales of the silver mine were as close to a legend as they had in this little town—before Grayson and his crew came.

"I think I remember my mother saying that the mine stayed open almost twenty years before it was boarded up. People kept hoping to find another mother lode, but all they ever got were just a couple of small veins that wound up petering out."

"We played there as kids." At the time, he'd never thought to go much farther than the mouth. It was during a period of his childhood when ghosts had held a real threat for him.

Hawk paused now, thinking about what might be ahead. Taking Carly along was just putting her life in jeopardy. "Listen, Carly, this could get really dangerous."

They were already in his car, ready to leave. "What's your point? I already know that."

He shifted in his seat to look at her. "Maybe what you don't know is that I don't want to risk you getting hurt."

Then don't leave when this is all over, she thought. Annoyed with herself and her moment of weakness at a time like this, she pushed the thought aside. "It's my sister we're rescuing. If anything you should be the one staying behind." She gazed at the makeshift sling she'd insisted he use. "You've only got one good arm."

"One's all it takes," he assured her. One hand to aim and shoot.

Hawk took out his cell phone and glanced at the screen. For once, the indicator said he was receiving a decent signal. He'd already gotten in touch with Jeffers, Patterson and Rosenbloom yesterday, instructing the agents to get a SWAT detail out as quickly as possible from Cheyenne because they were going in to take down a potential killer. He even had the excuse covered for going in: it had conveniently been provided for him by Charlie Rhodes. Since Carly had identified Grayson's second in command as the man who had tried to kill him, they were coming to arrest him, wedding ceremony or no wedding ceremony. Attempting to kill a federal agent was not a crime to be lightly shrugged off with a slap on the wrists. If convicted—and why wouldn't he be?—Charlie could be facing a great many years in prison.

With backup alerted, all that was left was to execute the main plan—which hinged heavily on gaining access to the center from within.

"You sure I can't talk you into holding down the fort here?" he asked one final time. He really did have enough on his mind without adding someone else to worry about to it.

There was no reason to "hold down" anything and they both knew it. Anyone who was anyone would be attending this wedding—at Grayson's behest. And no one crossed Samuel Grayson.

In response to his query, Carly gave him a long, penetrating look, which felt as if it went clear down to his bones. "What do you think?"

"I think I'd feel better if I had eyes in the back of my head, because I really don't like taking you into the thick of things like this," he said, setting his mouth hard as he stared out through the windshield for a moment. He didn't like the idea of actually bringing her to a potential crime scene. A crime scene, ironically, that had yet to become one.

"You're not 'taking' me anywhere," she informed him as they finally started heading to the cave. "If anything, I'm taking you," she pointed out. "I'm the one who remembered the tunnels and knows how to get to them."

There really was no point in arguing. He would lose, and it was just a waste of time. "I keep forgetting how damn stubborn you are," he said under his breath. The statement was accompanied by not-quite-silent grumbling.

"I like the word *resourceful* better," she informed him.

Potato, po-tot-toe, he was still not happy about having her come along with him.

They arrived at the mine shaft in a short amount of time.

Carly was right, he thought. She knew every shortcut in this underdeveloped region. Armed with flashlights, they went in. Hawk insisted on going in first.

This way, if there was trouble, he'd be the first to know. That left her room to escape—as if she would even try. Carly had already proved that she was the type to stand shoulder to shoulder with someone she cared about, not flee at the first sign of trouble.

It was, Carly thought at one point, like moving through the bowels of hell. The area was stuffy, dark except for the twin, thin beams of light cast by their separate flashlights. She just *knew* they were sharing the crammed space with umpteen rodents, which could come swarming around them at any moment.

She'd had great affection for all animals, big and small. But when it came to rats, she and the animal kingdom parted company. Rats made her flesh creep.

A little like the way Grayson did, she now thought. How could that man hold so many people under his thumb? It had to be some kind of aberration of nature.

They continued walking.

An uneasiness began to grow as she started thinking that perhaps she hadn't been right, that the mine shaft just led farther and farther into the mine and not into the center of town. Just when she was about to voice her concern to Hawk, suggest that they turn back, she heard a strange, thundering noise echoing overhead.

She looked at Hawk, a question in her eyes.

"Sounds like footsteps to me," he acknowledged. "Lots of footsteps." He let out the breath he'd been holding. "I think we've arrived, Columbus. Have to admit I had my doubts there for a while."

The man was nothing if not honest. And she hadn't

been when she sent him away, she thought as the guilt flared inside her.

"You weren't the only one," she murmured more to herself than to him.

Light was seeping in up ahead, coming in where the storage room door didn't quite meet its frame. She was about to open it when he put his hand up, silently cautioning her to stay where she was. He might not be able to talk her out of coming, but at the very least, if for some reason they wound up walking into a trap, then he wanted to be the first one to go down, not her. It would buy her enough time to get away.

Not that he was about to say any of this to her, because it would only result in yet another argument. The woman just didn't know the meaning of the words *staying safe*. But he intended to teach her—if it was the last thing he ever did.

Reaching the door, he turned the doorknob ever so slowly and eased the door open. They were in a storage room all right. It appeared to be a catchall for discarded items that had lived out their usefulness from the various rooms and offices. Apparently someone didn't seem to have the heart to throw them out just yet.

That was how pack rats got started, he thought. As for him, he was a minimalist. The less he owned, the less those things owned him. Turning, he beckoned for Carly to follow him—not that he actually had to. She'd seemed practically one step ahead of him all morning.

The hallway looked clear, so they advanced, making their way to the room where the ceremony was about to take place.

As they turned a corner, they surprised one of Grayson's henchmen—obviously playing the part of a groomsman/guard. Momentarily getting the drop on the man, Hawk acted swiftly, grabbing him by the head and twisting it—hard. Fresh pain shot through his bandaged shoulder.

There was a sickening snap.

Carly didn't ask if the man was dead. She knew. When Hawk released him, the guard fell bonelessly to the floor.

Carly waited a second, thinking that a surge of remorse would overcome her at any moment but it didn't materialize. These were the people who had come in and stripped her friends and neighbors—her *sister*—of not just their worldly possessions and their integrity but their very souls. She felt nothing about eliminating them before they had a chance to do the same to people she cared about. Death here was the great equalizer, not unlike the weapon she still carried with her.

"You okay?" Hawk asked, his eyes sweeping over her face.

"Don't worry about me," she told him, waving him on. "We've got a wedding to stop."

It seemed almost like poetic justice that the words, "If anyone knows why these two should not wed, speak now—" were the ones being said just as Hawk pushed open the doors, causing everything to come to a stunned, crashing halt.

"Everybody freeze," Hawk ordered. "I'm a federal agent!"

"I do," Carly cried, addressing Grayson who, under

the guise of "minister," was performing the ceremony. "I object."

She noted the angry look on her sister's face a second before she heard Grayson whisper something to the best man. Color drained from Mia's face. She'd heard what was being said.

The next moment, as if in slow motion, Carly saw Charlie Rhodes pull a gun from beneath his tuxedo jacket—he'd apparently tucked it into the back of his waistband, she realized—and fire in her direction.

She heard Mia scream her name just as she slammed against the floor. Not because she'd been hit but because Hawk had thrown himself over her, protecting her with his own body as he pushed her out of the line of fire.

"Told you to say behind!" he bit off as he rolled forward to return fire. Charlie hadn't been the only one who had brought a gun to the ceremony.

It still might have gone very badly for them, Hawk reflected later, had he not thought to "invite" his own "guests" to the wedding.

Just as the gunfire began being exchanged, the doors on the other side of the room burst open and Rosenbloom, Patterson and Jeffers, along with several other FBI agents, all wearing Kevlar vests, took over the room.

"Nobody move!" Hawk ordered again, getting up from the floor. This time, caught between two lines of fire, everyone obeyed. Hawk paused, his eyes and weapon trained on Grayson as he extended his hand to Carly.

Wrapping her fingers around his hand, Carly rose to her feet.

"You all right?" he asked.

She was bruised where she'd hit the floor, but she wasn't complaining. All things considered, she'd gotten off lucky. "Never better."

"Carly! Carly, did he—did Charlie—did Charlie shoot you?" Mia cried almost hysterically. Her arms filled with taffeta and organza, her sister came rushing over to her as fast as she could. Her face was still as pale as her wedding dress. "He tried to kill you," she said, stunned and clearly very shaken by what she'd just been forced to witness.

"Not exactly a quality one wants in their best man," Carly quipped. She wrapped one arm around Mia and hugged her. That was when she realized that Mia was trembling. "Are *you* all right?" she asked, even as more agents kept coming in, surrounding the wedding guests and ordering everyone over to a corner of the banquet room.

"I don't know," Mia answered honestly. She seemed dazed and confused as she looked up to meet her sister's eyes. "I thought everything here was finally so perfect. That my life was going to be so perfect." A bottomless sadness became evident in her voice. "He was going to kill you," she repeated numbly.

It was unclear if she meant Charlie or Grayson, but now wasn't the time to ask. It was enough that Mia finally understood that there was a viciousness here that threatened her very existence.

"I know," Carly replied quietly, keeping her voice at a calm, soothing level.

Mia appeared to sink further into her confusion and feelings of remorse and depression. "You came to save me, didn't you?"

"I told Mom I'd take care of you," she reminded her younger sister. "This was part of that promise."

She looked at Mia, trying to get a handle on what was going on in the younger girl's mind. Mia looked as if she was very close to a breakdown. And why not? Paradise had just blown up in her face.

Her sister would need help processing all this and coping with it, Carly thought. Grayson had done a number on Mia's head. It would take someone professional, versed in deprogramming, to bring her sister around with a minimum of consequences, she decided with regret.

But at least they'd gotten her out of Grayson's clutches. And Mia hadn't married Carrington. All in all, this was a very good day, Carly silently congratulated herself.

"Why don't we get you out of that dress and into something a little more comfortable?" she suggested to her sister.

Mia stared down as if she wasn't sure what she was wearing. "There's blood on it," she murmured, noticing the thin line of red across the bodice. "Is it Charlie's?" she asked.

Acting quickly, Hawk had brought the baby-faced man down with a single shot. Carly pressed her lips together and nodded. "Yes."

"Good," Mia said with feeling, then quickly raised her eyes to Carly's before lowering them again.

Maybe more than a little help, Carly thought. Her sister appeared as if she was retreating into a shell.

Looking around, Carly saw the agent Hawk had introduced to her as Tom Jeffers nearby, and she called him over now. When he crossed to her, asking if he could do something for her, she turned Mia over to him.

"Could you please take my sister back to her room?" she requested. "She needs to get out of those clothes."

About to protest that this wasn't part of what he was doing right now, Jeffers took one look at the distraught young face and changed his mind.

"Sure." Jeffers put his elbow out in an exaggerated fashion, indicating that Mia should take it for support. She looked as if she needed it. "Why don't you show me where it is?" he coaxed.

Mia nodded. "It's upstairs," she told him. The agent very gently led her away.

With Mia taken care of for the moment, Carly searched for Hawk. She finally saw him talking with several other agents. He was clearly the one in charge, and she felt a sense of pride watching him. Her initial instinct to make the supreme sacrifice and send him away had been the right move to make after all. Hawk was very much in his element here. This was where he belonged, leading people who ultimately made a difference and took pride in doing it.

Hawk was born to be what he was, a special agent with the FBI.

Drawing closer, she immediately recognized one of the men.

Ford McCall wasn't one of Hawk's people, he was from around here. A local deputy. One who, she now realized after she'd heard him making several arrests, was not corrupt the way that the police chief, Fargo, clearly was. The latter belonged to Grayson. Ford was obviously his own man. Thank God.

Nodding at Ford now, she turned toward Hawk. "How's your arm?" she wanted to know.

"Aches, but I'm still standing." And after what had just taken place in the past half hour, that was definitely an accomplishment.

As she looked around, it occurred to Carly that Grayson was nowhere in sight. Had he left? Or better yet, had he gone down in the cross fire? "Are you arresting Grayson?" she asked.

A frustrated expression came into his eyes as he did his best not to change his expression. "Right now, we don't have anything that'll stick."

She looked at him, stunned. "But he's behind all this," she cried. "Behind the murders. Maybe he's even had Susannah killed," she said, thinking about the conversation she'd had with Samuel the other day.

"Believe me, I'm not part of the man's fan club, either. I'd take him down in a heartbeat, if I could," Hawk told her. "He probably had his own brother killed. It wouldn't be the first time one twin murdered the other," he added grimly.

There'd still been no word from Micah. As soon as he got finished here, he would personally hire a private investigator to try to locate the missing would-be informant. He still firmly believed that Micah wouldn't have called him, then just vanished without a word.

Hawk surprised her by changing his tone of voice and looking directly at her as he said, "Looks like I've got a lot to keep me here in Cold Plains."

Was he saying more than she thought he was saying? "For how long?" she asked.

He spread his hands wide. "Right now, it's openended. I'm still trying to find out who killed those women and why. Jane Doe's identity is still a mystery, Grayson's brother is still missing—"

"Don't forget Susannah Paul and her baby. They couldn't have just disappeared like that," she reminded him.

"Right, there's that, too," he agreed. Drawing her over to an empty corner, Hawk lowered his voice as he continued talking. "Samuel Grayson is the key to all of this, and I'm not going anywhere until I find out just how he's connected. And when I find out, I intend to take him down."

She liked the sound of that. But she liked something else more. "So I guess I'll be seeing you for a while."

"I guess so."

Looking away for a second, Hawk blew out a breath. He was playing it safe again. Damn it, he was tired of playing it safe. He hadn't played it safe earlier when he'd put himself between Carly and the bullet meant for her. Somewhere, on some invisible tally, he was certain that he was running out of second chances, so he had better take advantage of this one before his luck ran out completely.

"Especially if you marry me," Hawk said to her out of the blue.

It was a minor accomplishment that she'd kept her jaw from dropping like a brick. It took her a good, long second to collect herself. When she did, she stared at him.

"Did you just say—"

"Yes," he answered, cutting her off.

No, not this time. This time, the *I*s were going to be dotted and the *T*s were going to be crossed. Just this once, their abilities to end each other's sentences wouldn't cut it.

She needed this spelled out.

"Let me finish," she insisted. "Did you—" She stopped abruptly as she pressed her lips together. Her mouth had suddenly gone dry mid-word. Regrouping, she tried again. "I think my hearing's going, because I thought I just heard you ask me to marry you."

He grinned at her, amusement dancing in his eyes. "Well, if your hearing's going, maybe I'd better reconsider my question. But for the record, yes, I did ask you to marry me."

"Why?"

"Why did I ask?"

"Yes." She nodded for emphasis. "Why did you ask?"

He thought a moment. "Because dragging you by the hair to my cave isn't the way it's done anymore." Before she could comment on his Neanderthal reference, he took her hand in his and became very serious. "I got a second chance when I wound up coming back here. And another second chance when you saved my life the other night. The way I see it, whoever's in charge of handing out second chances is going to think they're being wasted on me, and I'll be left out in the cold. I don't want to be in the cold anymore," he told her sincerely. "I want to be with you. If that means spending the rest of my life as a farmer in this two-bit town, I'll adjust."

"No way," she told him adamantly. "I like the idea of my husband being an FBI special agent." She smiled and succeeded in lighting up his entire life. "It has a nice ring to it."

"Your husband," he repeated, savoring the way that sounded.

She watched his face, trying to get a handle on what he was thinking as she answered, "That's what I said."

He raised his eyebrows hopefully. "Then your answer is yes?"

For once in her life, she wasn't going to be straightforward. For once, just once, she was going to be cagey. "Depends on the question."

Now he *really* didn't understand. "But I just asked you—"

"No, you didn't," she pointed out. "You mentioned it. In passing. You *didn't* ask." She turned her face up to his. "A woman likes to be asked. Formally."

He could understand that. "All right." He took her hand. "Carly Finn, I'm tired of feeling as if something's missing. I'm tired of missing you," he said with feeling. "Will you marry me and make me whole again?"

She slid her arms up around his neck, and he held her

to him with his one good arm. Her eyes danced. This was fun, and she savored her moment. "What do you think?"

"I've learned not to second-guess anything," he answered honestly.

"Okay," she said. Tilting her head up, she told him, "Then read my lips." Before he could pretend to look at them closer, she rose up on her toes and pressed her mouth against his.

Hawk had his answer.

He made the most of it.

Epilogue

"You're so much more of a beautiful bride than I was—or almost was," Mia amended as she fussed over Carly's train. She wanted to make sure that when her sister walked out onto the newly constructed patio that Hawk's FBI friends had just finished working on three days ago, the appliqué on the material wouldn't bunch up or accidentally snag.

"What are you talking about?" Carly cried loyally. "You were a gorgeous bride—despite the horrible circumstances."

Determined to make her point, Mia angled the tri-winged mirror on the wall over the bureau so that her older sister could get an actual good look at herself. Satisfied that the lighting was just right, she gestured toward the mirror while standing behind her sister.

"Look," she ordered. "You're positively glowing. I

didn't have that really happy glow. I just had a hazy look on my face," she recalled. There was no remorse, no regret. It was an episode in her past, and it was over. She was moving forward. That was the lesson she'd taken away from her weeks in the deprogramming center. "I can't believe what I almost did," she admitted, shaking her head. The only remorse she felt was for what Carly had had to put up with.

"I'm sorry for what I put you through," she said honestly. Then her apology broadened. "And I'm really sorry I didn't have enough time to get you a wedding present."

Carly turned away from the mirror and looked at her sister, her eyes brimming with love—and a few tears. "Having you back, just being you, is the best present I could possibly ask for," she assured Mia.

Mia had just arrived very early this morning, having completed her stint at the deprogramming facility that Hawk had found for her. It had been an intense, accelerated program, done at Hawk's behest because he knew how important it was for Carly to have Mia there for the wedding—and he wanted to get married as quickly as possible.

He'd gone to the facility and brought Mia back the minute the program was over. She was his wedding-day surprise for Carly. He'd kept it a secret, pretending that Mia wasn't going to be able to make it because of a last-minute delay, then sprung his surprise that morning.

Carly doubted that she had ever loved Hawk more than she did right this minute. He really was one of a kind. And he was hers.

Mia inspected Carly one last time. The ceremony was almost ready to begin. She caught her lower lip between her teeth and broached a delicate subject. It was now or never.

"I know this probably sounds awful, but would you mind very much if I stayed here for a couple of days?" Before Carly could answer, she quickly added, "It's just until I can figure out where I'm going to go."

"Go?" Carly echoed, confused. "You're not going anywhere. This is your home, Mia. You're going to live right here with us."

Mia laughed and rolled her eyes. "Right. I'm sure that'll make Hawk very happy," she cracked.

"As a matter of fact," Carly informed her, pressing her hand over the butterflies that had suddenly materialized in her stomach, "we've already talked it over, and he's fine with this."

"And what did he say *after* you untied him?" Mia deadpanned.

"I still said 'fine,'" Hawk confirmed, his voice floating in from the hallway.

Mia's eyes widened as she whirled around. She quickly crossed to the door. "Stop!" she cried. "You can't see the bride in her wedding dress before the wedding! It's bad luck!"

But when Hawk walked in the doorway, he had his hand covering his eyes. "I can't see anything," he promised. "See? I've got my hand over my eyes."

"What are you doing here?" Mia asked, peering at him to make sure he hadn't splayed his fingers apart enough to catch a glimpse of Carly.

"Heard you two talking and I came to back up my lovely bride-to-be. You're staying here, Mia," he said with finality. "It'll make us both happy. Besides, I've never had a little sister before. Might be fun," he added with a grin.

Strains of the *Wedding March,* courtesy of Patterson and a portable keyboard he'd brought along—who knew the man could play?—came drifting into the bedroom. "I believe they're playing your song, Carly," Hawk said, still covering his eyes. He turned on his heel, one hand braced on the doorjamb. "I'd better get to that make-shift altar Jeffers and Rosenbloom made for us."

Carly smiled when she thought of the men arguing as they'd worked feverishly to complete the altar where they were going to exchange their vows. "You know some very talented agents."

Hawk laughed. "Yeah, go figure. And they're special agents," he reminded her.

"Yes," Carly wholeheartedly agreed, "they certainly are."

"Go, shoo, get ready," Mia instructed, putting her hands on Hawk's back and gently pushing her almost brother-in-law out of the room.

"Yes, ma'am," Hawk answered obediently. In a moment, he was gone.

Mia gave it to the count of five, then looked at her sister. "Ready?"

Carly took a deep, fortifying breath. "I've been ready for ten years," she confessed.

Mia smiled at her. "Well, then," she said, ushering her sister out of the room, then picking up the edge of her train and following behind her, "it's high time we got you married."

Carly couldn't have agreed more.

* * * * *

Get back in the house!

And the tiny voice inside her, echoing nearly as loud as Grandfather's roar: *Run, run, run!*

Heart thudding, vision blurring, she spun around and dashed away. Dimly she heard a dog bark, a man shout, but she didn't slow. Her arms swung, her legs pumping, her strides closing the distance, but, God, not fast enough.

He caught her, arms wrapping around her, holding her close. His breathing was loud in her ears, his voice unfamiliar as he murmured, "It's okay, Reece, it's okay. Just an old memory. It can't hurt you. They can't hurt you. It's just you and me and Mick. You're safe."

She inhaled sharply, intending to scream, but the scents caught in her nose: soap, shampoo, cologne, dog. She knew those scents. She trusted them.

Jones. Mick.

Pivoting, she wrapped her arms around his neck and held on as if only he could chase away the fear, the ghosts, the memories. Only he could make her feel safe.

She held on for dear life.

Dear Reader,

I've always liked things that go bump in the night—in theory, at least. I don't like to be scared in real life, though having someone like Jones to hold onto could make the shivers more fun.

Jones is the kind of guy who could make everything better. He's the sort who falls fast and hard; once he gives his trust, it's *given;* and he's kind to crotchety old women and needy puppies. He couldn't possibly be any more perfect for Reece!

Marilyn

COPPER LAKE
SECRETS

BY
MARILYN PAPPANO

First published in Great Britain 2012
by Mills & Boon, an imprint of Harlequin (UK) Limited,
Eton House, 18-24 Paradise Road, Richmond, Surrey TW9 1SR

© Marilyn Pappano 2011

2in1 ISBN: 978 0 263 89517 9

46-0412

Printed and bound in Spain
by Blackprint CPI, Barcelona

Marilyn Pappano has spent most of her life growing into the person she was meant to be, but isn't there yet. She's been blessed by family—her husband, their son, his lovely wife and a grandson who is almost certainly the most beautiful and talented baby in the world—and friends, along with a writing career that's made her one of the luckiest people around. Her passions, besides those already listed, include the pack of wild dogs who make their home in her house, fighting the good fight against the weeds that make up her yard, killing the creepy-crawlies that slither out of those weeds and, of course, anything having to do with books.

To my husband, Robert, who is also kind to crotchety
old women and needy puppies. (Even if they do have
you wrapped around their pinkies.)

Chapter 1

One, two, three, four...

Counting in her head, Reece Howard moved thirty-eight steps along the ancient brick wall, then counted out another six before reaching the gate recessed into the wall. She counted a lot, but only steps. She'd done it for as long as she could remember—which was only fifteen years with any clarity, a little more than half her life—but who knew why? Maybe she was obsessive-compulsive with that lone manifestation. Maybe she was just freaking nuts. Maybe, her boss suggested—teasingly?—she simply liked numbers.

If that was the case, then she must *really* like the number thirty-eight. That was as high as she went. No more, no less.

It was a warm October afternoon, and Evie Murphy was keeping her regular appointments in the courtyard of her French Quarter home. Evie was many things to

Reece: friend, confidante, counselor, advisor. Officially her title was psychic, and she was very good at what she did, but even her talents had limits.

Evie was waiting at a wrought-iron table and chairs near the fountain. Playing in the grass a few feet away were Jackson, her four-year-old son, and Isabella, her two-year-old daughter. Eight-month-old Evangeline was asleep on a quilt in the nearby shade.

"Aunt Reece!" Jackson flashed her a wicked smile, the very image of his father, and Isabella wandered over, looking around with anticipation. "Puppies?"

"I had to leave the puppies at home today, sweetie. Next time I'll bring them, okay?" Reece slid into the chair across from Evie, who was looking calm and serene and beautiful. Not in the least like the dark, mysterious "Evangelina" who told fortunes for tourists in the shop that fronted the house.

"How are you?"

A lot of people asked the question, Reece reflected, but few put the sincerity and interest in it that Evie did. She was the only one Reece answered honestly. "Terrible. I had the dream again last night. I woke up soaked in sweat with all three dogs staring at me as if I were possessed. And I didn't remember a thing except that it had to do with my time at that place."

She'd used the same words in a recent conversation with her mother, who'd scoffed. *Your time in that place? You spent four months with your grandparents in a beautiful Southern mansion, and you make it sound as if you were incarcerated. Really, Clarice.*

"Your dreams got worse when your grandfather died. Maybe he's sending you a message."

"Like what? I'm next?" Reece retorted. The response startled her, both in its content and vehemence.

Evie's gaze steadied on her face. "Why would you think that?"

Good question. Why *would* she think that Arthur Howard wanted her dead? Besides those months she'd spent in his house, she hardly knew the man. When she tried to picture him, she couldn't bring his face to mind but only images: large, hulking, menacing. And numbers: *one, two, three, four...*

And fear.

"Damned if I know," she replied to Evie's question. "I look at pictures of him, and it's as if I've never seen him before. He's just this blank in my memory." A large, menacing blank.

"You have a lot of blanks in your memory." Evie touched her, her hand warm and grounding. "How many people know what happened that summer, Reece? Three? Maybe four? Your grandfather's death made it one less. If you ever want answers…"

Go to Fair Winds. Ask your questions.

They'd had the conversation before, but the idea of returning to Copper Lake, Georgia, to the Howard ancestral home on the Gullah River, tied her stomach into knots. Maybe she didn't really want to know. Her mother was convinced that the best thing she could do was forget the past and move on in the present.

Of course, her mother—Valerie—wasn't the one missing three months of her life, or facing the nightmares, or so full of resentment and distrust that every potential relationship became a burden too cumbersome to manage. Reece was twenty-eight years old, and her only real friends were Evie and Martine Broussard, her boss, and they made it easy for her. They didn't ask for too much; they understood her as much as anyone could.

Much as she loved them, she wanted more. She didn't have grand dreams, but she wanted to fall in love, get married and have children. She would like to make a difference in someone's life, the way her father had made a difference in hers. She would like to be a part of something special, something she'd had in the years before Dad's death had taken it from her: a family.

She wanted, she would like…she *needed*. Answers.

"Ah, Evie, I swore I'd never go back there again."

"You were thirteen."

"I didn't even go back for Grandfather's funeral."

Evie echoed the words Reece had only thought earlier. "You hardly knew the man."

Reece offered her last feeble excuse. "I have to work."

"As if Martine wouldn't let you off at a moment's notice."

Tension knotted in her gut. All these years, her refusal to return to Fair Winds had been a source of anger, frustration and more than a few arguments, but it had been a constant. Valerie had wanted to spend Christmases there; Reece had refused to go. Grandmother had invited them to Mark's wedding; Reece said no. Grandfather had unbent enough to ask her personally to attend Grandmother's seventy-fifth birthday celebration. Reece had stood her ground.

Valerie thought she was childish and melodramatic—ironic insults coming from the woman who embodied both. Grandmother thought she was stubborn and selfish. And Grandfather had told her that her father would be ashamed of her.

Not as much as he would be of you, she'd retorted before slamming down the phone. She believed that wholeheartedly. She just didn't know why.

She was tired of not knowing.

Across the table, Evie was waiting patiently. If something bad would come of a trip to Georgia, surely she would sense it. She warned people of danger; she helped them make the right decisions. If she thought Reece should go…

Reece huffed out a sigh. "Okay." Then… "I don't suppose you'd want to go with me."

"And leave Jack alone with the kids? His idea of day care would be sticking them in a holding cell while he interviewed suspects." She squeezed Reece's fingers. "You can call me anytime day or night, and if you need me, I'll come."

A knot formed in Reece's throat, and she had to work to sound casual. "At least you didn't say, 'And take my kids to a haunted house.'"

Her brows drew together. Yes, she had a psychic advisor; yes, she worked in a shop that sold charms, potions and candles to true believers. But ghosts, haunting her father's childhood home? The mere thought should make her laugh, but it didn't. It felt…like truth.

"A place that old, that was worked by slaves, is likely to have a few spirits, but generally they won't harm you."

Maybe. Maybe not. It was impossible for Reece to know what she feared about Fair Winds and her grandparents without knowing what had gone on during those months she lived there.

Grimly accepting, she got to her feet. "All right. I'll go. But if something happens to me while I'm there, Evie, I swear, I'll haunt you for eternity."

Evie stood, too, and hugged her. "I'd enjoy it, sweetie. Now, I'm serious—if you need anything, you call me."

"I will." Though, as she hugged Jackson and Isabella goodbye, she acknowledged she lied. Fair Winds was an evil, forbidding place, and she wouldn't expose these kids' mom to that for anything, not even to save herself.

It was a quick walk from Evie's to the building that housed Martine's shop on the first floor and both her and Martine's apartments on the second. When she walked in, the faint scent of incense drifted on the air, sending a slow creep of calm down her spine. The tourists browsing the T-shirts and souvenirs glanced her way, and she automatically flashed them her best customer-service smile as she passed through to the back room.

"I suppose you're going to ask me to take care of those mutts of yours while you're gone." Martine's back was to Reece as she collected specimens from the bottles and tins that lined the shelves behind the counter. Some customers thought she had a sixth sense, maybe seventh and eighth ones, too, but Reece knew there were mirrors discreetly placed along the tops of the shelves.

"My puppers are not mutts."

Martine sniffed. "What's their breed? Oh, yeah, Canardly. You can 'ardly tell what they are."

"And they love their Auntie Martine so much."

Another sniff before she turned, laying ingredients on the counter. "When are you leaving?"

"What are you, psychic?"

"iPhone and I know all." Martine's wicked grin was accompanied by a nod toward the cell on the counter. "I'll have everything you need in an hour."

Everything included charms, amulets, potions and notions. Reece couldn't say from personal experience that they would ward off evil or work to keep her safe, but they sure as hell couldn't hurt. "Then I'll leave in an hour and five minutes."

"You don't waste any time, do you?" Martine asked drily.

The answer was a surprise to Reece, as well, but she knew if she put off her departure for even one day, the dread and anxiety that were tangled in her gut would just keep growing. The drive would give her plenty of time to think of all the reasons this was a bad idea; no use giving herself additional time to wuss out.

"I wish you could go in my place. Grandmother hasn't seen me in fifteen years. She might not notice the difference."

How did Martine make a snort sound so elegant? "Oh, sure, we look so much alike. Maybe the woman's gotten deaf, blind and stupid in addition to old."

Reece grimaced. Though they were about the same height and body type, she was light to Martine's dark: fair-skinned and blond-haired. Having lived all her life in Louisiana, Martine had a pure and honeyed accent, while Reece's frequent moves had left her with a fairly nondescript voice.

"Okay." A sickly sigh. "I'm going to pack and tell the puppers that Auntie Martine will be taking care of them. They'll be so excited."

As she slipped through the rear door and trudged up the stairs, she wished she could dredge up a little excitement.

But all she felt was dread.

Thin streaks of moonlight filtered through the clouds to silver the landscape below, glinting off the stick-straight spears of wrought iron that marched off into the distance on both sides of the broad gate. Spelled in elaborate curls and swoops was the plantation name: Fair Winds.

Though this night there was nothing resembling *fair* about the place. Trees grew thick beyond the fence. Fog hovered low to the ground. No birds sang. No wildlife slipped through the dark. Silence reigned inside the wrought iron.

Jones had been in town for two days and had found plenty of people willing to talk. They said the place was haunted. Strange things happened inside those gates. On a quiet night, wailing and moaning could be heard a mile away.

This was a quiet night, but the only sound drifting on the air came from the dog beside him. Jones laid his hand on Mick's head, scratching behind his upright ears, but it didn't ease the quivering alertness that had settled on the animal the instant he'd jumped from the truck and scented the air.

Mick would rather be in town at the motel or, better yet, back home in Louisville. He liked traveling; he went with Jones on most of his jobs. But he didn't like spirits, and *here, there be ghosties.*

It was his father's voice Jones heard in his head, a voice he hadn't truly heard in fifteen years. His father was loving and generous and good-natured, but he wasn't forgiving. He nursed a grudge better than the meanest of spirits. His two middle sons were dead to him and always would be.

It appeared that Glen really was dead.

Absently Jones rubbed his chest as if that might make the pain go away. He'd been cold inside since he'd heard the news that everything Glen had owned in the world had been found buried under a pile of ancient brush outside Copper Lake. Clothes, books, driver's license, money, photographs, hidden no more than thirty yards from where Jones had last seen him. Maybe Glen would have gone off without his books or his license, even without the clothes or the money, but not without the photos of Siobhan. He'd been crazy mad in love with the girl, had intended to marry her. He never would have left her pictures behind.

And it was partly Jones's fault. All these years, he'd thought Glen was doing the same as him, making a life for himself that had nothing to do with family tradition. All these years, he'd been wrong.

Jones had rushed through his last job when he'd heard the news, then driven straight through from Massachusetts to Georgia. He'd had hours to come up with a plan, but after two days in town, he still didn't have one. All he'd been able to do was think. Remember. Regret.

Had his life been worth everything he'd given up? Doing what he wanted, being what he wanted? If he hadn't gone along with Glen, would his brother still be alive?

Their granny had been big on fate. Things happened as they were meant to, she'd insisted, and he'd been eager to share her belief. After all, that absolved him of responsibility. So he'd broken his mother's heart; it hadn't been selfishness but fate. He'd turned his back on the life his family had embraced for generations because fate had meant him to. He'd denied his heritage and lived for himself because that was the cosmos's plan for him.

But had fate decreed Glen should die before his eighteenth birthday?

Jones didn't think so. Someone else had made that determination, and he wanted to know who.

He figured he already had a pretty good idea of why.

Beside him, Mick gave a low whine. His ears were pricked, his tail stiff, his rough coat bristling. He was staring through the gate at the mists that formed, swirled, then dissipated, only to re-form a few steps away. Ghosts, essence, imprints—whatever you called them, Jones believed in them. His work took him to centuries-old houses all around the country, and every one housed at least one spirit. He didn't bother them, and they returned the favor.

Mick whined again as an insubstantial form separated from the shadows of the live oaks that lined the drive and stepped into the moonlight. Jones's jaw tightened with annoyance. Who would have expected the elderly and recently widowed owner of Fair Winds to be out haunting the place at nearly midnight?

She wrapped fragile fingers around one of the bars on the gate. "Who are you, and what are you doing on my property?"

Mentally kicking himself for coming to the place unprepared, he slid from the tailgate to the ground, felt his wallet shift and immediately knew his approach. As he walked to the gate, he pulled the battered leather from his hip pocket and silently handed her a business card.

It gleamed white as she tilted it to read his name, then tapped it on the bar. "I've heard of you."

He wasn't surprised. The business of historic garden restoration was an insular one. Word of mouth was still the best advertising; a satisfied client was happy to pass on his name to anyone who might be in need of his services. The subject was likely to have come up at least a time or two with the owner of Fair Winds, once home to the most spectacular gardens in the South.

"I've heard of you, too, Mrs. Howard." Then he gestured behind her. "Actually, more of the gardens." It was true. Because of the time he and Glen had spent at Fair Winds, he'd always paid attention when the name had come up. He'd researched the gardens while completing his degree, had seen plans, photographs and praise lavished by guests at the house during the gardens' prime in the 1800s.

"Humph. They haven't existed in the fifty years I've lived here."

"But they're legendary."

"That they are." She tapped the card again. "But that doesn't explain why you're sitting outside my gate close to midnight."

"No, it doesn't." He shrugged. "I'm between jobs, and I found myself in this area. I was curious."

"Curiosity killed the cat, don't you know?"

His smile was cool. "Do I look like a cat to you?"

She stared tight-lipped at him for a moment, then folded her fingers over the card. "Come back tomorrow. You can see more in the daylight." Turning, she took four steps and disappeared into the shadows. The only sound of her passing was the crunch of footsteps on gravel that quickly faded away.

Mick whined again, and after a moment staring into the darkness, Jones faced him. "You're just a big baby, aren't you? Come on. Let's go back to town. We've got work to do."

When he opened the pickup door, the dog jumped into the driver's seat and started to settle in, grumbling when Jones nudged him over the console to the passenger seat. Jones had picked up the shepherd mix

at a job in Tennessee. One day he'd appeared at a stop
sign, looking into every vehicle that came along before
sinking back to the ground. He'd stayed there for days,
growing thinner and more despondent, waiting for the
owner who'd dumped him to return. Knowing what it
was like to be alone and on your own and not sure you
were up to the challenge, Jones had begun taking food
and water to the stop sign.

On the eighth day, after he'd delivered the meal,
Mick had eaten, then walked back to the house with
him. They'd been together since.

He followed the hard-packed road to the highway,
then turned south. Copper Lake was just a few miles
away, but he and Glen had camped on Howard property
for a month without going into town once.

Not that it was a bad little town. Once past the
poorer neighborhoods on the north side, the town
was neat, easy to navigate and excelled at small-town
charm. It was home to more than a few magnificent
historic houses that made him itch for a sketchpad and
pencil.

If he couldn't talk his way into Fair Winds, maybe
he could drum up another job as an excuse for staying
in the area awhile.

Most of the motels in town were on the lower end,
with The Jasmine Bed-and-Breakfast at the high end.
He'd picked one in the middle—clean, comfortable,
high-speed wireless—and they didn't object to Mick.
He parked in front of his end room, let the dog do his
business in the narrow strip of grass nearby, then they
went inside and he booted up his laptop, calling up the
file he'd put together in college and carried with him
since.

Fair Winds Plantation.

The place where his life had changed. Where his brother's life had ended. Where he intended to find the truth.

A horn blared, long and angry, as a logging truck blasted past, the winds buffeting Reece's small SUV. Dawdling on a two-lane highway wasn't the safest driving she'd ever done, but she couldn't seem to help it. Every time she saw a mileage sign for Copper Lake, her foot just eased off the gas on its own.

Taking a deep breath, she loosened her fingers on the whcel and pushed the gas pedal harder. Once the speedometer reached the posted limit, she set the cruise control. There. The speed was out of her foot's—or subconscious's—control.

She'd spent last night in Atlanta, sleeping badly, tossing through one dark, malevolent dream after another. She was tired, her body hurt, and she had the king of bad headaches. If it were any farther to Copper Lake, she'd be physically ill before she got there.

And yet here she was doing her best to make the trip last.

As the road rounded a curve, a beautiful antebellum mansion appeared on the left, and Reece's fingers tightened again. That was Calloway Plantation. According to the map she'd studied, the turn to Fair Winds was less than a half mile south of Calloway.

Sure enough, there it was, identified with plaques set discreetly into the brick columns on either side. She braked, turned onto the broad dirt road, drove a hundred feet and stopped.

Could she do this?

Evie thought so. Martine did, too. The only one with doubts was Reece herself. Hand trembling, she reached inside her shirt to lift a thin silver chain that Martine had given her. Dangling from it was a copper penny. Appropriate, she thought unsteadily, since she was outside Copper Lake and the taste of both blood and fear, according to people who knew, was coppery.

Evie's calm, confident voice sounded in her head. *If you ever want answers...*

She did. Desperately.

If you need me, I'll come.

And Martine: *I'll have everything you need.*

"Except courage." Reece's voice was shaky. "But Grandfather's dead. I'm not thirteen. I can handle this."

She repeated the words in her head as she slowly got the car moving again. Tall pines grew dense on either side of the road, testament to the lucrative logging business that had taken the original Howard's fortune and increased it a hundredfold. As far as she knew, Grandfather had never worked in logging or any other business. He'd managed his investments from his study on the first floor and done whatever caught his fancy. She vaguely remembered fishing poles and rifles and shovels, and the glare every time he'd looked at her...

Before she realized it, she'd reached the gate. It stood open in welcome. She drove through, and the hairs on her nape stood on end. Was it quieter inside the gate than out? Did the sun shine a little less brightly, chase away fewer shadows? If she rolled the windows down, would the air be a little thicker?

"Oh, for God's sake. Valerie's right. I *am* being melodramatic. It's a house." As it came into sight, she amended that. "A big, creepy, spooky house, but still just a house. I haven't entered the first circle of hell."

At least, she prayed she hadn't.

Live oaks lined the drive, huge branches arching

overhead to shade it. The house and its buildings—a guest cottage, the old farm manager's office and a few storage sheds—sat at the rear edge of an expanse of manicured lawn. The brick of the pillars that marched across the front of the house had mellowed to a dusky rose, but there was no fading to the paint on the boards. The colors were crisp white and dark green, but still looked unwelcoming.

A fairly new pickup was parked near the cottage— silver, spotless, too high for a woman of Grandmother's stature to climb into without help. Its tag was from Kentucky, and she wondered as she pulled in beside it if some stranger-to-her relative was visiting. The recent generations of Howards hadn't been eager to stick around Copper Lake. Her father had left at twenty, his brother and most of their cousins soon after.

When she got out of the car, Reece was relieved to note that the sun was just as warm here as it'd been outside the gate and the air was no heavier than anywhere else in the humid South. It smelled fresh like pine and muddy like the Gullah River that ran a hundred feet on the other side of the gate.

She was closing the door when she felt eyes on her. Grandmother? Her housekeeper? The driver of the truck? Or the ghosts her father insisted inhabited Fair Winds?

Ghosts that might have been joined a few months ago by Grandfather's malevolent spirit.

Evie's voice again: *Spirits generally won't harm you.*

Oh, man, she hoped that was true. But if Arthur Howard's ghost lived in that house, she'd be sleeping with one eye open.

The gazes, it turned out, were more corporeal. Seated at a table on the patio fifty feet away, just to the left of the silent fountain, sat a frail, white-haired woman and a much younger, much darker, much... *more*...man, both of them watching her.

Reece stared. Grandmother had gotten *old,* was her first thought, which she immediately scoffed at. Willadene Howard had been frail-looking and white-haired for as long as she could remember, but the frailty part was deceiving. She'd always been strong, stern, unyielding, and in spite of her age—seventy-seven? no, seventy-eight—she certainly still was. She didn't even show any surprise at Reece's appearance out of the fifteen-year-old blue as she rose to her feet. When Reece got close enough that Grandmother didn't have to raise her voice—Howard women never raised their voices—she announced, "You're late."

Maybe she didn't recognize her, Reece thought. Maybe she was expecting someone else. She thought of the responses she could make: *Hello, Grandmother. It's me, Reece, the granddaughter you let Grandfather terrorize.* Or *Nice to see you, Grandmother. You're looking well.* Or *Sorry I missed your birthday party, Grandmother, but I thought of you that day.*

What came out was much simpler. "For what?"

"Your grandfather's funeral was four and a half months ago."

There was nothing Reece could say that wouldn't sound callous, so she said nothing. She walked closer to the table, knowing Grandmother wouldn't expect a hug, and sat on the marble rim of the fountain.

Grandmother turned her attention back to the man, who hadn't shown any reaction so far. "This is my granddaughter, Clarice Howard, who pretends that she sprang full-grown into this world without the bother of parents or family." With a dismissive sniff, she went on.

"Mr. Jones and I are discussing a restoration project we intend to undertake."

Reece's face warmed at the criticism, but she brushed it off as the man leaned forward, his hand extended. "Mr. Jones," she greeted him.

"Just Jones." His voice was deep, his accent Southern with a hint of something else. Black hair a bit too long for her taste framed olive skin and the darkest eyes she'd ever looked into. *Mysterious* was the first descriptor that leaped into her head, followed quickly by more: *handsome. Sexy.* Maybe *dangerous.*

She shook his hand, noting callused skin, long fingers, heat, a kind of lazy strength.

He released her hand and sat back again. She resisted the urge to tuck both hands under her arms and laid them flat on the marble instead. Rather than deal with Grandmother head-on, she directed a question to the general area between them. "The house appears to be in good shape. What are you restoring?" Left to her, she would be tearing the place down, not fixing it up.

"You can't judge a house by its facade. Everything gets creaky after fifteen years." Grandmother's tone remained snippy when she went on. "Mr. Jones is an expert in garden restoration. He's going to bring back Fair Winds' gardens to their former glory. Not that you ever bothered to learn family history, Clarice, but a few generations ago, the gardens here were considered the best in all of the South and the rest of the country, as well. They were designed by one of the greatest landscape architects of the time. They covered fourteen acres and took ten years to complete."

She waited, obviously, for a response from Reece. The only one she gave was inconsequential. "I go by Reece now."

Grandmother's lips pursed and her blue gaze sharpened. Across the table from her, Jones was making a point of gazing off into the distance, looking at neither of them.

"Gardens. Really." Too little too late, judging by Grandmother's expression. The only flowers Reece had ever seen at Fair Winds were the wild jasmine that grew in the woods. Her mother had told her their name and urged her to breathe deeply of their fragrance. Not long after, Valerie had left, the emptiness in Reece's memory had begun and the smell of jasmine always left her melancholy.

A shiver passed over her, like a cloud over the sun, but she ignored it, focusing on the stranger again. Did *just Jones* look like a landscape architect, or whatever his title would be? She'd never met a landscape architect, but she doubted it. He seemed more the outdoors type, the one who'd do the actual work to bring the architect's plans to life. His skin was bronzed, his T-shirt stretched across a broad chest, and his arms were hard-muscled. He was a man far better acquainted with hard work than desk-sitting.

"Sit," Grandmother commanded, pointing to an empty chair as she got to her feet without a hint of creakiness. "Entertain Mr. Jones while I get some papers from your grandfather's study. We'll let him get started, and then we'll talk."

Reece obediently moved to the chair, automatically stiffening her spine, the way Grandmother had nagged her that summer. *Howard women do not slump. Howard women hold their heads high. Howard women—*

The door closed with a click, followed by a chuckle nearby. Her gaze switched to the gardener/architect wearing a look of amusement. "That last bit sounded like a threat, didn't it?"

And then we'll talk. It *was* a threat. And even though she'd come there just for that purpose, at the moment, it was the last thing in the world she wanted to do.

Swallowing hard, she tried instead to focus on the rest of Grandmother's words. She might have trust issues and abandonment issues and a tad of melodrama, but she could be polite to a stranger. Her mother required it. Her job required it. Hell, *life* required it. But the question that came out wasn't exactly polite.

"So…is Jones your first name or last?"

Chapter 2

"Does it matter?" Jones asked, aware his lazy tone gave no hint of the tension thrumming through him. She didn't appear to recognize either him or his name, didn't appear to realize she'd asked him that question once before, the first time they'd met. Had he been so forgettable? Considering that he and Glen had saved her life, he'd think not…but she was, after all, a Howard.

Or was she just damn good at pretending? At lying?

He'd thought he'd lucked out when he returned to the farm this morning to a job offer that would give him virtually unlimited access to the Howard property, but having Clarice Howard show up, too… If there were a casino nearby, he'd head straight there to place all sorts of bets because today he was definitely *hot*.

He'd looked for her on the internet and had found several Clarice Howards, just not the right one. He'd asked the gossipy waitress at the restaurant next to the motel about her, but the woman hadn't recognized the name, didn't know anything about a Howard granddaughter. She'd had nothing but good, though, to say about the grandson, Mark, who lived in Copper Lake.

Mark, who, along with Reece, was the last person Jones had seen with his brother. Mark, who had threatened both Glen and Jones.

"I take it you don't live around here," he remarked.

"No." That seemed all she wanted to say, but after a moment, she went on. "I live in New Orleans."

"The Big Easy."

"Once upon a time." Another moment, then a gesture toward his truck. "You're from Kentucky?"

"I live there." He was *from* a small place in South Carolina, just a few miles across the Georgia state line. He'd been back only once in fifteen years. His father had begun the conversation with "Are you back to stay?" and ended it a few seconds later with a terse "Then you should go." He'd followed up with closing the door in Jones's face.

Big Dan was not a forgiving man.

"What brings you to Georgia?" he asked.

Reece didn't shift uncomfortably in the wrought-iron chair, but he had the impression she wanted to. "A visit to my grandmother."

"She was surprised to see you. You don't come often?"

"It's been a while."

Then her gaze met his. Soft brown eyes. He liked all kinds of women, but brown-eyed blondes were a particular weakness. Not this one, though. Not one who, his gut told him, was somehow involved in Glen's disappearance.

"What made you think Grandmother was surprised?"

"I'm good at reading people." Truth was, he'd heard Miss Willa gasp the instant she'd gotten a good look at Reece. *Lord, she looks like her daddy,* the old woman had murmured. *I never thought...*

She'd ever see her again? The resemblance to her father couldn't have been that surprising. She looked the same as she had fifteen years ago, just older. She still wore her hair short and sleek; she still had that honey-gold skin; she still had an air about her of... fragility, he decided. She was five foot seven, give or take an inch, and slender but not unappealingly so. She didn't *look* like a waif in need of protection, but everything else about Reece Howard said she was.

But appearances, he well knew, were often deceiving.

Deliberately he changed the subject. "Do you know much about the old gardens?"

Despite the change, the stiffness in her shoulders didn't ease a bit. Would she be against the project? Was she envisioning her inheritance being frittered away on flowers and fountains? "No, Grandmother's right. I didn't learn the family history the way a proper Howard should."

History could be overrated. He knew his own family history for generations, but that still didn't make them want any contact with him. They didn't feel any less betrayed; he didn't feel any less rejected.

"I've seen photos from as early as the 1870s," he went on, his gaze settling on the fountain beside them. Built of marble and brick, with a statue in the middle, it was silent, dirty, the water stagnant in the bottom. "They were incredible. Fountains, pools, terraces.

Wildflowers, herb gardens, roses… They covered this entire area—" he waved one hand in a circle "—and extended into the woods for the shade gardens. Fair Winds once had more varieties of azaleas and crape myrtles than any other garden in the country."

"And you're going to replant all that." Her tone was neutral, no resistance but no enthusiasm, either.

"Probably not all, but as much as we can. We have the original plans, photographs, detailed records from the head gardeners. We can make it look very much like it used to."

"What happened to the gardens?"

He shrugged. "Apparently, your grandfather had everything removed. The pools were filled in, the statues taken away, the terraces leveled. Miss Willa didn't say why, and I didn't ask."

Reece muttered something, but all he caught was *mean* and *old*. She'd missed the funeral, Miss Willa had said. Grandfather or not, apparently Reece wasn't missing Arthur Howard.

Shadow fell over them, and the wind swirled with a chill absent a few seconds earlier. A few brown leaves rattled against the base of the fountain, then grew still as the air did.

As Reece did. She sat motionless, goose bumps raised all the way down her arms. He considered offering an explanation—a cloud over the sun, though there were no clouds in the sky; a gust of mechanically-cooled air from an open window or door, though he could see none of those, either—but judging by the look on her face, she didn't need an explanation. She knew better than him the truth behind the odd moment.

Here there really were ghosties.

Did she know what he'd come to find out? Was one of them Glen's?

Before he could say anything else, the door to the house opened and Miss Willa hustled out, her arms filled with ancient brown accordion folders and books. He rose to carry them for her, but she brushed him off and set them on the table. "These are all the records I could lay my hands on at the moment. Clarice may be able to find more in her grandfather's boxes while she's here."

A look of distaste flashed across Reece's face—at the use of her given name or the thought of digging through her grandfather's files?

"Here's the code to the gate—" Miss Willa slapped a piece of paper on top of the stack, then offered a key "—and the key to the cottage."

Surprise replaced distaste in Reece's expression, and witnessing that took Jones a moment longer to hear the words than he should have. Frowning, he looked at Miss Willa. "What cottage?"

"That one." She pointed across the road. "There's no place in town worth staying at for more than a night or two besides The Jasmine, and I certainly don't intend to subsidize The Jasmine when you can stay here and keep your attention on your work."

He generally liked staying at or near the job site. On long-term jobs, he often moved into a small trailer, which beat a motel any day. But he didn't particularly appreciate being told where he would stay, or the assumption that he needed to be told to stay focused on his job. He was a responsible man, and while Miss Willa might well be accustomed to giving orders, he wasn't accustomed to following them, except in the narrow scope of the job.

But he wasn't stupid enough to argue, not when her high-handedness fit right in with his needs.

"I appreciate the invitation." His sarcasm sailed right past Miss Willa's ears, but earned a faint smile from Reece. "I should warn you, my dog travels with me."

"Keep him quiet, keep him away from my house and clean up after him, and we'll be fine." Miss Willa shifted her gaze then to Reece. "Lois is fixing dinner. We'll talk when that's over." With a nod for emphasis, she returned to the house.

The action surprised Jones. Miss Willa hadn't seen her only granddaughter in years, and yet she casually dismissed her?

But wasn't that what his own father had done with him? Hell, Big Dan hadn't just dismissed him; he'd sent him away. Though Jones had betrayed Big Dan. Did Miss Willa think the same of Reece? And was there more to it than Reece missing the old man's funeral?

Reece *wasn't* surprised. Idly she opened one of the books on the table, an oversize title with musty yellow pages and decades-old plates of the most impressive gardens of the post–Civil War South. Jones had a copy in his office back in Louisville. "Grandmother doesn't like to discuss unpleasant matters at the dinner table," she said by way of explanation.

"What could be unpleasant about her granddaughter coming for a visit?"

"A long-neglected visit. I haven't been here since…" Her attention shifted from the book to the house, her gaze taking in the three stories of whiteboard siding and dark green trim, the windows staring back like so many unblinking eyes. "Since I was thirteen," she finished, the words of little more substance than a sigh.

The summer he and Glen had been there. Why?

What had happened to keep her away all that time? A falling-out between her mother and grandparents? A petty argument that had grown to fill the years?

Or something more?

With a slight tremble in her fingers, she closed the book and smiled, but it lacked depth. "Fair Winds isn't my favorite place in the world. It's…"

He let a heartbeat pass for effect. Another. Then he softly supplied the word. "Haunted?"

She startled. Her gaze jerked to him and her arms folded across her middle as if to contain the shiver rippling through her. "You believe in ghosts, Mr. Jones?"

"I told you, it's just Jones. No *Mister*. Why wouldn't a house like this have ghosts? It's nearly two hundred years old. Dozens of people have lived and celebrated and suffered and died here. Some of those spirits are bound to remain."

"You've encountered such spirits before?"

"I have, and lived to tell the tale."

He grinned, but the gesture didn't relax her at all. Instead, a brooding darkness settled around her. "Wait until you've met Grandfather, if he's still here. He might change that."

Jones tucked the security code into his hip pocket, picked up the books and papers, then twirled the lone key on its ring around his finger. "He can't scare me too much," he said mildly as he started across the patio to the road. "After all, he *is* dead."

Dead, but not forgotten, and still possessing the ability to frighten.

At least, he could still frighten Reece.

She watched until Jones had disappeared inside the cottage, wishing she could have claimed it for herself

before Grandmother offered it to him. It was a minia-
ture replica of the house, with a huge difference: it was
memory-free and nightmare-free. Reserved for visitors,
it had been off-limits to her and Mark that summer. At
the moment it seemed the only safe place on all of Fair
Winds.

But Jones had it, so she was going to be stuck in the
house where Grandfather had lived.

And expected to go through his boxes, too. A shudder tightened her muscles as she recalled the one time
she'd gone into his study. Only in the house a few days,
she'd still been learning her way around, and Mark had
told her that heavy dark door that was always closed
led into a sunroom filled with beautiful flowers.

There'd been nothing sunny or beautiful about the
room. Dark drapes pulled shut, dark paneling, the thick,
heavy smell of cigars and age, and Grandfather, glow-
ering at her as if she'd committed an unpardonable
sin. He'd yelled at her to get out, and she'd scurried
away, slamming the door, to find Mark laughing at the
bottom of the stairs. Grandmother had chastened her,
and Valerie had, too, and she'd felt so lost and lonely
and wanted her dad more than ever.

Oh, God, she wasn't sure she could do this, not even
to find out what had happened those three months. Over
the course of her lifetime, they added up to what? One
percent of her time on this earth? Nothing. Inconsequential.

Except the months did have consequences: the nightmares, the fear, the distrust.

She breathed deeply. Across the drive, Jones came
out of the cottage, climbed into his truck and drove
away. She felt his leaving all the way to her bones.
Aside from Lois, who must be Grandmother's current

housekeeper, there was no one left on the property but her and Grandmother.

Not a thought to inspire confidence in a drama princess.

Another deep breath got her across the patio and into the door. Dimness replaced bright sun; coolness replaced heat. Instead of pine, the lemon tang of wood polish drifted on the air, along with the aroma of baking pastry. A voice humming an old gospel tune came from the kitchen, ahead and to the right. Lois, Reece was sure. She'd never heard Grandmother hum or sing, had rarely seen her smile and couldn't recall ever hearing her laugh.

No wonder Daddy had left the first chance he got.

She ventured farther along the hallway that bisected the house north to south. A glance through the first set of double doors showed the table in the formal dining room, set for two. Opposite was Grandmother's study, a small room with airy lace curtains, a white marble fireplace and delicate-appearing furniture that looked hardly a year of its century-plus age.

The rooms were small, the ceilings high, the furnishings mostly unchanged. A broad hallway, easily as wide as the rooms themselves, cut through in the middle from east to west. The stairs rose from this hall, and portraits of early Howards—and, in one case, an early Howard's prized horse—lined the walls. None of Grandfather, Reece noted with relief. His memory was enough to haunt her. She didn't need portraits, too.

The salon was empty, the door to Grandfather's office closed. Presumably Grandmother was upstairs. Readying a room for her? Gathering items Jones might need in the cottage? Or getting ready for the noon meal? After all, Howard women dressed for meals.

Reece paused outside the study door. The house was oppressive. So many rules, so little laughter. Her father had loved to laugh. Elliott Howard hadn't taken anything too seriously. He must have felt so stifled within these walls.

She was about to go upstairs, left hand on the banister, right foot on the first tread, when a creak came from the study behind her. Another followed it, then more: the slow, steady sounds eerily similar to a person pacing. Her fingers tightened around the railing until her knuckles turned white, but she couldn't bring herself to let go, to turn around and walk across the faded Persian rug to the door.

It was probably Grandmother, looking for more papers for Jones, having thought better of the idea of trusting the search to *her*. If she'd wanted company, she would have left the door open; she would have—

"Well, don't just stand there. Either come up or get out of the way."

So much for the theory of Grandmother. The old woman was standing on the stair landing, hair brushed, makeup freshened, a string of pearls added to the diamonds she always wore.

Reece glanced over her shoulder at the study door. The room was silent now. Just her imagination running wild. It always had, according to Grandmother. *That girl lives in a fantasy world,* she'd often complained to Valerie. *Thinks she sees ghosts everywhere.*

Heard them. Reece had never seen a ghost. She'd simply heard them, and felt them.

She loosened her grip on the banister and backed away as Grandmother descended the stairs.

"Dinner is served promptly at 12:30. Supper is at 6:30. If you miss the meal, you fend for yourself—and clean up after yourself." With an arch look, Grandmother passed her and headed for the dining room.

Reece followed her and took a seat at the polished mahogany table as a woman about her mother's age began serving the meal. There was iced tea in crystal goblets that predated the War, salad and rolls served on delicate plates her great-great-and-so-on grandfather had brought from France when he was still a sea captain in the early 1800s, roasted chicken and vegetables, and pie. Much more than the po'boy or muffuletta she usually had for lunch back home.

The conversation was sporadic, nothing more interesting than general comments about the weather or the food. It was ridiculous, really, to chitchat about nothing when they hadn't seen each other in so long, but Reece was no more eager to have a serious conversation than Grandmother was willing to break her dinnertime rules.

It would have been nice, though, to have been greeted with a little more pleasure—a hug, a kiss, an *I'm happy to see you*. Valerie didn't have much patience with her, but even she managed that much every time they met.

Finally, the meal was over and Grandmother, taking her tea along, led the way into her study. It was the brightest, airiest room in the house, but it was stifling in its own way. The furniture was uncomfortable, and Grandmother didn't relax her rules there. A settee that didn't invite sitting, spine properly straight, chin up, ankles crossed and Grandmother with her own rigid posture didn't invite confidences or intimacy.

Grandmother had apparently exhausted her store of chitchat and went straight to the point. "All these years, all those invitations you turned down or ignored, and suddenly you show up without so much as a call. What changed your mind?"

She could claim tender feelings, but Grandmother wouldn't believe her. Reece had always tried to love her; weren't grandmothers supposed to be important in a girl's life? But loving someone who constantly criticized and lectured and admonished... Fearing Grandfather had been easy. Feeling anything for Grandmother hadn't.

Reece gave a simple, truthful answer. "Curiosity."

"Curiosity killed the cat."

How many times had she heard that? And Mark, always out of the adults' earshot, creeping up beside her, his mouth near her ear. *Meow.*

"You look well," Reece said evenly.

"I am well. Your grandfather, however, is dead. Your mother came for his service. Your aunt Lorna came, and Mark and his family were there. Several hundred people were there, in fact, but not his one and only granddaughter."

The desire to squirm rippled through Reece, but she controlled it. Howard women met every situation with poise and confidence. "I couldn't come."

"You mean you wouldn't."

"It's not as if we were close."

"And whose fault is that?"

His. He never said a nice word to me. He yelled at me. He scared me. He threatened—

Reece stiffened. Threatened? She didn't recall Grandfather ever actually threatening her, not with tattling or spanking or anything. Was that part of what she couldn't remember? Part of *why* she couldn't remember?

"It was my fault," Reece said. She would take all the

blame Grandmother could dish out if it helped her get a few answers. "That summer I lived here, I was frightened of him. He wasn't exactly warm and cuddly."

To her surprise, Grandmother nodded. "No, he wasn't. But he was a good man."

Maybe in the overall scheme of things. Reece couldn't deny that Mark had adored him. Maybe Grandfather hadn't known how to relate to girls. Maybe he'd never forgiven his older son for leaving and transferred that resentment to her. Maybe asking him to deal with his son's death and a grieving thirteen-year-old girl at the same time was too much. She did look an awful lot like her father.

"That summer," she hesitantly began.

"What about it?"

What happened? Why do I still have nightmares? Why can't I remember? The questions seemed so reasonable to her, but she'd lived with them for fifteen years. Would they sound half so reasonable to Grandmother, who hadn't been much better at dealing with a grieving thirteen-year-old than her husband?

"I've been thinking a lot about that summer lately," Reece said, watching Grandmother closely for any reaction.

She showed none. "It was a difficult time for everyone. Losing your father that way… Your uncle Cecil passed four years ago. A mother's not supposed to outlive both her children."

The last words were heavy, as if she felt every one of her seventy-eight years, and sparked both sympathy and regret in Reece. She couldn't imagine losing a child…or having a loving grandmother. If things had been different, if Daddy hadn't moved to Colorado, if Reece had had a chance to know both her grandparents before Daddy's death, would that summer have had such an impact on her?

But Daddy had had issues of his own with Grandfather, so their visits had been few. They'd been practically strangers when she and Valerie had come to stay.

And there was no wishing for a new past. It was done, and all that was left was living with the consequences.

"I'm sorry about Cecil," Reece said, meaning it even though she hadn't met the man more than twice that she could recall.

Grandmother's unusual sentimentality evaporated. "He ate too much, drank too much and considered riding around a golf course in a cart exercise. It was no great shock that his heart gave out on him. His doctor had been warning him for years about his blood pressure and cholesterol, but he wouldn't listen. He thought he would live forever." Her sharp gaze fixed on Reece. "How long are you planning to stay?"

"I don't know. A few days." No longer than she had to. "If that's all right with you," she added belatedly.

"Of course it's all right. Fair Winds has always been known for its hospitality. I already told your cousin Mark that you're here, so he'll be by to say hello."

Reece swallowed hard. "He lives around here?" That was one thing she hadn't considered. Much as she wanted answers, she wasn't sure she wanted to face her childhood enemy to get them.

"In town. He moved here after college. He and Macy—she's from a good Charleston family—they have one daughter and another on the way. He runs the family business and checks in on me every day."

Reece smiled weakly. "Wonderful."

Grandfather's dead. I'm not thirteen. I can handle this.
If she repeated it often enough, maybe she would
start to believe it.

Jones stopped at the grocery store to get the five
major food groups—milk, cereal, bread, eggs and
chips—before going to the motel to pick up his clothes
and Mick. When he let himself into the room, the dog
was stretched out on the bed, the pillow under his head,
the blanket snuggled around him. He lifted his head,
stretched, then rolled onto his back for a scratch, and
Jones obliged him, grumbling all the time.

"You are the laziest animal I've ever seen. You eat
and sleep all day, then snore all night. You've got it
made."

Mick just looked at him, supreme satisfaction in his
big brown eyes.

"We'll be bunking in a new place for a while. There
will be room for you to run as long as you stay out
of Miss Willa's way. She doesn't strike me as a dog-
friendly person." Jones considered it a moment. "She's
not a particularly people-friendly person, either. But
we've dealt with worse."

And there was the consolation prize of her granddaughter, whose own eyes were as brown as Mick's
but way less happy and a damn sight less trusting. He
didn't think it was just him, either. She didn't seem the
type to warm up to anyone quickly, if at all.

That was okay. Pretty as she was, all Jones wanted
from her was information. She was still a Howard, still
a part of Glen's disappearance, and he was still the
kid who'd been taught wariness and distrust of country people—anyone outside of his people, regardless of
where they lived—from birth.

But she was awfully pretty, and she did have that vulnerable-damsel thing going on that neither he nor Glen had ever been able to resist.

But he would resist now.

After loading his bags and Mick into the truck, Jones slid behind the wheel and left the motel, turning west on Carolina Avenue. Catching a red light at the first intersection, he drummed his fingers on the steering wheel until, beside him, Mick whined. Jones glanced at the dog, an admonishment on his tongue, then forgot it as his gaze settled on a man in the parking lot twenty-five feet away.

He was about Jones's age, an inch or two taller, maybe thirty pounds heavier, and he wore a light gray suit so obviously well made that even Mick would recognize its quality. He was talking to a young woman, a briefcase in one hand, keys in the other, and he stood next to a Jaguar. He was fifteen years older, a whole lot softer and a hell of a lot better dressed, but Jones would have recognized him anywhere.

A horn sounded, and Jones's gaze flicked to the traffic light, now green, then back at Mark Howard. The sound drew his attention, and he looked at Jones, their gazes connecting for an instant before Howard dismissed him and turned back to his conversation.

Hands tight on the wheel, Jones eased the gas pedal down, resisting the urge to turn the corner, pull into the lot, grab Howard by the lapels of his custom-tailored suit and demand the truth about Glen. There would be a time and a place to talk to the man, but this was neither.

By the time he'd turned north on River Road, a bit of the tension had seeped out. He liked Copper Lake. It was the quintessential small Southern town, war me-

morials in the square and the parks, beautifully restored
antebellum homes. The people were friendly and happy
to answer questions. No one had treated him with suspicion…though so far he hadn't asked any questions
that sounded suspicious. He hadn't brought up the subject of Glen's disappearance or the discovery of his belongings or his gut instinct that the Howard family was
responsible. If he started asking that sort of question,
they were likely to close ranks and protect their own.

Mick sat straighter in the seat when Jones turned off
the highway onto Howard property. Shutting off the
AC, Jones rolled the windows down, and the mutt immediately stuck his head out to sniff the air. When they
drove through the gate, though, Mick drew it back in,
let out a long, low whine and moved to the floorboard
to curl up.

"Baby," Jones accused, but Mick just laid his head on
his paws. The dog knew the place was unsettled. Reece
knew it. How the hell could Miss Willa not know, or if
she did, how could she continue to live there?

The road continued past the cottage, leading to the
other buildings. Jones drove past the small house, then
pulled onto ground covered with a heavy layer of pine
needles. The spot would block the view of his truck
from any casual visitors to the house—maybe not a
bad thing once Miss Willa's grandson and others found
out she was planning to spend a ton of money on their
grand project.

"Come on, buddy, let's get settled." Jones climbed
out and stood back, but Mick didn't stir. "Mick. Out."

The dog gave a great sigh, but didn't move.

"C'mon, Mick, out of the truck now." He stared at
the dog, and the dog stared back.

He'd never had a battle of wills with an animal that

he hadn't won, and today wasn't going to be the first. He snapped his fingers, an unspoken command that Mick always responded to, but the mutt just whined once and hunkered in lower.

"I guess we know who's the boss in this family."

Jones started. He'd been so intent on the dog that he hadn't even heard the crunch of footsteps on the gravel, and apparently neither had Mick. He reacted now, though, stepping onto the seat, sniffing the air that brought a faint hint of perfume and smiling, damn it, as he jumped from the truck and landed at Reece's feet.

She offered her hand for Mick to sniff, then crouched in front of him, scratching between his ears. "You're a big boy, aren't you? And a pretty one. I don't blame you for wanting to stay in the truck. I don't much like this place, either. But we do what we gotta do, don't we, sweetie?"

Jones watched her slender fingers work around Mick's ears, rubbing just the way the dog liked. Hell, Jones liked a pretty woman rubbing *him* the same way, and Reece certainly was pretty crouched there, her khaki shorts hugging her butt, her white shirt shifting as her muscles did. For the first time since she'd climbed out of her car a few hours ago, she looked almost relaxed, and he doubted he'd ever seen her look that trusting.

Did she ever offer that much trust to a human being? To a man?

"He's usually not that stubborn," Jones remarked, leaning against the truck while Mick offered a toothy smile. It was almost as if the mutt was gloating: *I've got her attention and you don't.*

"Animals are sensitive."

"You have dogs?"

"Three. All throwaways. Like me." The last two words must have slipped out, because her gaze darted to him, guarded and a bit anxious, and a flush colored her cheeks. He knew from Glen that she'd had abandonment issues that summer. Her father hadn't chosen to die in that accident, but the end result was the same: he was gone. And her mother had preferred Europe with her friends over taking care of her daughter.

Jones could sort of relate, except from the other side of the matter: he was the one who'd done the abandoning. Had it cost Reece's mother as much as it had him? Did she share even a fraction of his regret?

"Mick was dumped near a job site. When he got tired of waiting for his owners to come back, he decided to live with me."

"Lucky you. After I fed the first stray outside the store where I work, he brought two more with him the next day. They've been living with me ever since."

"Too bad you couldn't bring them with you." Traveling with dogs could be a hassle, but their company was worth it.

"Dogs in Grandmother's house? And not even pure-breds?" She scoffed as she stood.

Reaching into the bed of the truck, he took out his suitcase and laptop, then started for the porch. To his surprise, the rustle of plastic told him she'd taken out the grocery sacks and was following.

Mick jumped onto the low porch while Jones and Reece went to the steps in the center. He propped open the screen door, unlocked the door, then stood back so she and the dog could enter first.

The door opened directly into the living room, with the kitchen a few feet to the right. To maximize space, there was no hallway, just a door off the living room that went into a bedroom. He guessed the bathroom could only be reached from that room.

"I always wanted to see this place." Reece set the grocery bags on the kitchen counter and automatically began unpacking them.

He laid his own bags against the wall. "You lived here and never came inside?"

The refrigerator, a recent model, closed with a thud after she put the milk and eggs inside. "Did I say I lived here?"

The undercurrent of wariness to her voice stirred its own undercurrents in Jones. He, who'd always been cautious of what he said to country people, never should have made such a stupid slip. "I just assumed you grew up around here."

She considered the words a moment as she crumpled the plastic grocery bags together, then shrugged. "I stayed here for a few months when I was thirteen. My cousin Mark was here, too, that summer. This cottage was off-limits to us. Grandmother said it was for guests, not hooligans who ran wild."

He forced a grin. "Hooligans? She actually called you hooligans?"

Her own smile was half-formed. "She did. Grandmother had—has—very exacting standards that we often failed to meet."

Jones didn't know about Mark, but apparently Reece was still something of a failure in Miss Willa's opinion. The old woman certainly didn't approve of Reece's long absence or missing her grandfather's funeral. That was the sort of thing that got a person disinherited by a prideful woman like Willadene Howard.

Was that why Reece had come now, because her grandfather was dead and her grandmother was nearing eighty? Did she want to get back in Miss Willa's good graces before she passed and left everything to cousin Mark?

Or maybe she'd heard about Glen's stuff being found. Maybe she wanted to make sure there was no suspicion, no effort to find out what happened to the boy who'd saved her life and, apparently, lost his own as a consequence.

Jones watched her wander through the living room, giving Mick on the sofa an affectionate pat as she passed, and hoped neither suspicion proved to be true. Maybe she had come to realize over the years that family was important. Maybe she regretted not making peace with old Arthur before his death and didn't want similar regrets when Miss Willa was gone.

God knew Jones had regrets about his family. He liked his life. He loved his job. But if he could do it all over again, he couldn't say he would make the same choices. There was a lot he hated about his family's way of life, but…he'd missed so much. He hadn't gotten to stand up at his brothers' and sisters' weddings. He had nieces and nephews he'd never met. Birthdays and holidays and anniversaries, celebrations and funerals, good times and bad…

Reece broke the silence. "The furniture looks like it's been here since the cottage was built."

"It probably has. There's a fortune in Chinese antiques in this room alone." He opened the drapes, letting in the afternoon light, before sitting on an unpadded imperial rector's chair. "The Howard who originally settled here was a sea captain. There's a maritime phrase, *Fair winds and following seas.* A wish for good weather. That's where the name comes from."

Head tilted to one side, she sat beside Mick, resting

her hand on his back. "I didn't know that. I told you, I didn't learn the family history."

"He acquired treasures from all over the world. I'm sure Miss Willa's given you the rundown of some things in the house."

"Some. I was always terrified, using lamps and dishes and furniture that were irreplaceable. Being afraid made me feel clumsy and insignificant."

There it was again—that hurt. Vulnerability. She'd grown up. She'd gone from cute and awkward to beautiful, from a child to a capable woman, but it didn't seem as if time had done a thing to change that part of her.

Seem. Which meant it wasn't automatically true. She could be a world-class manipulator. After all, she still hadn't acknowledged that they'd met before. She hadn't asked the obvious question: *How is your brother?* After all, she'd spent a lot more time with Glen that summer than with Jones.

Leaning back in the chair, he rested his ankle on the other knee. "Those months you stayed here…this must have been a great place to run wild. All the woods, the creek, the river…you and Mark must have had some fun times."

"Not particularly."

"You didn't get along?"

A jerky shrug. "He was a fourteen-year-old boy. I was his thirteen-year-old girl cousin. I think we were genetically predisposed to not get along."

"So what did a thirteen-year-old girl do for fun out here alone?"

Her expression shifted, darkness seeping into her eyes, caution into her voice. "I read a lot. Spent as much time away from the house as I could."

The reading part was true; she'd been lying in a

patch of sunlight near the creek reading the first time he and Glen had seen her, and she'd always brought books along every other time.

"Didn't you have someone to play with? A neighbor's kids?"

The caution intensified before she answered on a soft exhalation. "No."

Realizing he was holding his own breath, Jones forced it out and did his best to ignore the disappointment inside him. Okay. So she was a liar. It wasn't a surprise. It wasn't even a real disappointment. She was a Howard, and Howards were part of that segment of rich, powerful people who felt money raised them above everyone else. They weren't bound by the rules that applied to everyone else. They were, as Miss Willa made clear at every turn, *better*.

Truthfully, though…he *was* disappointed.

Chapter 3

"So…did you and Miss Willa have that talk?"

Reece studied the contented expression on Mick's furry face, feeling homesick not for her apartment, but for her dogs. It sounded trite, but they loved her in ways no human ever had, besides her dad, and he'd left her.

"We did. It was all warm and fuzzy." She grimaced to let him know she was grossly exaggerating, then quickly changed the subject. "Where do you start on this project?"

"Studying the history. Walking the property. Making sketches. Figuring a budget." He paused before asking, "Do you think it's a waste?"

"The place could only look better with gardens." The beauty of the gardens would offset the ugly creepiness of the house…maybe. Or the creepiness of the house might turn the gardens brown and lifeless, like itself.

"I mean the money."

Reece gave a little snort, a habit she'd picked up from her dad that neither Valerie nor Grandmother had been able to chastise out of her. "It's her money. Why should I care?"

"Because when she passes, presumably it becomes your money. At least, part of it."

The concept of family meant a lot to Grandmother, but she drew the line at rewarding the weak, the flawed or the obstinate. Reece had never given it any thought because she'd just assumed Mark and his mother—the good Howards—would inherit the bulk of the estate. She doubted there was any heirloom indestructible or worthless enough for Grandmother to entrust it to her.

"She took care of us after my father died, and she paid for my college." Two years at Ole Miss before Reece had gone to New Orleans for a weekend and never left. "She's done her duty to us."

"Do you think your cousin will feel the same?"

The muscles in her neck tightened. "I don't have any idea how Mark will feel. I don't know him."

"But you said he was here the summer you were."

"And I avoided him as much as possible."

"You haven't seen him since? Talked to him?"

She shook her head, though, of course, that would soon change. No doubt, he would be here before too long, for both his daily visit and to scope out the reason for *her* visit.

"Not real close to your family, are you?" Jones asked wryly.

"I see my mother two or three times a year. I talk to her once a month. That's close enough." Again, she turned the conversation to him. "I suppose you come from one big, happy family. Every Sunday when you're home in Louisville, you all get together after church for dinner, mint juleps and a game of touch football in the backyard, and you talk to your mama every day like a good Southern boy."

She expected acknowledgment, or a chuckle. Instead, shadows passed over his face, and his mouth thinned. "It would have been South Carolina, after Mass for barbecue and beer, then watching a game on TV. But no, we're not close. I haven't seen them in a long time."

Discomfort flushed her face. She wouldn't have said anything if she'd known that their two replies together would cast uneasiness and regret over the room as surely as a thunderhead blanketed the sun. At the moment, this room felt no more secure than the big house.

Except for Mick, snoring beside her. Abruptly he came awake, ears pricking, a ruff of skin rising at the base of his neck. He jumped to the floor and padded to the screen door, where a low growl rumbled in his throat.

At the sound of a vehicle approaching, Reece's gut tightened. Moving with much less grace, she joined the dog at the door, grateful for the deep overhang of the porch roof that granted some measure of camouflage.

The car coming slowly up the drive—no need to let speed throw up a chunk of gravel to ding the spotless metal—looked expensive, though if it weren't for the sleek cat captured in midpounce as a hood ornament, she couldn't have identified it. But Howards—all of them except her and her dad—liked luxury in their vehicles. Valerie switched between a Mercedes and a Cadillac every two years. She wouldn't even ride in Reece's hard-used SUV.

Without making a sound, Jones came to stand behind

her, not touching but close enough that the heat radiating from his body warmed her back and the scent of his cologne replaced the mustiness of the cottage in her nostrils.

Together they watched, Mick trembling with alertness beside them, as the Jag parked next to her truck. Reece's breath caught on the lump in her throat when the door opened and the driver appeared in the bright sunshine.

Curiosity killed the cat.

Meow.

She might not have seen him in fifteen years, but she had no doubt it was Mark. He'd gotten taller, carried too much weight in his midsection and his hair was thinning, but he still possessed the ability to make her hair stand on end, to raise goose bumps down her arms and to make her stomach hurt.

"Want to go say hello?" Jones murmured.

Both she and Mick looked back at him only briefly before focusing on Mark again. The dog growled, a quiet, bristly sound, and she felt like doing the same thing.

But she had no choice. She would have to face him sooner or later. Besides, he was a grown man now. He'd probably changed. And he well might have some of the answers she was looking for.

Drawing a deep breath, she laid one hand on the screen door.

"Want company?"

Going out there with Jones at her side—better yet, in front of her—sounded so lovely and *safe*. But he would probably have to face his own run-in with Mark once her cousin found out about the garden project.

"Thanks, but…I'd better…"

It took another deep breath to get her out the door and down the steps. She'd reached the drive before something made Mark turn in her direction. He stopped near the fountain, just looking at her as she approached, then slowly a smile spread across his face and he extended his hand, moving the last few feet to meet her. "Clarice! God, it's been a long time."

The instant his fingers closed around hers, he pulled her into a close embrace. Panic rose in her chest, but she controlled it, holding herself stiff. After just a moment, he released her, stepped back and gave her a thousand-watt smile. "You're no longer that skinny little kid I used to torment. Of course, I'm no longer that snotty little brat who liked to torment. Grandmother must be ecstatic about having you here."

Not so you'd notice.

Nor did he notice that she didn't answer. "Grandmother's kept me up on you. Living in New Orleans, still enjoying the single life. I'm married, you know. We were sorry you couldn't come to the wedding, but Valerie told us how busy you were. We have one kid, Clara, and another on the way." He pulled out his cell phone in a practiced manner and called up a photo of a brown-haired chubby-cheeked girl. She was about eighteen months, sweet and looked far too innocent to carry her father's blood.

"She's a doll." Reece's voice was husky, her tone stiff.

"Yeah, she's my sweetheart. Next one's going to be a boy, though. Just think of the fun I'm going to have with him." He returned the phone to his pocket, then settled his gaze on her again, his features settling into seriousness in an instant. "I made life pretty awful for you, didn't I? I'm sorry about that. I was a dumb kid, and I was so jealous of you being here. It was *my* summer visit, too, and I wanted Grandfather and Grandmother all to myself. I behaved with all the maturity of…well, a dumb kid. It's a wonder you didn't beat the crap out of me back then."

Something passed through his blue eyes with the words. Chagrin? Regret? Or something a little more… hostile?

Reece was sorry she couldn't be unbiased enough to tell.

Then he shrugged, a careless gesture she remembered well. As a kid, he had literally shrugged off everything—her pleas, Grandmother's requests, Valerie's infrequent attempts to admonish him. The only person he'd never tried it with was Grandfather. They'd been two of a kind, the old man had laughed.

"Let's go in and find Grandmother," Mark suggested, taking her arm. "I try to check on her every day. She's not as young as she thinks she is. Macy and I have asked her to consider moving into town—we have a guest cottage at our place that we built just for her— but you know how stubborn she is. She's convinced that she can do everything she did thirty years ago, but we worry about her out here alone."

Half wishing she could pull away and make a wild dash for her truck, Reece let herself be drawn across the patio to the door. Everything inside was just as it had been when she'd left a half hour ago: cool, dim, quiet, oppressive. Maybe a little more so than before…or was that her imagination?

Grandmother was at her desk in the salon, spine straight, fountain pen in hand. Reece hadn't seen a computer in the house, and no doubt Grandmother would disapprove of any correspondence that didn't include Mont Blanc and her favorite ecru shade of engraved Crane & Co. stationery. She'd been raised in a different era, and with the kind of money both her family and the Howards had, she could get away with remaining firmly rooted in the customs of that era.

When they entered the room, she finished her note, put the pen down and lifted her cheek for Mark's kiss. The affection between them—as far as any affection with Grandmother went—was easy, almost natural.

Mark claimed he'd been jealous of Reece. For a moment, she was jealous of him. She would have liked having a normal relationship with a normal grandmother who didn't constantly find her lacking.

"So you two have got your greetings over with," Grandmother stated as she moved from the desk to the settee with Mark's gentlemanly assistance. "And did you meet Mr. Jones while you were out there?"

"Mr. Jones?" Looking puzzled, Mark settled in beside her while Reece chose a spindly-legged chair opposite. "Is he traveling with you, Clarice?"

"I guess she didn't tell you she answers to Reece now." Grandmother's quiet little huff was all she needed to say on that subject. "No, Mr. Jones is a landscape architect whose specialty is restoring old gardens."

Mark stopped short of rolling his eyes. "That again, Grandmother? I've never seen anyone so fascinated by gardens she never laid eyes on. They're gone. Dug up. Grown over. You can't bring them back."

"*I* can't, obviously, but Mr. Jones can. He has quite an admirable reputation in this field."

Mark's eyes started another roll but stopped again. "Grandfather had those gardens removed for a reason, Grandmother. It was important to him. Have you forgotten that? Are you actually considering disregarding his very clear feelings on the matter?"

Grandmother gazed out the window for a moment as if lost in time, then replied with every bit of the stubbornness Mark had mentioned earlier. "Yes, I believe I am. Not just considering it, in fact, but doing it. Mr. Jones started work today."

Reece watched Mark closely: the faint fading of color from his cheeks, the thinning of his lips, the distress that settled over his face. "You've signed a contract with him? You've committed to this—this insanity? Grandmother—"

Her arch look silenced him. "Of course I haven't signed a contract with him." But just as relief sagged Mark's shoulders, Grandmother went on. "Robbie hasn't had time to draw it up yet. First Mr. Jones has to present me with plans and costs, and that will take some time. It's an enormous job, putting back everything Arthur undid. It will take a great deal of time and, yes—" her sharp, accusing gaze moved from Mark to Reece, then back again "—a great deal of money. But it's my money, at least until I die, and I'll spend it as I please."

Reece resisted the urge to raise both hands to ward off the warning. She didn't want the old woman's money. Sure, a windfall would be nice. Having the cash to get a place of her own where the dogs could run free—and where she could take in more homeless dogs—would be fantastic. But she earned enough to live on and to support a few luxuries—Bubba, Louie and Eddie—and she'd never expected anything more.

Mark, clearly, expected more.

"Grandmother, you can't be serious. Do you have

any idea how big those gardens were? How much they cost?"

"Yes, I do. As someone who's been *fascinated* by them since I came to live here, I know quite a lot about them, and so does Mr. Jones. Restoring Fair Winds will be a major coup for him. He'll have more business than he can handle after this."

Reece suspected he already had plenty of business. A man didn't get...how had Grandmother put it? *Quite an admirable reputation* without some major clients. No matter whose gardens he'd worked on, Grandmother would, of course, consider hers the most important.

"But, Grandmother—"

She interrupted him, something she considered rude and common—a sign of how determined she was to see this plan through. "Have you forgotten, Mark, that I'm in charge of my own affairs? When I want advice, I'll ask for it, and I'll ask an expert, not you. At this moment, I'm not asking. I'm simply informing you of my plans. Don't worry. There will be money left over for you and Macy and the children. You'll have your inheritance, but I will have my gardens."

Moving far more spryly than most women her age, Grandmother rose from the settee and left the room.

The silence was heavy, and just a bit darker as clouds blocked the sun and the windows fell into shadow. Uneasiness creeping up her spine, Reece wanted to make her exit, too—right out the door and onto the patio—but something kept her in her seat.

"Oh, my God." Mark dragged his fingers through his hair, the gesture drawing attention to how much it had thinned in fifteen years. Another five, and he'd likely be completely bald on top, as his father had been. As her father might have been if he'd lived long enough.

Forever couldn't have been long enough to suit her.

"Did you know about this?" Mark asked suddenly. "Is that why you just showed up after fifteen years without so much as a call?"

There, faint in his voice, in his eyes, was the hostility she remembered. Along with the shadows, it lowered the temperature in the room a few degrees.

"No. Jones was here when I arrived. They had pretty much completed their discussion by then."

"Sorry." Actually sounding it, he ran his hand through his hair again. "I can't believe… I thought I had talked her out of… We can't let her do this. I'll talk to Robbie Calloway—he's her lawyer—and see what we can do to stop her. Do you have any idea how *much* this will cost?"

"It won't be cheap." Martine shared the tiny courtyard of her building with Reece and the dogs, barely big enough for a fountain, two chairs and all the plants they could cram in, with a few patches of grass for the four-legged residents. Lush and lovely as it was, she doubted it would cost more than $100 to replant the entire thing.

"Wow, you have a way with understatement." Mark gave her a rueful smile. "We're talking tens of thousands, hell, probably hundreds of thousands of dollars. For some stupid flowers and bushes. What in hell is she thinking?"

Reece made her voice mild. "I imagine she's thinking that it's her money and she should spend it on what makes her happy."

The flash of friendliness disappeared under the weight of a scowl. "Maybe you're happy living in an apartment in the French Quarter, but that's a few hundred grand that I'd rather have in my kids' college fund than in the dirt out here."

Then his gaze turned distant. "Though she does comment on how beautiful the flowers are every time she comes to the house. Macy has a real green thumb. She planted the whole area around the guest house just for Grandmother."

How many young men would include separate living quarters at their houses for the day an elderly relative could no longer live on her own? How many young wives would embrace the idea? If someone told her *she* had to take in Grandmother or even Valerie to live, she'd pack up the dogs and disappear lightning-quick.

"You think she should go ahead with this foolishness."

Reece nodded. "I do."

"But she might not even live to—to see it done."

"She knows that." Though Willadene Howard had never answered to anyone on earth besides her husband; she might not answer to death, either, when it came calling.

"So I can't count on you to help change her mind."

"It's not my place. I haven't been here in fifteen years. I can't just show up and start telling her how to spend her money."

"I guess not." He stood, leaned across and tugged her hair. "I've got to get back to town. See you tomorrow."

"I'll be here." Unless Grandmother or the ghosts or the fear she'd lived with so long ran her off.

Out in the hall, he paused long enough to shout, "I'm going, Grandmother. I'll be back tomorrow."

A moment later, Reece saw him through the window, striding to the car as if he'd had nothing but the most pleasant of visits. She was turning back when a flash of movement at the door caught her attention. "Grandmother?"

The only answer was the soft whisper of footsteps on the wood.

"Lois?"

A breeze stirred the curtains, blowing one strip of filmy lace hard enough that it caught on her shoulder before drifting down again and, almost lost on that unseen wind, came a long feline whisper of sound. *Meow.*

Shivers racing through her, Reece stood and hurried to the door. *One, two, three, four, five...*

On summer jobs, where the temperature could be unbearable by noon, Jones usually tried to get a really early start on the job site by the time it was light enough to see. When excessive heat wasn't a problem, he took his time, actually sitting down to eat his breakfast, checking his email, catching up on the news.

That was what occupied him Tuesday morning when Mick trotted to the open door and snuffled. His tail was wagging in a broad enough swath to take down any antiques within range—the reason Jones had spent a good part of yesterday afternoon moving all breakables to a safer place.

After he'd stood at the door the entire time Mark Howard was inside the house. When Mark had come out, he'd looked satisfied, as if he didn't have a care in the world. Had the meeting with Reece gone that well, or was he just really good at hiding his emotions?

Even after Mark had left, Jones had stood there, watching, but Reece hadn't come out again. Neither had Miss Willa.

Now, though, it looked as if he'd have a chance to find out how the reunion had gone, because Mick wasn't wagging his tail so eagerly for the old woman who didn't care for dogs.

Shutting his laptop, he went to the door, unlatching the screen. Mick shot out, barking and bounding down the driveway toward the barn. Sure enough, Reece was a few hundred yards down the road, wearing the short pants his secretary called capris and a bright orange top, her stride long but easy, as if she didn't have a particular destination in mind.

Upon hearing Mick's approach—something similar to a freight train—she turned, then braced herself for any excited leaping. Jones grinned. No jumping was the first lesson he'd taught the dog. He'd guess her own dogs hadn't learned it as well.

Mick immediately sat down in front of her, and she bent to scratch him. Her mouth was moving, but Jones couldn't hear the words until he got closer.

"...such a good boy. You're so pretty, and look at that face. Who wouldn't love such a handsome face?" Her tone was softer than usual, gooier than usual. She was a sucker for four-legged guys, even if the two-legged ones made her a little wary.

"You're gonna spoil my dog rotten," he said from a few yards away.

Her gaze lifted, and wariness did enter it, just a bit. "He deserves to be spoiled. He's a good boy."

"You headed someplace in particular?"

She shook her head.

"Mind if I join you?" At her hesitation, he went on. "I told you yesterday, one of the things I need to do is walk the property. We need to know what conditions we'll be working with, if there are better ways in or out, where we can stage equipment when we're not using it, that sort of thing. Maybe you can show me around."

She was quiet for a time. She glanced at the old barn ahead, then past it where the road trailed off. Regretting that he'd ruined her plans for a quiet morning walk? Or was there something more to her walk this morning? Was she planning to revisit old haunts? Maybe to check that things out there hadn't been disturbed?

Things like Glen's grave?

She shrugged. "I'm not sure how much showing around I can do, but you're welcome to come along. I really don't remember much about the place."

"I thought you said you spent as much time away from the house as you could."

"I did, but it was a long time ago. I was a kid. I didn't pay much attention." She started walking again, and he fell into step with her. Mick raced on ahead, regularly looping back to encourage them onward.

Curious why she was lying about something as simple as knowing her way around the woods, Jones continued subtly probing. "I understand that a creek runs through here somewhere before it empties into the river, and that there's a pool deep enough to swim in."

"Really." She spared him a glance before shifting her gaze down again. The road had petered out and the ground was getting rougher. "I don't like to swim. I can't remember the last time I was in the water."

Jones's muscles tightened. Now *that* was a flat-out lie. He couldn't even count the number of times she and Glen had met at the pool to swim, and she'd done it like a fish. And how the hell could anyone forget the time they went swimming and their cousin tried to drown them?

"You're kidding." He hoped his voice sounded more

natural to her than it did to him. "Everyone likes to swim. What's better on a hot summer day than jumping into the water?"

Her smile was small and unsteady. "Anything, for me. I don't like the water. I'd rather swelter."

Her tone was just short of fervent, but her expression: eyes narrowed, teeth clenched, muscle twitching in her jaw... Was she doing a poor job of lying, or telling the truth with large parts left out?

He couldn't say. He wasn't an expert at detecting liars. If he was, he wouldn't have fallen for the stories of one customer and the beautiful blonde he'd dated a few years back. In their own way, both of them had cost him quite a chunk. Was Reece lying to him? If so, she sure lacked the finesse of the customer and Elena.

As they walked deeper into the pines, he asked, "How did it go with your cousin yesterday? Was he happy to see you?"

"He seemed to be. He apologized for being such a brat."

Was that what the oh-so-superior Howards called attempted murder: being a brat? He'd hate to see how they truly defined a crime.

"I'm kind of surprised he didn't go to meet you when he left the house. Grandmother told him about her plans."

"And he wasn't happy." Jones laughed. "You'd be surprised how often the extended family *isn't* happy. It's a lot of money, and a lot of families would rather see that money in their pockets rather than mine."

"He plans to change her mind. But good luck with that. I think Grandmother is constitutionally incapable of changing her opinion. She doesn't waffle, never sits on the fence and never backs down once she's reached a decision."

"Sounds like my dad. Big Dan has standards, and anyone who fails to meet them is out of his life."

Reece looked at him, her gaze both curious and sympathetic. He realized he'd said more than he meant to, but he didn't try to explain away the words. He was grateful, though, that she didn't ask questions. *What standards did you fail to meet? Is that why you're not close? Did you disappoint him?*

Standards regular people would applaud him for turning away from.

But his people weren't regular people. If they were, he'd probably still be there in South Carolina, living close to the family, a part of their everyday lives.

To fill the lull, he gestured around them. "Did you know your family used to be in the logging business? That's why these trees are planted in rows."

"I did know that." She sounded relieved for the mundane subject. "How do you know about Fair Winds?"

"I visited here once a long time ago, when I was a kid." He watched her peripherally, but no reaction crossed her face. "When I went to college, I came across some articles on it, remembered it and began collecting information."

"You must have been excited when Grandmother contacted you about redoing the gardens. What a coincidence, huh?"

"Not at all. I contacted her. I was in the area, my crew doesn't need me at our other job sites, and I wanted to see the place again. When I told her what I do, she offered me a job."

"It's that easy to get such a large contract?"

"Not usually. Must have been fate." Like Granny always said.

A shape took form in the woods ahead to the right, shadowy, its sharp, straight, man-made lines softened by the vines that grew over and around it. With a touch on Reece's arm, Jones steered her in that direction and onto the faint remnants of a rarely used trail.

Wrought iron encircled the Howard family cemetery, its paint faded and peeling where it poked free of the vines. Two brick pillars marked the gate, with another in each of the four corners. In the center stood a marble bench, and rows of markers marched away from it in all four directions. The rusted gate was propped open, and he walked through it, getting to the third row of headstones before realizing that Reece still stood at the gate, looking distinctly uncomfortable. Mick sat beside her, apparently understanding this was a place he shouldn't go.

"Ghosts rarely haunt cemeteries," he said quietly. "They attach to places or people that were important in their lives, not their deaths."

She moved forward enough to lean against the brick. "Do your clients know you believe in ghosts?"

"Unless the place has its own ghosts, it usually doesn't come up." He gazed over the oldest markers: 1821, 1845, eight from the Civil War. Most were elaborately carved: name, spouse, sometimes children, date of birth, date of death, a bit of poetry or Scripture. One had a carving of a galloping horse, another a sculpture of a fallen tree. The infants' graves bore hearts or angels.

"Is that Grandfather's grave?"

He didn't have to hear the quaver in Reece's voice to know she was uneasy, didn't have to see her gesture to locate the newest grave toward the back of the plot. The earth was no longer bare. Grass had grown over, and a tendril of vine from the nearest fence was beginning a slow curl around the base of the stone.

"It is. Arthur Belvedere Howard." He was reading the marker, massive, granite—a hard stone for a hard man—when Reece slowly came to stand beside him. She stared at the grave as if she feared the old man might reach up through the ground and yank her in.

"When my mother told me he had died, all I could feel was relief." She spoke so softly that Jones could barely hear her despite the quiet around them. "I hardly knew the man. I don't remember much about him. But I just thought, 'Oh, good. He's gone.' Valerie—my mother—pitched a fit when I told her I wasn't coming for the funeral. She kept saying, 'He was your *grand-father*,' as if that meant something, but when my only response to his passing is, 'Oh, good,' how much can it possibly mean?"

Jones studied her—the sheen of sweat on her forehead, the moisture glistening in her eyes, the faint quiver of her lower lip, the insubstantial voice, as if she was afraid to say out loud the things she'd just murmured—and his gut tightened. Was it possible… Had the old man…

They were ugly words: abused. Molested. Hurt. He didn't want to think them. But it would explain her feelings toward her grandfather. It would account for her avoidance of family and this place for fifteen years.

It could also explain her insistence that she didn't know her way around Fair Winds, her not recognizing him and her denial that she'd had contact with anyone else that summer. A kid whose father had just died, whose mother abandoned her, whose cousin tormented her and whose grandfather molested her... Any one of those could be reason enough to block that time from her mind.

He turned away from the headstone, revulsion making him queasy.

"What made you decide to come back now?" he asked as he started back toward the gate.

She caught up with him at the brick pillars, and they set off into the woods again, following the path of least resistance. "Truthfully?"

"Call me strange, but I always prefer the truth." In an effort to lighten the gloom from the cemetery—and chase those ugly thoughts from his mind—he wryly added, "Except about Mick. Don't tell me my dog is homely or has bad breath."

"He's a beautiful boy, and his breath smells just like doggy breath should." She swiped away the sweat on her forehead, then detoured around a fallen pine. "My psychic—who also happens to be one of my best friends—suggested it."

She walked on a few feet before looking at him. "No laughter? No horror? No 'Uh-oh, she's crazy'?"

"I told you, I believe in ghosts. Why should I think going to a psychic is crazy?" Besides, he had generations of female relatives who'd made decent money in fortune-telling. Most of them had been frauds, but there had been a few true seers in the bunch. His granny had been one of them.

"Evie's legit. I know they all claim they are, but she really is. And she's a good friend, too. She knows I have some...issues, and she thought coming here would be good for me."

Jones heard her words, but right after "issues," he stopped paying attention. They'd reached the easternmost side of the farm, marked by a wooden fence that had long ago been painted white, gleaming even out here in the woods out of everyone's sight. He recognized the small hollow between the trees, the not-too-distant trickle of water from the creek, the lone crooked pine that grew at a forty-five-degree angle over the fence.

This was where he and Glen had camped during their time at Fair Winds.

This was the last place he'd seen his brother.

Chapter 4

Reece felt as if she'd intruded someplace she wasn't wanted. It wasn't a new feeling, by any means, just unexpected. Jones had been so friendly from the start; she hadn't expected him to suddenly forget she was there.

She looked around, wondering if it was something about the place that had yanked his attention away, but there was nothing remarkable about it: a small clearing surrounded by trees. The creek ran nearby, and they were close enough to the highway to hear passing traffic. Other than that, it was woods, like the rest of the property.

She stayed where she was while he walked into the open area, then slowly turned. For a moment, he stared off to the northeast, and she had the strangest sensation that he'd left her. Sure, his body was there, but *he* wasn't. She was alone.

Just as slowly, he completed the circle, then looked

at the ground, the bent tree, cocked his head and listened to something—the creek? The breeze? A ghost?

After intense scrutiny, his exhalation was loud enough to startle her. He realized that she was watching him, but he didn't try to brush off the odd moment. "This place…" he murmured.

"Is haunted."

His smile was thin, almost…sad. "Yeah."

They didn't talk much after that. They tramped through the woods, Mick staying close most of the time, running off on occasion to trail some forest creature. Reece tried to open herself to the place, searching deep inside for a familiar memory. She didn't find it, not in the trees, the trails, the creek or the pool where it widened to an idyllic swimming hole.

Jones suggested they stop there, and they sat at opposite ends of a crude bench, one long slab of wood hammered atop two shorter ones. It looked old enough to have been built by the very first Howard, but she guessed it was probably Mark's work when he was younger. He'd liked swimming, fishing, hunting—those guy things he shared with Grandfather—while she'd had nothing in common with the man but blood.

The thought made said blood run a little cold.

"You mentioned your other job sites," she said at last. "How many jobs do you have going at once?"

"No more than one major one, usually, like this, but we've got a lot of smaller jobs. Enough to keep me busy and on the road most of the time."

"You like being on the road?"

He grinned. "It's in my blood. My father and grandfathers have spent a large part of their lives on the road."

"And your mother and grandmothers?"

"Wait at home."

"Nice, I guess. If you don't want to actually spend time with the man you're married to." It wouldn't work for her. She'd been looking a long time for Mr. Right. Once she found him, she'd like to share her bed with him more often than not.

"They spent enough time together. Both my grandmothers had seven kids, and Mom and Dad had six." Leaning forward, he scooped up a pinecone, broke off a chunk and tossed it into the water, where the current danced it out of the pool. "You ever come here before?"

"Not that I recall. I told you, I don't swim."

"Yeah, but what kid can resist throwing things in the water?" He tossed another small piece, then a second. As they bobbed along, an old memory came to mind: her and her dad at the duck pond in Denver. How many hours had they spent on a concrete bench not much better than this one, tossing in stale crackers and chunks of bread for the ducks and talking about the wonders of life? Of course, to a nine-year-old, everything was pretty wondrous.

The wish that it still was ached deep in her chest.

"This one," she answered in response to his question.

With a grin, he shook his head. "You must have read an entire library's worth of books that summer."

Maybe. In dire need of escape to a world where things still made sense, she'd read a lot those first weeks, when she wasn't crying and trying to convince herself it was all a horrible nightmare and she would wake up soon. After that…

Well, that was why she was here. To find out.

For the hundredth time, she wondered if knowing was really important. It didn't take a psychiatrist to know that there was a *reason* she'd blocked that summer out. Something bad had happened that her thirteen-year-old mind had deemed unbearable. Was she any better equipped to deal with emotional trauma at twenty-eight?

Evie thought so. Martine did, too. Sometimes so did Reece. But sometimes…

She was about to suggest they get moving again when a wind blew over them. Elsewhere around them, the air remained still; the leaves didn't rustle; the branches didn't sway. The current was icy and bore hints of smells: sweat, brackish water, fresh dirt, rain, tobacco. Goose bumps raised on her arms, and she hugged herself tightly to contain a violent shudder.

When she managed a look at Jones, he was watching her. The skin on his arms was pebbled, too, but he wasn't shivering. He sat as still as stone.

As quickly as it had stirred, the wind stopped. For an endless moment, the woods were silent as a morgue, until one brave bird chirped. Another swooped from one tree to the next, and the usual chatter slowly resumed.

Jones stood, his movements smooth and easy, and extended his hand. She wasn't sure she could have stood without his help. Her legs were unsteady, her hands trembly and her insides awhirl.

They'd gone a hundred feet, her hand still clasped inside his big, warm one, before he spoke. "Now that's something you don't experience every day."

She laughed, just a little, enough to ease some of the tension making her vibrate. "I think it's safe to say that most people don't experience ghosts every day." As relief and calm seeped into her, self-consciousness flooded her, and she eased her hand from his and put a few more feet between them. "My father used to tell me stories about this place. Grandmother said they were all nonsense, and Grandfather...well, he thought pretty much everything about Daddy was nonsense. They didn't get along. The first time I can remember coming here for a visit, I must have been five or six. As soon as we walked into the house, I started asking, 'Where are the ghosts, Daddy?'" She shook her head. "My grandparents were not amused."

"Did you see anything?"

"I never actually see them. I hear things. Feel things. Footsteps, that wind, creaking, emotions." She looked up. "Do you see anything?"

"Sometimes just wisps or vague shapes. But usually not."

The conversation might have struck anyone else as ridiculous, but not Reece. Besides her own sensitivity to other presences, Evie talked to spirits and they talked back, and Martine had her own experiences with things otherworldly. It was a common thing in their small circle.

"But Miss Willa doesn't believe."

"Oh, no. So if you have any trouble with the ghosts when you start digging up the yard, don't expect her to understand."

"I'll keep that in mind."

The trees thinned ahead, allowing the sunlight through, and the house became visible. Jones's gaze fixed on it. "It's a beauty, isn't it?"

Reece tried to appreciate the house from a purely architectural view. The symmetry of windows and doors was nice. The porch that stretched across the front was shady and cool in the morning, sunny and warm in the afternoon. It was a wonderful place for watching storms sweep across the river. The bright white and the crisp green paint contrasted starkly with each other, and the faded brick softened the whole effect.

It was exactly how a plantation-era house should look.

But where Jones saw beauty, she saw despair. In every one of those windows reaching three stories high, she saw unhappiness. Gloom. Unsettledness. Cold. It was the most unwelcoming place she'd ever been and, having grown up with Valerie, that said a lot.

"I'm afraid I'm too biased to answer that fairly."

A slight figure rose from one of the rockers on the porch and faced their direction. Grandmother. It was too early for lunch, so probably a good time to talk to her. Reece had tried a couple of times the afternoon and night before, but it was just so hard to start the conversation.

Her experience with Valerie didn't make it any easier. Every time the word *summer* came from Reece's mouth, even if it was something as innocuous as a mention of summer vacation, her mother tensed, lines appeared at the corners of her mouth and a look passed through her eyes. *Here we go again.*

But Reece hadn't tried three dozen times to get any information from Grandmother.

"Mick and I are going back to the cottage to get to work," Jones said, his path angling toward the back of the house.

"Coward," she murmured.

"I heard that."

Her own steps slowed until she was barely moving. Once she realized it, she gave herself a mental shake and picked up the pace. As she walked across acres of neatly mown grass, she wondered what had possessed Grandfather to tear up the gardens that had been such a large part of Fair Winds' legend. Surely he hadn't resented the staff needed to care for them. And it couldn't have been a financial decision; he'd had more money than God.

What problem had flowers and shrubs and fountains caused that led him to destroy them?

Long before she was ready, she reached the house. Grandmother had seated herself again, a book open on her lap. Dressed as formally as ever, she slid her gaze over Reece's shirt, capris and sneakers, and her nose crinkled in the slightest *humph,* though she said nothing about Reece's appearance.

She gestured to the nearest chair, green wicker with a floral-patterned cushion. "Have you been getting Mr. Jones acquainted with the property, Clarice?"

"Getting both of us acquainted with it." Reece didn't correct the names. That Jones preferred no *Mister* preceding his name and she generally answered only to Reece was of no consequence to Grandmother. *She* was the arbiter of what was correct and it wasn't open to discussion.

"You spent enough hours out there in those woods. I don't see how you could possibly have forgotten any part of it. Of course, that was a long time ago."

It was as good an opening as any Reece was likely to get. Shifting enough to make the wicker creak, she tried to project a casual attitude, in both voice and posture, as she said, "There's a lot I don't remember about that summer."

"There wasn't much to remember. You got up in the morning, played outside until mealtime and you went to bed at night. Once a week you went to town with me to shop, and on Sunday mornings we went to church."

"All of us?" It was hard to imagine Grandfather putting on a suit, going to church and being sociable.

"You, Mark and I. Your grandfather believed in God. He just thought he was more likely to find Him out there—" she gestured toward the property "—than in some stuffy church."

More likely he'd been afraid that God might strike him down if he stepped through the doorway of the sanctuary.

"So nothing memorable happened that summer."

Grandmother gave her a chastising look. "Obviously not, or you would have remembered it." Gripping the book with both hands, she lifted it from her lap. "I've brought this for you. It's a history of the Howard family. Your great-grandfather commissioned it shortly before he passed. You should know from where—and from whom—you come."

With reluctance Reece took the book. It was heavy, bound in leather, its pages yellowed and its fragrance musty. She couldn't imagine much more boring than a family history where the family chose which facts to include and which to leave forgotten. No doubt every Howard in the book appeared as highly intelligent, benevolent, compassionate, heroic and generous, and from her limited experience, she knew better.

"I'll look at it this afternoon." Not a lie. She would look at it. She just might not open the cover. Though knowing Grandmother, there would probably be a quiz later.

"Did Mark and I get along that summer?"

Grandmother's gaze was directed westward, toward the river barely visible through the live oaks. "Of

course you did. You were cousins. He might have been
something of a pest, but you were rather spoiled and
had a tendency to cry."

*Of course I did! My dad had died and Valerie had
left me here where I hated it!*

"We'd hoped you would grow out of it, and you did
stop tattling fairly quickly, but you were still prickly.
Comes from being an only child, I suppose."

Mark was an only child, as well—and a brat. He'd
gotten her in trouble, blamed her for his own actions
and scared her more times than she could count. But
he'd been the grandchild they knew, the one they could
handle.

The silence had gone on awhile when abruptly
Grandmother spoke again. "I blamed your mother, you
know."

"For spoiling me?" Wrong person. Valerie had been
okay as a mother, but it was Dad who had indulged
Reece. He'd been like a kid himself, finding wonder in
everything they did. He'd loved being silly and making
her giggle, and he'd usually found a way to give her
things Valerie had said no to, without upsetting Valerie, either. He'd had a knack for getting his way without upsetting people.

Which made his estrangement from his parents seem
that much odder.

"For your father's death," Grandmother answered.
"If she hadn't come to Georgia for college…if she
hadn't insisted on going back to Colorado…if Elliott
had been here where he belonged, he wouldn't have
been on the highway that day. He wouldn't have been
hit by that speeding truck." Her voice softened to a
whisper. "He wouldn't have died."

Pain stirred in Reece's chest. One thing she did remember from that time was the *if* game. *If I'm a good girl, Daddy will come back. If I do everything I'm supposed to do, they'll tell me it was a mistake. If I pray hard enough tonight, when I wake up in the morning he'll be here.*

But there had been nothing conditional about it. Her dad was dead, and there was nothing she could do to change it.

"Dad didn't leave Georgia because of Valerie." She was staring out across the yard, too, but she felt the sharp touch of Grandmother's gaze. After a moment, she looked at her. "You know it's true. He left because of Grandfather." He had never deemed Reece old enough to hear the whole story, and all Valerie would say was that he and Arthur had *had issues,* but that was the reason they'd moved to Valerie's hometown of Denver. It was the reason for their infrequent visits and why Dad had little contact with his mother and virtually none with his father.

Plum-tinged lips drew into a thin, hard line, but Grandmother didn't argue. Did she regret that she'd let her husband cost her so much time with her son?

Reece didn't have the chance to find out. Grandmother abruptly stood and started to the door. There she turned back. "Read the book. There will be discussions later."

After leaving Reece, Jones did work on the project for a while, making a few preliminary sketches, compiling lists of plants needed, including virtually every variety of azalea and crape myrtle known to man. It was always fun at this stage, pretend-shopping with someone else's pretend money. The final budget, of course, dictated what they could actually buy, but in the beginning, on a project of this scope, anything was possible.

He had an appointment at one, so he worked with one eye on his watch and about half his senses tuned outside. There'd been no company this morning and, more importantly, no sign of Reece since he'd left her to face her grandmother. He wondered how that chat had gone.

Assuming that someday he got married and had kids, then grandkids, he didn't want to be the type of grandparent who deserved the name of Grandfather. He had one grandpa and one papaw, and either one was good enough for him.

At noon, he knocked off work, drove into town and downed a fast-food burger, then headed north on River Road. His destination was a construction site just north of the turnoff to Fair Winds. His truck bounced over the rutted road that cut through a thick stand of tall pines before opening into a cleared area not visible from the road. White pickups bearing Calloway Construction logos were parked around the site, along with heavy equipment that was gouging up the earth.

Russ Calloway was studying plans spread out in the tailgate of his truck while a huge black dog stood in the bed, front paws braced on the side and head up as if it were supervising the activity.

Beside Jones, Mick straightened and pressed his nose to the window as they stopped next to Calloway. He and the black exchanged looks, then barks before Mick pawed at the door. "Stay," Jones commanded.

Mick didn't look happy about it, but he obeyed.

The machinery made easy conversation out of the question, so Russ gestured to the south, and they began walking that way. Twenty acres of trees had been taken down on the site, and five houses were going in. The construction would be excellent—Calloway Construction was known for top-quality work—and the houses would be expensive, with big lots, swimming pools and room to park monster RVs and boats. The new owners would spend small fortunes having mature trees brought in to replace those dozed down, but not pines. Oaks, likely, maybe a few pecans and sweet gums.

Little work had been done at the southern tip of the site. The ground had been graded a bit, and a brush pile, there fifteen years or more, had been moved, stick by stick, thirty feet away. Sprigs of weed were starting to poke up from the bare earth.

"This is where the surveyor and I found the backpack," Calloway said, gesturing to the new weeds. "It was stuffed in underneath the top layer of brush. Looked like it had been there a long time. It was faded, parts of it rotted."

It was easy for Jones to imagine Glen hiding the pack that held everything he owned. In the weeks they'd camped on Fair Winds—just through the trees and across the fence—they'd routinely hidden their belongings before leaving camp, especially after they'd seen three Howards—Reece, Mark and their grandfather—roaming the woods. They might have gotten caught and chased off, but no one was going to steal their stuff.

"We called the sheriff," Calloway went on. "Once they confirmed that the owner of the backpack hadn't been seen in years, we cleared out the brush pile to make sure…"

That Glen's body wasn't under there, as well. Jones swallowed hard.

"You, uh…know the guy?"

Jones stared at Fair Winds, barely able to make out the crooked pine, barely able to hear the creek. He had asked a lot of questions since he got to town, but all of them about the Howards. No one had reason to suspect his real interest in the area.

Exhaling a heavy breath, he met Calloway's gaze. "I'd prefer people not know for obvious reasons, but… he's my brother. And you're right. The family hasn't seen or heard from him in fifteen years. Not since he was here."

Calloway's expression turned both sympathetic and awkward. "Sorry. We didn't find anything else. He wouldn't have just gone off and left his stuff, I guess."

Jones shook his head. His people were all about survival. Glen could have survived without his belongings, but it wouldn't have been easy. He'd handled those pictures of Siobhan so much that he'd just about rubbed the color off of them. If he'd left Copper Lake, he would have taken them and the backpack with him.

If he were alive, he would have contacted Siobhan.

"Who owned this property back then? Do you know?"

"My grandmother owned it, but it was leased to Arthur Howard. He didn't do anything with it, though. Some Calloway two or three generations before her had leased it to the Howard family for logging. The Howards got out of that business, but they kept renewing the lease." Calloway looked back at the site as if checking on his crew. "My grandmother used to say that Arthur kept writing those checks because he wanted as much land between him and the world as he could get."

Interesting theory. Was the man just antisocial? Or had he had something to hide?

As they started back to their trucks, Jones asked his

next question. "How chatty is the sheriff's department around here?"

"You want to talk to them about your brother without everyone else finding out he's your brother?" Calloway drew a wallet from his pocket, thumbing through it for a business card. It was white, embossed in gold with the badge for the Copper Lake Police Department. "Tommy Maricci's a detective in town. He knows everyone on the sheriff's department, so he can help you out. He'll make sure it stays private."

Jones accepted the card, holding it lightly between his fingers. Seeking assistance from a cop...what would Big Dan think of that?

It wasn't as if he could slip much lower in his father's respect.

He offered his other hand to Calloway. "Thanks. I appreciate your time."

On the way to town, he called the cell number on the business card. Maricci answered on the third ring, sounding distracted. Jones introduced himself, then dropped the Calloway name. It didn't take a stranger more than a day in Copper Lake to realize that the Calloways were important to the area. Their name opened doors or, at least, stirred interest.

They arranged to meet at the coffee shop on the town square. Mick's ears pricked at the mention. Jones had had coffee there every day since coming to town, and every day the pretty barista had given him a treat for Mick, waiting outside.

"You know, she might not be there," he warned. It didn't wipe the anticipatory look from the dog's face.

"I spend more time talking to a dog than I do to people," Jones muttered to himself as he found a parking space down the block. "Of course, most people aren't as smart as you, Mick."

Three small tables occupied a portion of the sidewalk in front of A Cuppa Joe. Jones left Mick at the nearest one while he went inside to order his coffee. He got the plain stuff—dark roast, sugar, one cream. No foam, no ice, no exotic flavorings. Armed with that and a dog biscuit, he returned out front to find that Detective Maricci, identifiable by the shield embroidered on his shirt and the gold one attached to his belt, had arrived and was sharing the table with Mick, who'd climbed into a chair for a better view.

"Pretty dog," Maricci commented.

"Yeah. He gets away with a lot because of that face." Jones showed Mick the biscuit, and the dog immediately sat, his tail thumping steadily. "Sit down there," he commanded, pointing to the ground.

All Mick did was follow the biscuit with his gaze.

Jones set his coffee down, then gave the dog a shove. As soon as his paws hit the sidewalk, he sat again, quivering, and Jones gave him half the cookie.

"My kid responds well to bribes of cookies," Maricci observed.

"Don't we all." Jones settled into Mick's chair and removed the lid from his coffee to let steam escape. Nothing smelled better, he decided, than a freshly brewed cup of coffee.

Except maybe a woman.

"I talked to Russ after you called. So the missing guy is your brother. You have any idea what he was doing out there?"

"Traveling. Camping."

"Did he have a car or was he hitching rides?"

"A little hitching. Mostly walking." Not many drivers had wanted to give rides to two teenage boys, and they'd been wary of the ones who did.

"Do you know for sure he was in this area? Maybe someone stole the backpack elsewhere and ditched it here."

Jones shook his head before taking a sip of coffee. "No. He was here. He told me."

"When was the last time you spoke to him?"

"August 12. Fifteen years ago."

"And what did he say?"

"That he liked this area and was going to stay awhile." There had been more to it than just that. Glen had wanted to stay because of Reece. He'd figured she needed someone on her side if her cousin tried to kill her again. Mark had been scheduled to return home a week later; then, Glen had said, he would leave, too.

Atlanta had been his destination. He was going to get a job and a place to live, then send for Siobhan. Their families would have been appalled that they'd turned their backs on their heritage, even more so over the two broken marriage contracts, but Glen and Siobhan had been prepared for that.

Mark had eventually left, but Glen never had.

"Why didn't your family report him missing at the time?"

"I left home that summer. I didn't know he'd disappeared until the backpack was found. I guess our family thought he'd gone with me, so they didn't know until then, either."

Maricci's gaze narrowed. "Where did you go?"

"I headed out west. About the time I reached the California coast, I turned eighteen and joined the navy. After that, I used the G.I. Bill to get through college and settled in Kentucky."

"You didn't think it was odd you didn't hear from your brother all that time?"

Jones's smile was more like a grimace. "I haven't heard from any of my family. The one time I went home, my father closed the door in my face. Every time I call, as soon as my mother recognizes my voice, she hangs up. The only exception was when she told me Glen's backpack had been found."

"So your family took your leaving hard."

Tension knotted Jones's gut and turned the coffee bitter. Carefully he set the cup down, leaned back in his chair and laced his fingers together. He was about to admit something he hadn't told anyone in fifteen years and hadn't really believed he ever would. But if it helped find out something about his brother... "The address on Glen's license was North Augusta, South Carolina, but we actually lived in Murphy Village. Just off the interstate, big houses, trailers, lots of statues of the Madonna. Are you familiar with it, Detective?"

Just for an instant, Maricci showed surprise—something, Jones would bet, he didn't often do. Quickly his expression went blank again, and his tone was perfectly neutral when he spoke. "What law-enforcement agency in the region isn't? So you and your brother...are...were Irish Travelers."

Watching traffic on the street, Jones swallowed hard, then absently reached down to slip the second half of the biscuit to Mick. Touching the dog's fur, feeling him breathe, hearing his gung ho crunch, eased him a bit.

Then he forced his gaze back to Maricci's. "Yes. But that's not what Glen was doing here that summer. It had nothing to do with the family business." *Business* included just about every scam a man could think of: resurfacing driveways, putting on new roofs, sell-

ing stolen property, construction. Wheeling and dealing and stealing.

There was an art to the business, Big Dan always
said. A man needed charm and sincerity, an ability to
bullshit and a little bit of acting. The men hit the road
in spring and stayed gone into fall, always doing business far from home. They didn't run cons where they
lived—another of Big Dan's rules.

"It's my understanding the older boys travel with the
men. Why weren't you and Glen doing that?"

"We asked for one summer off to do whatever we
wanted. We'd always done what we were told to. We
were good workers. Glen had already quit school, and
they'd decided I'd finished my last year, too." He'd
gotten one more year than his brothers and most of his
cousins, but it hadn't been enough. He'd wanted to learn
more—to learn a different life. "Our family agreed to
it."

"And you used the time to get the hell out of the
South."

Jones nodded.

"Was Glen planning to go back?"

"No." Grimly Jones recounted his brother's plans,
leaving out mention of Siobhan by name. She'd gone
through with the arranged marriage—to one of Jones's
cousins—and had a half-dozen kids. Most likely, no
one even suspected she'd intended to run away, and
he'd prefer to keep it that way. Glen had found enough
trouble. No use spreading it to her.

"How long was he here?"

"A few weeks. Three, maybe."

"And the last time you saw him—where was that?"

"Right around where the backpack was found. He'd
made camp and was going to stick around awhile. I

went on without him." The biggest regret of Jones's life. If he'd stayed...

"What was his routine? Did he keep to himself? Hang out in town? Did he try to pick up a few dollars somehow?"

"We stayed out of town as much as possible. If there was fishing to be done, we did that. If there was a creek to swim in, we did that. We didn't mess with people." His jaw tight, he deliberately disregarded the last question. He and Glen had saved as much money as they could for the trip, and their father had given them some, but, yeah, they'd stolen when the opportunity was too good to resist—cash a few times, food a few others. They'd both wanted to live more law-abiding lives, but they'd been willing to do whatever was necessary to get to those lives.

Maricci was quiet a moment, then he pushed his chair back. "I'll talk to the sheriff's investigator who caught the case. Where are you staying?"

"Fair Winds. I'm putting together a bid to restore the gardens there."

"Really. I've heard about those gardens from my grandfather. He said people used to drive out there just to look through the gate at them." His gaze turned speculative. "What does Miss Willa's grandson think of the plan?"

"He's not thrilled, or so I've heard. I expect to hear from him sometime soon."

"I expect you will. I'll be in touch, too." Maricci stood, offered his hand, then gave Mick a scratch before walking away.

Chapter 5

After an excruciatingly stiff dinner with Grandmother and Mark, Reece retired to her room upstairs for a little light reading. The book she'd been instructed to study lay open on the bed, about as interesting as a six-month-old newspaper. The writing was as pretentious as the title—*Southern Aristocracy: The Howards of Georgia*—and the musty odor was giving her a headache.

Restlessly she got out of bed and went to the windows. The nearly full moon cast its eerie light, giving a ghostly glow to the objects it reached directly, casting deep shadows elsewhere. Out front, except for distant lights across the river, everything was dark. On the side, a lone light shone on the patio, but the cottage was in darkness. Everyone was asleep but her.

There had been more talk at dinner about the garden project, Mark trying repeatedly to get her to side with him. She hadn't, which had frustrated him, but he'd continued to argue his case until Grandmother had flatly told him to shut up or leave.

After that, conversation had fizzled out. He had asked a few halfhearted questions about her life in New Orleans, talked a bit about his daughter, then murmured on his way out, "Thanks for the support, Clarice."

After the door had closed behind him, Grandmother had drily repeated, "Yes, thanks for the support, Clarice."

It's none of my business. She hadn't said the words out loud, but she'd shrieked them inside.

As she stared out the window, movement caught her attention in the shadows across the driveway. She squinted, trying to find focus in the lack of light. Was it merely leaves rustling? A bird fluttering past? Maybe Mick, out for a middle-of-the-night bathroom break.

She couldn't make out anything, and trying just made her head hurt worse. With a sigh, she began to rub her temples, but her hands stilled as a thud sounded downstairs.

It was likelier one of the resident ghosts than Grandmother. Still, after a moment, she started toward the door. She would really rather lock herself inside, crawl into bed and let the book bore her to sleep, but there was no lock on the door, and what if it *had* been Grandmother? What if she'd gone downstairs for something and fallen?

Opening the door, she looked quickly down the hall. Grandmother's door was closed, but that didn't mean anything. It was always closed.

She stepped into the hallway and softly called, "Grandmother?"

No response from upstairs, but the quiet click of a

door came from below. Just as the bedroom doors were always closed, the doors downstairs were always open, except the kitchen door...and the one that led to Grandfather's study. Reece took the few steps necessary to reach the top of the stairs, then crept to the landing, where the study door became visible, and the hairs on her arms stood on end.

Faint light seeped out underneath the door, and distant footsteps shuffled. Unable to breathe, unable to do anything at all but cling more tightly to the stair rail, she watched the shifting light as those footsteps paced slowly to the left, then slowly back again. *One, two, three, four, five...*

Maybe it was Grandmother. Maybe she felt closer to Grandfather in his study than anywhere else, so she went there when she couldn't sleep.

But to convince herself of that, Reece would have to go down the stairs, across the hall and open the door.

She couldn't.

...six, seven, eight, nine...

Chills swept over her, creating shivers that left her barely able to stand. She wanted to throw her stuff in the truck and drive home without stopping. She wouldn't feel safe again until she was curled up in her own bed with Bubba, Louie and Eddie all snuggled close.

Abruptly the footsteps stopped and the light winked out. The house seemed unnaturally quiet, all the normal sounds gone. There was the light rasp of her breathing, the thudding of her heart and nothing else.

She couldn't say how long it took to steady her legs or to uncurl her fingers from the banister. Afraid to turn her back on the study door, she backed up the steps and down the hall, pivoting when she reached her room. She closed the door noiselessly, leaned against it and gave a great exhalation.

When she breathed again, she caught the faint hint of tobacco smoke on the air. Her stomach knotted once, then did it again as her gaze took in the book she'd left open on the bed, closed now and resting on the dresser. Then, slowly, she looked upward to the message barely visible on the mirror.

Go away.

It appeared as if it had been written on wet glass, fading as the moisture dried. Even as she watched, it disappeared, not leaving so much as a smudge behind.

Which resident ghost was the message from? Was it friendly advice…or a threat?

Moving to the bed, she shoved her feet into a pair of flip-flops, then hastily left the room again. She tiptoed down the hall to the back stairs—anything to avoid the area around the study—then switched off the patio light and let herself out the side door. Moonlight was illumination enough for her tonight.

It was a little too cool for the thin cotton shorts and T-shirt she wore as pajamas, but she didn't care. Out here she could breathe. She could think. She could feel, if not safe, then saf*er*.

As she settled in one of the chairs with her back to the house, her shoulders sagged with release. It wasn't her first encounter with a Fair Winds ghost. She hadn't been in danger. Someone was just telling her to do what she very much wished she could: say goodbye to this place forever. If the message had been a threat, any ghost could have come up with more ominous words.

If it was just a warning, though, it could have at least said *please* or *for your own good.*

Or someone could have just been making mischief.

A weird sense of humor in life would likely follow its owner into death.

Across the road came a little creak, and her muscles started tightening again before she saw Mick leap off the cottage porch and trot toward her. There was no other sign of movement from the place; she guessed Mick had awakened Jones and he'd let the dog out and was waiting half-asleep inside.

"Hey, sweetie," she murmured, offering a scratch to the dog.

He put his paws on her leg, stretched up and licked her chin, then hunkered down again, practically vibrating with pleasure as she rubbed the base of his ears and down his neck. He reminded her of how very much she missed her dogs. They were probably all stretched out on her bed right now, snoring loudly, pushing against each other as they rambled in their dreams.

"I wish I had a treat to give you, but I haven't trespassed into the kitchen yet. I don't know if Lois would mind, but there's no doubt that Grandmother would." She'd found the kitchen the most welcoming room in the house fifteen years ago, and Inez, the housekeeper then, the most sympathetic person. But once Grandmother had caught her slipping in there, both Reece and Inez had been warned.

Mick didn't seem to mind affection in place of treats, so she continued to rub him, leaning forward as he slowly sank onto the ground, then rolled onto one side to expose his belly.

"Don't forget you already have three at home. You can't have mine, too."

She startled, but just a bit, nothing like the scare she'd already had. Jones did indeed look only half-awake. His hair was mussed, he wore the same shirt and shorts he'd worn on their walk that morning, and his feet, like hers, were in flip-flops.

"I'm not trying to win over your dog."

"You're doing a pretty good job of it for not trying." He sank into the nearest chair and propped his feet on the fountain rim. "I wondered what was taking him so long. I should have known. If there's a pretty girl with magic fingers around, he forgets it's the middle of the night."

Pretty girl. The warmth that settled over her was far too much response for the casual compliment.

"Sorry I kept him out." But she wasn't. She'd needed the peace Mick provided, even it was just for a few minutes.

"Trouble sleeping?"

"Yeah, a bit."

"I never have trouble sleeping. Mick doesn't snore, but he does have this loud, rhythmic breathing when he sleeps. It just kind of draws you in. I'm usually out ten minutes after he is."

"Lucky you." Though, usually, falling asleep wasn't her problem. The rude awakening from the nightmares was. Nothing like a few bloodcurdling screams to put the end to a much-needed rest.

"I saw your cousin leaving after dinner. He didn't look like a happy man."

That was a good description for Mark, at least on the subject of the garden plan. He'd told Grandmother he was worried and didn't want anyone taking advantage of her. Grandmother had retorted that it was her *money* he was worried about, not her, and not to worry, that she wouldn't let *anyone,* including her grandson, take advantage of her.

"Has he talked to you yet?" Reece asked. "Tried

to send you away or make it worth your while to convince Grandmother you can't fit her into your schedule? Or maybe he'll decide she can have a smaller—much smaller—garden."

"Not yet. He's probably checking out his options. First he'll try to change her mind. When that fails, he'll either bring in other family members—"

Reece interrupted with a snort that made Jones grin.

"—or talk to his lawyer to see what legal steps can be taken."

"He mentioned Grandmother's lawyer." The thought of that kind of interference irritated her. Having been married to Grandfather for fifty-some years certainly entitled Grandmother to spend her money on anything she wanted, even if it was clowns performing every day in a combination water/skateboard park on the front lawn. "Has it really come to legal action on any of your jobs?"

"Just once, in Florida. Old man with grown children and a new bride. He left the bulk of his estate to his kids, but the wife got to spend pretty freely while she lived. The kids insisted she was trying to bleed the estate dry to punish them. The thing is, the kids were going to get about $20 million each, and they paid their lawyers more than the project was budgeted for to fight over the cost of a five-acre garden."

Uncomfortable in her crouching position, Reece sat up, then scooted to one side before patting the seat. Mick crawled up with her, the front half of his body across her lap. "Twenty million dollars. Wow. You could do a lot of good with that kind of money."

"Not those people. Money had never made them happy, and it never would."

Had money made Grandmother and Grandfather

happy? Did it make Mark happy? After considering it a moment, Reece decided she couldn't reconcile the notion of her grandparents and happiness. They just weren't the smiles-and-joy type.

Mark, on the other hand… He'd always had money and had taken it for granted. She would bet the idea of not being wealthy had never crossed his mind; it was literally unthinkable. And, like many overindulged children, he'd grown into an adult for whom, apparently, the more he had, the more he wanted.

What about Jones? She watched him, gazing into the darkness. "Does money make you happy?"

His gaze flickered to hers, and a thin smile touched the corners of his mouth. "Money's important. I won't deny that. There have been times, back when I was in college, when I could barely pay my rent or buy groceries, and the last few years I've made more than I can spend. I definitely prefer the extra cash. But there's a lot more to being happy than that."

"So *are* you happy?" It was a nosy question, too personal to ask someone she'd known less than forty-eight hours. Valerie would admonish her; Grandmother would remind her that Howard women never pried. But Jones was free to ignore the question or tell her it was none of her business. She wouldn't be offended.

He was quiet a long time, as if it wasn't an easy answer for him. Finally, he exhaled loudly. "Yeah, I guess. For the most part."

What parts of his life was he unhappy with? Besides his estrangement from his family, what would have to change to make his answer a simple *Yes, I am?*

He turned the question back on her. "What about you? Are you happy?"

"Yes," she said immediately, then, feeling a flush of

guilt for not being totally honest, she added, "For the most part. I, uh …" She looked at him, then focused her gaze on the dog settled so contentedly in her lap. "I don't get along with my mother, I'm not close to my grandmother and cousin, and I'd like to get married and have kids someday though I've never met anyone I'd remotely consider tying myself to. But other than that and…that summer, yes, I'm happy. I like my job. I love my dogs and my friends. I can pay my bills, and I'm in good health. That's a lot."

Halfway through her response, his gaze had zeroed in on her. She could feel it as surely as she felt Mick's warm, comforting weight against her.

"What happened that summer?" His voice was low and comforting, too, with its blend of accents. It was a perfect voice for talking in the dark, for lulling an edgy woman into relaxing all those taut muscles, for making her feel safe.

God, she'd been using that word a lot lately. Yearning for something she couldn't regain until she faced the fears that had taken it from her.

Unless remembering stole it from her for good.

Jones watched her, her fingers lightly stroking Mick's fur. Her head was tilted so little of her face was visible to him, but that was enough in the silvery light to know that her expression had gone blank. The suspicions that had reared their ugly head that morning came back, prickling his spine, making him sit straighter in the chair.

He thought she wasn't going to answer and didn't blame her at all when slowly she lifted her head and met his gaze. "I don't know."

"What do you mean?"

She shrugged. "I don't remember most of the time I spent here. I remember coming with my mother. Mark arrived soon after we did for his summer visit, and Valerie left again not long after that. She didn't even tell me goodbye. I got up one morning, and she was… gone. The next memory I have after that day, she and I were back in Colorado."

Truth? It was impossible to tell with an accomplished liar. But something about the look on her face, the way she said the words…it *felt* like truth.

He knew from fifteen years ago that her mother had just bailed on her. She'd told Glen the story, and he'd repeated it angrily, wondering how a woman could do that to her child. In their culture, family came first… unless two restless sons ran off to experience a different life.

"Where did she go?" he asked, though he knew the answers to that, too.

"Grandmother said she left to take care of things back at home, but she was gone a long time. There wasn't that much to take care of."

That had been Miss Willa's first explanation. Later, she'd told Reece that her mother had gone to Europe with friends. Glen had shaken his head in disgust. *Can you believe that? Leaving her own kid to go on* vacation?

"What did Valerie say when you asked her?"

Reece's brow furrowed. "She would never talk about it. Even now, if I ask her anything about that summer, even about my father's death, she says the past is past and she's not going to waste any time discussing it."

That was cold, when your daughter still had questions. *If* the daughter really did have questions. But leaving your grieving thirteen-year-old daughter for whatever reason was pretty damn cold, too.

"So you really don't remember anything? Swimming in the creek? That old cemetery? Hanging out with your cousin?"

She shook her head. "I remember enough from the first few weeks to know that Mark and I didn't hang out. He was mean."

Mean wasn't the half of it.

If she was being honest, she didn't remember Jones and Glen.

She didn't remember Mark trying to drown her.

She didn't remember anything her grandfather might have done to her.

She had no answers to give him.

She was of no use to him.

If she was being honest.

He could be honest even if she wasn't. He could tell her why he was here, what he remembered of that summer. He could appeal to her conscience, could trade answers to some of her questions for some sort of closure for the family regarding Glen.

Silently he snorted. If Glen was dead, knowing was better than not knowing, but it wouldn't provide closure. It wouldn't make the knowledge any easier to bear. It damn sure wouldn't ease his guilt for leaving his brother there. Yeah, Glen had been older; yeah, he'd been stubborn as a mule. But Jones should have stayed with him. After that threat from Mark...

It had been such spoiled-juvenile bluster. *I'm gonna tell my grandfather that you're trespassing out here, and he'll call the sheriff to put you in jail.*

Reece, dripping wet, eyes huge and still shaking

from her near-drowning, had gotten in his face. *You say a word, and I'll tell him you tried to kill me.*

Mark had put on a good show of bravado—*He'd never believe you over me. He loves* me, *not you!*—but his voice had quavered and a look of pure panic had come into his eyes before he'd run off through the woods.

None of them had believed he would really tell, or have the nerve to confront either Glen or Jones again.

The whisper of cushions and a grunt from Mick drew his attention back to Reece, shifting to a more comfortable position. As soon as she settled again, so did the dog, looking utterly content.

"Did I mention that I had a visit from a ghost tonight?" she asked, the lighter tone in her voice signaling the end of the other subject.

"It must have slipped your mind. What happened?"

"Just light. Footsteps. A book moved from where I'd left it a few moments before." She paused. "A note written on the mirror telling me to leave."

"Not a very friendly ghost, huh."

She shrugged carelessly, though Jones wasn't too convinced by it. "Maybe he doesn't like sharing my room with me. Or maybe he thinks if I couldn't bother to visit while he was alive, I'm not welcome now that he's dead."

"He? Your grandfather?"

She shrugged. "I smelled tobacco. Though I doubt he's the only Howard who liked his cigars."

The presence at the creek that morning had smelled of tobacco, too. Arthur Howard had dominated the place while he lived. It was no surprise he'd hang around now.

"You planning to spend the night out here instead of inside with him?"

She made a *pfft* sound. "If Grandmother had a chaise with a nice thick cushion on it... He didn't waste any time on me when he was alive. I doubt he'll give me much more of his attention now."

"That would be my guess." Jones yawned, then nudged Mick. "Come on, boy, I need to get some sleep."

He half expected the dog to open one eye, give him a blank look, then close it again. Instead, Mick stepped lightly to the ground, stretched, then trotted for the cottage. Reece laughed at his fickleness. "Yeah, good night to you, too, Mick. You're welcome for all the scratching."

"Sitting with you is comfortable," Jones said as he stood. "Stretching out on the bed, though, is his idea of the way to spend a night. See you tomorrow."

He crossed the road into the shadows that hugged the other side, listening for some sound that Reece was going inside, too. It didn't come. When he stepped inside the cottage, he turned back to fasten the screen door and saw her still sitting there.

He intended to lock up, strip down to his boxers and crawl back into bed, but the sight of her held him there. She seemed so alone and vulnerable. She *was* alone: no family that counted, no man to stand beside her, just friends back in Louisiana.

That wasn't too different from his life, the cynic in him scoffed, and he wasn't alone or vulnerable.

But no one had abandoned him. No one had ever wanted him dead.

After a few minutes, she stood and, like Mick, stretched. Her back arched, her breasts pushing against her thin shirt, the hem of the shirt rising up over her middle. She held the position long enough to make his mouth dry, then straightened, looking at the house for a time before finally walking to the door. She really didn't like the place. But why should she, when all the memories were bad?

He stood there in the dark, just watching, until she disappeared inside. A moment later the patio light came on again. Soon after that, a shadow appeared in the only room lit up, then those lights went out, too.

Rubbing at the unease cramping his neck, Jones closed and locked the door and went to bed.

Reece awoke even more tired than when she'd finally fallen asleep. She hadn't had any screaming-to-wake-the-dead nightmares, but her sleep had been restless, her dreams haunted by Grandfather's fierce scowls, Mark's taunts and angry words.

If you say a word...
Curiosity killed the cat.
Meee-oww.

She felt a little better after a long shower. After dressing in jeans and a shirt, she picked up the family-history book from the dresser, her gaze fixing on the mirror. Leaning forward, she blew out her breath on the glass, curious to see if the message might reappear in the fog. It didn't.

Grandmother had already eaten breakfast and was in her study, her back to the door, when Reece tried to slip past. Without glancing up, she said, "It's about time you got out of bed."

Reece grimaced before turning into the room. Grandmother could hear the faintest creak of a floorboard when someone was trying to sneak past, but never heard any of the thumps and thuds from the ghosts. How was that? "Good morning."

The old lady turned, and displeasure wrinkled her nose. She disapproved of jeans—Reece had heard that on her first day in the house fifteen years ago—and shorts—Reece had learned that on her second day. And she *certainly* disapproved of Hawaiian shirts with bright red flowers on a royal-blue background.

Some days a girl just had to dress to suit herself, and today Reece really needed the lift from the vividly colored shirt.

"I'm going to a meeting in town today," Grandmother said once she was certain the censure had been recognized. "As Mr. Jones is going to restore the gardens, I believe joining the garden society is in my best interests. The meeting is today, and there will be a luncheon afterward. I gave Lois the day off, so you'll be on your own for lunch."

"That's fine." Reece wasn't a fan of eating out by herself, but this would give her a chance to go into town and see if anything jogged her memory. She doubted it, since the bulk of her time had been spent here on the property, but hey, it was an excuse to get out for a few hours, right?

Grandmother tucked her handbag under one arm and bypassed Reece on the way to the door. When her gaze fell on the book Reece held, she gave a firm nod of approval.

Reece followed her into the hall. "Do you need a ride?"

"Of course not. I am fully capable of driving myself where I want to go." Grandmother cast a sharp look over one shoulder. "I may be approaching eighty, but I'm as able-bodied and sharp-minded as ever."

Her snippy tone made Reece draw back emotionally if not physically. "I never suggested you weren't."

"Your cousin suggests it quite regularly."

"He worries about you." Heavens, she was defending Mark. Who would have imagined it.

As she stepped outside, Grandmother shot her another scowl. "When he's got something genuine to worry about, I'll tell him."

When the warm morning sun struck her, Reece felt a moment of relief. A gentle breeze blew from the west and smelled faintly of wood smoke. On the far side of the river, a thin plume of smoke circled lazily into the sky, and an unseen boat putted on the water. It seemed such a normal scene that, for a moment, *she* felt normal.

As Grandmother passed the fountain, heels tapping on the brick, Reece drew her attention back. "I only offered because I hadn't seen a car around."

"It's in the garage, where we've always kept the cars."

Garage? Reece glanced around, her gaze lighting on the storage sheds that stood between the house and the barn. She'd walked right past them yesterday, paying them no mind, but now she saw the keypad on the nearest one, and the overhead door.

A faint memory stirred: that door standing open, Grandmother's big old Cadillac gone, Grandfather's beat-up pickup inside. The tailgate was down, the bed littered with dirt and holding a tarp stained with something dark and wet. Grandfather, filthy and sweating, yelling at her to get back to the house, and Mark…just standing there, a look on his face. Fear? Excitement?

Goose bumps covered her arms, and she shivered violently, hugging herself to ward off the sick dread.

She'd seen that feverish, gleaming expression in Mark's eyes before, one day when he'd…when she'd…

The memory was there, so close, so elusive. She focused inward, trying to grab it before it slipped away, but she was too late. Like fog struck by burning sun, it disappeared.

Like the message on the mirror last night.

"Do you intend to follow me all the way?"

Grandmother's impatient voice brought her back to the moment. They were halfway to the garage, when Reece couldn't remember crossing the patio. She looked at the garage, then back at the house, and gave herself a mental shake as she stopped. "No, of course not."

"The spare key and the code to the gate are on my desk. If you go somewhere, be sure to lock up. And if you do go somewhere, change clothes. Howard women do not appear in public dressed so gaudily."

Reece stood where she was, book clutched in her arms, until the garage door had lifted, until Grandmother had climbed behind the wheel of a big old Cadillac—Lord, surely not the same one she'd driven fifteen years ago—until she'd backed out of the garage and driven past with a frown directed at Reece.

"Wow. That car's a classic. It's older than both of us."

Jones's words would have startled her if Mick hadn't run into view the instant before he spoke. She turned and watched the two of them saunter down the road from the direction of the barn.

He wore shorts again, denim, with a T-shirt advertising a nursery in Louisville. His hair was untidily combed, and dark glasses hid his even darker eyes. He looked friendly, approachable, sexy—and still, somehow, mysterious. It wasn't the way he moved, all smooth and easy, or the way he grinned, all open and boyish. It was just some aura about him. Some little bit of *something*.

"Everything else around here is ancient. Why not the car?" She greeted Mick with a quick rub, then asked, "Walking the property again?"

"Giving Mick some exercise. He'd sleep twenty-two hours a day if I'd let him." His gaze slid over her. "I like your shirt."

Glancing at the huge flowers, she smiled. "Me, too. It's hard to take life too seriously when you're wearing a Hawaiian shirt." If only that were true.

"Where is Miss Willa off to?"

Reece fell into step with him and headed back the way she'd just come. "She's joining the garden club in town. Now that you're restoring the gardens, it's her duty."

"She takes duty very seriously."

"Yeah." Except the duty of caring for her granddaughter when she'd taken her in. Had Grandmother been so disinterested that she hadn't noticed that something was wrong? Or had she just preferred Mark? After all, she'd described Reece as spoiled with a tendency to cry, while Mark was merely a pest.

"You've got a book again."

Again? He'd never seen her with a book. Oh, but she'd told him she'd read a lot that summer. "It's a Howard family history, bought and paid for by the Howard family."

"Lots of unbiased views and straightforward facts, huh."

"There's nothing like having total control over the final product. How's the work coming?"

"Great. I've done some preliminary sketches, and Lori, who works back in the office, is doing a search for the original statuary. I doubt we'll be able to buy much of it back, but Miss Willa wants to try. We're also putting together a list of—"

He stopped in his tracks, the words stopping, too. Reece looked at him, then in the direction he was staring: his pickup. It took her a moment to realize what was wrong with the picture: both tires on the driver's side were flat.

"Son of a bitch!" Jerking off his glasses, he lengthened his stride and Mick ran ahead, a low rumble coming from his throat.

When Reece caught up, she saw that the other two tires were flat, as well. With a jerk of his head, Jones muttered, "Yours, too," and she spun around to the same sight with her SUV.

"They weren't flat when Mick and I left the house. What about you?"

"I don't… I was talking to Grandmother, and I—I remembered something from—from before. I didn't notice the cars at all."

His gaze sharpened, and she realized his eyes were the biggest source of his mysterious aura. They were so dark, so intense. A lot of emotions could hide there. A lot of secrets.

He started to speak, but bit off the words and yanked his cell phone from his pocket instead. Finding the number he wanted, he gripped the cell tightly and walked a few feet away. "Hey, Calloway, it's Jones again. I just have a request this time." Tersely he explained the situation, said thanks and disconnected. "He's going to send a wrecker out."

Reece frowned as she walked toward her car. She'd heard the Calloway name before, and not just on the plantation she'd passed on her way here. Memory clicked: Mark had mentioned it. Grandmother's lawyer.

Why would Jones have Grandmother's lawyer's number in his cell?

"Robbie Calloway?" she asked, her voice reedy. "The lawyer?"

"No. Russ Calloway. Owns the biggest construction company around here."

She didn't realize she'd been holding her breath until she let it go. It seemed logical a landscape architect would meet the owner of a local construction company. Maybe Jones did a few small jobs on the side while working on big projects like this.

He passed her, walking a wide circle around her truck. "Your ghosts ever do anything like this before?"

She lifted one shoulder in a hapless shrug. "One of them moved my book last night. Have yours?"

He shook his head. "I've never run into a destructive one." He gazed up at the sky, rested his hands on his hips and flatly said, "Well, hell."

Well, hell, indeed.

Chapter 6

The tow-truck driver gave them a lift to a tire store in town, the one recommended by Russ Calloway. After talking with a service technician, Jones and Reece left their vehicles there and walked outside to the sidewalk.

"You hungry?"

When she didn't answer right away, he turned to see her staring around intently. There was nothing remarkable about the block: a '50s-era drive-in; Charlie's Custom Rods; a window treatment place; a chiropractor's office. Was she looking for something recognizable from fifteen years ago?

Or was it all recognizable?

"Reece," he said, and her gaze flew to his. "You want some lunch while we wait?"

"Uh, yeah. Sure."

"You have a favorite place here?" He half expected a

terse repeat of the claim that she didn't remember anything, but he didn't get it.

"No."

"Downtown's that way." He pointed, and they started
walking to the nearest northbound street. "There are a
couple places down here to eat—a deli, a steak house, a
home-cooking diner, Mexican, pizza, a riverside place
that's a little more upscale than the others. What do you
feel like?"

"Any place where I don't have to sit up straight on
the edge of my chair and deal with a full complement
of silver."

"Miss Willa still likes things a little formal, does
she?"

Her scowl was her only response.

Copper Lake was a nice little town, laid out around a
central square with a white gazebo, lots of flowers and
the usual war monuments. He pointed out a couple of
businesses as they walked the few blocks to the square,
then stopped across the street from the Greek Revival
mansion that sat just southeast of the square.

"That's where your grandmother is. The garden society meets there."

Reece looked at the house, then back at him. "How
do you know that?"

"My job basically boils down to gardening. I learn
these things."

"Beautiful place."

"The oldest house in town. Not rumored to be
haunted, though I assume it is."

She looked at the house a moment longer, its white
paint gleaming in the morning sun, the massive oaks
with their Spanish moss casting welcome shade. It had

been meticulously restored a few years earlier and was ready to face the next two hundred years with grace.

When Reece glanced back at Jones, her expression was troubled. "Do you think someone sneaked onto the grounds this morning and slashed our tires?"

"I didn't see any slashes." Or any footprints, though gravel wasn't likely to show much. "I'll bet they just let the air out."

"They who?"

He shrugged. "Ghosts? Your grandfather? Your grandmother?" A pause for effect, then, "You. Me."

Her face paled. "I didn't— Why would you—"

"I didn't, either." They crossed the street, passed A Cuppa Joe and continued northward. "I just can't see Miss Willa stooping to vandalism. For someone to come onto the property, he'd either need the code for the gate or would have to climb the fence, and in the middle of the morning, that's a bit of risk for very little gain. It isn't much of a warning. It isn't violent. Mostly it's just a nuisance. Why would a living, breathing person bother?"

A few yards passed in silence.

"Mark has the code," she said quietly.

"I figured that. And if he was seen, he'd have an excuse: he'd come to check on Miss Willa. But why? Like I said, it's not a big deal. If the tires had been slashed—" and he could see Mark doing that, quick, vicious work "—that would be different. We'd be out the money for new ones, and there's some element of threat there. But just letting the air out?"

She nodded as if agreeing as they turned at the next corner. Their destination, a little diner he'd found his first day in town, was in the middle of the block, a place that looked every bit its age. There were rips in the vinyl benches that had been repaired with duct tape, and the industrial carpeting on the floor carried a lot of stains. But the rest of the dining room was clean, the waitresses friendly and the food good.

He waited until they'd settled in a booth and the waitress had taken their order before he brought up the subject niggling at the back of his mind the past hour.

"You said this morning that you'd remembered something from before." He watched for a response and saw it in the clenching of her jaw, the shadowing of her eyes. "You want to talk about it?"

She looked as if she wanted to put it out of her thoughts forever, but after a sigh, she shrugged. "It wasn't anything much. Just I'd gone outside one morning and wandered over to the garage. Grandfather and Mark were in there, doing something with his pickup, and he...he *screamed* at me to get back in the house. He was angrier than I'd ever seen him. And Mark was so complacent."

Disappointment shafted through Jones. She was right: it wasn't much. From what he knew, Arthur had always been angry around her and Mark had almost always been a smug little bastard.

But if she recovered one memory, then the others could come back, as well.

And when she remembered him and Glen? How would she feel about him not telling her right up front who he was and what had happened? She would be pissed off. He didn't care. He could handle pissed off. He couldn't handle not knowing what had happened to Glen.

"What was the old man's problem with you?"

"I don't know. My dad moved away when he was in college—met my mother, finished the semester and transferred to a school in Colorado, where she was from. He hardly ever came back here." Her expression was mocking. "Howards didn't leave Georgia. This was where they belonged.

"But I think it was more than that. My dad was a good guy. People liked him, respected him. He got along with everybody. He was a high school teacher, and even his students loved him. But he couldn't get along with Grandfather. Even when we did visit, they rarely spoke."

"So Arthur extended his estrangement from your dad to include you?"

She shrugged, and he was struck again by the air of vulnerability. Every kid, he'd guess, wanted affection from their family. How did it feel when you couldn't have it, and not even because of something you'd done? Just because of who you'd been born to? Jones missed his family like hell, but he'd known he would lose them when he left the life. He'd considered the consequences a long time before he'd taken the action. And if he had a kid who wanted to know his grandparents, aunts and uncles, they would welcome him. They wouldn't hold Jones's sins against him.

"What about your mother's family?"

"Her parents died before I was born. No siblings, two uncles who traveled around the world on business. She hardly knew them, and I've never met them."

"Wow. Your family really sucks."

Her laughter surprised her as much as him. "I've got good friends. They're better than family."

The waitress brought their lunch, a silent invitation to lighten the subject. They talked about inconsequential things as they ate—a few of his more interesting jobs, the shop where she worked, their dogs.

They were trading funny dog stories when a new-comer to the diner stopped halfway to the counter to stare at them. Mark Howard.

He smiled when he saw Reece, then his gaze shifted to Jones, and though the smile remained, the warmth didn't. He turned cold enough to give a man the chills if he was the sort whose blood ran cold. Jones wasn't.

"Well, you're the last person I expected to see in town today," Mark said, his words directed to Reece but his gaze on Jones. "What brings you out?"

Some of her warmth drained away, too, replaced by stress that darkened her eyes. "Grandmother had a meeting and gave Lois the day off, and I needed to come to town, so…"

Mark frowned at the mention of Miss Willa's meeting. Afraid she might be with her lawyer drawing up a contract for the garden project? But he apparently decided to let it pass as he turned his attention to Jones. His gaze was steady, like a snake, his expression blank.

Did Mark recognize Jones? How could he forget the faces of either kid who'd stopped him from killing his cousin, especially the one who'd knocked the snot out of him? Especially when, back then, no one told him no and got away with it. Maybe he was waiting to see if Jones acknowledged him first, or willing, if Jones was, to pretend they'd never met.

Or maybe he really didn't recognize him. Maybe he'd dismissed Jones and Glen as nuisances who'd temporarily gotten in his way, who weren't worthy of a place in his memory fifteen years later. Maybe the snakelike look was for Jones the garden designer trying to do business with Miss Willa, not for Jones the kid who'd once thwarted him.

He came closer, his intent to sit down showing

when he'd actually lowered himself to Reece's bench.
A shiver danced up her arms and she slid, in record
time, to the far end of the bench, giving Mark plenty
of room. She didn't relax, either, Jones noted, when he
left plenty of that room between them. She was trying
to hide it, but she still looked trapped.

"So you're the gardener looking to part Grandmother
from her money."

Jones picked up his glass, rattling the ice in the tea.
He didn't bother to correct his occupation—that would
just let Mark know he'd gotten to him—but instead said
evenly, "I'm the one she approached about her project."

"You don't feel guilty?"

"For what?"

"Entering into a deal with a senile old woman."

Jones would have coughed up tea if he hadn't already
swallowed. "Little woman? Five foot nothin', ninety
pounds if that? White hair, sharp gaze that doesn't miss
a trick? Proper and determined and stubborn as hell?
I just want to be sure we're talking about the same
woman, because there's *nothing* senile about the one
I'm dealing with."

Color tinged Mark's cheeks. "'Senile' was a bad
word choice." Before anyone could ask him what word
he would substitute, probably digging himself a deeper
hole, he went on. "You have to admit this plan of hers is
ridiculous. She's almost eighty, for God's sake. Spending all that money, and for what? Some silly gardens
that don't belong that she might not even live long
enough to see completed."

"I don't think it's ridiculous at all. The gardens were
there longer than they've been gone. To most historians, Fair Winds without its gardens is just a shadow of
its former self."

Mark snorted. "I don't give a damn what most historians think. It's not their property. It's not their money."

Very quietly, still pressed against the wall, Reece said, "It's not yours, either."

Mark turned his scowl on her. "Of course you're siding with Grandmother, trying to get back in her good graces." Then his gaze shifted between them, turning speculative. "Or is there more to it than that? Isn't it a coincidence, the two of you showing up here at the same time, him wanting to take thousands of Grandmother's money, you encouraging her every step of the way?"

Just the accusation was enough to turn Reece's cheeks a guilty pink in spite of her rigid denial. "I'd never met Jones until the day Grandmother introduced us."

Which Mark knew, of course, was a lie. Jones watched anger ripple through the other man as he struggled to control it. Mark may have grown up. Adult responsibilities and a family of his own may have made him regret the sins of his youth. He may have become a better person, one who matched the stories Jones had heard since arriving in town.

But he still had that sense of entitlement.

And he still had that temper.

"Never discount the power of fate," Jones said mildly, drawing Mark's attention back to him. "I've always been interested in the Fair Winds gardens, since I was a kid. And Reece's, ah, friend was the one who persuaded her to come back now."

"Friend?" Mark echoed.

She forced an almost natural smile. "My psychic advisor."

For a long time Mark simply stared at her. Then he

laughed. It was unexpected and hearty and broke the tension at the table. "You see a psychic? Does Grandmother know that? Oh, my God. When Macy was pregnant with Clara, she went to a psychic here in town just to find out if everything was all right, and Grandmother about pitched a fit. You'd've thought she'd had a voodoo priest kill a chicken for her and drank its blood, the way Grandmother carried on."

"Grandmother doesn't know everything," Reece replied, "and she doesn't know Evie."

Mark dragged his fingers through his hair. "Look, I'm sorry. I don't like this whole idea. Grandmother brought it up while Grandfather was alive—repeatedly—and he was adamantly against it. He hated those gardens enough to destroy them, and whatever his reason, I think we should respect his wishes. Just because he's passed is no reason to forget everything he said." His gaze moved to Jones. "And it *is* a hell of a lot of money. And she *is* old. I just hate to see…"

"What about respecting Grandmother's wishes?" Reece shifted on the bench to face Mark.

The question flustered him. He seemed to take good care of Miss Willa, as much as she needed it, but he'd always been closer to Arthur, Jones remembered. It was Arthur Mark had complained to, Arthur who encouraged him to think he was lord of everything and everyone around him.

Arthur he'd threatened Jones and Glen with.

Mark sat silent a long time, his expression growing more chastened by the moment. At last, after clearing his throat, he spoke. "Of course Grandmother's wishes matter. It was just *so* important to Grandfather that Fair Winds remain the way he left it."

"Why?" Reece asked.

Mark smiled ruefully. "Damned if I know. I just know he hated the gardens. He hated flowers in general—wouldn't have them in or around the house. I always thought maybe it had something to do with his father's death, because he tore out the gardens right after Great-grandfather passed. We didn't even have flowers at his funeral. Grandmother ordered that all arrangements be sent to the old folks' homes in town instead."

Arthur had been fairly young when his father died—twenty-four or twenty-five—Jones reflected. The old man, if he remembered the history right, had died one day in the garden—heart attack or stroke, no one had been sure. Arthur had been the one to find him, toppled over on a freshly replanted bed. If they had been very close, if the flowers had reminded Arthur of the heart-break of that day...

Jones supposed it was a plausible explanation. His uncle Kevin had never been able to eat fried chicken again, his wife's specialty, after her death. People handled grief in different and sometimes odd ways.

"I know Grandmother loves flowers. I just don't see why she can't be satisfied with a normal garden plot, like everyone else."

"Grandmother's never been satisfied with 'normal' anything. She's not like everyone else, you know. She's a Howard."

The dry tone of Reece's voice drew Jones's gaze. He'd bet his entire business that all she'd wanted in life was normalcy: father, mother, home, extended family. With the exception of her father, she'd gotten anything but normal, to the point that she'd basically written off her family and made a new one for herself with friends.

How hard had it been for her that summer, having to be a Howard and never getting it right?

Harder than it had been for Jones to be a Traveler. At least his family had loved him. The men in the family had taught him how to do everything except abide by the law, and the women had spoiled him. He'd disappointed them, but because of what he wanted, not who he was.

Reece had never been a proper Howard; it wasn't in her. And her grandparents hadn't let her forget it.

Mark's sigh was heavy and resigned. "I just hate…"

To see Miss Willa bury Arthur's wishes with heavy equipment, stonework and an entire nursery full of flowers? Or to see that money leave the family coffers? A bit of both, Jones suspected.

And it was going to be a hell of a lot more than just thousands. Jones didn't work on the budgets—Lori oversaw that—but he could give a ballpark figure for a project of this size. The final number, to do everything Miss Willa wanted, would knock ol' Mark flat.

Though most of Jones's clients rarely got exactly what they initially wanted. Even among the very wealthy, there were usually compromises.

Mark exhaled again. "All right. I'll accept Grandmother's wishes. I don't approve, but as she so succinctly pointed out, it's not my business." He stood, but paused before walking away. "Hey, Clarice, will you tell her I can't make it tonight? Macy's got some kind of mommy's night-out thing tonight, so I've got Clara. Since Grandmother believes small children should be seen and not heard, and Clara insists on being heard all the time, they don't spend much time together."

"I'll let her know."

With a grim nod, he went to the counter, picked up a foam container and left.

"I wondered how Grandmother got along with her great-granddaughter," Reece commented as she settled more comfortably on the bench. "It doesn't surprise me that she doesn't."

"She's not big on displays of affection."

She shook her head. "The first time we visited here, she was waiting for us on the patio. She air-kissed my mother, gave my father a stiff little hug, then looked down her nose at me, told me I was to refer to her as Grandmother—not Grandma, MeMe or anything else—and recited the rules for residence at Fair Winds, however temporary the visit might be. No running, roughhousing, loud play, interrupting, picking at food, raising one's voice, disturbing the adults…"

"So the first thing you did was go inside and shriek, 'Where are the ghosts, Daddy?'"

She smiled, unaccountably pleased that he'd remembered her comment from the morning before. "I can't tell you how many times during that visit he had to say 'She's just a kid' to all of them—Grandmother, Grandfather and even Valerie. And it wasn't an acceptable excuse to any of them."

Jones's features softened, reminding her again of how handsome he was. Watching him sitting there across from Mark, she'd been struck by their differences: total opposites, hard versus soft, tough and indulged, independent and very dependent, easygoing and quick to rile. By Howard standards, Jones was surely nowhere close to Mark's exalted status, but by *this* Howard's standards, he was head and shoulders above.

He was drop-dead-sexy handsome. He loved his dog.

He'd been nothing but friendly to her and respectful to Grandmother. And when he smiled...

He did it now, well aware of her scrutiny and amused by it. "You want to sit here while we wait for the garage to call, or would you prefer to see more of the town?"

"Let's hit the town." Maybe she would see something or someone that would jog loose another memory. And it would be harder for her to stare at him while they were moving.

Though he offered to pay her tab, she did so herself and he let her without arguing. She liked that.

Back outside, they turned west, strolling along the sidewalk toward the river. She gazed at storefronts and into offices, wondering if she'd ever walked this sidewalk before. Had she played in the square or been inside that beautiful house Jones had pointed out? Had she accompanied Grandmother on shopping trips to any of these stores?

The questions made her head hurt. For the thousandth time, she wished she were like most other twenty-eight-year-old women: average, everyday, with total recall of an average life. And for the thousandth time, she reminded herself that she wasn't.

Realizing that they'd covered nearly a block in silence, she grabbed at the nearest sight—twinkling diamonds in a jewelry-store window display. "Are you married?" The minute the question was out, it struck her as odd that she hadn't asked sooner. She'd just assumed he was single. Something about him—she couldn't even say what—gave the impression that he didn't have a wife and kids waiting back in Kentucky for him, that he wasn't missing a part of himself.

Not that all married men missed their wives. But

her father had, and she just had this sense that Jones would, too.

"No. Never have been."

"Why not?"

"Same reason as you. I've never met anyone I'd want to go home to or hate to be away from."

She kept her gaze on the store windows as they walked, too often catching a glimpse of his reflection in the glass. "Do you want to be someday?"

"I always figured I would. Isn't that kind of what we're taught to expect? We grow up, we get married, have kids and grow old." He shrugged, and his shirt rippled in the window glass.

The street they were on ended at River Road. One block to the left was the square; to the right were the types of businesses that seemed to line the main road out of any town. Straight ahead, starting next to the last building, was a park that filled the narrow space between river and road. She headed that way.

As parks went, there was nothing special about Gullah Park: no flower beds or fancy playgrounds. At this point, there wasn't even a parking lot, though a clearing to the north looked as if it might be for that purpose. There was just neatly mown grass, tall live oaks whose massive branches spread in every direction and a paved path for runners. She walked to the edge of the river, lowering herself to a cushion of grass, her toes just inches from the water.

Jones leaned against a tree branch that dipped so low it required man-made support to stop its own weight from crashing it into the river. Hands shoved in his pockets, he watched her.

She watched the lazy current and breathed deeply of the damp, earthy, fishy smell. "Each time we visited

Grandmother, Daddy took me fishing outside the main gate of Fair Winds. He was happier outside than in. We never caught anything—we splashed around too much for that—but it didn't matter. He said fishing wasn't about catching fish. It was about peace and quiet and freedom."

Jones pushed away from the tree and sat beside her. "Trust me, when you're hungry, it's about catching fish."

Resting her arms on her knees, she tilted her head just enough to see his face. "Have you been hungry?"

"A time or two. Not in a lot of years."

She looked back at the river. It stretched half a mile to the western bank, dotted with condos and large houses. There was a bridge to the south, nothing but water and trees to the north, save a boat anchored in the middle. Though a fishing pole was mounted on the side, the fisherman appeared to be snoozing.

"What happened between you and your family?" The words came out so softly, and he remained so still beside her, that she wasn't sure he'd heard. She'd decided she wouldn't repeat the question because it wasn't any of her business when he moved, just the blur of a shrug in her peripheral vision.

"They wanted me to continue with the family tradition, and I wanted something else. Like your dad. He wanted to do something, be something, other than a Howard, like all the men before and after him. Tradition was fine for my grandfathers, my dad, my brothers, but I wanted…more."

"And they've never gotten over it."

"Some things you just don't walk away from."

Family was one of those things. Some people who did it managed to salvage some sort of relationship, but she didn't think her family would. Her grandparents had never forgiven her dad for wanting something else; her grandmother wasn't going to forgive her for cutting them off. And if she was brutally honest, she'd never forgiven Valerie for abandoning her to her grandparents, or her grandparents for the way they'd treated her.

She stared harder at the boat. The man inside was slumped back, a floppy hat shading his face. A red-and-white cooler occupied the other bench, and the same colors bobbed on a plastic float, marking his line in the water. "Do you regret it? Would you go back and change things if you could?"

"I regret a lot," he said evenly, "but no. I wouldn't live the way they'd wanted me to. I couldn't."

What was it they'd wanted of him? Was his family like her grandparents—dedicated to a way of life so superior in their minds that nothing else was acceptable? Had it been a matter of occupation, religion, military service? When people were narrow-minded enough, stubborn enough, the slightest disagreement could become an unbreachable gulf.

"You mentioned brothers. How many?"

A shadow crossed his eyes. "Three brothers, two sisters."

"Wow. And all of them did exactly what was expected of them, which made your rebellion even harder."

"Yeah." He might have gone on, but at that moment, his cell phone went off, a straightforward *ring-ring*.

You could tell a lot from a person's ringtones, she thought, comparing that to the three she heard most often: *"Marie Laveau"* for Evie, *"Witchy Woman"* for Martine and an *uh-oh, trouble* dirge for Valerie.

The call was short, and Jones stood up as he dis-

connected. "That was the garage. The cars are ready."
He extended his hand to her, and she took it without
thought, as if it were the most natural thing in the
world. But what happened next wasn't natural at all.

His hand was warm, the skin calloused. His fingers
closed snugly around hers, sending heat and tingles and
something that felt very much like *life* seeping upward,
through her hand, along her arm, into her chest. The
sensation was both relaxing and disturbing, but in a
thoroughly pleasant way. Awareness. Connection. Intimacy.

And he felt it, too. It was in his startled gaze, in the
way his breath hitched. He stared at her, and she stared
back, surprised, anticipating...*something.*

Moment after moment they remained that way:
him standing, her sitting, hands clasped, gazes locked,
barely breathing. Slowly his muscles flexed, and her
body responded. He pulled her to her feet, so they
stood toe to toe, still staring. His scent blocked the
river's as she breathed hesitantly, then deeper, filling her lungs with his warm, steamy fragrance. She
couldn't say whether she leaned toward him deliberately or if it was primal attraction.

She *could* say that it took all her strength to stop, no
more than a fragment of space separating her mouth
from his. He raised his free hand, his fingertips almost
touching her cheek, but he stopped, too, before making
contact.

And the moment ended. She dropped her gaze, backing away, and he lowered his hand, also backing off.
When their intertwined hands tugged, he hastily let
go, flexed his fingers, then shoved both hands into his
pockets again. "We, uh..."

Her head bobbed like the fisherman's float on the river. "Yes, we should."

"I, uh…"

"Yeah, me, too."

They walked from the river to the garage in silence. Even that wasn't uncomfortable. When was the last time she'd walked three or four blocks with a man in complete silence without casting about almost feverishly for something to say? Never.

But she didn't need to say anything to Jones. She had plenty to think about, plenty to just feel…satisfied and curious about. That moment, that touch…and it had been a *touch* of far more than just hand on hand. It had been important. Intimate. So full of potential. Not once had her brain whispered a warning, a reminder that she couldn't get involved, that she needed answers before she could go blithely trusting anyone.

All true—at least, in the past. Still true now, except that something basic inside her, maybe the very core where her emotions lived, wasn't showing much interest in listening this time.

When they reached the garage, both their vehicles were parked to the side, with the same old tires, newly refilled with air. They paid the bills, then Jones walked to her SUV with her.

"Are you headed back to Fair Winds?"

"I'm going to drive around a little bit. See some of the places Grandmother says we used to go."

"Since you're not going home yet, I've got a couple things to take care of. If you get home before Miss Willa—" he headed around the SUV to his own truck, then looked back at her "—be careful."

Chapter 7

Jones waited in his truck until Reece had turned east out of the parking lot, then he headed south, his destination the biggest nursery in Copper Lake. He wanted to check the quality of the plants, get a feel for the operation. Miss Willa had stressed that she wanted him to buy locally wherever possible, and to hire locally, as well. Part of the Howard obligation to the community, he supposed.

The plant farm was just the other side of the city-limits sign, spreading along the road for a half mile and farther than that away from it. He pulled into the gravel lot and parked, only then becoming aware of the Jag behind him. He got out of his truck and waited as Mark parked, then climbed out.

"I was on my way back to the office after an appointment when I saw you. I hope you don't mind that I followed you." Mark removed sunglasses that probably cost more than Jones's entire outfit, including his favorite top-quality work boots, and gestured in front of their vehicles. "Can we talk?"

Outdoor tables, chairs and fireplaces were clustered in small groups in the section ahead of them, some on squares of grass, some on tile pavers, some on concrete patios. Mark chose a teak set occupying a tiled area, with a fireplace built of the same stone. The cushions were comfortable, warm from the day's sun, the prices posted excessive. Of course, not many customers could lay the patio and build the fireplace themselves, like Jones could, saving at least half the price.

Mark took a few moments to settle comfortably in the armchair, then he blurted out, "You remember me."

Then Mark remembered, too. It was nice to know that Jones had made such an impression back then. "I do."

"So why did Clarice say she'd never met you before Grandmother introduced you?"

It wasn't Jones's place to answer that question truthfully, especially when he didn't know the truth. Reece's claim of amnesia—real or scam? If it was true, who else knew that was why she returned? Was it a secret? Or had she already told Miss Willa, who probably would pass it on to Mark?

"She prefers Reece."

Mark blinked. "What?"

"She goes by the name of Reece."

"Huh. Can't say I blame her. Macy didn't want to name our daughter Clara, but some version of it— Clara, Claire, Clarice—has been in the Howard family for generations. Macy has called her Clary since she was born. Says it's a much better name."

He was silent a moment, his face softened by mention of his wife and daughter. He might be a Howard, Jones thought, but at least he knew how to show affection. He wasn't the sort who would avoid his own grandbaby because she was too noisy for his tastes.

Then Mark's expression turned puzzled. "So…why did Cla—Reece lie about knowing you?"

Jones could offer any number of answers: *I don't know. Ask her. It's not my place to tell.* But if he gave any of those answers, the next logical action for Mark would to be ask Reece herself.

And when—if—she denied it, his next logical statement: *You hung out with him and his brother for weeks that summer. They rescued you when you almost drowned in the creek. How could you have forgotten them?*

And if he was being really truthful: *I was the one who almost drowned you. His brother took care of you, and Jones damn near drowned me before he finished punching me.*

Then he'd threatened them. Jones had left town, and Glen had disappeared.

If Reece truly didn't remember, Jones would prefer to keep himself in that black hole of traumatic forgetfulness. No matter what the reason for his deception, she had some deep trust issues. She wouldn't take it well.

The last thing he wanted was Mark tattling around Fair Winds about Jones's presence on the farm fifteen years ago. Who knew how Reece would react? Worse, who knew how Miss Willa might react? And since Reece hadn't asked him to keep it between them…

He shrugged. "From what I understand, she doesn't remember much about that summer. Losing her father that way…" *To say nothing of being abandoned, end-*

*lessly criticized, tormented, possibly molested and
almost killed.* She had plenty of reasons for forgetting.

Mark stared. Counting his blessings? Thinking that
was one less thing he needed to apologize for? Wondering if Jones himself was the real threat here, and not
the garden project he was starting?

"And you haven't told her?" He sounded part dismayed, part satisfied.

Jones shook his head. She deserved answers, but he'd
come here for his own answers. Her remembering the
details of an ugly summer just didn't stack up against
his finding out what happened to his brother. How he
died. Where he was buried. Why.

Whether it was his fault.

Keeping his gaze focused on Mark, he said, "I'm
more interested in finding out about Glen."

"Glen…the other boy." Mark sounded fuzzier in his
recollection of Glen. Of course, the three of them had
only had that one run-in, and Glen hadn't bloodied his
knuckles on Mark. He'd been on the sidelines calming
a hysterical Reece.

"He left that day, didn't he?" Mark asked. "I never
saw him again."

"Neither did I," Jones said flatly.

"I never knew his name." Sheepishness crept into his
face. "Never knew yours, either, until Grandmother told
me she'd hired you and then I saw you this morning."

Mark murmured the name again, frowning, then
shook his head. "All that talk about telling Grandfather
and him calling the sheriff… I never did. I was just…
embarrassed and upset. I'd never meant to hurt Cla—
Reece. I was just messing with her—I always messed
with her—and suddenly there you were and things got
out of control. I *never* would have hurt her."

An explanation with more than a little finger-pointing. Jones called the memory to mind: him and Glen on the way to the pool, where Glen was meeting Reece while Jones went on to the river to fish. Hearing splashes, cries, agitated enough that they'd broken into a run. Seeing Reece in the water, her cousin's hands on her shoulders, pushing her down while she clawed her way up, shrieked, then went under again. Mark wearing a look Jones had never seen on anyone—fierce, angry, driven.

He and Glen had both jumped into the water, Jones grabbing Mark under the arms and jerking him away while Glen pulled Reece up sputtering and half dragged, half carried her out of the water. His victim gone, Mark had turned on Jones, landing several punches before Jones subdued him, then dragged him out a safe distance from Glen and Reece.

Mark had been spitting mad, livid at their interference, then abruptly, the viciousness disappeared and the anger became that of a boy, all but swallowed up in fear at the magnitude of what he'd done.

Things had been way out of control before Jones and Glen had arrived, but if that was what Mark needed to tell himself to live with his memories…

"I kept waiting on her to tell Grandmother," Mark went on. "I couldn't eat or sleep, and I kept my distance from her as much as I could. She never said anything, but she never trusted me again." Then he scoffed at himself. "She never trusted me before that. I'd been spending summers with our grandparents since I was five years old. It was *my* time, and I *hated* having to share them with her. It sounds selfish, but I didn't know her dad, so it's not like his death should have ruined my whole summer. I was such a jerk."

Jones didn't bother agreeing with that. "When did her mother come back?"

"A couple days later. She just showed up, no phone call, no nothing, and had the housekeeper pack Reece's stuff. As soon as Inez was done, they left. We never saw Reece again until now."

"Where had she been?"

"Aunt Valerie? Supposedly taking care of business, then vacationing, but..." Mark's mouth thinned, then he went on. "My father and his brother weren't close, and my mother never did care much for Aunt Valerie. I heard her tell Father once that she thought Valerie's vacation had been more of the very discreet rehabilitative kind than the spas-and-fun kind."

Jones considered that: a less-than-responsible woman, based on Reece's comments, suddenly widowed, finding it difficult to cope, especially when her mother-in-law and the housekeeper were there to take care of her child. Needing a little help to get to sleep and a little something to keep her steady when she was awake, to keep the enormity of her loss at bay. How easy it would have been to rely too much on pills prescribed by a helpful doctor and/or liquor that was readily obtained, to the point that rehab quickly became a very real necessity.

That would explain why no one had told Reece the truth. If Valerie had deteriorated that quickly, she wouldn't have wanted her daughter to know—*still* didn't want her daughter to know. And Miss Willa couldn't fudge and tell Reece her mother was sick and needed hospital care; that would have terrified a kid whose father had just died. Miss Willa was of an era where family secrets *were* secrets. She hadn't consid-

ered the psychological damage to Reece, believing she'd
been abandoned by her only parent.

Mark glanced at his watch before rising. "I'd better
get back to the office before my assistant—" His cell
phone interrupted his words. He glanced at it, muted it
and returned it to his pocket. "Your friend, Glen…you
think he might have stayed around here? Is that why
you took this job?"

"One of the reasons." Jones stood, too. "I'm pretty
sure he never left the area."

There was no significant change to Mark's expression. No worry, fear, anxiety. The possibility apparently
meant nothing to him. "I came back every summer
until college, but I pretty much kept to Fair Winds. I
wanted to spend as much time with Grandmother and
Grandfather as I could. But if he's in Copper Lake, he
shouldn't be hard to find. Just ask around."

The cell phone rang again, and he frowned. "I've got
to go. Thanks for your time."

Jones watched him leave, then headed away from the
furniture and into the broad aisles flanked by shrubs,
containers in trees and flowers. He'd always given himself credit for good instincts; all Travelers, especially
the men, relied on them. But his seemed more than a
little dull this afternoon.

Did he believe that Reece really had amnesia from
that summer? Maybe. Had the scene in the creek really
been horseplay that got out of control? Stranger things
had happened. Was Mark really a changed man? Who
knew what a man was really like inside?

But he couldn't quite shake the memory of that look
in Mark's eyes. The same cold look in the pictures
Jones had seen of Arthur Howard.

Being surrounded by plants usually put him on an

even keel. He liked the smells—flowers, earth, fertilizers. They spoke of potential, beauty and the cycle of life. He could plant a garden now that, with a little care, would still thrive long after he was dead, or trees that would still grow strong and straight long after his great-grandchildren had died. He could leave a mark.

But today he wasn't finding much of a sense of balance. The back of his neck itched, and an unsettled feeling kept slithering up and down his spine. An unknown person—or ghost—had let the air out of eight tires. A ghost had moved the family-history book—significant in itself?—and left a message on Reece's mirror.

Mischief? Warning? Threat?

If you have any trouble with the ghosts when you start digging up the yard...

Grandfather screamed *at me to get back in the house...*

And the echo of words Jones had used himself a few moments ago: *family secrets.*

Doing a 180, he headed back toward the parking lot. He could check out the nursery tomorrow. Right now he felt the need to return to Fair Winds.

And Reece.

Twenty minutes of driving around town gave Reece a good visual of Copper Lake. She located the hospital, the shopping mall, schools and probably most of the churches—and bars—in town. She even found the Howard church, recognizable from the huge addition fifty years ago paid for by and named in honor of the family.

She parked across the street from the church and sat on a bench that fronted a well-kept cemetery. Generations of Howards had attended the church, including her father—although not Grandfather. But there was no reminder of them in the marble and granite markers spread across the ground. All Howards were buried in the family plot at Fair Winds.

Except for her dad.

"I would have thought if you took the time to visit a cemetery, it would be the one where your own family is located, to say nothing of changing into appropriate attire before the visit."

Reece refused to feel guilty about her Hawaiian shirt and jeans, but when she lifted her gaze to Grandmother, she found herself automatically straightening her spine and shoulders as if she were dressed in her finest clothing.

"Of course, even if you did visit the family cemetery, you wouldn't find anything of your father beyond a marker, thanks to your mother."

Ghosts rarely haunt cemeteries, Jones had said, but attached to people or places important in their lives. Fair Winds hadn't been important to Elliott in his life, so it didn't matter in his death.

"Valerie carried out Daddy's wishes."

Grandmother *humph*ed. "Cremation, then scattering his ashes in *Colorado*... Never in the history of the Howard family—"

"It was what he wanted."

Reece's interruption earned her a tight-jawed look. "Death rituals are for the living, not the dead. It didn't really matter what he wanted."

That certainly explained Grandmother's refusal to be swayed on the garden project by Mark's insistence that it went against Grandfather's wishes.

Or maybe she'd just spent so many years giving in

to Grandfather's wishes that she'd decided it was time
for her own wishes to matter.

She seated herself on the bench, facing the opposite
direction. "Why are you here?"

"I came to look at the church."

"So you're sitting with your back to it."

Reece started to swing one leg to straddle the bench,
decided against the criticism sure to follow and stood
to turn around properly. "I remember it a little." Stiff
dresses, shoes that pinched her toes, best behavior, a
little white leather-bound Bible with her name engraved
in gold.

She couldn't recall ever seeing the Bible again after
that summer.

Granted, she'd never gone to church again, either.
Valerie had liked sleeping in on Sundays.

"Your father's memorial service was held here. Can't
rightly call it a funeral without a body, not even ashes."
Grandmother scowled at the steeple atop the church.
"Cecil's funeral was held here, also, as well as your
grandfather's. If you'd like to visit their graves, you
know where the family plot is."

Reece didn't admit to her visit with Jones the day
before. She certainly didn't admit that her only interest in Grandfather's grave was making certain he was
in it.

Abruptly, Grandmother stood, more energetically
and gracefully than most women half her age. "It's time
to go. Come along. You can follow me home."

Reece considered refusing just to be difficult, but
what was the point? She'd seen everything she wanted
in town, anyway, finding few memories of any substance, and all of them from her first month there.

The answers to that summer were at Fair Winds, with Grandmother, Mark, maybe even with the ghosts.

She stayed a comfortable distance from the Cadillac on the short drive home, then pulled into her usual space while Grandmother parked right beside the patio. Jones's truck wasn't in sight, but clearly he was home, since Mick lay curled on a sunny spot of patio, the warm stones of the fountain at his back. He opened one eye to identify the newcomers, then closed it again, unconcerned.

"You there," Grandmother said, opening the Cadillac's trunk as Reece crossed the road. "You can unload these flats."

Reece blinked, never having been referred to as *you there* by the oh-so-proper matriarch of the Howard family, then by the reference to flats. Had one or more of her tires been vandalized, as well?

Then Jones stood up in a shady spot of the patio, laying aside a laptop, and Reece saw the contents of the trunk: flats of pansies in yellow and blue, the shades ranging from palest pastel to vibrant, deep hues. The trunk was full, and a glimpse showed the backseat was, as well. Had pansies had a place in the Fair Winds gardens of old, or was Grandmother planning her own touches?

If so, Jones didn't seem to mind as he lifted the first box out. "Beautiful. Good, healthy plants."

"The garden society sells them as a fundraiser. Of course they're beautiful and healthy."

The snippiness in her voice didn't seem to bother him at all as he carried the flat to a protected corner of the patio. Reece watched him walk away, the light load no strain on his muscles, the long steps no strain, either, on his long, lean legs. When he turned but before he caught her watching him—she hoped—she shifted her purse under one arm and bent to pick up one of the flats herself.

Grandmother stood in her way. "Really, Clarice. Let the people who are paid to do the dirty work do it."

Some little devil made her imitate the tone. "Really, Grandmother. People who belong to garden societies tend to get their hands dirty in the garden. And you know what?" She leaned closer, lowering her voice. "It washes off."

Sidestepping Grandmother and Jones, whose grin disappeared before the old lady could see it, she deposited the flat beside the first, laid her purse on a table and came back for another.

Disapproving, Grandmother stood by and watched as they completed the unloading. "The beds nearest the front porch were always planted with pansies in the fall," she announced. "I realize it will be a long time before the entire garden is completed, but I'd like those beds done now. As I'm sure everyone's realized, I may not live to see the final results, but I will have flowers in this yard for at least one season."

She unlocked the door, then came back around the fountain, giving Mick an irritated look before pressing the keys into Jones's palm. "Return the car to the garage—the code is the same as the gate—then send the keys back to me with my granddaughter."

Reece might have been embarrassed by Grandmother's imperiousness if she hadn't become used to it so long ago. It was part of the Howard superiority over everyone else. Daddy hadn't had a drop of it in him and hadn't tolerated it from Valerie, either, but after his death, Valerie had proven almost as adept at it as Grandmother.

"Want to ride along?" Jones asked as he opened the driver's door with a sweeping gesture.

She didn't want to climb into the Cadillac where, unseen by their grandmother, Mark had so often pinched and poked at her, and she really didn't want to go to the garage. But she agreed, anyway, sliding underneath the steering wheel and across the bench seat to the passenger side. Jones was just a breath behind her, filling the space with broad shoulders and adding his scents of sun and cologne to the aroma of fresh earth and plants.

The drive took all of thirty seconds. Jones pressed the electronic opener clipped to the visor, and the door lifted with a slow creak. The lightbulb overhead provided just enough illumination to make the space shadowy, cavelike, creepy. Goose bumps raised along her arms, and she suppressed a shiver by keeping her gaze firmly settled on Jones's hands. Grandfather was dead. She wasn't thirteen. She could handle this.

Especially with Jones an arm's length away.

He eased the Cadillac into the space, squarely in the center. When he shut off the engine, the silence was overwhelming, the structure shadowier, creepier. Her mind's eye saw that old pickup, Grandfather and Mark, the truck bed holding clods of dirt, something wet—oil?—and a tarp-covered lump. And, in a voice as real as her own, she heard Grandfather's roar: *Get back in the house* now!

Chest tightening as it had that day, she fumbled with the door, then, too clumsy, she scrambled across the seat and climbed out the driver's side so fast that she slammed into Jones's solid back.

The impact knocked him a step off balance, but he recovered and reached back, taking hold of her arm,

steadying her beside him. "You in that big a hurry—"
His tone was light, to match his expression, until his
gaze connected with hers. She must have looked as pan-
icky as she felt, because his expression sombered and
he led her out into the warm afternoon sunshine, not
stopping until twenty feet of gravel and grass separated
them from the garage.

"Are you okay?"

She nodded, not yet trusting her voice.

He studied her a moment longer, then asked, "You
want to let go of me, or would you rather wait a minute?"

For the first time she realized her hands were
clenched around his arm, her fingertips whitened from
pressure. She tried to let go, tried to smile, to shake off
the reaction, but all she managed was a faint whim-
per. That was enough to bring him closer, his free arm
wrapping around her, pulling her until her body was
snug against his, his voice a quiet murmur above her
ear. *It's okay. I've got you. It's okay.*

Heat seeped into her, and security and comfort. After
a moment, the shudders faded, leaving her muscles tight
and exhausted. The chill faded, too, and the echoes of
Grandfather's shout. Her pounding heart slowed, her
legs steadied, her fingers unclasped and she thought
inanely how different a nightmare was, even a waking
one, when you had somebody to hold you and chase it
away. After her father died, she'd never had anyone…
until now. Until Jones.

She looked up at him and found him staring back,
concern making his already dark eyes even more so.
His other arm now loosed of her grip, he raised his
hand, brushing one finger over her face, fluttering her

eyes shut, skimming her cheek, feathering over her lips, as if he were wiping away the fright.

Then he bent closer still and kissed her. It wasn't the hottest kiss she'd ever had, or the hungriest or the sweetest, but it was the best, because she needed it, and he knew it.

After a long, gentle moment, he raised his mouth, his forehead resting against hers. "Better now?" Soft words, tender.

This time she managed a real smile, if somewhat shaky…though this time, the shakiness was from the kiss, the taste and feel of him, rather than fear. "I am."

Then *she* kissed *him*. She didn't warn herself off, didn't tell herself that this was a bad time and a worse place for any kind of intimacy. She didn't let herself think at all.

She just acted.

And he *re*acted.

Jones was no idiot. He knew it was possible for a kiss to go from nothing to burning-hot-need-to-get-naked in half a second, but he still wasn't prepared for it. Hell, he hadn't been ready for Reece to initiate a kiss at all. She'd needed calming, and that was what he'd offered: a hug and a nothing little kiss to settle her fears.

And now he was combusting from the outside in. His tongue was in her mouth, his erection pressed against her, his hands cupping her face while her hands roamed all over him. His blood pumped hot, fire licking along his veins, his only thought *now!* and his only need privacy. The cottage was closest and his befuddled brain was trying to direct his body that way, without losing contact with her body, when some small, still-functioning part of his brain spoke up.

"Miss Willa," he mumbled against Reece's mouth, trying as he spoke to put some space between them. It was hard when he didn't really want that space, and neither did she, judging by the way she clung to him.

His words, though, did the trick. Her hands still on his chest, one beneath his shirt, she drew back enough to focus her gaze on him. "When a man brings up my grandmother while I'm trying to kiss him senseless, I'm obviously not doing it right." Her voice was husky, tinged with amusement and tempered with impatience.

"I passed senseless a while ago." He tried for a rueful grin and thought he succeeded with the rueful part. "We're not exactly being discreet, and your grand-mother would give you hell for dallying with the hired help."

She looked at the house, where rows of windows stared down on them. Jones hadn't been inside yet, but he'd guess they could be seen there beside the driveway from at least two-thirds of the structure.

"She's given me hell plenty of times before," Reece said, taking a step back, then another. "It wouldn't be anything new. But she wouldn't fire you for dallying with her granddaughter."

The thought hadn't occurred to him. Once voiced, it gave him a moment's thought: leaving Fair Winds knowing no more about Glen than when he'd come.

But Reece was right, and it showed in her smile. "It'd be easier to send *me* away than to find another big-name landscape architect to handle her project." There was only the slightest hint of self-pity in her voice before she went on. "A name that I think, after getting more intimately acquainted, I should know."

He left her a moment to return to the garage and

close the door, then came back, took her hand in his and started toward the house. "You know my name."

"Jones. No *Mister.* Just Jones." She gave him a wicked sidelong glance. "Don't tell me your first name is Justin. Or Justice."

"Nope. Though that wouldn't be so bad."

She laughed at the idea of something worse than Justice Jones. "I don't even know whether Jones is your first or last name."

She'd asked him that twice, fifteen years apart. The first time he'd always been on the lookout for trouble, and never giving anyone his full name, or sometimes even his own name, had been one safety measure. The second time he'd thought she knew who he was.

Now he believed she didn't. He'd been wavering on the subject of her self-claimed amnesia, but at that moment he admitted he believed her. And she was right; after that, uh, intimacy, she deserved to know that much.

"It's my last name. My first name is between me, my lawyers, my accountant and my mother. Everyone else in the world just calls me Jones."

"Even your girlfriends?"

"When I have one."

"Do they get tired of waiting for you back there in Kentucky while you travel all over working?"

As they got closer to the house, he released her hand and, in silent agreement, they put a few extra inches between them. "You're assuming they all break up with me. That's not always the case. Besides, long-distance relationships aren't so tough anymore, not with the internet, smartphones and the money to make regular visits."

"Yeah, it worked for your grandparents and parents."

"And without the internet, smartphones or airlines."

"Is that what you want? A long-distance relationship? To always be saying goodbye, sleeping alone, waiting for the next visit? Putting business first, wife and kids last?" Scrunching her face into a frown, she shook her head. "You're no romantic, Jones."

Now it was him laughing. He'd learned all the gestures—the fancy restaurants, the flowers, the extravagant gifts, the celebrations for no reason. He could romance a woman with the best of them. It wasn't his idea of fun, but if it was what a woman wanted, and if he wanted her, he could do it.

He didn't think the gestures were what Reece wanted at all. Just genuine emotion. Knowing she was important and being shown in the ways that really mattered—the little ways. A massage. A shoulder to lean on when she was upset. A voice to ease the fear. Loving her dogs unconditionally.

Oh, yeah, and being there every night at bedtime.

"First, I'm talking about just a relationship at the moment, not marriage. And second, it's not ideal, but life usually isn't. Ideally, I'd want a wife who shared my interest in the business, who would travel and work with me. And ideally by the time we had kids, the business would be at a point where I could just run it and let other people do the traveling."

"If you're known well enough in this business to impress Grandmother, then you're in that position now," Reece pointed out as they reached the patio.

"I am," he admitted, then parroted her own words back to her. "I've never met a woman I'd remotely consider tying myself to. At least…not yet."

Their gazes locked, and again there was heat, need, hunger. It was sexual tension, he told himself. Lust.

Any man in the world who'd just shared that kiss with her, whose nerves were still humming with little electric shocks, would feel the same way.

It didn't mean she could be that woman. It didn't mean they could share any sort of relationship beyond a temporary one. It didn't mean she felt or wanted the same thing.

It didn't mean a damn thing at all except that he was in sorry shape.

"I—I'd better get the keys back to Grandmother." Reece's voice was unsteady again, just a little quaver that hinted of her physical response.

"I'd better start on the front bed." He handed her the keys and watched her go to the door. There she turned back to watch him until finally he forced himself to move.

Pansies. Flower beds. Mulch. Soil. Edging. Hard work.

Exactly what he needed.

Chapter 8

The clock in the hall chimed four o'clock, drawing Reece's gaze from the book. Grandmother was resting, something she'd done every afternoon as far back as Reece could remember, and the house was particularly quiet with the housekeeper gone.

Quiet didn't apply to outdoors, though. Shortly after she'd come inside, Jones had driven past on his way out. An hour later, he'd returned, parking the truck in the middle of the driveway about even with the porch. Yes, she'd gone into Grandmother's study to peek through the lace curtains. Behind him was another truck, bigger, loaded with pallets of brick and mulch, bags of concrete mix and some type of equipment. He and the driver had unloaded, shaken hands, then the truck left and Jones turned to the front yard.

The equipment—a tiller, she guessed, not that she'd ever had the opportunity to need one—was noisy and distracted her from her reading. She'd finished four chapters of *Southern Aristocracy* without remembering a word.

Now she closed the book and sighed loudly. It echoed in the salon, as if a dozen souls joined in. Setting the book aside, she stood and stretched, looked around as if seeking something else to do, then gave up the pretense and went into the hall. A slight hum from the refrigerator, the swish of paddle fans in the salon and Grandmother's study, the smells of wood polish and age and... Her nose twitched as she looked toward the front hall. She took a few steps toward the heavy closed door and sniffed again.

It was cigar smoke. Not the stale decades' worth of smoke Grandfather's study had seen, but fresh, almost sweet. She imagined as she stared at the door that she could even see the faint curl as the smoke escaped the room.

She took a few more steps, reaching the door in fits and starts. For a time she just looked, aware that everything in her had gone cold. The smoke was definitely seeping under the door in delicate wisps as if drawn out by an invisible vacuum.

Fingers trembling, she touched the door, solid ancient wood, neither warm nor cold, just a door. Slowly she slid her hand down and to the right, until her fingers brushed the intricate brass knob that the sea captain Howard had brought from India. She could turn it. Open the door. Go inside. Satisfy her curiosity that Grandfather assuredly wasn't there.

Meow.

She jerked her hand away, strode to the front door and clumsily undid the locks, stumbling in her haste to get out of the house.

Busy with the tiller, Jones didn't notice her less-than-graceful exit, giving her a chance to study him. He'd removed his shirt and tossed it onto the porch. Sweat sheened on his back, rippling as he worked the tiller in a north/south line, amending the beds he'd already tilled. His skin was brown, a deep tan adding to the rich olive hue he came by naturally, and muscles defined the long bare expanse, disappearing into the sweat-soaked waistband of his shorts. Her breath coming more shallowly, she raised her gaze up again, to where his dark hair curled wetly against his neck.

She saw handsome men every day in New Orleans. She saw handsome men half-dressed and sweaty every day, and while she always appreciated them, she didn't grow short of breath looking at them. Her fingers didn't itch to touch them, to feel the heat radiating from them, to comb through their damp hair. For heaven's sake, she was a twenty-eight-year-old woman, not a fifteen-year-old girl.

Sudden silence made her realize he'd seen her and shut off the machine. She strolled down the steps, absently counting *one, two, three, four,* then stopped at the bottom. "Marvin?"

Removing the ear cups that protected his ears from the tiller's noise, he quirked one brow.

"Is that your name?"

"Nope. But I have an uncle Marvin."

"Leonard?"

"Nope. He's my cousin."

"Homer?"

Grinning, he shook his head. "That's my grandpa."

"You're kidding."

"Nope. And my other grandfather's name is Cleland. I come from more Joneses than a census taker could count. Name a name, and I've probably got a relative who answers to it." He wheeled the tiller off to one side, then swiped his face on a bandanna he pulled from his hip pocket. "What do you think?"

She walked out into the grass to get the full effect of the new beds. There was one on each side of the steps, blocky, their straight lines broken only by diamond points in the center of each bed. The freshly tilled earth smelled rich and lush, an intoxicating fragrance, like the first whiff of coffee early in the morning. Again, she felt a yearning to dig her hands into the soil, grind it into the knees of her jeans, cake it under her nails. Which would just earn her more disapproval from Grandmother.

"I like the points."

"Every bed had them originally, except in the shade garden, which really didn't have any beds at all. Things just grew kind of wild."

"When do the brick people come?"

His grin was way too charming to leave any female unaffected, whether she was fifteen or fifty-five. "You're looking at him."

"You're just a master of all trades, aren't you?"

"When you work with different tradesmen on every job, it helps to know the job yourself. You want to help?" When she arched her own brow, he said, "I saw the gleam in your eye when you saw the pansies, and then when you got your first whiff of soil. Miss Willa and Valerie might not like getting their hands dirty, but there's a gardener inside you."

She didn't bother telling him that any gleam in her eyes lately had been inspired by *him*. Her kiss earlier had gotten that message across clearly. "I'll go change."

She jogged up the steps and went inside, nudging

the door shut behind her. As if yanked from her hand, it slammed, echoing through the house, and a puff of cigar smoke billowed around her.

Go away.

For a moment, she froze, then remembered Jones just outside. Batting at the smoke, she started up the stairs, but the words echoed again as she reached the top and an extraordinarily icy patch of air. "You go away," she whispered with a glance toward Grandmother's closed door.

Inside her room she started to strip off her jeans, hesitated, then grabbed the clothes she wanted and stepped behind the changing screen in the corner. She didn't want to be ogled by any ghost, but especially a smelly, bossy one who was likely related to her.

She'd replaced jeans with comfortable cotton shorts and was unbuttoning her shirt when a squeak came from the other side of the screen. Part of her job at Martine's shop included cleaning glass display cases. She knew the sound of moisture on glass.

Sticking her head around the screen, she watched an unseen finger write on the mirror, the words appearing slowly.

You may not live to regret the answers.

"Are you *threatening* me?"

The first message faded, then what sounded like a sigh—and smelled of tobacco—shivered cold air through the room. "Go home. Forget that summer."

These words were as clear as her own, the voice as curt and ominous in death as it had been in life. Then, after a long pause, came another word, one she doubted he'd ever said in life, certainly not to the annoying granddaughter who'd disrupted his home for four months.

"Please."

Slowly she withdrew behind the screen again, though she was certain Grandfather was gone. She removed her shirt and tugged a T-shirt over her head. *Welcome to New Orleans,* it read over a picture of Jackson Square. *Now go home.* The words struck her as…ironic? Prophetic?

With flip-flops and a ballcap to shade her eyes, she returned to the front yard without incident.

Her part of the work was easy. Jones prepared the base for the brick retaining wall that would enclose the garden while she followed his directions. They talked about inconsequential things, the topics two new co-workers might discuss…or a couple on their first date.

And this—helping to build a brick wall, albeit minimally—was more fun than any first date she'd ever been on.

He explained to her that each row of bricks was called a course, and showed her how to be sure the courses were level, how to slather mortar onto the bricks and position each one. She even laid a few herself, using his gloves that were too big and were damp from his own hands, because Portland cement was harsh on the skin.

They were taking a break, sitting in the shade cast by a majestic live oak and drinking bottles of cold water that he'd retrieved from an ice chest in the pickup bed, and she was thinking how out of shape she was for physical labor, when the front door silently swung open. Ghost or Grandmother? she wondered, then Grandmother stepped out onto the porch. Her gaze flickered over Reece, her mouth tightening, then she took in the progress Jones had made.

"You'll be ready to plant soon."

"Yes, ma'am."

She looked again, then made eye contact with Reece. "Supper is in fifteen minutes. If you delay, the leftovers will be in the refrigerator, and you will clean up after yourself."

"Yes, ma'am," Reece echoed Jones. As the door closed, she wrapped her arms around her knees, resting her chin. "Do you suppose she cleans up after herself on Lois's days off?"

"I imagine not. Though she's probably very neat by nature."

"You'd think I'm some sort of slob, the way she acts, but I'm not. Except for the clothes I left on the floor when I changed, but that wasn't my fault." She told him about Grandfather's visit.

When she was done, he gazed thoughtfully into the distance. "Have you considered taking his advice?"

"And going home? No. I came here to find out what happened that summer."

"Sounds like he wants his family secrets to stay secret." Jones stretched out his legs, leaning back on his elbows, and studied her. "What's the worst case? You remember a little less of your childhood than most people do."

"I have nightmares."

"Take sleeping pills. See a therapist."

She scowled at him. "I *want* to know."

"There's a reason your brain blocked it out to start with. You couldn't handle it."

"I was thirteen. I can handle anything now."

He tilted his head to one side, studying her before quietly asking, "Are you sure? Have you considered all the possible reasons you blocked it? Maybe you were attacked that summer. Or molested. Maybe you witnessed something."

"Like what?" Her voice didn't sound like the voice of a woman who could handle anything, she noticed, and clamped her jaws shut.

Jones shrugged. "An attack on someone else. A death. A murder." Another shrug.

She swallowed hard, wanting to protest that none of those things could possibly have happened. Something that significant would stand out in her memory, not disappear into blackness. She would have remembered.

But that was the point. She couldn't *remember*.

And if the event *had* involved an attack, molestation or someone else's death, was she sure she *wanted* to?

Yes. Knowing was better than not knowing. She could always deal with knowing, with the help of time, friends and maybe a therapist. But not knowing…for fifteen years, not knowing had been the worst thing in her life.

Very quietly she repeated, "I *want* to know."

Jones understood. Hell, he felt the same way about Glen. He needed to know what had happened to his brother. But he couldn't help but think he was better able to handle his own nightmare than Reece was hers. Which didn't make any sense. Neither of them had family to turn to for support, but at least she had a couple of best friends. He had a lot of buddies, but no one that close. And though she might not look it, she was tough. Coming back here proved it.

They worked until the sun was low in the sky. As they cleaned up, he caught her grimacing with the discomfort of muscles unaccustomed to his kind of work.

"You want to take a shower and ride into town with me for a burger?"

That wasn't at all what he wanted to offer, he realized the instant she turned toward him. The shower part, okay. They were both caked with sweat, dirt and cement dust, and he knew from long experience that he smelled about as bad as he looked.

But he didn't want to go into town. He didn't want a burger. He didn't even want to get dressed after the shower. And he wanted to take that together.

She removed the ballcap and ran her fingers through her damp hair. "I suppose I should eat whatever Lois prepared for Grandmother." A light flickered on, the dim illumination of a pole-mounted lamp above the driveway. She looked up, appearing to listen to its hum for a moment, then smiled. "I'll meet you on the patio as soon as I'm clean."

He watched her go into the house, and continued to watch for a while before a breeze stirred that brought his attention back. He gave the area around him an exasperated look. "If ol' Arthur can hang around and pass on messages, why can't you, Glen?"

There was no answer, no sight or sound out of place.

"You always did like to make me work for stuff." Giving a whistle for Mick, he headed for the cottage. The dog joined him from the spot where he'd been sleeping on the patio, trotted inside the house and climbed onto the sofa, settling in comfortably.

Jones was quick at showering and dressing. With five brothers and sisters, he'd had to be. He put out fresh water and food for the dog, then walked to the door. Mick followed him with a mournful whine. Jones told him no, told him that he was just taking Reece out for a burger. Whether it was the mention of Reece or the burger that excited the mutt, he wasn't sure, but some-how when he locked up and walked back to the house, the dog was beside him.

The only lights visible in the big house came from the downstairs hallway and Reece's front upstairs bed-room. Either Miss Willa's room was on the other side of the house, or she went to bed awfully early.

Before he reached the table that was his destination, the side door opened and Reece came out. She was dressed like him—jeans, T-shirt—and her hair, like his, was still damp. If she'd put on makeup, he couldn't tell—which was the point of makeup, his older sister had once told him. Though both his sisters had worn a lot of it, and his nieces, if he had any, had likely dipped into their mothers' cosmetics—and fashion style—about the time they started kindergarten.

One of the traditions he'd been happy to leave be-hind.

"Is your grandmother settled for the night?"

"She's in her room with the door closed. One of the first lessons I learned here was that meant leave her alone." Her smile was faint. "I left a note for her."

For the first time in Jones's memory, Mick will-ingly gave up the front passenger seat for someone else, jumping over the console to the rear seat, then sitting with his chin on the seat's back so Reece could scratch him. He thought of their conversation about relation-ships, when he'd silently listed what she was looking for: *loving her dogs unconditionally.*

He had to admit, he was pretty much a sucker for someone who treated Mick the way she did.

Instead of a hamburger joint, they wound up at a table on a small brick patio outside Ellie's Deli, where a friendly waitress named Gina supplied Mick with a chew toy and a bowl of water. She asked for their drinks, and Jones ordered a beer, Reece iced tea. When Gina returned with the drinks and took their dinner orders—they both got burgers, after all—he picked up the icy bottle and studied it a moment.

All afternoon he'd been wondering when to tell her what he'd learned from Mark. Well, not all afternoon, he corrected himself as he watched her lay the straw aside and lift the glass of tea to her lips, drinking long and slow. He'd spent a good part of it wondering when they would get to finish that kiss, because it wasn't done, not by a long shot.

But the conversation with Mark had been in the back of his mind, stewing there behind the lust and need. It wouldn't give her all the answers she wanted, and it was only gossip stirred by someone with a dislike for the subject, but Reece had a right to hear it. It was up to her what to do with it.

He gestured with his beer bottle to her iced tea. "Do you drink?"

"Not really."

"Is that on moral, religious or medical grounds?"

She shook her head. "My parents drank wine every evening and always celebrated special events with champagne. Grandmother liked wine with meals, too, while Grandfather drank good ol' Kentucky bourbon. The evening glasses of wine stopped for Valerie after my dad died. I guess it reminded her too much of him, that it was something they'd shared. I tried booze a few times, as most kids do in their teens, but I never liked the taste of it."

Jones watched a black Charger cruise past, then pull into the last parking space before River Road. Tommy Maricci got out, and Jones's nerves tightened. *I'll be in touch,* Maricci had told him. Was that his reason for stopping?

The detective walked up the sidewalk, giving them a polite nod as he climbed the steps and went inside. Through the open screen door, Jones saw him greet a pretty blonde with a kiss, then take a dark-haired child from her and give him a hug and a tickle. He was just meeting his wife for dinner. He had no news about Glen.

Jones breathed and refocused on Reece. "I ran into Mark again this afternoon. After we left the tire store."

"Lucky you. Trying to bribe you to leave Copper Lake?"

"No. He, uh, mentioned your mother—how she suddenly came back that summer and took you away. He said it was unexpected. She blew in and blew out with you in tow."

Her expression was thoughtful. "Did he say where she'd been?"

"He'd heard the same explanations you had. But, uh, his mother thought that your mother might have, uh, been…well, in rehab during that time." There. He'd said it. It had been harder than telling a client he was looking at a six-figure overrun. But with Lori keeping a tight control on the budgets, major overruns were almost always the clients' fault, and that was strictly business. He didn't get emotionally attached to clients.

And he was getting emotionally attached to Reece.

Reece's expression shifted—surprise? Understanding? Acceptance? "Rehab… That would explain…"

A lot. Why Valerie had given Reece's care totally over to strangers. Why she'd stopped having those evening glasses of wine. Why she refused to discuss the subject with her daughter all these years later.

"Rehab," she repeated. "She was so distraught about Daddy. You see families on TV, when a loved one dies, and they're sad but composed, dry-eyed, coping. That was Grandmother. She was stoic, like a proper Howard, but not Valerie. She sobbed for days. She was so fragile. The doctor had to sedate her after the ashes-scattering service in Colorado, and she didn't even get out of bed for a week after the memorial service here. She rarely came out of her room for more than a few minutes, and when she did, she was a mess. Rehab makes sense." She nodded slowly as if confirming it to herself.

He reached for her hand, cold and stiff, and folded his fingers around it. "Which means she didn't abandon you. Not intentionally."

She didn't say anything to that—just gazed into the distance—but her fingers tightened just a bit around his. Did hearing her aunt's gossip offer any comfort? Or was abandonment abandonment, no matter what the reason?

She didn't look as if she'd reached a decision on that when Gina brought their food. Squeezing his hand again, she murmured, "Thank you," before sliding her fingers loose and unrolling the linen napkin next to her plate. She didn't say anything else until they were halfway through their meal. "What kind of mother was your mom, other than fertile?"

"Fertility runs in the family. That's why Big Dan taught us boys to never even go near a female without condoms at hand." He took a bite of hamburger and chewed it while his mind wandered across the state line into South Carolina, to the big house just off Highway 25. They'd built the house when he was fourteen, but he'd never gotten to live in it. Tradition required a new house remain empty for a year before the family could move in, and by the end of that year, he'd been gone.

His mother had been proud of the fancy house, the new cars, the jewelry, of her husband and her children. She'd protected them fiercely, as fiercely as she'd protected the family traditions. He figured Big Dan would come closer to forgiving him than his mother ever would.

"She was a typical mother. She loved us even when we were getting on her last nerve. She wanted the same kind of life for us that she and our father had. We heard a lot of 'Wait till your father gets home,' but she was really the one who put the fear of God in us."

"And yet you walked away from that. What did you want that you couldn't get there?"

"Freedom."

"Was it worth it?" She smiled faintly. "Life is meant to be lived with family. Not just parents and grandparents and stepparents, but siblings, cousins, aunts and uncles, the more, the merrier. You gave all that up. Was it worth it?"

"Yes." He didn't hesitate over the answer, nor was he embarrassed by it, though some part of him felt as if he should be when she'd wanted a family and been denied a real one for more than half her life.

"Freedom to do what?"

"Freedom to *not* do," he replied. Finished with his meal, he leaned back in the chair. The streetlights were buzzing, voices sounded through the windows and on the sidewalks, and music came from a restaurant across the street. If the night were ten degrees warmer—and the conversation more casual—it would be the most comfortable he'd been in a while.

"My family had certain expectations for me. They couldn't accept that I wanted something more."

"What expectations?"

Jones sighed. He'd told Detective Maricci the truth. He could tell Reece. Hell, she might not have a clue who or what the Travelers were—their reputation, their activities. But he could guarantee Miss Willa knew, as surely as Maricci had.

"My family is very insular. My brothers and I were raised to follow in our father's and grandfathers' footsteps. My sisters' lives would be just like our mother's and grandmothers'. We'd be in the same business, live in the same community, teach our children the same values."

"Sounds like a religious cult," she said cautiously.

He grinned. Not a cult, but a clan. A very close-knit, like-minded, strict-living clan. "No, just plain ol' Catholics. I love my family. They're not bad people. They're just very set in their ways, and I wanted something different."

"And they can't forgive you for that?"

"I disappointed them. They don't forgive easily."

"Sounds like you shocked the socks off them." She sighed heavily, too. "Welcome to the club. Grandfather didn't know the meaning of the word *forgive,* and Grandmother might do it, but she never forgets. I think she'd find it easier if I said I was sorry for missing his funeral, but I'm not. I just couldn't face it."

"A reasonable person wouldn't expect you to." Even if the old man had never laid a hand on her—and God, Jones hoped that was true—the fact remained that Arthur had terrified and traumatized a kid. The child could be forgiven for the state of their relationship. The supposedly mature, responsible adult couldn't.

Reece laughed at his comment. "You expect Grandmother to be reasonable? She doesn't have to. She's a Howard, you know."

"So are you."

Her leftover smile faded. "Only in name, Jones. Only in name."

When Jones excused himself to go inside the restaurant, Mick moved to Reece's side, placing his head where she could easily rub the favored spot between his ears. The action was repetitive, soothing, and allowed her to let her thoughts wander.

Valerie an alcoholic. Yes, that fit. If she closed her eyes and looked back in time, she had vague images of her mother, totally undone, eyes puffy, face swollen, fingers clenching tightly a tall, clear bottle. She'd raged at everyone who ventured near—Reece, Grandmother, the housekeeper. The best Reece could remember, Grandfather hadn't tried to approach her, though he had retrieved that bottle from her room a time or two.

She could call Valerie and ask, but she would likely get the same response she'd always gotten: *Really, Clarice. The past is past.* And then she would change the subject to something inane and totally inconsequential.

Better that she ask Grandmother. It was less personal with her, so she was more likely to answer. Though only if she wanted to.

Movement near the screen door caught her eye, and she saw Jones talking to a muscular dark-haired guy. The guy was holding a child, two, maybe three years old. With its shaggy hair, jeans and a T-shirt, she couldn't tell whether it was a boy or girl.

Their conversation appeared serious until the child

broke in. Whatever he said made Jones grin and tickle his tummy, which made the kid squeal with laughter.

The simple action touched something inside Reece.

After a moment, Jones returned to the table. "I paid the check while I was inside. Ready to go?"

Mick leaped to his feet. Like with her dogs, *go* was a magic word. No matter how much Bubba, Louie and Eddie loved where they were, they were always thrilled to *go* somewhere else.

She stood, and Jones automatically reached for her hand. She naturally let him take it. It felt normal. Good. And just the mere presence of him felt promising.

She'd been hopeful in the beginning with other men, she reminded herself. Not every new relationship came with that sense of promise, potential, future, but a few had, and look what had happened: every one had ended. And those were with guys who lived in the same part of the country she did, never mind the same city.

This thing with Jones wasn't likely to be any different, even if he was open to the idea of a long-distance relationship.

A CD played quietly on the stereo on the drive home, classic rock, hits from a band that had peaked before either of them had been born. It was one of her favorites.

When they reached Fair Winds, he entered the code and the gate swung slowly open. With little moon and too much shadow, the place looked eerie—nothing new there. But she didn't feel the eeriness quite as sharply as she normally would have. Too bad she couldn't just attach herself to Jones and hold on to that safe feeling the whole time she was here.

Mists swirled in the shadows as they drove along the drive, despite the fact that the air was calm, and awareness hummed along her veins, as surely as if their voices were in her ears. It was just plain creepy, even if she *was* safe with Jones.

He parked beside the cottage, shut off the engine and looked at her. "Want to make out while we're here?"

With a laugh, she considered the broad console between them. "I don't think this truck is made for making out. That's a long way to lean."

"Or you could just come over here and sit on my lap." He tilted the steering wheel up and out of away, then grinned as he offered her a hand.

Making out was good. She'd never had any trouble handling that. She climbed across the console, wriggling and twisting to get comfortable, and drawing a grunt from him in the process. Once she was settled, he didn't kiss her right away, though. Instead, with one arm around her shoulders, he touched her face with his free hand. "You're a beautiful woman, Clarice. I always thought…"

When he fell silent, she prodded him to go on. "Thought what?"

He seemed lost for a moment, then his mouth quirked. "The girl my mother picked out for me to marry was a redhead with watery blue eyes, but I always had a weakness for brown-eyed blondes."

"Your mother picked out a bride for you?" she echoed. "Just how old were you when you left home?"

"Fifteen."

Her eyes widened. "You were just a kid."

"So were you back then," he retorted. "We've both grown up."

There was no denying that, not sitting the way they were, her on his lap and his fingertips just grazing the side of her breast. "So…what? She was your mother's best friend's daughter and they thought 'wouldn't it be great if our kids got married'?" Her voice hitched as those feathery little caresses continued.

"Something like that." There was some emotion in his voice, too—dark, deep, sending tiny shivers along her arms. But he didn't say anything more because he was kissing her, sweet nibbling tastes, starting with her forehead and working his way to the corner of her mouth, then the bottom lip, then the bow in the center.

She opened her mouth and his tongue dipped inside, and something deep in her dissolved. This was good. Promising. Full of potential and future.

They kissed leisurely, touched slowly, as if they had the entire rest of their lives to do nothing but explore each other. It was sweet and lazy, and the heat built slowly. They took it easy, a new experience for Reece with first-time sex. He wanted to get her clothes off—she could feel that tension thrumming through his body and into hers, could feel the erection swelling against her hip—but there was no rush. They could take the time to do it right.

In the backseat, Mick gave a little whine, then exploded in a frenzy of barking, hitting the seat with such force in an attempt to get out of the driver's window that it jarred Reece and Jones apart. "Hey," Jones started to complain, but he recognized before she did that this wasn't routine, want-out-of-the-truck barking. His muscles tightening, Jones twisted beneath her to look off to the east for the source of Mick's sudden alert.

By the time Jones started to lift her away, Reece was already scrambling onto the console. "There's a light in that shed," he said quietly. "It wasn't there when we pulled in. I would have noticed it. You stay here—"

"Like hell." When he slid out the open door, she was right behind him. He scowled at her, but Mick bounding out of the truck, hair on end, and racing toward the shed claimed his attention.

The shed was fifty feet past the garage, an identical structure with an overhead door and a smaller side door. The light shone through the panes of glass in the side door and leaked under the front one. Jones was right, she thought as she matched her strides to his. The light gleamed in the darkness; they would have noticed it when they'd come home.

Mick reached the shed far ahead of them and ran from door to door, quivering, snarling, nose to the ground searching for scent. Jones peered through the door glass, but it was covered—painted white, Reece abruptly recalled. To let light in and keep nosy looks out.

He silently tried the knob, but it was locked. Moving to the overhead door, he twisted the handle to unlock it, gave her a steady look until she backed away a few feet, then heaved it open.

The long-unused mechanism shrieked, and Reece clapped her hands over her ears, trying to ignore the queasiness in her stomach and the goose bumps popping up everywhere.

A naked bulb dangled overhead, its pull-chain swaying slightly, showing and shadowing the only items in the building: Grandfather's old truck, two shovels leaning against one wall and a pile of canvas tarps neatly folded on a rough-built shelf. Another tarp was hung to dry over the side wall of the pickup bed, an aged dark stain making it stiff where it should have draped.

Jones went into the shed, looking around the truck,

under it, inside the cab. There was no place for anyone to hide.

No place for Reece to hide.

Oh, God, what have I done? The words were years old, the tone so harsh and horrified that she couldn't recognize it.

And the response, too quiet to hear.

The heat of that long-ago August afternoon beat down on her as she stiffened in place, staring through the open door. Such anger, evil and hate—such utter coldness—emanated from the space.

She choked back a cry as she stumbled back a step, terror flooding into her very bones, drawing their attention to her.

Get back in the house!

And the tiny voice inside her, echoing nearly as loud as Grandfather's roar: *Run, run, run!*

Heart thudding, vision blurring, she spun around and dashed away. Dimly she heard a dog bark, a man shout, but she didn't slow. Her arms swung, her legs pumping, her strides closing the distance, but, God, not fast enough. He was chasing her—Grandfather? Mark? He was stronger, faster, and she was too slow, too clumsy. Her feet slid in the gravel, and she tripped over a hank of grass when she veered off the road.

He caught her, arms wrapping around her, holding her close. His breathing was loud in her ears, his voice unfamiliar as he murmured, "It's okay, Reece, it's okay. Just an old memory. It can't hurt you. They can't hurt you. It's just you and me and Mick. You're safe."

She inhaled sharply, intending to scream, but the scents caught in her nose: soap, shampoo, cologne, dog. She knew those scents. She trusted them.

Jones. Mick.

Pivoting, she wrapped her arms around his neck and held on as if only he could chase away the fear, the ghosts, the memories. Only he could make her feel safe.

She held on for dear life.

Chapter 9

Silently cursing, Jones scooped her into his arms, choking at the strength with which she gripped his neck, and walked to the cottage with long strides. What the hell had happened? Had the mere sight of the old truck brought that memory of her grandfather and Mark back to vivid life? Judging by the sheer panic in her eyes, he'd say yes. She hadn't been merely remembering. She'd been living it again.

Balancing her on one hip and against the door frame, he got the front door open and carried her to the couch. She was trembling, making a terrible keening sound that set his nerves on edge. It worried Mick, too, who stood beside the couch for only a moment before trotting back to the screen door to peer out, then trotted back to the couch. On guard, like a good dog.

Jones couldn't get her to let go long enough to set her down, so he sat instead, settling her on his lap. He'd never dealt with a hysterical woman before. He didn't know what to say or do, so he held her, stroked her, murmured promises to her. *It's all right. You're safe. I won't let them hurt you.*

He hoped he wasn't lying.

After a time, the keening stopped. Traditionally, he knew, it was a mourning for the dead. Was it purely an emotional response? Or had she witnessed a death? A murder. Glen's murder.

The shudders slowed, losing their violence, fading into occasional tremors before disappearing entirely. She lay limp in his arms, probably exhausted by the shock, and her voice, when she spoke, was weak. "The stain on that tarp, it's blood. I'm sure of it. I smelled it."

Glen's blood? Would it be possible to prove after all these years? Jones knew science as it pertained to plants, not people. But Maricci would know. He would know where to send it, and where Jones could give a sample if DNA was retrieved to see if it matched.

His muscles ached to set Reece aside and go now: get the tarp, jump in his truck, call Maricci on the way into town. But it was late, and he couldn't just set Reece aside. She needed him. The tarp had survived this long. It would keep until tomorrow.

He could put off knowing for absolute sure that Glen was dead for a little while longer. Though he felt it in his bones, as long as he didn't have definitive proof, some part of him could still hope...

"Whose blood?" he asked softly.

Staring into the distance, she shook her head.

"What did you see, Reece?"

"The same thing," she said dully. "Grandfather, Mark, the truck. It was August. So hot, so humid. There was such threat in his voice. I'd only seen him like that once before, when I…"

The thought seemed to strike them both at the same time. When she'd repeated the memory to him earlier, she'd said, *He was angrier than I'd ever seen him.*

Her gaze met his. "One day he caught me digging in the yard, and he was livid. He grabbed my shoulders and lifted me right off the ground and said, 'Do you know what happens to little girls who poke around where they don't belong?' Then he set me down and dragged me to the front door, where he bent down right in my face. He said, 'If you ever tell anyone…' And I didn't wait for him to finish. I ran inside and straight to Grandmother's study. I didn't say a word to anyone, but every day I looked at the bruises he'd left, then stayed as close as I could to Grandmother or the housekeeper, until they got tired of it and made me go outside."

Jones grimly stared at her. "Were you digging in the front yard? Where the garden used to be?"

She nodded.

Arthur Howard may have been a good man as far as his family, excluding Reece's father, was concerned, but he'd definitely had a secret to keep. His destruction of the gardens, his fury at Reece for digging there, his messages from the grave for her to get out…

Could that secret be Glen's body? Even though Mark said he'd never told his grandfather about Jones and Glen, that didn't mean the old man hadn't discovered Glen on his own. Hell, they'd seen him in the woods several times, striding about like a king surveying his kingdom. He'd felt so secure on his property that he'd never seemed the slightest bit aware that there were trespassers who watched him from the cover of low growth or sturdy tree branches.

And Glen had been worried about Reece. He'd intended to move his camp off Howard property, but he would have sneaked back close to the house to watch for her. If Arthur had caught him…

Had the old man really been violent enough to kill a trespasser rather than chase him away or call the sheriff? He'd deliberately, cruelly traumatized his own granddaughter. He'd had a cold, uncaring side, along with the strong sense of entitlement that came from being a Howard in a place where that meant everything. He'd been taught he could do what he wanted and that money, power and the family name would protect him.

What was it Russ Calloway's grandmother had said about him? That she believed Arthur had kept leasing that land where Glen's backpack was found because *he wanted as much land between him and the world as he could get.* Between his secrets and the world.

His head starting to throb, Jones shifted underneath Reece until they were both lying on the couch, face-to-face in the narrow space. "Why were you digging in the yard?"

"I don't know." She pushed back to give him an inch or two more of space, and he took it, moving until their bodies were snugly pressed together again. Her hand rested on his rib cage, her knee between his. "When I left here that summer, I dug a lot. I planted garden beds everywhere Valerie would let me. I also had nightmares, a new fear of deep water and counted."

"Counted what?"

"Steps. You know, when I walk. One, two, three, but only up to thirty-eight. Not all the time, but when I'm anxious or my mind's wandering or I'm thinking about that summer." She flushed. "It used to drive Valerie crazy because I did it out loud, so I learned to keep quiet, and she thought I stopped. Now my best friends, Evie and Martine, are the only ones who know."

"And me." It touched him that she trusted him with the secret. Shouldn't he trust her with his? At least he could explain the reason behind her fear of water, and maybe some prodding would help unleash other memories.

"Reece—"

She laid her fingers over his mouth. "No. That sounds like the start to more serious conversation, and I can't do it anymore tonight. Make me laugh, Jones. Make me feel good. Make me forget everything else in the world but you and me."

He pushed her fingers aside after pressing a kiss to them. "I don't know—"

She did laugh, not wholeheartedly but a little chuckle of amusement. "Oh, you do know. Like you were doing—*we* were doing—in the truck before Mick interrupted. Make me forget, Jones. Just for tonight."

He wanted to tell her no, this wasn't the right time, certainly not the right reason, but she looked so vulnerable and her hand was under his shirt, spreading heat across his skin, and they'd already been headed this way before the latest interference. He'd already wanted her, and she'd already wanted him, and they could make it the right time and the right reason. They could laugh together, feel good together, forget together…

And, tomorrow or the next day or next week, they could remember together.

They could do damn near anything together.

Reece awakened sometime in the night with a sense of well-being she hadn't experienced since the day she'd

driven out of New Orleans. It wasn't a nightmare that
had roused her—a happy exception—but the simple
need to change positions, to pull her covers a little
tighter, then go back to sleep. Good rest came rarely.
She would take advantage of it.

The instant she shifted her weight to roll over, something else in the room shifted, too. For just an instant
there was complete silence, sound conspicuous due
to its absence, then the noise she easily identified as
Mick's breathing started again, slow and easy.

For a moment she considered why Mick was in her
room, but realized the opposite was true from the heat
radiating behind her. Jones, his breathing as slow and
easy as Mick's. She turned carefully, trying not to dis-
turb him, and settled onto the pillow again, watching
him in the thin light. She couldn't really make out anything—the suggestion of a nose, the darker slash of eye-
brow, the rest too shadowy—but she didn't need to see
to picture him. Memories of him would stay with her
forever. The way he'd run after her, the way he'd held
her, the way he'd soothed her, the way he'd made love
to her, the way he'd fallen asleep holding her, making
her feel...

Good. She felt good. Because of him, she would survive this visit. She might return home without all the
answers she'd been seeking, but she would be better for
the things she'd learned.

Even if one of those things was that her grandfather
was a murderer.

A chill passed through her, and at the foot of the bed,
Mick lifted his head with a whine. He stood, stretched
all over, then hopped off the bed and trotted to the door.
There he looked back as if to make sure she was follow-

ing, then went into the living room. A moment later, he nosed the front door.

Homesick for her own dogs, she slipped from the bed, located her clothes and set them on the night table, then pulled on Jones's T-shirt and padded after Mick. She let him out into the cool night, hugging her arms to her chest, and watched as he sniffed around the truck, then lifted his leg at the corner of the porch.

The shed down the road drew her gaze. The light was off, the door closed. Jones had gone to lock it up after they'd made love the first time, and he'd returned looking puzzled. She'd known without asking that the shed had been shut up by the same whoever—whatever—had lit it up for them to find, and without the terrible screech of the overhead door.

Mist swirled, though the humidity was no higher tonight than usual, and she wondered if those ethereal shapes drifting about with purpose were spirits. A distant wail from the direction of the woods that sounded faintly like tears convinced her she didn't want to know.

Mick's nails clicked across the wooden porch, his fur brushing her legs as he eased inside. She was happy to close and lock the door behind him.

Dim light fell in a wedge from the kitchen into the living room. Reece paused midstep, certain she hadn't turned on the bulb over the sink. She had assumed the cottage was haunt-free—she'd never heard of anything happening there. But Jones had told her—as Evie had, as Martine had—that ghosts attached to places *or* people. Was Grandfather's ghost attaching to her, or was she mistaken in attributing all her otherworldly experiences to just one soul?

The light arrowed in on a small walnut table at the

end of the sofa, just strong enough to give the gilt lettering of its title a bit of gleam. *Southern Aristocracy.*

She was more than certain she hadn't brought the book to the cottage.

Restlessly she picked up the book, her nose wrinkling at the musty smell, and flipped through the pages. The first time she found nothing. The second time, the pages of the middle third opened to reveal a piece of thick ivory linen writing paper.

He isn't what he seems.

After reading the single line a half-dozen times, she shifted her gaze to the bedroom door. Was Jones the *he* Grandfather meant? As if she would trust his opinion on anything. He'd terrorized her for half her life. Even dead, he was still trying to frighten her away, not only from Fair Winds but now from the only person who'd made any effort to help her. The only person she'd felt something...*real* with in years.

But what do you really know about him?

She couldn't tell whether the voice echoing in her head was her own or Grandfather's or, hell, even someone else's, and she flushed hot with guilt. She knew enough.

His own family wants nothing to do with him.

"Oh, please." Slamming the book shut, she set it back on the table. "Like that makes him the bad guy? My father wanted nothing to do with you, and that was *your* fault. *I* wanted nothing to do with you, and that was your fault, too."

Silence met her whisper, and after a moment of it, she was sure she was alone again. She went into the bedroom, where Mick was already snoozing again on a blanket folded under the window and Jones was sprawled across most of the bed, covers down to his waist.

He isn't what he seems, the note echoed.

She thought of him, of the way they'd connected, of the way he'd cared for her. Taken care of and with her. No one had done that in so very long.

Why shouldn't she trust him? He had nothing to gain from a relationship with her, and she had nothing to risk besides her heart. Sometimes that was a risk worth taking.

Slipping out of the shirt, she climbed into bed. As she snuggled close, Jones wrapped his arm around her waist, left a sleepy kiss on her neck and settled her in with a soft, contented, "Umm."

Definitely worth a risk.

She dozed a few more hours, and when she awakened again, the quality of the darkness had changed. It was dawn, everything quiet outside, everything mostly quiet in, but she wasn't the only one awake. Opening her eyes, she found Jones lying on his side, watching her, his expression deep and intense.

"If you don't want Miss Willa to know you spent the night here, you'd better go now." His voice was a rumble in the shadows, husky, comforting.

"I don't care if she knows, though it may be easier for you if I go now."

"I don't care if she knows, either." After a moment, he raised one hand to stroke her hair back. "Are you okay?"

"You mean, have I adjusted to the fact that my grandfather was probably a murderer?" She tried to smile, but it came out more of a grimace. "Before I even understood what evil was, I sensed he was bad. Valerie said I let Daddy prejudice me against him. Well, yeah.

My father loved everybody, but he could hardly bear to look at my grandfather. He only brought us here when the pressure from Valerie and Grandmother got too much for him, and he always kept our visits short."

She paused, a detail becoming clear that she'd long forgotten. "He never left me alone when we were here. Whatever I did—fish, explore, read—he did it with me. Always. Do you think he *knew* that his father had killed someone and did nothing about it besides keep us far away?"

"No." Jones didn't hesitate. "You said he was a good guy. He probably just suspected there was something *off* about your grandfather. If he'd known the truth, he would have gone to the authorities, even if they were family, even if he wanted to protect his mother. That's what good guys do."

Nodding, she relaxed against the pillow again. Daddy *had* been good. He was the one everyone turned to for help, the one who couldn't drive past a car broken down on the side of the road without offering assistance, the one who mentored troubled kids and mowed yards for neighbors who couldn't do it themselves and volunteered at the soup kitchen. It wasn't in him to sit back and do nothing.

"The man I was talking to at dinner last night, the one with the kid, he's a detective in Copper Lake. I'd like to show him the tarp—see if there's a chance of proving the stain is blood, maybe proving whose it is."

She swallowed hard. She didn't know whether they could legally turn it over to the authorities, but Grandfather was dead; he couldn't be taken to trial. And if it was blood, if the victim could be identified, didn't his family deserve to know?

"All right," she murmured. "But maybe I should call

your detective friend. Maybe you should stay out of it. It's no big deal if Grandmother throws me out."

His grin was faint. "It's no big deal if she fires me, either. In fact, if she did, there are some damn fine gardens in New Orleans that I've been meaning to visit."

The tightness in her chest eased a bit. He wanted to see her after they left here. She wasn't just an on-site diversion.

"I'll call Maricci," he said.

"If he needs to come out here and you want me to keep Grandmother occupied, just let me know." Pushing back the sheet, she swung her legs over the side of the bed and shimmied into her panties. Her shirt came next—had she not worn a bra or just hadn't found it?—then her jeans. She was zipping up when tires crunched on the gravel outside. She glanced out the window though the driveway wasn't visible. The faint "Goodbye" drifting on the still air identified the arrival as the housekeeper, calling to her driver before closing the door.

Reece reached the bedroom door before turning back. "You'd go all the way to New Orleans just to see some gardens?"

"Maybe. But I'd definitely go to see you."

She grinned, waved and hustled across the living room, grabbing the book from the end table on her way. As she clenched it in one arm, she swore she could actually *feel* the warning note inside, drumming. *He isn't what he seems, he isn't what he seems.*

He is, she firmly argued. She believed that. She trusted him. *Trusted,* she who always had issues with trust.

She returned to the house, changed clothes and had breakfast—coffee, toast and an orange—on the front porch. Grandmother had stuck her head out when she finished her own meal for a stern hello, then retreated back inside to do whatever it was that filled her days.

When Reece's cell phone rang, it startled her. She carried it with her from habit, but this was the first call she'd gotten since leaving New Orleans. Evie's voice sounded cheery and energetic.

"No frantic calls saying, 'I need you!' so I'm guessing everything's going…well, if not great, then tolerably. How is your grandmother?"

"She's fine."

"And the ghosts?"

"They're in fine form, too."

Evie's tone grew more serious. "And you?"

Reece gazed across the lawn toward the river. Back when the gardens were magnificent, the grounds between fence and river had been maintained, too, so it was visible from the porch. Now scrub blocked all but the briefest views. "I'm okay. I've remembered a few things, got an answer or two. My cousin, Mark, lives in town, and he doesn't have horns and a pitchfork after all. Grandmother's as warm and fuzzy as ever. And…"

"And…?"

Reece drew her feet into the cushioned seat and said softly, "There's a guy here. His name is Jones, and he's doing a project for Grandmother." Though, as far as she knew, no contract had been signed yet.

"I take it he's gorgeous and wickedly sexy."

"He is."

"Do you remember him?"

"No. He lives in Kentucky. He's just here working."

"Oh, of course. Tell Sister Evie more. Was last night incredible?"

Reece grinned. Sometimes there were disadvantages

to having a psychic for a best friend. It was hard to keep secrets. But considering that half her life had been about secrets, maybe that was a good thing. "It was."

"Tell me the best thing about him."

Evie had made the request before, regarding other relationships Reece had gotten into—and, always, out of. Usually her answers were glib or average: *He's funny. He has great taste. He has great abs. He's gone.*

This time she answered earnestly. "I trust him."

After a moment of utter silence, Evie murmured, "Wow."

That was another thing about having a psychic for a best friend: it was hard to surprise her. But Reece had managed.

"Wow," Evie repeated. "I knew you should, but I didn't think *you* would know you should. Not yet. He's a good guy, Reece. In spite of everything else, trust that. Believe that."

Reece's fingers tightened. "I do," she answered automatically, then just as quickly asked, "In spite of what else?"

In the background came a shriek so shrill that Reece tilted the cell a few inches from her ear. "*Mama!* Isabella broke my car!" Jackson shouted over the wail.

"Isabella! Jackson! I'll have to talk to you later, Reece, okay? If you need me—" The decibels surrounding her spiked, making her sigh almost indistinguishable. "Really, think about needing me, will you? Love you."

"Love you, too." Reece disconnected, torn by the conversation. She was glad to hear Evie's endorsement of Jones, and always glad to have her friend agree with her assessment of someone. But what had she meant by *in spite of everything?* Being estranged from his family? Probably having to do some tough things to get by when he was just fifteen and on his own?

"'Love you, too,' hmm? I hope that was Valerie or Evie or Martine." Jones didn't bother with the center steps but climbed onto the porch at the end, his calf muscles flexing. His khaki shorts and T-shirt were both well-worn, as were the running shoes that looked as if they could walk on their own. He'd shaved the stubble from his chin, but had combed his hair with his fingers.

He looked incredible.

"Valerie and I aren't exactly the endearment type. That was Evie. She said you're a good guy."

His brows arched as he crouched in front of her, a post at his back. "How would she know— Oh, yeah, she's the one with the gift." The surprise settled into a grin that warmed her from the inside out. "She's right. I am a good guy."

"Do you want me to stroke your ego by agreeing?"

"I'd rather you stroke…" He broke off, and a dull tinge flushed his cheeks. "Sorry. I didn't mean to say that out loud."

She laughed. Laughter was such a rare thing around Fair Winds that she was half surprised the spirits hadn't come flying to see what was going on.

"I talked to Maricci. He's on his way out. If you don't mind distracting Miss Willa… I somehow don't think she's going to give him permission to poke around, especially if she has any clue what Arthur did."

That was another thought that had niggled at Reece since last night. She'd believed Jones's assurances that her father would have taken action if he'd known, but what about Grandmother? She'd been married to the man for more than fifty years. Could she really not have known what he was capable of? Or could he have been that good at fooling people?

Grandmother only acknowledged what she wanted to know, and Grandfather had only shown what he wanted to show. She had to live—and he'd had to die—with the choices they'd made. Their actions, or inactions, were their responsibilities.

"I can always ask her questions about family history. Better yet, we can have the conversation we haven't quite managed yet." She uncurled her legs, and Jones stood, offering her a hand up. His fingers gripped hers a minute longer than necessary, sending heat and assurance and strength her way. *A good guy.* She had a weakness for truly good guys.

When he released her hand, she gathered her dishes and went inside, taking one last look at him for encouragement.

A hum came from the door to Grandfather's study, reminding her of angry bees. Traveling the length of the hall, she passed through a couple of cold spots and steadfastly ignored creaking and rustling from the rooms she passed. Grandmother was in her study, a thick sheaf of papers on the desk in front of her. Reece waited to be acknowledged, which she got with a brief, dry look.

"I would like to talk to you if you have time."

Grandmother made an impatient gesture. "Seat yourself."

"Not here. In the salon." The driveway ran twenty feet from the study windows. There was no way Grandmother would miss a stranger's arrival there.

"Why the salon?"

"Because it's a lovely room that's rarely been used in the last century." In her limited experience, it seemed everyone had had their favorite places: Grandmother and Grandfather their studies, Valerie her bedroom, Mark wherever Grandfather was, Dad wherever Reece was and Reece outside. The only place they'd gathered as a family was at the dinner table.

Grandmother looked as if she might refuse—she was so accustomed to doing that—but instead she rose and led the way down the halls to the salon. "Every single piece in here came from distant lands. That chandelier is from France, those tables from India, the vases from China. The rugs are Persian, the lace is from Brussels, that glasswork from Murano. Captain Howard never made a voyage that he failed to bring home some treasure for the house he intended to build."

Reece seated herself in an uncomfortable chair that looked as if it might have come from France, as well, and immediately asked her first question. "What went wrong that my father left this house intending never to return?"

Grandmother's posture stiffened even more than its usual boardlike state. "He fell in love with your mother."

"People fall in love and move away from home all the time and still go back for summer visits, holidays, birthdays."

"Your father came back."

"How often in the sixteen years he was away? Twice? Three times? And he couldn't even speak to Grandfather when he was here."

Grandmother's scowl was stern, her gaze sharply disapproving, and would have made adolescent Reece quake and flee. Not this time. "Elliott and his father had some silly falling-out. With the misguided passion of youth, Elliott never forgave him, and then…it was too late."

"Is that Grandfather's description? A silly falling-out? Because my father didn't hold grudges over silly falling-outs. He was a loving and forgiving man. Whatever happened to him was serious, and it was Grandfather's fault."

Grandmother managed an inch more rigidity in her bearing. "You will not speak of your grandfather like that in his house. Whatever happened between him and Elliott was their business, not yours, not mine. Now, if that's all you want…"

Gazing at her, Reece realized the old woman meant what she'd said. Maybe she'd actually believed it all along, or maybe Grandfather had told her that so often over the years that she'd come to accept it as fact. But the *falling-out* had cost *her* a relationship with her son and granddaughter, as well. How could that not be her business? How could she have not wanted to know why?

"No," she said abruptly as Grandmother began to rise. "That's not all. The summer I lived here…you told me Valerie had left to take care of things back home. Was that true? Or was she receiving treatment for her drinking?"

Grandmother's mouth pursed as if she'd sucked a lime. "You have a habit of asking the wrong people your questions, Clarice."

"Well, Daddy and Grandfather are dead, and Valerie doesn't discuss the past. Since you're the one who told me the lie…"

She soured even more. "Yes. Your mother had to enter a rehabilitative program. I insisted. She was a weak woman. Between the medicines the doctor gave her and the alcohol she took from Arthur's study, she was barely able to get out of bed. But she begged me not to tell you, so I didn't. I had no idea that keeping a promise to her would offend you all these years later."

"I thought she had abandoned me, like Daddy. I thought she'd left me with people who obviously didn't want me any more than she did."

"Your father didn't abandon you, Clarice. He died." Grandmother didn't bother to dispute the last part of Reece's statement, sending an ache through some small part of her that still wanted... Instead, shaking her head, she scowled. "I'd hoped you would outgrow this melodramatic bent, but you obviously haven't. These things happened years ago. Why are you making a fuss about it now?"

Reece wanted to give in to that melodramatic bent and stamp her feet, throw a few priceless antiques and scream, *I was a child! A mourning, distraught, terrified child! I needed love and reassurance and to believe someone wanted me!*

But her grandmother's response would likely be one she'd given before: *You always were rather spoiled.*

"I'm making a fuss now," Reece said, imitating Grandmother's stony calm, "because I can't remember most of that summer, because something happened then, something besides my father dying and my mother leaving me. Something that gives me nightmares, that—" She paused, considering the wisdom of going on, then did it, anyway. "Something that Grandfather's spirit wants to keep secret. He's been warning me away since I got here."

"Oh, really, Clarice." Grandmother put more scorn in those three words than Reece would have believed possible. She rose from the sofa, looking inches taller and way too imposing. "His spirit…for heaven's sake. I blame your father for this, encouraging you to believe in ghosts, and both your parents for this self-centered, inappropriate and hysterical behavior. Your grandfather wanted nothing to do with you in life, and he certainly wouldn't change that in death. As if such a thing were even possible." At the doorway, she turned back. "I do believe you should consider ending your visit here soon. Welcomes do wear out, you know. Sooner for some than others."

Chapter 10

"It's human blood."

Jones was standing in the shed door, Maricci beside him, watching silently as the lab geek who'd come with the detective performed her test. Marnie Robinson wasn't much of a living-people person, Maricci had told him, but she was very good with dead people and all things pertaining to them.

Now, at the certainty in her voice, Jones's gut tightened. He'd known it was blood. Reece had been positive of it. But hearing it confirmed made it that much more real.

It *could* be Glen's blood. He could be one step closer to knowing what had happened to his brother.

"Is it as much as it looks?" Maricci asked.

Marnie gazed at him owlishly. "Losing this much blood would be incompatible with living."

"Can you get DNA from it?"

"Depends on the degree of degradation. Can I take the tarp back to the lab?"

Maricci shifted his gaze to Jones, who walked a few yards off to the east, where the building hid them from any view inside the house. Maricci followed. "If we take it without permission from Miss Willa or a warrant, the results will be inadmissible in court, and if there's any way it implicates her husband, she's not likely to give permission. There's a missing-persons case open on your brother. The sheriff's investigator has probable cause to get a warrant."

"The old man is dead. Kind of limits any legal action that can be taken against him."

"If he's the killer."

Everything pointed to Arthur, and Reece was certain it was him warning her away. "Who else would it be? Miss Willa? Mark? Reece? An old woman or a couple of scrawny kids?" Glen had been too wiry, too strong, too used to fighting with bigger and smaller brothers. No way he could have been overpowered by any of those three, unless they'd bashed his skull from behind, and no way any of them could have crept up and caught him unaware.

"I've heard stories about Arthur Howard," Maricci said. "That he was scary, menacing, more than a little odd. I don't have trouble believing he could lose his temper and kill someone."

"You're a detective," Marnie said from the doorway of the shed. "You don't have trouble believing anyone could do anything. Do I bag the tarp or not?"

Both of them looked at Jones. He and Reece had been led to the shed for just that discovery, but not to prosecute a dead man. Not to destroy Miss Willa's life—and besmirching her respected family name would do that—or any chance Reece might have a relationship with her only grandmother. All *he* wanted was answers: Was it Glen's blood? Had he died here at Fair Winds? And maybe, if God took pity on Jones, where was his body?

Maricci turned to Marnie. "Bag it. And get a DNA sample from him for comparison."

Surprise flickered across the woman's face, but she nodded and disappeared back into the shed.

In a few minutes, they were driving away, the tarp and Jones's DNA sample both bagged and tagged. He closed the door, wincing at the metallic shriek, then started toward the house. The tarp's discovery didn't change the fact that he had a lot of work to do.

He was mixing concrete in a wheelbarrow with a hoe when Reece came out the front door. The instant he saw her, some of the tension left his shoulders and jaw, and a smile came automatically. She wore the same clothes as the afternoon before, with smears of dirt, sweat and mortar on both shirt and shorts.

"I didn't bring any real work clothes with me," she commented as she approached, "so I'm already stinky and dirty."

And beautiful.

"How did it go with the detective?"

"It is human blood, and taking the tarp without a warrant means anything they find is inadmissible in court."

She made an obnoxious sound. "Like that matters in this case."

"How did it go with Miss Willa?"

"She confirmed that Valerie was in rehab those months. She also said I was hysterical, melodramatic and unwanted when I was here then, and that I had worn out my welcome now and should consider leaving. Of course, being a proper Howard, she won't throw me out. Not just yet, at least."

Jones stared at her, then took her hand, but she wouldn't let him tug her around the wheelbarrow so he could hold her. Her eyes bright with tears, her fingers holding tightly to his, she forced a smile. "It's nice to know where one stands, isn't it?"

So much for preserving some kind of relationship between them, he thought bitterly. "You don't need her."

"I know." She shrugged. "I never really had her in my life. Just the possibility that someday... But it's okay." She sounded as if she meant it. There was disappointment in her voice, but acceptance, too. Not resignation—that would have been painful for both of them—but simple acceptance.

"Families suck sometimes, don't they?"

She laughed. "Yeah, they do. That's why God gives us the chance to make or pick our own."

They finished the last course of bricks on the south bed, then moved to the bed north of the steps. The sun was warm, the air smelling of the river and the pines that edged the yard but lacking the crisp scent of fall Jones had become accustomed to on many of his jobs farther north. Sometimes he missed the change of seasons, but not enough to move someplace where the months brought drastic weather.

In fact, he might be willing to consider relocating farther south instead, where the biggest seasonal difference was warm versus hot, damp versus suffocatingly damp.

New Orleans would do nicely.

If he had the proper incentive.

Around eleven, Miss Willa drove past in the big old

Caddy, never glancing in their direction. Jones watched Reece's expression, but saw nothing more than momentary curiosity. Soon after, the housekeeper brought out a tray of chicken-salad sandwiches along with two dainty dishes of salad and a pitcher of iced tea. "I fixed the food before Ma'am told me about her appointment with Robbie Calloway," she announced, "and she won't eat leftovers, so I'm not letting it go to waste."

Reece didn't say anything, so Jones thanked the woman. After she returned inside, they gave their hands a cursory wash with the hose, then sat on the porch steps, the tray between them.

"Robbie Calloway is her lawyer," Reece said before picking up a sandwich half. "Either you're getting your contract at last, or I'm getting officially disinherited, if I wasn't already."

"I don't know if I still want the contract." He wasn't sure he'd ever actually wanted the project. His work had been a way to gain access to Fair Winds, to find answers about Glen. If that tarp provided at least some of those answers, and he had this knot in his gut that said it would, would he want to stay around for months on end, working for the widow of his brother's murderer?

Even if he didn't get answers, his opinion of Miss Willa had taken a serious hit today. He wanted to pursue this thing with Reece. How much trouble would it cause if he was working for the grandmother who'd deliberately caused her such needless pain to restore the place that gave her such nightmares?

"Maybe someone who works for you could oversee it," Reece remarked. Then she shook her head. "Strike that. Grandmother isn't the sort to settle for the number-two guy. She'd want your attention twenty-four hours a day until the job was done to her satisfaction."

"Yeah. Some of my clients think a contract with my company entitles them to that." He grinned. "I charge them a little extra for attitude."

She finished her sandwich, then picked up the delicate crystal plate and heavy silver fork, both elaborately monogrammed with an *H*. "I don't see the point of salads like this," she remarked. "A small serving of mixed greens, one slice of cucumber, two cherry tomatoes and raspberry vinaigrette. I like plain old lettuce, and I want lots of stuff on it, all topped with rich, thick blue-cheese dressing. You know, a salad of substance."

"The difference between you and Miss Willa. She's superficial. You're about substance."

"Thank you," she said with a wry smile. "Right now I'm about embracing the differences. It's hard to imagine that my dad came from these people."

"Because he made a conscious decision to leave here. To leave them."

"Like you did with your family."

It was the perfect opening to tell her about his family, both good and bad. He'd rehearsed different openings in his head, ways to tell her his background without making his family seem nearly as bad as hers, because they weren't, honest to God. But the opening came and went without a single word making it from his mouth before she returned to the subject of the contract.

"What happens if you decide you don't want a project? You've got a lot of time in here—these beds, the research, the sketches, all the preliminary work. You just write that off and move on?"

He grinned. "I don't know. I've never turned down a job of this size and significance."

She gazed into the distance a long time, then abruptly

said, "I think you should do it. You and Grandmother both said the gardens here were historically significant. Even if you don't need it on your résumé, who could turn down the chance to bring history back to life?"

"And to thwart Arthur in the process?"

Her smile was sunny. "Well, yeah, there's that, too."

"Pursuing it could bring disaster into Miss Willa's life. Gl—whoever's blood is on that tarp might not have been your grandfather's only victim. Once we start digging out here—" His words broke off as ice rushed through his veins, appropriately chilling to the image of mounds of dirt and piles of bones.

As she looked across the expanse of yard, her gaze darkened. Imagining how many bodies could be buried there? Wondering if her grandfather could have been that kind of monster?

After a moment, her hand unsteady, she gestured toward the two new beds. "At least we haven't uncovered any bodies so far."

He met her weak smile with his own, choosing not to point out that so far, the digging had been relatively shallow. If Arthur were burying a body permanently, surely he'd dug deeper than two feet, as the heavy equipment would. "It would shake Miss Willa's world to its foundations, having to face the truth about her husband."

"That's on Grandfather, not you. If he really did kill someone—maybe multiple someones—those families have the right to know. The world has a right to know what he was." Sounding less certain, she added, "Grandmother would deal with it. She's a Howard. Besides, I could be wrong. That could be Grandfather's blood, or Mark's, from an injury they suffered while out hunting or working."

Jones didn't repeat Marnie Robinson's comment about the blood loss being incompatible with life.

"It was August," Reece remarked.

His gaze jerked toward hers. "What?"

"The day I surprised Grandfather in the garage. It was August. And the truck was in the garage, not the shed."

Glen had disappeared in August. What were the odds that someone else had disappeared from the area at the same time and not been missed?

Not good.

Leaning his head against the pillar, Jones closed his eyes, easily calling his brother's image to mind. Dark-haired and dark-eyed, Glen had usually been smiling, often laughing, always feeling whatever he felt with passion. Jones had wanted a different life, but it had been Glen who first suggested actually trying for it. He and Siobhan were in love, but they'd both been promised to someone else since they were kids. They'd decided on the runaway plan, and Jones had jumped at the chance to join in.

If they had changed their minds, if Jones had warned their parents, if *anything* had happened differently...

Things happen as they're meant to. Granny's voice echoed in his head.

Opening his eyes, he looked at Reece. "Do you believe in fate?"

She wasn't quick to answer. She finished her tea, then stood and walked to the bottom of the steps before facing him again. "I do most of the time, but sometimes I wonder. Was it fate that Daddy died so young? That Valerie wasn't the best mother? That I wound up here that summer?" She shrugged, an easy, graceful movement. "I do believe things happen for a reason, that good comes out of bad, but I also believe we have influence, too. We can make decisions that can alter our fate. Though then, Martine asks, how do you know you weren't fated to make that decision?" She smiled faintly.

"What good came out of your father's death, your mother's deficiencies and your summer here?"

Again she smiled, but this time it was the real thing, the kind that involved her entire face and affected him like a punch to the gut. "I met you." She turned, tossing a look back at him over her shoulder, as she sashayed— no other word fit that sassy, sexy sway of her hips—to the work site.

Warmth spread through him, easing doubts and guilts and fears in its path, and for the first time in a very long time, he realized, he was falling for a woman. It was too hard and too fast, at least if a man wasn't prepared for it.

But his subconscious had been preparing for it even if his conscious mind hadn't. All that talk about long-distance relationships, all that wanting—needing—to take care of her, all that thought about relocating to New Orleans... Oh, yeah. Some part of him had been headed this way without his even realizing it.

It was a realization he was very comfortable with.

With the brick border finished on the second bed, they returned to the first one, using spades and rakes to work amendments into the soil. By the time they were ready to plant, the wind had come up and the northwest sky had turned dark. Thunder reverberated slowly across the ground, a low, threatening rumble.

"Great," Jones muttered. If they went ahead and planted before the storm broke and it was a hard rain, it could damage the new plants. If they didn't plant and get the mulch down, the rain would pound the soft soil into mud, complete with rivers and gullies. At least there would be no loss if they didn't plant, just more work for them when the ground dried out.

With the wind whipping into a frenzy, they put away the tools, then, as the first rain fell, took cover on the broad porch. Reece stomped the dirt from her shoe soles on the top step. "Watching thunderstorms was the only thing I liked doing here. A couple times, when we were here, Daddy and I snuggled up in that chair—" she pointed to a wicker rocker "—and we'd count the seconds between the thunder and lightning. Once he told me the scientific reasons for storms, but usually he'd have some silly story about giants bowling or lightning bugs getting refills of light so we could chase them at night."

Jones sat down in the chair she'd indicated and held out his hand. She didn't hesitate at all, but curled immediately, trustingly, in his lap.

Trustingly. When she didn't know some of the most important things about him.

He held her loosely, his hands resting on her hip, and quietly said, "I was here that summer, Reece."

Reece's brows drew together, and her stomach muscles clenched. Surely she'd misunderstood. If he'd been at Fair Winds fifteen years ago, why would he wait until now to say so? Why would he listen to all her angst over not remembering without telling her?

Why would she have trusted him?

His arms tightened around her, and he said, "Wait, Reece, hear me out," before she realized she'd made an effort to stand. She pushed at his hands and he let go, leaving her free to move away, and immediately she felt the loss of his embrace, his warmth, the sense of security he'd always given her.

Security? From a liar?

Folding her arms across her middle, she stalked to the nearest column, then faced him. "You forgot to mention that until now?" Her tone was snide, sarcastic, reminding her of both Grandmother and Mark. Maybe she really was a Howard, after all.

"When we met, I didn't know if you just didn't remember me, if Glen and I weren't important enough to have registered with you or if you knew who I was and were pretending not to. I thought it would be better if I waited until I did know to say anything."

"I told you Tuesday night that I didn't remember," she said heatedly, then chilled just as quickly. "You didn't believe me."

He pushed out of the chair with enough force to set it rocking and paced to the end of the porch. "I wasn't sure. I wanted…I needed to be sure."

Borne on the force of the wind, rain splattered her back, but she didn't move deeper into the porch's cover. "What do you mean, you were here? You weren't staying at the house. Grandmother would have mentioned— Mark would have mentioned it."

"I never saw your grandmother back then, and Mark had good reason to keep his mouth shut."

She waited, but when he didn't go on, she flung both arms out. "What reason?"

It was obvious in every line of his body, in his eyes, in the rigid set of his jaw, that he didn't want to answer, but he would. If she had to strangle the truth from him, she would, by God. She even took a step toward him, but stopped when he spoke.

"Your fear of water. Mark tried to drown you that summer. Glen and I stopped him."

It was an outrageous claim. Mark had been a spoiled brat, and there'd been no love lost between them, but *drown* her? He'd picked on her, pestered her, tormented her, but he hadn't hated her that much.

Had he?

Because…it didn't *feel* outrageous.

"In the creek," Jones went on. "Where it forms a pool. You and Glen were meeting to swim, and I was with him, and we saw him holding you under, saw you fighting him. We…jumped in. Stopped Mark. Got you out."

Slowly her arms lowered to her sides. It felt—it felt like truth. As if everything inside her remembered it even if her brain didn't.

Mark had tried to kill her. Yeah, that would explain the memory loss, the determination to never return to Fair Winds again, cutting off contact with her father's family. He'd tried to kill her, and her grandmother, with her talk of melodrama, never would have believed it—if Reece had even bothered to tell her—and her grandfather… He'd probably given Mark tips on how to succeed the next time.

Numbly she went to the chair Jones had vacated and sank down with a creak of wicker. Just a few minutes ago, she'd felt safe in this chair, just as she had all those years ago with Daddy. Now…

She raised her dull gaze to Jones's. "Who is Glen?"

Anguish crossed his face, then disappeared. "My brother. He and I were camping out there near the cemetery. We ran into you one day on our way to the river. You were hurt and scared and so sad, and he always

liked fixing things—machines, animals, people—so...
he was your friend."

"Where is he now?"

The stark emotion flashed again. Her hand lifted, her
fingers reaching out to comfort him, but there was too
much distance between them, and she couldn't bring
herself to close it.

"I think he's dead," he said in a monotone that hinted
at how deep that thought hurt him. "I think that blood
on the tarp we found is his."

Dead. Murdered. Right here at Fair Winds. By her
grandfather.

Dear God.

She pressed her hand to her mouth, as if that could
stop the sickening thoughts, but words spilled out, anyway. "You think—you're here—you think we might
find his body. That's why you're here. That's why—"
Helplessly, she waved a trembling hand at the lawn.

He continued in that flat, hard voice. "A few weeks
ago, Glen's belongings were found hidden back there
in the woods, just off Howard property. I left without
him that summer. I figured he was out there somewhere
living his life, just like me, until I heard that news. I
came here hoping to find something, to learn something. When your grandmother asked me to redo the
gardens, it was too convenient. I couldn't refuse."

Of course not. It gave him a reason to hang around
and ask questions. And she just happened to choose the
same time to come back herself. What lousy luck. *Or,*
whispered Martine's voice in her head, *was it fate?*

"You could have told me," she said, accusation heavy
in her tone.

"Not at first. I didn't know what you might say to
your grandmother. I didn't trust you."

Reece smiled grimly as the rain poured harder. She was the one famous for trust issues; she feared betrayal and abandonment and disillusionment, and yet he hadn't trusted her. Ironic.

"So you didn't trust me at first. Do you now?"

"Would I have spent last night with you if I hadn't?"

Some pettiness inside her wanted to retort that she didn't know since he was so obviously good at keeping secrets, but she knew better. Last night hadn't been just sex. They'd both had their share of casual sex, and they both knew the difference.

"So why didn't you tell me sooner? Once you decided I was trustworthy, why didn't you say something?"

He crouched in front of her chair, the column at his back. "I tried last night. But you said, 'Make me forget everything else in the world but you and me.' And I wanted that, too, so…"

That sounds like the start to more serious conversation, and I can't do it anymore tonight. She'd meant the words with all her heart. If he'd insisted, if he'd told her any of this then, she would have had a meltdown right there on his sofa, and even he might not have been able to put her back together.

His gaze was steady, intense. Though he was trying not to show too much emotion, it was there in his eyes: sorrow, anger, regret, concern—and that concern was for her. *He's a good guy,* Evie had told her. *In spite of everything.*

Something else Evie had said flashed into her mind. *Do you remember him?* Had Evie known in her woo-woo way that Jones was connected to her past? Probably.

She didn't remember him. But he and his brother

would have been the only friendly people in her life fifteen years ago. Maybe that knowledge somewhere deep inside her explained why she'd so quickly come to feel comfortable with him. To trust him.

"So this thing between us…"

A little of the tension around his mouth eased. "Would have happened no matter where or when we met again."

"*If* we met again."

He shook his head. "When."

She was considering the possibility that everything in their lives had happened in order to bring them together, that they were meant to be. That when Daddy had said he and Valerie were meant to be, it hadn't just been a romantic notion but a fact of life. Even for someone who believed in fate—most of the time—it was an enormous idea to take in.

"I wasn't honest with you from the start, Reece, but I like you a whole lot." His mouth quirked. "I think I'm falling in love with you. Whatever happens here, I still want to see you. Be with you. Be a part of your life."

Honesty forced her to admit that she wanted to be with him, too. She wanted at least a fair chance to have a normal relationship with a good guy—with *this* good guy. She wanted to see if she was falling in love with him, too. All her emotions suggested so, but she'd never trusted any man enough to risk her heart, so it was a totally new experience for her.

And she did trust Jones. Even though he'd misled her.

She gazed past him to the flower bed, where the rain flooded out crevices and puddled and washed away much of the work they'd done, then slowly brought her gaze back to him. "I've always had an interest in gardening."

She saw by his expression that he understood the reference to his earlier words: *Ideally, I'd want a wife who shared my interest in the business.* Tension drained from him, and he rocked forward onto his knees. "I've always had an interest in New Orleans."

"You would visit me there?"

His hand closed around hers, and he eased to his feet, drawing her with him as he stood, holding her close. "Honey, I'd relocate there. I'm no fool. I don't want a long-distance relationship. Always saying good-bye, sleeping alone, waiting to see you again? It might have worked for my parents and grandparents, but not for me."

She wrapped her arms tightly around his neck and felt...peace. Welcome. As if she'd come home.

Chapter 11

Jones was still holding her, his cheek pressed against her hair, his eyes closed, his gut taut with gratitude, when the air around them crackled. The hairs on his neck stood on end an instant before lightning struck the nearest live oak alongside the driveway. The sound was deafening, the scent crisp. He looked up in time to see a massive branch explode from the tree and across the road, leaving a charred, ragged wound on the ancient trunk.

Still in the circle of his arms, Reece twisted to face the tree, her nose wrinkling at the smell of ozone. "Wow."

"That tree's taken its hits." He let go long enough to point out an old scar a few feet from the new one. "It lost a big branch there, too, at some time."

"When I was here." She said the words casually, but the instant they registered with her, her body stiffened and her next words came slowly, hesitantly. "Right after I came. It was the first thunderstorm since I'd arrived, in the middle of the night. The lightning strike woke me. The windows in my room were open, and that smell… I didn't know what it was. I didn't know what had happened."

Jones could imagine her, already unhappy in this place, getting jerked from sleep by a violent storm and with no one to turn to—no father to hold her and tell her silly stories, no mother to comfort her, no caring grandmother to tuck her back into bed.

"I got up to close the windows, and then I stood at the front window and watched. The lightning was constant, lighting up the entire sky, so bright sometimes that it made my eyes hurt, and the thunder went on and on until it felt like it was inside me. I was about to get back in bed and pull the covers over my head when I saw…"

She was silent so long. His mouth close to her ear, he quietly prompted her. "What did you see, Reece?"

She eased away from him and walked to the first step. "Grandfather. It was pouring rain, and he was carrying something over his shoulder, something heavy wrapped up. He carried the—the—it over into the yard—" she pointed west of the second flower bed "—and laid it down and picked up a shovel and began covering it."

Stopping beside her, Jones watched her hand tremble in the air before wrapping his fingers around hers. Her skin was clammy, the shivers so strong that they vibrated through his own hand. Slowly he lowered their hands, but she didn't seem to notice. She was staring fifteen years distant into the rain, her cheeks pale, her

voice losing strength, reminding him of the girl she'd
been then.

"I watched until he was finished. He took the shovel
and disappeared around the house again. I was always
too curious, Valerie said. I wanted to know what was so
important that he'd had to bury it in the middle of the
night in a terrible storm. So the next morning, I went
out front to look. Before he'd dug the—the hole, he'd
cut the grass out in big squares, then pieced it back together. Grandmother wouldn't have noticed. I wouldn't
have if I hadn't been looking for it."

He could see the scene easily: the bright, sharp-
edged light that followed a cleansing storm, the air as
damp as the ground, the sad little girl with the pixie
haircut sneaking out of the house, curious but totally
clueless about the aftershock of what she was about to
do.

"I got a stick that had blown off in the storm, and I
was crouched there, poking this stick into the ground,
when Grandfather caught me. He lifted me off the
ground and said, 'If you ever tell anyone…'"

Anger roiled through Jones at the old man for terrifying his granddaughter. Relief that the body she'd
watched him bury couldn't have been Glen's, since it
occurred before they'd arrived at Fair Winds. Revulsion that Arthur Howard must have killed more than
once. Concern about how Reece would bear this.

"The next time I came outside again after that, the
first thing I did after making sure Grandfather was
gone was stand at the bottom of these steps and pace
off the distance to the—the grave. Twelve steps out and
twenty-six to the right. I was terrified of him and angry
with him and one day I was going to find out what he'd
buried and show everyone."

She looked at him, her eyes glittery with uncried tears and a faint, unhappy smile on her lips. "That's why I count."

The rain still fell, easier now, but the lightning had passed and the thunder was nothing more than an occasional rumble. He'd worked in the rain before, for far less important reasons.

For a long time they stared at each other, and finally she nodded. "You get the shovel. I'll count. I'm good at it."

He retrieved a shovel and gloves from the tools covered with a tarp near the drive. When he returned, she'd already taken the first twelve steps and was walking north. "How tall were you when you were thirteen?"

She held up one finger, took a dozen more steps, then stopped. "I don't remember, but I was the tallest kid in my class." Opening her arms, she faced the house. "This is thirty-eight steps for me now. Do you want to allow for shorter legs?"

"Just a little." He sank the shovel into the dirt a few feet closer to the house. It went easily through the first couple waterlogged inches, then required more effort.

How deep did a monster dig when he was burying a body in his own front yard? At least two feet. More than three?

Soaked within minutes, he dug a decent-size hole to three feet. A years-old skeleton didn't make much of a target, so after a few more scoops, he moved again at an angle to the house and started over. He'd stopped to sluice his hair back from his face when Reece asked, "What if it wasn't a body? What if there's nothing left of whatever it was to find?"

"What else would he bury in the middle of the night in a storm?" He muscled the shovel into the dirt, tossed out a scoop of mud sitting atop dry dirt, then stomped it in one more time.

It hit something solid.

His jaw clenched, his fingers knotted on the handle, he loosened the dirt in the area, dropped to his knees and shoved his hand into the hole. About two feet down, he found the object, long and cylindrical, worked it free of the loosened soil, then brought it out.

He recoiled, dropping it to the ground, then swiping his muddy glove on his jeans. Reece didn't show such dismay, instead kneeling in front of him and gently picking it up. "It's a bone. Too short for a leg." She held it alongside her own arm, several inches shorter, and studied it before looking at him. "An arm?"

One nod. That was all he could manage.

"We should call—" Sliding his gloves off, he patted his pocket where he normally kept his cell, but of course it wasn't there. He'd left it on the charger in the cottage, where he'd left Mick, too, asleep on the couch. Reece didn't have hers, either. Her wet clothes were plastered to her body, making that obvious.

"You shouldn't have disturbed the dead."

The voice came from behind them, the tone as friendly as if he'd simply commented on the weather. Reece's fingers clenched tightly on the bone as Jones stood, then turned. The Jaguar was parked in the driveway, just short of the fallen limb, and Mark was striding toward them.

He was dressed down for the middle of a business day, in khaki trousers and a polo shirt, looking as if he'd come from the golf course instead of the office. The elegant-casual look contrasted sharply with the length of pipe he held in his left hand and the small pistol in his right.

"Haven't you heard the old saying 'Let sleeping dogs lie'?" he asked, as polite as any well-bred Southern gentleman could be.

"That's not a dog," Jones replied.

"No, it is not. How about this one: 'Curiosity killed the cat'?" He smiled at Reece and added, *"Meow."*

Cat, meet Curiosity.

Looking very unkittenish, still holding tightly to the bone, Reece moved to stand beside Jones. "You knew about this body?"

"Of course. I knew about that one." He pointed where they'd found the grave. "I knew about that one." This time his finger shifted three feet away. "And that one. And that one and that one. I know about all of them."

Jones's stomach heaved. "How many are there?"

"I never bothered to count them. Besides, the number changes. After today, there will be two more."

"Grandmother will be back any moment," Reece bluffed.

"No, she won't. She had lunch with Macy and me at the country club after her meeting with Robbie Calloway. Macy convinced her to attend the historical-society meeting with her. They won't be done for several more hours. Do you know why she went to see Robbie?"

"To cut me out of her will?"

"You were already out of it. Grandfather took care of that when you refused to attend her birthday party." He grimaced with fake sympathy, then scowled. "She put you back in. Can you believe it? She said it was only fair, you being Elliott's daughter, even if you were a ridiculous little drama queen."

"And what? If I die before she does, the money goes back to you?"

"Me and my children."

Reece scoffed. "You can have it. I don't want anything from the Howard family. I don't even want their name anymore."

Though he rested the pipe on the ground, Mark's aim with the pistol remained steady. "I'm supposed to believe that? That you'd turn your back on a fortune because you don't like the people who had it first? I'm not stupid, Clarice. Besides, that's not the only reason you have to die. You're nosy. You always have been. You never learned to respect other people's boundaries. Snooping in the yard, in the garage, spying on Grandfather and me. You want to call the police about that bone, don't you? Let them come out here and dig up the entire property and tarnish Grandfather's name and traumatize poor Grandmother. I can't let that happen."

He moved a few steps closer, and all trace of pleasantness disappeared beneath a cold, angry, insane smile. "I *won't* let that happen."

Reece's knees were unsteady, her lungs tight. She'd accepted that her grandfather was a murderer, but her cousin, too? What the hell was the Howard motto? *The family that kills together...?*

Oh, God, this couldn't be real. None of it. She wasn't standing here in the rain holding all that was left of some poor stranger's arm while her childhood tormentor pointed a gun at her and Jones. Mark had outgrown that behavior; he was an adult, a husband, a father, a likable, respectable man. He couldn't really intend to kill them, could he?

The gun drew her gaze like a magnet. Yes, apparently he could.

"Then your objection to the garden restoration was never about the money," Jones said quietly.

"It was always about the money. But it was also about protecting my family."

"She's your family."

"No, she's not," Mark said.

"I'm not," she insisted. She'd always known the family was a bunch of snobbish, entitled elitists, but now she knew they were also all crazy. She had some personal issues, but insanity wasn't one of them.

She looked at Jones, utterly motionless in the light rain, and thought she'd be damned if she'd let a crazy man kill her when she'd just found the man who could help her deal with those issues.

"So...what?" she asked. "You plan to shoot us and add us to your boneyard? You think no one will notice? No one will wonder?"

Mark shrugged. "Grandmother told you to leave. You left. And when he—" he jerked his head toward Jones "—realized he wasn't getting the contract for the garden project, he left, too. What happened to you after you drove out that gate is anyone's guess."

"That's pretty lame."

"We're Howards. No one would ever suspect us of wrongdoing." He gestured with the pistol. "Let's take a walk."

Reece's feet actually started moving, but Jones didn't budge. "Let's not."

Mark's expression was comical for a moment, then he waggled the pistol. "Man with a gun here. The way this works is I tell you what to do, and you do it."

"That only works if you're undecided about killing us. But you've already made the decision, and you expect us to cooperate? To make it easier for you?" Jones shrugged, looking far less scared than Reece felt. "Dead is dead, whether it's here or in the woods. I vote for here."

What was he thinking? That maybe the housekeeper would come out and Mark would have qualms about killing *her?* That Grandmother would return home early? Or maybe that Detective Maricci would come back with information or new questions? Any of those seemed about as likely as another bolt of lightning coming out of the dreary gray sky and striking Mark dead where he stood.

Furtively Reece glanced around. The nearest cover was the corner of the house, too far to reach before Mark shot them, and the only possible weapons were the shovel a few yards away and the bone in her hands. She couldn't imagine Mark coming close enough for the shovel to be of any use or that the bone would do much, if any, harm before it broke.

If Jones was looking for a way out, too, it didn't show. He looked as calm as Mark, as if this was just any old discussion on a fall afternoon. "You're wrong that no one would suspect you. You know Tommy Maricci?"

"The cop? Of course."

"You remember that tarp out in the shed with the old man's pickup? The one with the big, dark stain?"

Mark's brow wrinkled. "I didn't realize Grandfather kept that truck. He hadn't driven it for years. We had some good times in that truck."

"Yeah, well, Detective Maricci has that tarp. They've already identified the blood as human."

Mark started shaking his head halfway through

Jones's statement. "Grandmother would never let a police officer take anything from this property."

"You're right, she wouldn't. So Reece and I gave it to him. It may not be admissible in court, but all these remains will be."

Two details struck Reece at the same time: Mark's confidence was shaken by that news, and Jones was edging away from her, moving so slowly that she hadn't even noticed. Her first impulse was to follow him, to stay right at his side because she always felt safer there, but she forced herself to not only stay, but to shift just the tiniest bit away.

"You had no right." That cold, imperious Howard tone came through in Mark's voice, making him sound eerily like Grandfather.

Another shrug. "One of these bodies is my brother's. That gives me every right."

Sorrow washed over Reece. She'd forgotten about Glen for a moment. She wished she remembered his face, his friendship, his saving her life, but there was just that big blank. But Jones remembered. He would never forget.

"Where is Glen?" she asked softly.

"Somewhere out there." Mark indicated the expanse of lawn. "We only kept track of graves to know where to dig the next one. But you'll be seeing him soon."

We only kept track of graves to know where to dig the next one. God, he sounded so normal, so sane, as if murder was simply a hobby he'd shared with Grandfather, the way other boys fished with their grandfathers, keeping track of which lures brought better catches.

Reece edged another half inch to the right. "Why did Grandfather kill him?"

"He didn't. I did. He didn't respect boundaries, either. He interfered with my plans—snooping around, trespassing, probably stealing anything that wasn't nailed down. That's what gypsies do, you know."

Her stomach tightened and heaved. Mark had been fourteen years old when Glen died, barely into his mid-teens, and he'd murdered a boy. How could she not have known he was so cold, so damaged?

Because she'd been thirteen. The idea of one kid killing another had been totally foreign to her. Though now she knew rationally it happened, it still felt foreign.

She pushed the ugly thought from her mind, focusing instead on his last comment, stealing a glance at Jones. Gypsies? That was the family tradition he'd run away from? He'd wanted to live a life without the scams and cons and prejudices that were his heritage?

"'Gypsies' is a word the uninformed use," Jones said blankly. "We were Irish Travelers."

Mark shrugged impatiently. "You say Irish Travelers. Everyone else says lying, thieving bastards."

The shovel was within Jones's reach. One quick lunge...and then what? Charge Mark and hope the element of surprise kept her cousin from shooting him? Reece had no idea. All she did know was that she needed to keep Mark's attention on her. Outwardly bold, inwardly quivering, she began walking toward him. The pistol in his hand swung around, aimed straight at her.

"You killed Glen because he stopped you from killing me."

"Yeah. And because I could. He was so arrogant. He stayed to look out for you. He thought he could protect you from me." Mark snorted. "He never even knew what hit him. One instant he was there, hiding behind that tree—" he jerked his head toward the oak that had suffered the lightning strike "—and the next…lights out."

After a thoughtful moment, Mark gestured. "I don't have all afternoon to chat. I'm going to count to three—" he thumbed back the hammer on the weapon "—and if you aren't headed toward the woods, I'll kill you here. One."

Reece swallowed hard. Her feet wanted to obey, but Jones was right. If he was determined to kill them, the last thing they should do was cooperate. Damned if she'd die easily for him.

"Two."

Her mouth was dry, her palms damp. The arm bone she held visibly shook.

Mark's index finger began to tighten on the trigger. "Thr—"

In an instant, an icy wind swirled around them, giving voice to an inhuman roar as dark and menacing as the vortex surrounding them. Reece staggered from the force of the gale, stumbling, and would have fallen to the ground if Jones hadn't grabbed her, supported her. Their wet clothes whipped around them, her hair standing practically on end. Dust swirled in the air, stinging her skin, making it difficult to see, to breathe.

Jones tried to move; she felt his muscles straining, and she tried to herself, but the wind held them in place, rushing with fury, pelting them with rage. With one hand cupped around her eyes, Reece saw the terror on Mark's face as the pipe was snatched from his hand and sent soaring across the yard. He spun in a circle, cursing, searching, then stiffened, his eyes widened, his nose wrinkling. She did the same, smelling dirt, damp and cigar smoke.

"Holy God," Jones whispered.

A figure was taking form at the core of the fierce wind that shook her to her very core: large, threatening, the center of her nightmares for fifteen years. It hovered, shaking so violently that its outlines blurred, and a long, drawn-out rumble vibrated the air. *Nooo mooore!*

Helpless against the spirit's force, Mark managed to squeak out one pleading word. "Gr-grandfather?"

I told you no more!

"But—but, Grandfather—" Mark's protest broke off with a shriek as his gaze shifted to his hand. Slowly, moved by an invisible force, his hand twisted, the barrel of the gun pivoting toward him. His elbow jerked out, as a wooden doll's might under the control of an angry puppeteer, and the gun pulled upward.

His expression turned panicked. "Grandfather, no! I was just doing what you taught me! I was just protecting you! No, you can't—"

The gunshot echoed as Jones pushed Reece's face against his chest.

As quickly as it had come, the storm dissipated and the air cleared. Unnatural quiet settled around them, heavy enough to make Reece's ears ring, then slowly she became aware of the rapid tenor of her breathing, the thud of her heart, the slow control of Jones's breaths.

She didn't want to look. Didn't want to see Mark lying lifeless on the ground. She wasn't sure she *could* look. It took all her strength to stay on her feet, clinging to Jones as if she would never let go.

His body was solid, his arms strong around her. "It's okay," he whispered. "It's okay, sweetheart."

Gradually her trembling eased, and she lifted her head just enough to meet his gaze. "Grandfather…"

He nodded.

"He saved our lives." The man who'd terrorized her in life had protected her in death, and he'd done it by... "Mark was his favorite. They were so much alike. And he killed him."

Jones glanced past her, his expression grim, then nodded again. "He wanted the killing to stop."

I told you no more. And when Mark had ignored him, Grandfather had taken matters into his own hands. Oh, God, what would this do to Grandmother and the rest of Mark's family? He had a mother, a wife, a daughter, another one on the way. They would be devastated. Grandmother, at least, would blame her, and probably the others would, too.

Not that it mattered. The important people—she and Jones—knew she wasn't guilty.

With a deep breath, she turned in Jones's arms to face her cousin for the last time. He lay on his back, his head turned to the side, his eyes closed. The entry wound was small, the exit, if there was one, not visible from her vantage point. Nothing about him screamed *He's dead!* He didn't appear particularly peaceful, or as if he'd just lived through the last moments of his own terrifying murder. He just looked like Mark.

Mark the pest, the bully, the tormentor. The murderer.

And this yard was his and Grandfather's burying ground.

Her fingers tightened on Jones's arm. "I'm so sorry about Glen."

Emotion shuddered through him. "I knew when I came here he was dead. I felt it. At least now we *know.*"

She understood the difference between knowing and

knowing. She'd known something bad had happened that summer. Now she *knew* exactly what.

Would it make a difference to him—that his brother had died because of her? Would it change the way he felt about her? She was trying to find the courage to ask when he sighed heavily, his arms tightening.

"Fate," he murmured. "Everything happens for a reason."

Her father's death, Jones's and Glen's desire for new lives, that horrible summer, her return at the same time as Jones's, Mark's secrets, Grandfather finally, for the first time, doing something to protect his granddaughter.

Fate.

She breathed deeply of rain-washed air, the damp of the river, the scents of sweat and soap and Jones and herself, then gently pulled from his embrace. "We'd better call Detective Maricci."

Hand in hand, they skirted Mark's body, circled around the house and headed to the cottage. As soon as the authorities arrived, she figured, the entire property would be declared a crime scene and she and Jones would have to leave. He might return here someday to work, but she never would. The past was over, and Fair Winds had no place in her future.

Even if it had brought her Jones.

She loved fate.

And she was pretty sure she loved *him*.

It had been a week since their discovery of the first body. The excavation had been slow going, but so far, more than forty bodies had been found buried in the front lawn. The authorities assumed the victims were mostly hitchhikers, runaways and homeless people—

the kind of people who could go missing without anyone noticing. They estimated the older graves at forty to fifty years old. Arthur Howard had started his hobby young, about the time he destroyed the gardens.

The thought repulsed Jones: What kind of man preferred moldering bodies in his yard over color, fragrance and well-maintained flower beds?

Glen's body hadn't been identified yet. DNA and dental matches could take a while with so many victims.

So many victims. Thank God he and Reece hadn't become two more in the Howards' lifelong killing spree.

Mark's funeral had been private, and Miss Willa had sent a message that Reece wasn't welcome. After the service, she and Mark's family had left Copper Lake for Raleigh, where his mother lived. No one knew whether she would return to the home that had meant so much to her or if the revelations would keep her away. Jones was betting she would be back.

But he wouldn't. There were too many other things he wanted to do. Get on with his work. Live his life. Spend every moment possible with Reece.

They were standing in the nearly deserted parking lot of the motel where he and Mick had first stayed in town. She lifted her suitcase into the SUV, then turned to catch him watching her. The smile that spread across her entire face warmed him from the inside out. She was beautiful. She was everything he could ever want in a woman. She was his fate.

"Are you ready?" she asked, reaching through the open pickup window to scratch between Mick's ears.

"I am." In less than forty-eight hours, they would be in New Orleans, where he would meet her friends, whose approval he wanted, and her dogs, whose approval he needed. He trusted his obvious love for her would be all Evie and Martine would have to know, and dogs always liked him. If Bubba, Louie and Eddie were a little hesitant, he could count on Mick—and plenty of treats—to smooth the way.

He kissed her, and the hunger that was always right there simmering beneath the surface flared. Reluctantly he stepped away, opened the door for her and waited until she was buckled in before he closed it again. After climbing into the truck, he leaned forward to see past Mick's wagging tail. "Hey, you said last week that you didn't want the Howard name anymore. You want to consider mine?"

For a moment, she gazed at him, expression blank. They'd done a lot in the past week: dealt with the cops, made love, discussed their pasts, their present, their future. He'd said *I love you,* and she'd said it, too, but neither of them had gotten around to bringing up marriage.

Then came that sweet, warm smile that danced along his spine and made him want to lose himself with her, and she responded with words he knew he'd hear from her again. "I do."

He grinned foolishly as she shifted into Reverse and backed in a big U around the truck, until they were facing each other again with only a few feet of pavement between them. "Tell me again…is Jones your first name or last?"

Without waiting for an answer, she blew him a kiss and drove away. He laughed as he shifted into gear to follow her. "Settle in, Mick. We're going home."

* * * * *

A sneaky peek at next month...

INTRIGUE...

BREATHTAKING ROMANTIC SUSPENSE

My wish list for next month's titles...

In stores from 20th April 2012:

☐ Rancher's Perfect Baby Rescue – Linda Conrad

& AK-Cowboy – Joanna Wayne

☐ Sudden Insight & Sudden Attraction
   – Rebecca York

☐ His Duty to Protect – Lindsay McKenna

& The Heartbreak Sheriff – Elle Kennedy

☐ Operation Baby Rescue – Beth Cornelison

In stores from 4th May 2012:

☐ Down River – Karen Harper

Available at WHSmith, Tesco, Asda, Eason, Amazon and Apple

Just can't wait?

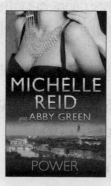

The World of Mills & Boon®

There's a Mills & Boon® series that's perfect for you. We publish ten series and with new titles every month, you never have to wait long for your favourite to come along.

Blaze® Scorching hot, sexy reads

By Request Relive the romance with the best of the best

Cherish™ Romance to melt the heart every time

Desire™ Passionate and dramatic love stories

Visit us Online Browse our books before you buy online at **www.millsandboon.co.uk**